BARBARA LAMPLUGH was born and grew ~~~~ London. She studied Language and English at York University ~~~~ where she lived on and off for over tw included an overland trip to Kathmar and a journey on the Trans-Siberiar months backpacking around Southeas in *Kathmandu by Truck* (1976) and *Trans-Sib...* published by Roger Lascelles.

Preferring variety to routine, she has worked as a librarian, a project officer for Age Concern, a volunteer bureau organiser, a teacher of English, an editor and translator and a journalist.

In 1999, spurred by the challenge of living in a different culture, she headed for Granada in Spain, where she still lives, inspired by views of hills and the Alhambra from her sunny terrace. As a regular features writer for the magazine *Living Spain*, she contributed around a hundred articles on numerous aspects of life in Spain. She has also written for *The Guardian, The Times* Educational Supplement and other publications.

Although her heart and home are in Granada, she makes frequent visits to the UK to spend time with her children and grandchildren in Bristol and Edinburgh.

Barbara
Lamplugh

SilverWood

Published in 2015 by SilverWood Books

SilverWood Books Ltd
30 Queen Charlotte Street, Bristol, BS1 4HJ
www.silverwoodbooks.co.uk

ISBN 978-1-78132-369-4 (paperback)
ISBN 978-1-78132-370-0 (ebook)

British Library Cataloguing in Publication Data
A CIP catalogue record for this book is available from
the British Library

Set in Sabon and Jellyka by SilverWood Books
Printed on responsibly sourced paper

For Tom and Corinne

Prologue

11th March 2004

They almost missed their train, the 'train of death' as it was later dubbed by the press. Deborah was to blame, of course, having crawled out of bed too late, spent all of ten minutes searching for a lost earring and still insisted on a 'quick' *café con leche* at the bar below Teresa's flat in Alcalá de Henares.

'Come on.' Teresa put two euros on the bar counter and grabbed Deborah's arm. 'You'll make me late for work. I thought the English were supposed to be punctual.'

'Just shows you can't believe the stereotypes. Anyway, I've lived in Spain long enough...'

The train doors were already starting to close when the two women dashed onto the station platform, both of them panting. Deborah leapt aboard and held the door open for her friend. 'I told you we'd make it,' she said, laughing at Teresa's agitation. She pointed to a couple of empty seats further down the carriage. 'We can even sit down.'

'*Uf*, my head hurts,' Teresa complained as they settled into their seats. 'Too much Rioja last night. How come you're not hung over?'

'Who says I'm not hung over? Why do you think I was so desperate for that coffee?' The train picked up speed and Deborah leaned back. 'So, now I want to hear what you've been up to in the three years since you left Granada because, if I remember rightly, I did all the talking last night.'

'That's true.' Teresa couldn't supress a smile. 'You and your liberated Moorish heroines. *Bueno*, the forty minutes into Madrid will be time enough to fill you in on my relatively mundane life.

'I miss Granada,' Teresa concluded as the train approached Madrid's Atocha station. She placed a hand over Deborah's and let it rest there. 'I miss *you*,' she was about to add but the time for words ran out when an innocuous-looking rucksack in the centre of their carriage erupted, its contents ripping into flesh and bone, glass and steel with a mighty blast, a roar from hell that made all words redundant.

Chapter One

Alice sat at her desk, too stunned to move. *Trust Deborah*. A first, fleeting reaction, no more than the ghost of a thought, but still unworthy: how could her sister be to blame? Her black mobile phone, once so inoffensive, was lying askew on the open pages of a neatly filled out housing benefit form, exuding malevolence. Nothing else appeared out of the ordinary. Around her in the open-plan office she sensed the movement of colleagues, a faint whiff of coffee, the whirr of the photocopier, a murmur of muted conversation from the far end of the room. She frowned at the phone, purveyor of tidings so terrible they could not be true. *No, No way, Impossible* resounding in her head, gaining strength with each repetition.

Even as she gabbled the news to Carol, her boss – *I have to leave immediately, a terrorist attack, my sister in Spain* – the words sounded hollow. They were mere sounds, meaningless syllables that had nothing to do with reality. And later, when she fetched Timmy from school halfway through the morning, repeating the story to his teacher, Alice was baffled by the look of horror on his face because it wasn't true, surely it wasn't?

No, Paco had been relaying fears, not facts; he had called long before anything could be verified. It was even possible she had misunderstood: one of those failures of communication caused by the language barrier. She tried to recall the exact words her sister's partner had used. Had he said she *was* on the train or she *might have been* on the train? Was his English sufficient to convey this vital distinction? And when he said the news was bad, did he mean in general, the terrible fact of the bombings, or in relation to Deborah specifically?

They would arrive in Granada to find everything perfectly normal.

Deb would emerge, reading glasses in hand, from her study in the *carmen* to greet her when she walked through the door. *It was a mistake, sorry to alarm you,* she would say. *I was on a different train.* She'd look fondly at Timmy, remark how he'd grown and bend down to kiss him. Then she and Deb would hug; almost certainly she would cry with relief. This was the scene Alice wanted to imagine as she checked flights, threw clothes into a suitcase, made arrangements for the cat. This, rather than the scenes she had glimpsed on TV before switching it off in horror – as if by pressing a button, she could erase those images, undo what had happened.

How to tell Timmy: that was the immediate problem. *There's been an accident, your Auntie Deborah...* How could you tell a nine year-old without frightening him to death that something as ordinary as a train journey could end in a massacre? They would both remember this day for the rest of their lives. Was it a mistake to take him? There had been no time to think, to weigh up the pros and cons as she usually did. And really what choice did she have? Now Mum was no longer alive with her cupboard full of toys and games, the dinosaur duvet (chosen many years ago by Mark) on her spare bed... Remembering how hard Timmy had taken Mum's death, how he had cried and cried. *But where is she? Where is Granny?* The endless questions she couldn't answer. And now, it seemed, their pitifully small family would be reduced even further. Now, he did not even have an aunt. Just a cousin, Mark, who was twenty years old, lived in a cave and took drugs. So if anything happened to *her...* Whenever this possibility crossed her mind – as it did from time to time – she became paralysed with fear as to what would happen to Timmy.

Mark. Too immersed in her own feelings, too preoccupied with Timmy, she had scarcely given a thought to her nephew until now. Yet it was Mark who would be hardest hit. She pictured him as he appeared in one of her photos taken last summer in the garden of the *carmen*. He was standing under the pomegranate tree, skinny and waif-like in faded jeans and a stretched T-shirt that hung loosely, barely covering his midriff, his blondish hair twisted into frizzy dreadlocks. Although it didn't show up in the photo, she remembered the dark caramel tone of his skin – darker than Timmy's, much darker than her own. A result, no doubt, of so much time spent outside. Poor boy, how would he cope with this? Twenty, but still hopelessly immature, still at the rebellious stage; 'wasting his opportunities', Deb had complained. And like Timmy, he was as good as fatherless, Charlie having proved himself a shamefully negligent parent. He would need her support: they might have to stay some time in Granada... Well, Bristol's housing department was hardly going to fall apart without her.

'Timmy, choose a few books to take,' she called to him, 'And a couple of games.' How to tell him?

She gazed at the clothes in her open wardrobe, unable to think clearly. Was Granada warm or cold in March? Would she need her winter coat or a light jacket? Boots or sandals? The difficulty of getting through to the airline had stretched her nerves so taut she had screamed at the man who finally answered her tenth or fifteenth call. 'Please calm down, Madam.' The voice was patient, not entirely unfeeling. 'We do have seats on this afternoon's flight to Málaga.' Ashamed, she had tried to explain, but then the words swelled in her throat, forcing her to stop and take deep gulps of air before she could finish the transaction. She had to read her credit card number three times before she got it right. *I'm not normally like this*, she wanted to say. *I'm a level-headed, organised person. I don't flap.* After putting down the phone, she had gone to the piano and poured out all her emotion through the keys. Ten minutes only but the Beethoven sonata had calmed her enough to carry on with what had to be done.

Timmy held out his Game Boy. 'Can I take this? I want to show it to Mark.'

'Here, put it in the bag. Then you can play on the journey.' She looked at his upturned face, so trusting, so innocent still. Her darling darling boy: the miracle of her life. Nine years on and she still had those moments when she marvelled at it. Ruffling his head of fuzzy curls, she remembered their hair appointments and picked up the phone again.

'Mummy, how long are we staying? I'm supposed to be playing in a football match next week against...'

'I don't know, my love. It depends.' She mustn't cry, not in front of Timmy. Not yet. Not till they knew for certain. Focus on the practical.

Weird, Mark thought, how he'd never really rated sleep; it was one of those things you just took for granted. Now he knew it was bliss, better even than sex. He'd still be sleeping now if Paco hadn't turned up to drag him out of it. Way too early so it's guaranteed to put a jinx on the day. One minute you're sleeping peacefully, the next you feel someone shaking you, yelling in your ear that you've got to get up and go to Madrid. Mark remembered telling Paco to fuck off and then to calm down, because he sounded deranged. 'They've bombed her train. Your mother was on the train.' He kept repeating the same words. You can shut your eyes but you can't shut your ears – not when someone's standing right next to you, bellowing that your mum's been blown up by a bomb. It was like a nightmare had lost its way and leapt out into daylight – or as near daylight as ever seeped into his cave. 'Wake up, Mark. Do you understand what I'm saying?' Why would he want to wake up? Not if it was true what Paco was telling him.

It *was* true. He'd followed Paco down the hill to the Albaicín, still only half-believing it, still only half-awake. But now he'd seen the mangled trains and panicked faces; he'd heard the death counts that kept nudging up and up, so he knew it was true. You couldn't argue with the TV. He looked around Mum's study at all her books and papers and junk; at the chair where she always sat.

The portrait of Walladah had been stuck on the cork board above her desk for as long as Mark could remember. Like a fucking pin-up. Every day as she worked, Mum must have stared at this thousand year-old *puta* like she was some kind of goddess. Her colours had faded but she still had that irritating smirk. It was time for her to go. Mark reached up and ripped her off the board. He scrunched up the paper and flung it across the room. If it hadn't been for Walladah, Mum wouldn't have been in Madrid. She wouldn't have been on the train. She wouldn't be dead.

He could hear Paco calling his name, shouting was he ready? Madrid was a four-hour drive from Granada, but why the rush? It was too late. She was dead. Blown to pieces. He made a run for the door into the patio, thinking he was going to throw up, but his stomach was empty. The retch just filled his mouth with a horrible sour bile. He spat and went back inside.

Paco was standing there, fumbling with a cigarette packet, trying to pull one out only his hands were shaking too much. He offered the pack to Mark, who took two and lit them both before handing one back.

'Have you packed some overnight things?' Paco asked. 'Ignacio will be here in a moment. We must be ready.'

'You go on your own.' What was the point? He'd seen enough on the telly. Blood, bodies, twisted metal, the train track covered in debris. He didn't want to see his Mum in bits.

'Mark, we don't yet know anything concrete,' Paco said. 'She may be alive, possibly injured...'

Mark didn't bother to answer. Teresa's daughter had said she was on the train: they'd both been on the train – his mum and hers. It was fucking obvious she was dead; otherwise she'd have been in touch, wouldn't she. He'd tried enough times to get through to her, letting the phone ring and ring, leaving messages... He'd said he was sorry.

Paco was pacing up and down, taking long drags on his ciggy. He looked really old, his eyes all pouchy and bloodshot, the whole of his face kind of slumped. He must have shaved in a hurry because there were two nicks on his chin, one of them oozing dark blood.

'We mustn't give up hope,' he said in a voice as flat as a board so you could tell he was just talking himself up and didn't believe it. Hoping was a mistake: Mark had learnt that years ago from his dad. It was one of the few things Charlie had taught him, though not intentionally. That hoping was risky: promises were easy to make and easy to break. Expect nothing, then if things turn out good, you get a nice surprise instead of being disappointed. He'd worked it out aged about seven. So, there was no way Paco was going to convince him now that Mum had got out alive.

*

After Paco had gone, Mark tried repeating the word to himself. He tried it in Spanish, then in English. *Muerta*. Dead. Either way, it sounded wrong. He knew Mum was dead but...somehow he couldn't quite get his head round it. She'd always been there. How could she not be – just like that, from one minute to the next?

It was a shit time for her to die. On the whole, they'd been getting on better lately, so why did she have to die just when they'd had a fight? Forty euros: that was all he'd asked for. It was nothing to her. If she'd just handed it over instead of winding him up, hassling him with questions... He wouldn't have got mad then; he wouldn't have sworn at her. What was it he'd called her? A mean bitch, it could have been... And then as he walked out the door: '*Vete a la mierda*!' He seemed to remember throwing that at her. He hadn't meant it, course he hadn't. But the thing was, she wouldn't have known that. And now it was too fucking late.

Go to shit: the last words he'd spoken to his mum. He thought of her dying with those words in her head and kicked at the stack of wood piled up in the patio. It collapsed and the logs rolled away in all directions. He wished now that he'd gone with Paco to Madrid. Just in case. He'd have been able to tell her then, if she *was* still alive. Tell her he didn't mean it. Tell her she was the best mum, really... What he couldn't hack though was sitting in the car with Paco and Ignacio for four fucking hours, talking about her, pretending it was going to be okay.

He wandered into the kitchen and opened the fridge just for something to do. It occurred to him he hadn't had any breakfast. Eating was the last thing on his mind – or had been – but now he was suddenly ravenous. No one had bought any bread: there was only half a stale *barra* from yesterday. He split it and stuck the two halves under the grill, then put on some coffee.

It didn't feel right sitting down to breakfast as if everything was normal. He picked up the oil jug then put it down again. It felt all wrong being in this kitchen, here where he'd grown up, where every day he used to have breakfast with Mum before going to school. It was like she was standing there by the sink, smiling at him or prattling on about her project while the milk boiled over. He thought about this jug of oil in front of him and pictured her filling it from the bottle, maybe spilling a few drops, wiping the greenish glass with kitchen paper. Might only have been yesterday: her last breakfast before she left for Madrid.

Grabbing the jug again, he poured oil onto his toast, watching it soak in and turn the bread gold. He gobbled it down in two minutes flat, not even bothering to wipe away the trickle of oil on his chin. He was still hungry. It was obscene to be thinking about food at this time but he couldn't help it. He remembered the cakes María had brought round a couple of days ago and found three left in the bag. He crammed them into his mouth one after another. What would Mum think if she could see him? Without any warning, a huge sob rose in his chest and forced itself out. He laid his head on the table and cried like a baby. Cried like he hadn't done since he was a little kid.

The phone kept ringing so he grabbed it off the wall and let it dangle; there was no one he wanted to speak to. It was bizarre: he'd never felt so alone in his life, yet at the same time he *wanted* to be on his own. If he went back to the cave, there'd be people about: José, Pierre, Tina; fucking Ed. It wasn't so easy to keep bastards like Ed and Dani out. Locking yourself in a cave was tricky. At least here no one would bother him. Not till Alice arrived with Timmy. He wasn't too keen on seeing them either but he'd promised Paco he'd stay to let them in, make sure there was something for them to eat. Later he'd have to go out and buy bread. Alice would be fussing, pestering him with questions, crying maybe. And Timmy... His little cousin thought he was cool. He'd probably want to play. Mark liked Timmy; it was just that today he wasn't in the mood.

He checked his mobile for the time. He couldn't believe how it was dragging, how each minute hovered like it had nowhere to go; forcing him to wait. Paco wouldn't even be in Madrid yet.

'Off on your holidays?' the taxi driver asked. 'Going somewhere nice?'

Alice stared out of the window and was grateful when Timmy answered for her.

'We're going to Granada.'

'Sunny Spain, eh? Lucky you.'

It was worse on the plane, trapped in her seat, still not knowing if Deb was alive or dead or horribly injured; wanting to prepare Timmy but forced instead to listen to the woman next to her wittering on about her daughter and grandchildren in Fuengirola; suffering all the boring routines of flying: the useless safety demo, the trolley of expensive refreshments, the warning not to smoke in the toilets. As if this were just a regular holiday flight like any other. *Thank you for choosing to fly with us, we hope to see you again soon.*

At Málaga airport a blast of loneliness hit her as the vision of an earlier visit lodged itself in her mind: Deb running forward to greet her in the Arrivals hall, grabbing her in a ballroom hold and waltzing her around, oblivious to the stares and smirks of others. It must have been before Timmy, yet the memory remained vivid.

The two-hour bus journey to Granada seemed interminable. Timmy pulled at her arm, chattering away, excited about seeing Mark. Not understanding. Outside the window, dotting the hillsides, would be those straight rows of olive trees that from a distance always reminded her of crochet; brown signs naming the dry rivers they crossed; small villages of whitewashed houses with a church in their midst. But it was dark: she could see none of this, only distorted reflections of herself, Timmy, the other passengers in the overheated bus.

The road wound on: they passed an illuminated sign for Granada, still eighty kilometres to go. Why did Deb have to live so far away? She'd always known it was a mistake for her sister to leave England, with Mark – still a toddler – in tow. He was so small, so helpless, it wasn't fair... She'd told Deb, who had laughed at her fear that some calamity would strike them; but now it had. Alice realised her fists were clenched tight; her fingernails had made deep grooves like smiling mouths on her palms. Mocking her.

You see? It's all worked out. When was it Deb had spoken those words? Perhaps only a year after emigrating. Much too soon. She attracted trouble like a magnet: one drama after another ever since her teens. Moving to Spain hadn't changed that; quite the opposite. What was she doing in Madrid anyway? An early morning commuter train in Madrid struck Alice as an unlikely place for her sister to be. She tried to remember what Deb had said. Was it something to do with her book, with the Spanish translation?

The bus slowed down and came to a stop in Loja; a few passengers alighted. Now they were drawing closer, Alice began to dread their arrival. She imagined getting out of the taxi and walking along the narrow cobbled street towards the familiar house. The wisteria that draped the outer wall of the patio could be in flower already. She would breathe in its divine scent even before reaching the *carmen* named after it. *Carmen de la Glicina*, the house Deb had lovingly renovated, a house brimming with memories of her sister. She imagined arriving to the hollow pit of her absence.

Paco was in Madrid, waiting for news... She checked her phone again and tried to convince herself that no news was good news.

'Timmy...' She put an arm round his shoulders and hugged him to her. 'Mark might not feel like playing, certainly not this evening. We're all very worried about Auntie Deborah. You must be patient.'

'Is she dead?'

Despite her reticence, he had understood. 'We don't know yet, darling. We're hoping not.'

Timmy was silent for a while. Then he said, 'She's Mark's mum, isn't she.'

Tears sprang to Alice's eyes and leaked out, wetting her cheeks. She wiped them away with her hand and kissed Timmy's forehead. 'Yes,' she said, 'Auntie Deborah is Mark's mum.'

*

Alice was preparing for bed when Paco phoned at last. Her mobile trilled much too loud, jarring her nerves with its crassly upbeat tune. She reached for it, her hands shaking as she held it to her ear. He sounded numb – or perhaps just exhausted, the Spanish accent stronger on the phone. Deborah was alive, he said, alive but unconscious. The prospects were not good. He was sorry to be so brief. He would return to Granada tomorrow with more information.

Timmy was already asleep. Unusually quiet and compliant, he had gone to bed with no fuss after just a cup of hot chocolate and some toast. Much to his disappointment, Mark had left within moments of their arrival. Alice could feel the tension in her nephew's body when they hugged; she noticed the soreness around his eyes that told her he'd been crying. Longing to offer him some comfort, she held him close but he slipped out of her embrace, saying he must go. She had a strong suspicion he planned to get drunk.

After Paco's call, Alice pushed doors open, flooded each room with light in a vain attempt to alleviate the terrible bleakness. It was no longer a home, just a house, an empty shell full of lifeless objects. In Deborah's study – what she referred to as her sanctum – Alice paused, recalling the urgent task she had set herself. Anxiety and grief had pushed it to the back of her mind, but it refused to stay there. She was loath to admit it even to herself but concern for Deborah had not been the only reason for her panic, her desperation to reach Granada that same day. Guilt mingled with her grief, clouding it; making her feel selfish. Her sister was in a critical state. Nothing else should matter.

It shouldn't matter but... Now she was standing here surrounded by the chaos of books and papers and computer hardware and twisted cables that, amazingly, didn't seem to bother her sister, she realised this might be her best opportunity to hunt for the diary. A diary she wasn't even sure existed. But knowing Deb and her compulsion to write everything down... If there was a diary, she must find it; find it fast and destroy it before the truth came out and wreaked havoc on all their lives.

As Alice surveyed the accumulated clutter of God knew how many years, wondering where on earth to start, a wave of exhaustion swept over her. It surely wouldn't hurt to wait till morning, would it? After a few hours' sleep, she might feel better able to face the task of rummaging through all Deborah's junk. Tomorrow then. First thing.

Chapter Two

'I heard it on the radio. Every morning I listen to *Cadena SER*, this is my habit... Madrid, three trains, I hear, then four. All is confusion. Then Teresa's daughter, she calls me. They took the train from here, she says, from Alcalá de Henares...'

The words spilled from Paco's mouth, unstoppable; slowed only by the effort it took to express himself in English. Alice sat facing him across the table, nursing her glass of insipid, milkless tea. She was still struggling to put meaning to his words. He might as well have been talking in Spanish: her brain couldn't cope with it. Why was he so determined to bombard her with unnecessary details when she was still trying to take in the dreadful fact that Deborah was...not dead apparently, but as good as? She needed to lie down, to sleep, to shut out the visions Paco was conjuring up. She had spent the whole of the previous night tossing and turning in the narrow spare bed, tortured by memories of her last visit when one evening she had sat on this very same bed with Deborah, talking, laughing, reminiscing about their childhood, never dreaming it could all suddenly end.

This morning, wandering from room to room in the *carmen* as if searching for her sister; seeing her books piled in untidy heaps, her clothes spilling out of drawers, a fringed shawl flung over a door. She had not changed: the room they'd shared for so many years as they grew up had been equally shambolic. She was always tidying up after her older sister. Deb hadn't cared. Careless: she'd been careless of her possessions; careless of her life.

If she had kept a diary, she would have been careless with that too.

19

But last night's panic now seemed not just inappropriate but callous, hysterical even. What was the rush? No one was going to start rooting about amongst Deborah's possessions at this awful moment. Why should they? They knew nothing.

'I ring her mobile, many times but she does not answer,' Paco continued. His hands would not be still. They held a cigarette packet, which danced from one hand to the other as if it were alive. 'I try to call Mark but you know in the cave there is no signal so then I must go to Sacromonte, to his cave. Of course he is sleeping... I have to wake him, make him understand. *Ay*, first he is angry. To be woken with this news... He cannot believe it. We must go to Madrid, I tell him. Now, immediately.'

The last time she saw her sister... October it must have been. She had come to Bristol on the train straight after meeting her publisher, thrilled at the prospect of seeing her work in print. But it was too late. All those years she had spent on the project and now she might never see the fruits of her labour – a labour of love that had occupied her for a decade or more, longer than most of her other passions.

Alice recalled their last walk together the day before Deb left. The Forest of Dean: a favourite place of hers for as long as she could remember. Waking to blue skies, unexpected autumn sunshine gilding the leaves that were just beginning to fall from the trees outside her window... The decision had been spontaneous, mutual.

On a familiar path through ancient beech and oak forest, they had strolled – in silence at first, listening to the birdsong, spotting squirrels that darted up the tall trees at their approach – while Timmy ran on ahead.

As they entered a small clearing, Deb stopped and turned to her. 'Can you believe it, Paco and I have almost reached the proverbial seven years? And it's still getting better. I believe I've found my true *media naranja*.'

'Your what?'

'You know, my half-orange.' She took Alice's arm and added, with that husky smoker's laugh of hers, 'I think he's tamed me.'

And Alice had shaken her head, said she doubted it.

When Timmy came running back, Deb grabbed his hand and the three of them veered off to crunch through piles of crisp brown and ochre leaves. Stamping them down just as they had in their childhood; laughing at themselves. She could not imagine Deborah tamed. She could not imagine Deborah dead.

'I spoke with the doctor.' Paco's voice was hoarse, breathy. 'She was thrown across the carriage, he says. The head injuries indicate this. Miracles happen, but I should not expect... She is in a coma, this may last many weeks or months and even if she does emerge, the damage to her brain...'

Only politeness stopped Alice clapping her hands over her ears. He had already described the scene at the temporary mortuary they'd set up, the scanning of lists, the bodies laid out for identification, the crying relatives. How in the face of his own relief at not finding Deborah there, he had tried to comfort Teresa's daughter, who clung to him, sobbing. Then the dash from hospital to hospital, each time seeing the same faces, all equally desperate for information. And how he had found her finally at the fourth hospital...

The horror was written in his every trembling movement: in the nervous flicker of his eyes, the quivering lips, the twitchiness of his hands as they painted the scene. *Be still*, she wanted to scream. *Be quiet, just for a moment.* She recalled Deb enthusing about his 'serenity', the way he could calm her down with a mere look, or a touch. It was one of the qualities she most admired in him. 'He starts the day by meditating for fifteen minutes: every morning without fail. He's so disciplined.' Then she had voiced what Alice was already thinking: 'They say opposites attract.' And they'd both laughed.

'It is possible they can transfer her to a hospital in Granada.' Paco's voice now was anything but serene. 'This is not certain. There is a risk it could cause further damage, the doctor said. And in any case it would take time to arrange... Tomorrow I will return to Madrid. You'll come with me? We can take a flight, it's only one hour. Your son could stay with friends of ours here.'

Alice remembered the aloe smell and soft, squishy texture of her sister's skin when they kissed goodbye at the airport that October day. Spanish style, right cheek, left cheek – she had got it right for once, she remembered. The expression on Deb's face – a less pudgy and rather more lined version of her own, similar enough, it seemed, for most people to recognise them as sisters – when she tasted the airport coffee (or was it the price that had caused her to wrinkle her nose in disgust?). So alive. Deborah had always been fully alive, buzzing with life; a *livewire*, people used to say.

Paco had dropped a grey worm of ash on the sleeve of his sweater. She wanted to reach across and brush it off for him. He was a neat man who looked after his appearance. There was nothing sloppy about him: on any other day, ash on his clothes would have bothered him, she thought. He was waiting for an answer.

'I'm not sure. Leaving Timmy with people he doesn't know...' Although the need to see Deborah was compelling, it had become a reflex to consider every decision in the light of Timmy's best interests rather than her own. 'If we come back the same day, perhaps Mark could look after him... Or will he come with us?' Even as she spoke, doubts began to surface about Mark's reliability as a babysitter.

'Mark...' Paco stubbed out his cigarette and sighed, that long-drawn out Spanish *ay* that even Deborah had acquired as part and parcel of her enviably fluent Spanish. 'You will have to ask him. But in my opinion he is not in the best state to take responsibility for a child.'

'Of course, I'm not thinking straight. It wouldn't be fair on either of them.'

Right on cue, Alice heard the clang of the gate and a moment later Mark appeared – breathless, as if he'd run all the way up the hill.

'You know what?' he burst out. 'Fucking Aznar and his lot, they've been lying. It wasn't ETA at all. It was al-Qaeda. They don't want to admit it because it's their fault – for dragging us into this fucking war with Iraq that no one wanted. Fucking liars they are, blaming it on ETA.'

Alice hated the way Mark talked, repeating that ugly f-word all the time. Timmy looked up to his cousin. Unless Mark moderated his language, Timmy would be swearing like a trooper by the time they left Granada.

'You know what it's about: they're afraid of losing the election if people realise. They thought they could fool us, keep the lie going till after the vote on Sunday.' Mark grabbed the remote and switched on the TV. 'But their plan's backfired. Look, everyone's out on the streets – in Madrid, Barcelona, all over the country. I've just come up from Plaza del Carmen. There's hundreds of people down there.'

On the television, scenes of angry crowds chanting seemed to confirm what Mark was saying, though Alice couldn't understand their words. The shock she felt had less to do with the news than with Mark's perverse fixation on politics at this time. Had he forgotten Deborah? The insistent blaring of the TV was a torture; more than she could bear. Her head ached with exhaustion. There was too much to deal with all at once.

Now Mark: she couldn't figure him out. He knew, of course. Paco had called him from Madrid immediately there was news. Yet he hadn't even mentioned his mother, hadn't asked Paco a single question. She put a hand to her temples where the throbbing was worst, pulled at her tired eyelids. How long since she had slept properly?

'Mark, please turn it off now,' Paco said, noticing her gesture. 'And sit down.' The sudden silence came as a huge relief. Alice glanced at Mark, leaning back in his chair, legs stretched out. There were rips in his jeans and on one leg an irregular-shaped patch in darker blue sewn on with large, untidy stitches. His defiant look had vanished, exposing the vulnerability, the fear. Tears welled up in her. He was so young; a lost child.

'*Bueno.*' Paco rested his elbows on the table and leant forward. 'Tomorrow.' He looked at Alice. 'If you agree, I call Robin and Leonor now. They are good people, friends of Deborah for many years. Robin is English, there will be no problem to communicate. They have two sons so they are used to boys. For them it will be a pleasure to take care of Timmy for the day.'

Alice nodded. She felt incapable of making decisions. 'Okay.'

'And you, Mark. Will you come to Madrid with us? We must book the flights.'

'I dunno.' His lips tightened and distorted as he struggled to stay in control of his emotions.

She itched to hold him, the way she held Timmy when he was hurt or upset, but she didn't quite dare. Turning to Paco, she said, 'Book three tickets,' and Mark bent his head in a just perceptible nod.

He should have taken a candle for Mum. One part of the square outside the Town Hall was all lit up with little flickering flames where people had put candles down on the paving slabs. Two hundred dead, he heard someone say. It would be two hundred and one if Mum died. He was praying she wouldn't die before they got there, before he could make it right with her. He hadn't prayed since his *primer comunión* when he was about nine. Mum had tried to stop him going to the classes – she didn't agree with it – but in the end he'd persuaded her. Why should he be the only one in the school left out, specially when it came to the presents and treats? It didn't matter whether you believed or not; that wasn't the point. The priest told them they'd have to confess their sins before Jesus would accept them. He couldn't think of any sins so Mum said to just make up a few. He could think of some now...

If she got better, if she made a miraculous recovery... It happened. He had heard stories about people being written off for dead and proving all the doctors wrong, living for years and years after. There was this one guy he'd read about who'd been laid in a coffin and then suddenly he sat up and waved his arms about. *What the fuck's going on?* Or something like that. He could just see it: Mum staging an act like that, making everyone gawp. He almost smiled, imagining it. So, if she did recover, what would he do? He'd give up drugs, he'd study, he'd quit his cave and move back in with her and Paco; whatever she wanted. If she recovered. In his head a voice was telling him: *Yeah, yeah, get real.* He told it to shut the fuck up.

More people drifted into the square; placards and banners were waving about above the sea of angry faces. *El pueblo llora, el gobierno miente*, one banner said: The people cry, the government lies. Too fucking true. He felt like smashing something, preferably that smug face with the moustache, Aznar. Even seeing it on some of the placards made him want to spit. Those cowards in the Town Hall wouldn't come out and face the crowd. People were shouting: 'Assassins! Liars! Enough manipulation! We want the truth before we vote!' He joined in the shouting for a few minutes but then he didn't feel like it any more; he just wanted to be quiet.

He pushed his way through the mass of demonstrators to where the candles were. A couple had been blown out so he lit them again and thought about Mum. He thought about flying down a hill with her in the snow, using a plastic bag for a sledge, both of them laughing like drunks. It must have been one Christmas when they were staying with Gran in England. He thought of them cramming their gobs with cherries from some orchard out in the country (not really stealing, she said) till they looked like they had lipstick smeared all round their mouths. He thought of her singing some silly song about *alegría*, rhyming it with *mamma mia*, that she'd made up on the spur of the moment, then twirling him round till he was dizzy.

She was cooler than the other mums. He wasn't the only one to think so: he remembered how Antoñito and some of the other kids liked to come over and play because his mum was more fun. But their mums hadn't got blown up, so what use was it in the end? She should have just stayed in Granada and talked to the translator on the phone. That's what phones were for, wasn't it?

Some of the candles were burning down but new ones kept replacing them. Paco might be back from Madrid by now. Best get up to the Albaicín, see if there was any more news. Then he could tell Paco what he'd decided about tomorrow: that he'd go to Madrid to see Mum. He'd been there a few times. Once, when he was about twelve, Mum had taken him to the *chocolatería*. It was late at night, packed out with people dunking their *churros* after an evening in the bars. It was the best hot chocolate ever. Maybe Mum had been planning to go there for breakfast – before or after meeting the translator. He didn't want to think about that. His bum was cold from sitting on the ground: he only noticed when he got up. Once he'd cleared the crowd of people in the square, he broke into a run – partly to get warm, partly because he wanted to reach the house quickly now.

Timmy was curled up on his side, lips slightly parted as he slept. Alice bent over him, feeling the warmth of his breath on her cheek, resisting the temptation to kiss him in case he woke. She hated the idea of leaving Timmy with strangers but there was no question of taking him to Madrid, to the hospital. And it was irrational to feel nervous just because they were in Granada rather than England. She tried to remember Robin and Leonor. The names rang a bell: quite possibly she had met them on one of her previous visits. Deb was always introducing her to 'friends' then running off, leaving her stranded to dredge up her few words of Spanish with people who spoke even less English.

She crouched over her suitcase, still only half unpacked. It was difficult to see in the dim light from the bedside lamp, which was made from goat or perhaps camel skin crudely painted with geometrical designs in red and yellow. Deb must have bought it from one of the Moroccan shops on the way down to town. What did you wear to visit someone in a coma, a sister who might or might not be aware of your presence? Certainly not the black she had brought just in case... Thinking about it now, she realised black would be utterly inappropriate even if it came to a funeral. Deb would want bright colours, flamboyant, life-affirming outfits, not dreary black. She had been through a black phase in her early twenties but since moving to Granada, she had taken to wearing all kinds of strange, haphazard combinations – clashing colours and styles that you had to admit were striking, if unconventional. It would not come to a funeral: she must take the optimistic view, use every ounce of willpower and positive thinking to spur her sister to recovery.

The bedroom felt cold. Central heating was a basic comfort she took for granted, but here, according to Deb, it didn't exist. There was no piped gas, she'd explained, only the *butanero*, who came with his truck and carried the orange gas bottles to the house on one shoulder. Alice became aware too of feeling hungry. She had scarcely eaten today. There was little food in the house and in her distracted state of mind, shopping seemed one challenge too many. She had made egg and chips for Timmy while she picked at some leftover broad beans with ham she found lurking in the fridge, not even bothering to heat them up.

Neither Paco nor Mark had shown any interest in eating; they appeared to be living on cigarettes. Even here in the bedroom, a faint whiff of tobacco smoke hung in the air. It always irritated her, despite Deb's habit of throwing windows and doors open. The three of them smoked like chimneys. Smoking had killed Dad at sixty, as she used to point out, fearing Deb might also succumb to an early heart attack. As so often, she had worried about the wrong thing.

On her way to the kitchen, she passed the open door of Paco's study. He was on the phone, his eyes half-closed, forehead creased in a deep frown. '*Sí, sí, claro.*' He spoke in a dull whisper, the voice of despair.

Mark was sitting at the kitchen table, preparing to roll a joint. She decided to ignore his methodical laying out of paper, tobacco, cannabis.

'Have you eaten?' she asked.

'I grabbed a *shawarma* on my way up,' he said.

'A what? You know my Spanish is non-existent.' Exhaustion was making her irritable, she realised with shame. 'Sorry, I didn't mean to snap.' She sat down opposite him.

'It's not Spanish,' he said with more patience than she deserved. 'Most likely Arabic. You must know what they are, those kebabs in pitta bread...'

The Moroccan influence was inescapable – no longer just a reminder of Granada's Moorish past like the Alhambra but part of the present. It made her uneasy, though she knew such feelings were absurd.

She rummaged in the cupboards and found some tins of tuna, a jar of red sauce, labelled *tomate frito*, and a packet of spaghetti.

'I'm making some pasta so if you're still hungry, there'll be plenty,' she said, 'For Paco as well.'

Mark finished assembling his joint and lit it. 'You want to share this?' he asked, holding it out to her.

For one crazy moment she felt tempted to accept, though her experience of smoking dope was limited to the odd party in her teens when she'd wanted to look cool. Without inhaling, so the effect was nil. Deb had been much more daring in her experimentation – until a couple of bad acid trips put her off.

'No thanks,' she said, making an effort to keep her voice and expression neutral.

Mark sat there smoking his joint in silence while she prepared the simple meal. *It'll be alright*, she wanted to say, but he wasn't a child with a grazed knee. He knew as well as she did that the nightmare of waiting could drag out interminably and that when it was finally over... If she lived, Deb would never be the same again. A billow of grief surged up without warning. She dashed out of the kitchen before her tears spilled over into the sauce and embarrassed Mark. Finding the wooden spoon still in her hand, she gripped it tightly as she tried to regain control. She must be strong for Mark, support him all she could through this tragedy. Going to pieces would help no one. Alice took a deep breath and then another and another until she felt calm enough to return to her cooking.

The three of them ate in near silence. The flights were booked, Paco said. Robin would come to collect Timmy first thing in the morning. Mark should sleep here tonight. There was no more to be said. Or, rather there was too much – which came to the same thing.

Chapter Three

The hospital smelt of bleach and bad news. There were too many people scurrying about, getting in the way. Mark didn't like how they huddled in tight little groups whispering together and swarmed into the lifts so he was squashed up close, with their sweat and perfume almost making him gag. Paco had been here yesterday but he'd forgotten the way to Mum's ward. His mind had gone blank, he said. Alice had to ask at two different desks and then a nurse took them to Intensive Care.

He'd lied to Mum about the money. That was the main thing on his mind as he followed the nurse down the corridor. Not that he ever took much, just ten or twenty euros now and again to keep those bastards off his back. It wasn't as though she was going to miss a few euros but still, it was wrong of him. He wished he hadn't taken it; he wished he hadn't lied about it. She knew he was lying, that was what bothered him most.

He'd planned to tell her everything when he got to the hospital: all the bad things he'd done and felt sorry about. How he was going to make it up to her, be a good son like Robin and Leonor's boys (or so she was always telling him). But when he saw her all wired up to machines like a body not a person, the words just dried up. There seemed no point when she wasn't going to hear a thing he said. They'd given her a label, which was just as well because you could hardly recognise her; she might have been anyone.

Alice looked like she was going to burst into tears any moment. She held Mum's hand and whispered stuff to her. He moved away, not wanting to hear. Paco just stood there jiggling about like he needed a pee and rubbing his eyes. At one point Mum shifted a bit in the bed and he went ballistic, grabbing the nurse, asking was it a good sign, did it mean she was coming round, but the nurse said no, it didn't mean anything. He leant over Mum and said her name over and over: 'Deborah, Deborah *mi amor*, I'm here, I love you.' He fiddled with the covers – to try and make her more comfortable, he said. As if that would make any difference. He tried to stroke her hair but half of it had been shaved off. She looked terrible.

All the fucking medics could say was *'no se sabe'*. They were supposed to be the experts but they didn't know. Most likely they were lying. They didn't want to admit they were fucking clueless about how to bring her round. Or else they were just scared to tell the truth, to say she was as good as dead.

Mark walked over to the window. Down below, the street was busy with traffic, *motos* weaving in and out, a beer lorry unloading crates of *Cruzcampo* at a bar, wheeling them in on a trolley. He watched the people walking past. Some of them looked ancient: a bent old man dragging himself along with a stick, a shrunken woman with wisps of white hair, leaning on her daughter's arm. They were fucking years older than Mum and they were still alive, still out and about. It wasn't fair. Three men in suits – business types like his dad – were standing together waiting to cross the road. Mark heard one of them laugh like a hyena. It made him want to punch the guy.

Did Charlie know? He thought about sending a text message; it might get him some sympathy. He pictured his dad: tall and straight like a policeman, with his snooty voice and his stubbly grey hair that he must get trimmed every bloody week. Fuck it, he didn't need Charlie's sympathy. What if he came over? The last time they met, Dad had tried to talk him into moving to London, offered to set him up with some crappy office job. As if.

It was stupid but he couldn't help it, the pathetic little scrap of hope that Charlie might still change, might start to be like other dads – like Robin or Juan Antonio, for instance. That instead of just sending him a twenty-pound note (that he had to take to the bank and swap for euros) on his birthday and forgetting about him the rest of the year, he might actually show some interest in his life, make an effort to like him even. But what Charlie wanted was a clone of himself, which Mark would never ever be. When he was little, he used to imagine he had a proper dad – one who played football with him and lifted him up on his shoulders so he could see the three kings in the *Cabalgata* procession.

A couple of years ago in England, Mark had taken his cousin on the Avon Valley Railway and Timmy had asked him about his dad. He thought Mark was lucky having a dad, even a useless one. He'd never met his own dad. Alice refused to talk about him or even tell Timmy his name. Mark thought that was mean: it wouldn't hurt to give him a name. He'd gone away to a different country without knowing she was going to have a baby, Alice told him. He could be anywhere in the world: finding him would be impossible.

Mark felt sorry for Timmy. At least *he* had Paco for a substitute dad. Paco was okay; he'd been around since Mark was thirteen. Alice didn't have boyfriends like Mum. Well, she used to, she'd been married even. But she'd given up on men, Mum said. He wondered if she was a lesbian but he didn't think so, seeing as she'd had Timmy.

Alice was hovering, not knowing where to put herself while Paco talked to Mum. People said she and Mum looked alike. He'd never thought so. There were little things about her that reminded him of Mum: the way she cupped her chin in her hand and made her eyebrows go up; certain expressions she used, like *funnily enough*. They both said that a lot. They had matching noses, turned up at the tip – not like his that was a broad triangle same as Charlie's – but apart from that and the bluey-grey eyes... Alice was all straight lines: the cut of her hair, her mouth, everything about her neat, like it was drawn with a ruler. Mum was the opposite: she was kind of chaotic, but she had style. She was someone you couldn't help notice.

Also, Alice never changed: she'd looked the same all his life with that hair the colour of walnut shells (except now there were grey streaks in it), same length, same straight fringe. Whereas Mum was always experimenting. She'd get fed up with her hair and dye it black or cut it short like a punk; once she had a thing about purple and dressed in different shades of it for months on end; another time it was sparkly silver and gold stuff with sequins she went crazy about. Alice's face was less wrinkly but Mum looked younger somehow. He thought it could be because she had more fizz. He glanced at the bed and had to concentrate so he wouldn't cry. *Used to have more fizz.*

When Alice came over and put a hand on his arm, he pulled away like he'd been stung because for some reason that little touch made the tears shoot out all of a sudden.

'Paco and I are going for a cup of tea,' she said. 'You should talk to your mum. 'She may be more aware of people around her than we think. Hearing your voice might help bring her out of the coma.'

Mark didn't think it would help. It might even make her worse if she was still angry with him about the fight. 'Okay,' he said, mainly so Alice would leave him alone. Then, when he saw the two of them had gone, he thought: no harm in trying. He forced himself to go up close. He put his hand in hers like he used to when he was a little kid. Mainly he was curious to see if it would be warm or cold. What happened then spooked him out. She gripped it; gripped his fingers. But her face stayed exactly the same: eyes closed, blank like she wasn't really there at all. Nothing else moved. He didn't know what to do so he just leaned down and talked in her ear. He said he was sorry about the money and about the fight and about slagging her off. She was a brilliant mum so she'd better bloody well pull through. Then he got all choked up and couldn't say any more. He sat on the chair by her bed counting the tiles on the ceiling while he waited for Paco and Alice to come back.

Alice sat opposite Paco in the crowded cafeteria, leaning across the table to hear better amidst the general hubbub. The doctor had explained to him that moving Deborah would be too dangerous. The next few days were likely to be critical: swelling of the brain could occur, which meant constant monitoring of the intra-cranial pressure. They might have to drill a hole, drain some fluid.

As Paco conveyed this news, translating the doctor's words in a slow, deliberate way that only served to drag out the anguish, she stared at the bulge of his Adam's apple moving as he spoke; at the folds of his neck; at the open collar of his denim shirt, one side of it curling slightly. Anything to avoid looking directly into his eyes and seeing her own pain reflected back to her.

'Will you stay?' she asked.

'For the moment, yes.' He stubbed out his cigarette. 'And you? What will you do?'

'I must go back to Granada and take care of Timmy. But I won't return to England until...' The unfinished part of her sentence hung heavy in the air between them. 'I want to be there for Mark too. I'm afraid he might fall apart at some point. If my sister shows any change... you'll let me know, won't you?'

'Of course.' Paco stood up. 'You have drunk your tea? Come then.'

*

Alice had hoped that actually seeing Deb would dispel the visions, stop her obsessive imaginings of the train, the bomb...but as the plane levelled out over central Spain, the scene of the tragedy forced itself yet again into the forefront of her mind. What had Deborah felt? Each time she tried to imagine her sister's last moments of consciousness, the details changed. Did the roar of the bomb, of clashing metal and screaming passengers interrupt a conversation with her friend, Teresa? Or was she absorbed in a book? Possibly she had dropped off to sleep after staying up late and rising early. Did she have time for thought when the explosion blasted the train apart? Time to think *I'm going to die* as she flew through the air and slammed into the hard surface of the carriage roof (or door or seatback – so many hard surfaces in a train)? Metal would be fused into unrecognisable shapes by the heat of the explosion, jagged splinters of window glass transformed into deadly missiles... Would Deb have choked on fumes of burning plastic, the sickly odour of blood and seared flesh?

Alice picked up the in-flight magazine and flicked through its pages of adverts and articles, all equally meaningless to her. It was ironic, she reflected, that if what Mark claimed was true, Deb's injuries should be the result of Islamic terrorism when she had fought so hard on behalf of Muslims in Granada. With typical passion, she had campaigned for a mosque in the Albaicín, had thrown herself into defending their rights. 'People here are so prejudiced against Arabs, you've no idea! As if half of them weren't descended from what they call *moros*.' She had even learnt Arabic – for the purposes of her research, she said, rather than to communicate with Hassan, who spoke perfect Spanish. Alice remembered her sister raving about the eight hundred years of

Muslim civilisation in Granada: how advanced they were in medicine and science and agriculture and how Christian architecture couldn't compete in beauty and sensuality.

Mark raised his head from the newspaper he'd been immersed in since take-off. 'Paco's going to miss voting,' he said. 'Bloody shame.'

Wrapped up in her own thoughts, she had almost forgotten his presence. 'Yes, it's a pity,' she agreed, humouring him. 'If only we had the ability to be in two places at once.'

'Yeah well...' He flipped over a page of the paper but then abruptly closed it and turned to her again. 'Do you think Mum will get better?' He was fingering the woolly ropes of his dreadlocks that Deb called *rastas*. 'Don't lie to me, Auntie Alice. I'm not a kid any more. Tell me honestly what you think.'

Alice hesitated before replying. 'I'd say her will to live is as strong as anyone's. If that counts at all...'

'Too right. You know what? I've just remembered something. We were in town a few weeks ago and Mum nearly got flattened by a car, trying to cross the road on red. The driver had to brake so sharp, the car behind ran into the back of him – no damage, but still everyone was yelling at Mum. When the lights changed and we got across, she grabbed me and made me promise not to tell Paco. You know what she said? "I can't die yet – not before my book comes out."'

Was that what went through her mind as the blast hurled her across the carriage? *Oh please, not yet! I want to see my book in print.* Alice heard Mark mutter something under his breath. It sounded like 'fucking Walladah'. She ignored it.

'Then she can't die.' Alice tried to keep her voice light. 'I remember how ecstatic she was about finding a publisher. She told me what her editor had said: "With so much post-9/11 Islamophobia, the world needs examples of liberated Muslim women." I remember the words exactly because she repeated them at least three times.' Glancing at Mark, she was pleased to see the trace of a smile on his face.

'June,' Mark said. 'It was supposed to be coming out in June. She must have told me about fifty times. So she's got to come round by then.'

The plane had started its descent: the snowy peaks of the Sierra Nevada were already visible in the distance.

'Why don't you stay at the house for a few days?' she said. 'Then if there's any news... I gather you don't have a mobile signal in the cave.' When he failed to respond, she added, 'Come up for meals if nothing else. Timmy would be glad of your company.' She was aware that her motives were not entirely altruistic. If Mark were there she would feel less vulnerable.

'I dunno.' He opened his newspaper again. Conversation closed.

Her thoughts returned to Timmy. She was itching to get back to him, to reassure herself he was alright. As soon as they arrived at the airport she would ring Robin.

It was in the Granada newspapers about Mum. Tina had showed him the page in *Ideal*. They'd got their facts wrong, stupid buggers. Deborah Hardy, an English writer who had lived in the Albaicín since 1990. It was 1985, not 1990. Critically injured, they said, but in the photo she was laughing. Where the fuck had they got that picture from? It was a rubbish one that looked nothing like her. It must have been from years ago and she looked half cut. It was taken with flash, maybe at some party in a bar.

Tina said she was sorry. So did about half a dozen other people he passed on his way home from voting. Some of them he didn't even know, though they seemed to know him. What was he supposed to say? *Gracias*? He couldn't really see what there was to thank them for but he said it anyway. He'd managed to avoid Ed and Dani – that was one good thing. They wouldn't be sorry. If she died, they'd probably be fucking celebrating, seeing as they'd always dissed her. Just for having a nice house and more money than them. If it hadn't been for Dani threatening to slice him up like a rabbit, he'd never have taken the forty euros.

Being able to vote was cool. It was his first time. He was glad now that he'd gone to all the hassle of getting Spanish nationality. Being officially English was a joke when he'd lived here since he was one. It was Mum who said he should apply but Paco had helped him loads. Without Paco, he'd most likely have ripped up all that fucking paperwork. He wouldn't have had the patience.

At the polling station you could spot those who were voting PP by their shifty look. He reckoned they were ashamed, because now everyone knew about Aznar's lies. The train bombs had been the government's fault and that was a fact. They were fucking murderers as well as liars. If it hadn't been for them, Mum and all those others... He noticed the paper he'd bought at Madrid Airport yesterday lying open on the floor with a photo of the new PP leader, Rajoy on the page. He stamped on it, then ripped it in two right across his ugly mug. They'd better not get in again... The votes would be counted tonight; he'd have to get himself to a bar and see the results.

Mark looked around the cave. It was a mess: beer cans lolling all over the floor, plates and mugs he hadn't bothered to wash, a pan with some leftover rice from days ago that had gone off; his mattress piled up with clothes and bedding. The plastic jerry-can of water was nearly empty; he wished it wasn't such a long trek to fill up.

Timmy wanted to see his cave. Probably he imagined something spooky with water dripping from the roof and prehistoric bones. He'd asked if there were bats, like in the one he'd been to on his school trip. He'd be well impressed when he saw there was a bed and chairs, rugs on the floor, a gas stove. Or maybe he'd be disappointed. He was just a kid.

It was still morning. The day seemed to be stuck, like it had a flat tyre. He wasn't used to so much waiting. He should tidy up, fetch some water, go and get Timmy...but he couldn't be arsed. He lay on the bed. Waiting. If time could just stop dead like this, you should be able to make it go into reverse too. He thought about time travel. Just going back was no use. You'd have to be given a second chance so you could change things. He thought about fortune tellers, old women with crystal balls. If Mum had known... Once, when she was young, she'd had her palm read. It was on a train in some other country, not Spain or England. This man with a turban and staring eyes had grabbed her hand and examined it. 'You'll go far,' he told her. 'You'll have children.' Obvious things like that. The man must have been a fake because he said nothing about her getting blown up by a bomb.

The questions kept coming back to him like hiccups that wouldn't go away. Had Mum heard what he said? And if she *had* heard, did she believe him? There was no way of knowing: that was the worst thing. He checked his phone and found a missed call from his dad. Someone must have told him. Mark didn't think he'd care about Mum, though he might pretend to. He'd never been able to figure out how Charlie and Mum got together in the first place: they had fuck all in common. Remembering how the last time they met, Dad had slammed him for not studying, for living in a cave, for looking like a scarecrow (incredible, those were his exact words!) – just because he'd turned down the 'fantastic opportunity' of a job in London – and how he'd blasted Mum as well for not bringing him up right, he decided no way, no fucking way did he want to talk to his dad now.

'It's like a real house, Mummy, with a door and windows and a chimney sticking out of the hill. Mummy, can I sleep there one night? Mark said I could.'

'We'll see.' Alice baulked at the idea of Timmy joining, even for just one night, the ragtag bunch of hippies and drug-addicts and dropouts who populated the Sacromonte caves. Although she hadn't seen it herself, she could well imagine the insalubrious state of Mark's cave home without running water or a toilet of any kind. It would be much better for all concerned if Mark came and slept here at the *carmen*.

'He has to light candles at night because there's no electricity and sometimes, when it's cold, he builds a campfire outside and bakes potatoes in it. He calls them *papas*.'

'I'm not making any promises now.' Alice cut a generous slice of pizza and put it in front of him, hoping the food would serve as a distraction.

She had ventured out to shop at the little supermarket in the Albaicín where no language was needed. She remembered Deb's disappointment when – several years ago – it was modernised from the kind of grocery store where you had to ask for everything at the counter. 'It's so much more impersonal now,' she had complained. While Alice stood waiting in the checkout queue, sandwiched between the arguing (or were they merely gossiping?) local women, her mobile rang.

'Your sister follows the same,' she heard Paco say just as her turn came up.

Struggling to make sense of his words, she repeated them. 'Follows the same?'

'No change,' Paco said and she stared stupidly at the elderly man behind the till to whom she had given a twenty-euro note.

Then, as she was passed a handful of coins, her mind cleared; she understood what Paco was telling her. 'Oh,' she said, and realising how much gloom that lone syllable must have conveyed, 'So no deterioration then. That's good.'

Human beings were programmed for optimism, it struck her as she trudged back to the *carmen* weighed down by two plastic bags of shopping. In some hidden niche of her mind, the possibility of a miracle must have been lurking. Otherwise she would not have felt so dispirited by Paco's call.

Later, while Timmy was still out, she had roamed around the house, touching things, examining them as if she were in a museum. Everything had been chosen by Deb. In the early days she'd teased her sister about going native. She meant things like the *brasero*, that heater nesting under the table, and the long felt tablecloth you were supposed to pull up to your waist to keep the warmth in; the uncomfortable, bolster-like pillows on every bed; the lack of a kettle, which seemed nothing short of perverse. Deb's irritation at what was intended to be a light-hearted remark had been out of all proportion. 'Oh for God's sake!'

Family photos greeted Alice in every room: the familiar faces of her parents, Deborah, Mark at different stages of his childhood. Younger, mostly smiling, versions of herself – with Deb or with Timmy – gazed back at her from the frames, each one assaulting her with a maelstrom of emotions and memories. The picture taken by a friend of Deb's on her first visit to Granada with Timmy when he was two (she had labelled it *Sisters and Sons* in her own album); a later one of the two boys with their granny in England not long before she died; and on the bookshelf in a seventies-style fabric frame, a photo of herself and Deb as teenagers, their faces fresh and unscarred by painful experience. As always, she noted how gawky and graceless she looked next to Deb. Not fat but big-boned. How she had envied her sister's slim, elegant build.

Still nagging at her mind now as she watched Timmy eat was the mission she had been postponing for too long already. The diary – if one existed – must be found. Deb had written a journal since childhood. It was private, she had boasted to Alice at age fifteen, gloating as she waved it in front of her sister, hinting at secrets too scandalous to share. She kept it hidden but Alice had found it easily and one day when Deb was out, she had read every page, horrified to find several scathing or, at best, dismissive references to herself. Being unable to confront Deb without giving away her own sneaky behaviour made it worse. The humiliation stayed with her for a long time.

They'd done it! Zapatero had won and the PP were out. It was fucking brilliant. That would show them what came of their lies, what came of dragging the country into Bush's fucking war in the first place. Bush, Blair, Aznar, they'd lied about everything. There were no weapons of mass destruction in Iraq. And all that shit about ETA...but people had seen through it and now the PP's lies had got them kicked out. Zapatero was going to bring the troops back first thing. He'd promised.

Mark flicked the top off another bottle of beer from the plastic bag at his feet and tilted it to his throat. It was the last one. Time to get himself home while he could still walk straight. The bars were emptying now, no one exactly celebrating because how could you when two hundred people had died? Still, he was glad the PSOE had won.

He looked round for Tina and José. They'd been with him till a few minutes ago but somehow he'd lost them. He started walking down the hill, pausing every few minutes to take a swig from the bottle. Along the Camino de Sacromonte, a *moto* came round the bend too fast, nearly knocked him over. The guy swore at him, like it was *his* fault. Mark gave him the finger and carried on. He'd been planning to take Tina back to his cave; he felt like some company tonight. She had a lovely body, just thinking about her was making him hard. He hoped she hadn't gone with José. Mark wouldn't put it past him to try it. Sly bastard. He had the hots for her, you could tell.

Mark chucked the empty bottle into some bushes and carried on. The urge to throw up hit him out of the blue. He doubled over by the side of the road and heaved. Afterwards he sat on the wall for a few minutes, thinking he didn't have the strength to make it back to the cave. Puking had sobered him up – much too quickly. He didn't want to be sober. He didn't want to see visions of Mum in the hospital looking more dead than alive. If she carried on like that they might write her off and take out a few of her organs for transplants.

The wall felt damp through his jeans. He eased his bum off it and plodded the rest of the way home. He didn't care any more about Tina. She could sleep where the fuck she liked. There was no one he wanted to see; they could all go to hell.

Alice waited till Timmy was asleep before starting her search for the diary. Deb's study seemed the most sensible place to begin. As she stepped into the room, her foot caught one of the many piles of books ranged around the floor. It tottered and fell, shedding a few torn strips of paper used as markers. Crammed bookshelves lined three walls while her sister's desk and a filing cabinet took up a large part of the window wall.

Alone in the house, there was no logical cause for stealth but she approached the desk with soft step and all her senses alert, as if she might be apprehended at any moment. Surrounding the computer monitor, files and loose sheets of A4 lay in untidy heaps, while smaller scraps of paper with scribbled notes and references in Deborah's handwriting were pinned to a cork board on the wall. One of the desk drawers was jammed slightly open. She yanked at it, freed the obstruction and closed it again, unable to face the chaotic jumble of plugs, cables, CDs and yet more papers she had glimpsed within. Deborah was scatty but she would surely have chosen a less obvious hiding place.

Alice surveyed the bookshelves, hoping to find a blank spine or a slim exercise book squeezed in discreetly between the tomes of history and fiction and philology. Her eye was drawn to several but none of those she tugged out were diaries. Absently she retrieved a screwed-up ball of paper lying on the floor and flattened it out. A woman aged about thirty, self-assured and strikingly beautiful, returned her look with a faint smile, challenging, almost defiant. She was wearing a long, fairly plain dress with a gold-bordered bodice and sat with legs spread, her long dark hair topped by a close-fitting cap adorned with beads and a floppy fringe. Glancing at the caption, Alice realised this was Walladah, Deborah's 11th century idol. How strange to find her chucked on the floor, discarded like a piece of trash.

Giving up on the bookshelves, Alice began to rummage through the dizzy pile of papers on the desk, some already yellowed with age. Nothing. She looked out of the window at the view that must have greeted her sister each day as she worked at her desk: the red-tiled patio and overhanging it, the big mimosa tree still bright with yellow blossom. In the garden beyond, a few decaying fruits from last year hung on the branches of pomegranate and persimmon trees; the foliage of jasmine, honeysuckle and wisteria clung to trellises and railings. Would Deborah ever sit here again to gain inspiration from all this loveliness?

A piece of paper, its edges tattered, protruded untidily from the pile. Alice pulled it out and cast her eye over the page. Mark's childish handwriting, alternating with Deb's familiar scrawl, suggested it dated back some years and was a game of Consequences. *Hassan meets Alice at the beach*, she read. *He says, 'The moon is bright, let's dance tonight.' She says, 'You stink.' They hide behind the mimosa tree. The police send them to prison.*

Hassan. It was disconcerting to see his name associated with hers. But how spookily prophetic, because he *had* gone to prison a couple of years ago. She wasn't sure what crime he had committed. Deb seemed to think it was all down to paranoia in the aftermath of 9/11 and he was probably quite innocent. As she tore up the page, dropping the pieces into a crammed wastepaper bin, Alice remembered the surge of relief she had felt at the news. It might be unjust but with Hassan out of the way, they were all safer.

The filing cabinet next: she must not let herself be distracted. Ten years had passed since she and Deb made their pact of secrecy. To protect it, the diary had to be found. At stake was everything she valued. Even if Deb had eventually given up recording the serial dramas punctuating her life, she had always written obsessively when going through emotional crises, and in the turmoil of that year when so much had to be hidden, her need to write would have been greater than ever. Writing was Deb's equivalent of the piano: a way of expressing her innermost feelings. Alice remembered how furiously she had scribbled in her teens, alone in their bedroom, refusing to come to meals, after that explosive row with her best friend, Jane Brock, and when Stephen Helliwell, her first love, dumped her for another girl.

Systematically, starting at the top, Alice flicked through the nondescript files in each drawer, trying not to lose heart. Could her instinct be mistaken? Squatting to tackle the bottom drawer, she pulled it open and stared at a typical Deborah clutter of seemingly unrelated objects. A large shoebox at the back of the drawer held the only promise. She lifted it out and removed the lid. Her breath quickened as she took in its contents and recognised that same sense of triumph mixed with guilty self-justification she remembered from her early teens. She tipped the six exercise books, each labelled with dates, onto the floor and opened one at random.

21st September 1989

The days are getting shorter but still warm, the earth parched, waiting for the rain to bring relief. I'm sitting here in the patio, the light beginning to fade now. From inside I can hear him playing... I love to listen to those plangent notes so resonant with emotion, some unbearable sorrow from deep in the past, it seems to me. Where does it spring from: the instrument or the player, the oud or Hassan? If I could play an instrument, the music would be joyful, exultant, brimming over – like my singing in the shower these September mornings! *Luna de miel*, moon of honey, sweetness of love.

Strange how I considered myself perfectly happy before Hassan came into my life. Now I realise how incomplete that 'happiness' was.

Hassan again; she couldn't escape him. The madness of a new relationship, new love. That soaring joy she recognised from her own early days with Simon, with Michael, even – if somewhat muted – with Andy. Was disillusion, the souring of love, inevitable from such a high point? She thought of Deb and Paco and knew the answer was no. But she was wasting time. She picked up the next volume, the crucial one covering those months Deb had spent in England. The rest of the diary could wait.

'I don't believe...' She was startled to find she had spoken the words aloud. For it seemed that Deb had for once done the sensible thing. A whole wad of pages had been torn out: the last three months of 1993 and the whole of 1994 were missing.

Perversely, her relief was tinged with disappointment. She had always been curious: it seemed weird that Deb had shown so little feeling at the time. She had 'closed down emotionally' or that was how Mum interpreted her apparent stoicism. Suffering in silence was not Deb's usual way. Had all her pain been concentrated in these missing diary entries? After the event, she had returned to Spain in a matter of days and by mutual agreement they did not meet again for over two years. How she had fared during that time remained a mystery.

The diary resumed in a new exercise book dating from months after her return to Granada. Scanning the pages of this volume, Alice noticed that here and there lines had been blacked out so thoroughly that nothing was left legible. In some places Deb had obliterated whole chunks of writing, in others just a few words. It was impossible to know when. Had something alerted her to the danger of leaving written evidence of their lie?

Sometimes a lie was for the best. And yet... There would be consequences: sooner or later she would have to pay a price for what they had done.

Chapter Four

One week. It seems like a month that I've been here. So many new impressions to absorb, my senses are assailed every hour of the long luminous day, the vibrant night. I feel fully alive; my skin tingles as if I'd been making love for hours. Granada. I love the sound of it, rolling the 'r', almost losing the 'd', imitating Lola and Ramón who own this little apartment in the Albaicín. Ridiculously small but it's fine, perfect for Mark and me. I knew as soon as I saw it: tiled floors, pine shutters at the windows, everything compact, modest, charmingly Spanish. Comparing it to our house in London (Charlie's house now) makes me smile. I don't need so much space, nor so many possessions. Reducing ourselves to this diminutive space, these few belongings, is a liberation.

Deep inside me, I've known for a long time that this was what I needed: a place with light and warmth and soul. Becoming a mother has changed my priorities but they were already ripe for changing. A slow, stress-free life should be easy here. I don't need to worry about work for the moment; that can wait. For now, I just want to be, to absorb everything; and to give my full attention to Mark after all he's had to put up with in his turbulent year and a half of life.

24th April 1985

So many small things give me pleasure. From our window we can look out on the cobbled street and across to the houses opposite, their balconies filled with pots of geraniums. Yesterday a mule loaded with panniers of rubble passed by, led by a builder working on one of the houses further down. I could hear the clip-clop of its hooves as it plodded down the steps to the little square.

Mark loves watching all the bustle of the morning market in Plaza Larga, the noisy chatter and clatter in the bar where everyone has breakfast and people actually talk to each other, shouting above the din of the coffee machine.

¿Qué te apetece? Pepe asks. What do you fancy? Then he shouts your order for toast to the woman in the kitchen. *¡Dos tostadas con tomate!* He's small and round and he knows everyone. All the staff make a fuss of Mark, sit him up on the counter and play with him. The customers too. *Qué guapo es.* How handsome.

2nd May 1985

Suddenly it's cold enough for jumpers again – quite a shock after the hot sunshine of the last few weeks. Lola says it's normal to have 'cold-waves' at this time of year and that soon we'll all be complaining of the heat.

I already feel part of this small world, the Albaicín. People recognise us in the street and say hello (or sometimes goodbye when they don't want to stop and chat).There's such a mix here: stout housewives with loud, bossy voices, perfectly coiffed hair and shapeless dresses (though sometimes you see them wandering about in dressing gown and slippers), their menfolk stolid and mostly silent, seated on benches in the plazas, from where they observe the bustle and activity around them; gypsies – the men dark and proud with hair to their shoulders and gold jewellery, the women heavy-hipped after a certain age, and fierce-looking; a few hippy types with long unwashed hair and what must appear to the locals rather outlandish garb, who I'm told live in the caves on the other side of the old medieval wall, up near San Miguel Alto.

I love the way I'm greeted with '*hola guapa*' or '*hola joven*' in the street and in the shops. It makes me feel prettier or younger, even though I know it means nothing, it's just like saying 'hello love' in England. In the bank they sometimes address me as *Doña* Deborah, which sounds so funny I struggle to keep a straight face.

Alice knew she shouldn't be reading the diaries, not while Deb was still alive. She had opened the first notebook intending just a peek at the earliest days before replacing all six books in the shoebox and returning it to the back of the filing cabinet. But once she'd started, the words seemed to hypnotise her, compelling her to read on. The words *were* Deborah. Alice could hear her voice, see her in the apartment, in the market place... Reading these pages brought her sister closer. Deb would forgive her, surely?

13th May 1985

I'm beginning to anticipate the reaction when I admit to being husbandless and far from my family. Pity predominates. Older men – Ramón included – become protective. The younger women think I'm brave and regard me with awe. Most people probably think I'm mad – to have left not just my husband but all my family too and come here alone by choice. Or if I'm not insane, I must be running away from something, a crime perhaps? In the end they shrug and put it down to my being from the alien and incomprehensible culture of northern Europe, a foreigner.

28th May1985

Lola works so hard in the house, always cleaning, washing, ironing, preparing food; she never stops. Not that she seems unhappy. Sometimes I even hear her singing. I'm quite sure she doesn't feel exploited but sees it as her role. Ramón is early retired due to some medical condition to do with his digestion that Lola explained to me in graphic detail but I still didn't quite grasp. Needless to say, he does little to help Lola – just a bit of shopping. Their daughter got married last year and she told me how much she looks forward to grandchildren. My mother must be very sad, she commented. To be so far away from Mark and with no other *nietos*... By the time she finished her empathising, I felt horribly guilty for depriving Mum.

5th June 1985

It strikes me how everything in my life has changed in the space of not much more than a year. I mean EVERYTHING. Last spring I was still married to Charlie. Now I'm single and free. I was working in a high-powered job in the centre of London. Here I'm not working at all. I've moved from a large luxurious house full of expensive furniture, the latest in gadgets and all sorts of costly but useless 'things' to a small rented apartment in the Albaicín where I'm living this simple, tranquil life with practically nothing in the way of possessions. And I'm happy!

More important, Mark has adapted and seems to be thriving in this environment. Alice thought it was selfish of me to 'drag' Mark out here. I can't wait for her visit, so that she'll see how wrong she was. When friends ask if I've any regrets, the answer is a resounding NO.

17th June 1985

It's a delight after London to feel so safe. I can walk around at any hour of the day or night without the slightest fear. The only real danger is from objects, not people. Everything is rundown – the houses, the streets, all in terrible disrepair. Poor Mark – he was such an early walker, steady on his feet by eleven months – but here he's forever falling over and hurting his knees. I've stumbled several times myself. But my indignation at the neglect lasts about ten seconds. Then I'm seduced once again by the charm of my new world, which more than makes up for the occasional grazed hand or knee. The craggy old man who comes by with a bucket of golden honey from his bees in the mountains, shouting *Miel*! *Miel*! and out you go with your jam jars for him to fill and weigh on the old-fashioned spring balance he carries around with him. Then there's the knife-grinder I've seen once or twice on his motorbike – which somehow powers the grinding wheel. He plays a few notes on a mouth organ to announce his presence and people come running from their houses with knives to be sharpened.

22nd June 1985

I've been showing off 'my' city to Alice, enjoying her delight in the beauty of the Alhambra (my fifth visit), the sights and sounds of the Albaicín, the generous free *tapas*. I found her a lot more relaxed than when we last met. She sees that the split from Simon was necessary, that their marriage was never going to mend. Most relationships have a natural time-span, whether it's four weeks or forty years. Recognising it and giving up that seductive, happy-ever-after dream is the hard bit. People change, circumstances change. I'm happy to be on my own for now but I've got Mark. Being single doesn't suit Alice; she needs to find the right man and start a family. Although she hasn't said so, I'm sure it's what she wants. There was a guy at work who liked her but the revolting way he ate, 'like an alligator', turned her off completely, she said.

Alan the Alligator: Alice had forgotten all about him. She could picture him now, open mouth chomping on a sandwich that oozed mayonnaise and shreds of lettuce; tomato seeds stuck to his lip or lodged, half camouflaged, in his short reddish beard. The idea of a romance with him was a joke. He had been no more than a smokescreen.

It was another colleague, Michael she had loved and waited for, keeping all her feelings locked inside. Michael, who had let her fall for him, flirted with her and given her every encouragement, neglecting to tell her until it was far too late (*after* those three magical nights in her bed) that he had a girlfriend who worked away during the week and came home at weekends. Magical at the time; later excruciating to recall.

She had ended the affair at once but changing her feelings was another matter. What madness it seemed now, to have wasted five years of her life pursuing that happy-ever-after dream when it was obvious he would never leave his girlfriend. She should have changed jobs but she *wanted* to see him every day, keeping the hope alive, persisting against all logic, all common sense. Every smile, every kind word or look of affectionate regret reignited her fantasies of a future together. None of her colleagues had any idea. Only her best friend, Ginny knew what a fool she was.

The right man. As if it were that easy. When she'd married at twenty-two, she had assumed it would be for life. But with Simon too she had stuck it out longer than she should. They were simply not suited. Everyone thought her marriage broke up because Simon spent so much time working away. They were wrong: his absences were the easy part. She didn't even mind his occasional flings. It was the times they spent together that were difficult: his homecomings that she always tried to make special but that so often backfired, causing her bitter disappointment and frustration. Bottled up, those feelings would slip out in the form of snide criticisms or pointless bickering. Before each separation, they managed to be nice to each other for a few days, giving her cause for optimism. Until she realised the part played by relief – on both sides – at his imminent departure.

Was it all down to luck? Deb had been lucky to meet Paco. Until then, she had hardly chosen well: Charlie, Hassan...both disastrous. Her own choices hadn't rivalled Deb's on the disaster scale but the fact she was alone now spoke for itself. Not that it bothered her; not any more. Timmy was her comfort, her joy in life.

12th July 1985

I'm gradually getting to know the few other foreigners living here. There's Monika, a German artist, Kay from Essex, who teaches English and has been in Granada four years. Through her I've met one or two others. Most of the foreigners are married to Spaniards so their children grow up bilingual. Robin, for example, whose Spanish wife Leonor teaches yoga (I thought she was a dancer, she moves with such enviable grace). They have two little blond boys, the younger one about Mark's age. I'm thrilled at the speed with which Mark is picking up Spanish (complete with the local accent) alongside his English – quite effortlessly just from hearing it all around him. No need for me to find a Spanish husband then. Just as well, because that is definitely NOT on my agenda.

Standing back from the cave entrance to survey his new security measures, Mark felt proud of the afternoon's work. He'd been dead lucky finding this old door dumped by the bins – even if dragging it up from the road had nearly killed him. It was worth the effort: the blanket had been no fucking use for keeping people out. They might finally get the message now – that when he told them to fuck off, he meant it. He wanted to be alone. He wanted to concentrate, remember everything from the beginning; from as far back as he could go. Otherwise it'd be lost. He had water; he had *tabaco* and a little stash of *maría*; he'd stocked up with beer and food. If he felt like it, he could stay up here for days. He lay on his back, staring at the low curve of the roof, its knobbly surface still snowy white from when he and Tina had set to with a bucket of thick *cal* last summer. He closed his eyes. He had to focus, block out all the other shit getting in the way. It was bloody hard.

England...he's seen pictures: photos of the house in London with the green front door, where they used to live; him lolling in a buggy, him holding a furry rabbit, one of Charlie spooning baby food into his gob. He can't remember any of it though, it's just the photos. He was still a baby when they came to Granada. A toddler, Mum said, because he could walk.

He can remember living in Lola and Ramón's apartment. There was a bird in a cage on their wall, a yellow canary. Once they let it out and it flew around the room and sat on a shelf and Mum screamed when it brushed past her hair. At Christmas Lola gave him wrapped *polvorones*. Mum said the word came from *polvo* and they tasted like dust but he liked all the Christmas sweets: *turrón, mazapan, mantecados*. Not any more, but he did when he was little. He was a greedy kid.

He thought it was fun dropping his toys off the balcony. Sometimes Ramón picked them up and wagged a finger at him but mostly it was Mum who had to go and fetch them. Maybe he'd been told that but he definitely remembered the time he threw a cup down and it broke. Mum got mad at him and slammed the window shut. He lay on the floor and bawled like it was the end of the world. He hadn't meant to break it.

What he can't get away from, the hardest thing, is that it's always him and Mum, the two of them: she's always there like they're twins... No, that's stupid. Course they're not twins but she's like...like a shadow or something; she's half his past. So she can't just fucking die on him.

Mark got up and lit a couple of candles so he could see to roll a joint. Someone was beating out a rhythm on the *tambor*, most likely Pierre. It was never totally quiet up here: there was always music, shouting, some *loco* laughing.

He remembers one day in winter. He must be about four years old. Mum's buying fruit from Trini's stall. She suddenly pokes him in the ribs. 'Look,' she says, and points to a group of kids running around these two women, who're yakking away. One of the boys has grabbed the ends of both their shawls and he's tying them together. They haven't noticed; they're too busy gossiping. So we stand there waiting till they finish their chat and try to move off. The kids have done a bunk by this time; I can see them peeping round the corner of Calle Agua. It takes the women ages to undo the knots, cursing and swearing all the while, not knowing which kids to blame for the trick. Me and mum, we're pissing ourselves laughing and so are half the other people in the *plaza*.

Another thing he remembers: Mum letting him sleep in her bed so Auntie Alice could have his. There must have only been two beds. In the morning he burrowed down under the covers and pulled at Mum's feet to wake her up. Alice brought him some coloured play-dough and helped him make little animals – or maybe that was another time. There was a giraffe but after they baked it in the oven, the neck broke.

He'd felt odd having only one aunt. All the other kids had hundreds of relations: aunts, uncles, cousins, granddads... Laura's granddad used to fetch her from school most days and he was always seeing them together around the Albaicín. Pedro bragged he had fifteen cousins and in the summer the whole lot of them, aunts and uncles as well, would go off to the beach for a month or two. Mark didn't even have a brother or sister. Once, when he was quite little, he'd asked Mum if they could get one. He must have thought you could buy them in a shop like toys. She just said no in an angry voice so he never dared ask again. It was good when Alice had Timmy: a cousin was okay, better than nothing.

31st July 1985

After a week back in England it feels wonderful to be 'home' again. Hanging out in Plaza Larga, buying my fruit and veg from Trini. '¡*Dos piñas 20 duros!*' she was shouting today. Two big juicy pineapples for 100 pesetas, the equivalent of 40p. And waiting to be served at the little fish stall close by, I learnt a new word: *chiquitillo*. I just love saying it. A bossy Albaicín housewife was pointing to the sardines being scooped up for her by the fish lady and demanding smaller ones: *más chiquitillo. Chico, chiquito, chiquitillo*, the equivalent of small, tiny, minute – except that their use is quite random.

The fish stall. Alice had considered buying fish yesterday but even passing by the open-fronted shop made her nervous: the shouting fish lady with her custard-blonde hair (surely the same one Deb was referring to); the local women pushing and shoving to be served, then buying enough fish to feed what must be vast extended families. The counter piled with slippery squid, with prawns large and small in varying shades of pink and translucent grey, whole fish of countless unknown varieties, their ugly fat lips and glassy eyes reminding her of storybook hags... Much easier to buy chicken instead.

> *20th September 1985*
>
> I'm learning new things all the time. I've just realised what's going on with the man from Sevillana, the electricity company, why he makes such a racket when he comes round to read the meters. '¡*Sevillana, Sevillana*!' he yells at the top of his voice as he moves down the street. It's to give people time to turn back their meters!

Deb's diary writing, like everything else she did, was erratic. Flicking through, Alice found gaps of weeks or even months without a single entry, followed by periods when she wrote nearly every day. What struck Alice as she read was that her sister had no fear. Everything was unfamiliar, uncertain, unpredictable, yet she wasn't in the least intimidated. On the contrary, she embraced her new life with passionate enthusiasm, seeing the positive in everything. How did she manage it? Or did she only write on the good days?

> *22nd September 1985*
>
> Rain is a novelty after so many months without. I think Mark had almost forgotten what it was. People complain about the heat and the cold, but the rain is welcomed. The parched earth soaks it up like a libation. I couldn't resist running down to the patio and letting the soft splashes fall on my bare arms. Feeling wetness on my face rather than the dry dust of summer was like a cleansing.

> *20th October 1985*
>
> Robin and Leonor are members of La Platería, a *flamenco peña* housed in a beautiful old building here in the Albaicín. I went along as their guest, quite unprepared for the thrilling experience in store. La Paquera, a singer from Jerez (a gypsy like most flamenco artists) was performing. She held the entire audience spellbound. No one moved,

no one spoke except to shout *Olé* and *Bravo* and other such encouragements. This was a club for serious *aficionados* and I was privileged to be there, as several people told me afterwards in the bar.

Last night my sleep was haunted by the clapping of palms and stamping of heels, by dark gypsy eyes and above all, the passionate and powerful voice of La Paquera. So in the morning I took myself to Sacromonte, the gypsy *barrio* of Granada where most of the homes are caves gouged out of the rock. Snatches of guitar drifted from one of them; I heard a man's voice singing a lament and turned a corner to see him sitting at the bottom of a flight of steps, dressed all in black. A flounced and frilled dress, blue with white spots, billowed in the wind from a line strung up in the cobbled street.

3rd December 1985

Keeping warm indoors is a colossal challenge. Mark has chilblains on his fingers and toes. My nails are brittle as potato crisps. We pile on the jumpers, wrap ourselves in blankets. The only warm place is in bed. Once this week we were so cold we sought refuge in a nice cosy bar with a *chimenea*, a roaring open fire. Everyone takes their children to bars and restaurants. Leaving them with babysitters is something Spanish parents wouldn't even consider. And if for some exceptional reason they have to leave the children, there's always a willing grandmother on hand.

Alice snuggled down under the bedcovers. So Deb too had found the house cold; her toughness had been a sham, designed to make Mum and herself feel like pathetic wimps. She would never forget that horrendous Christmas they had spent here in 1991. Horrendous for reasons that had nothing to do with the icy temperatures, but they made it worse. Cold rose from the tiled floors, penetrated the walls, crept in around poorly sealed windows and beneath doors. She remembered the daily torture of slipping off her fleecy pyjamas and exposing her bare flesh to the arctic chill; the toilet seat so cold she had to brace herself before sitting down. They had colluded in putting on a brave face to Deborah but behind her back they had grumbled and griped to each other, shivering despite the innumerable layers of clothes they piled on each morning –

half of them borrowed from Deb, who claimed not to feel cold at all.

The diary spoke with more honesty. Of course, it was not intended for other eyes. Yet the very fact that she was reading it now proved that anything set down on paper was unsafe. So full marks to Deborah for destroying the most sensitive section.

Out of the blue, she was assailed by a more disturbing possibility. What if it were not Deb who had torn out those pages? *Oh for God's sake! Who else would it have been? Some mystery blackmailer?* She must stop tormenting herself. There was only one person with the power to ruin her life and it was ridiculous to think that he... Timmy stirred in his sleep. She switched off the light before lifting the mattress and pushing the diary underneath. Secrets were dangerous; lies were dangerous. Alice had always known that. Known it and accepted the risks. She would not allow herself to become paranoid now.

Chapter Five

What could be worse than waiting for someone to die, waiting with the knowledge there was nothing you could do? Paco had phoned this morning to say the doctors held out little hope, given the extent of the damage to Deborah's brain. Nevertheless, he preferred to stay in Madrid for the time being, just in case.

Conscious of the need to occupy herself, Alice set to cleaning the house. It felt grubby and neglected. Deb was hopeless: she claimed not to notice dirt. For a while one of the neighbours had come in to clean but judging by the state of the house now, this arrangement must have ended. The dust here was like nowhere Alice had ever lived. It amassed on floors and surfaces in thick pinkish-grey clumps that magically reappeared within moments of being swept up. Sweeping, scrubbing, mopping at least passed the long restless hours. She heaved aside a heavy bookcase in Deborah's study and poked with the broom at a ball of screwed up paper lying behind it. She was about to chuck it away when some sixth sense, a flicker of recognition made her hesitate. The paper was coated in dust but underneath she could see that this was the same paper as the pages of Deborah's diary, the same slightly shiny paper ruled into tiny squares. Smoothing out the creases, she cast her eyes over the words her sister had written.

16th September 1994

Last night I had a dream, such a sweet dream. If only I could recall it better. I saw him; I held him in my arms. He smiled at me and his smile revealed no trace of sadness or reproach. Yet I was convinced he knew and I felt happy as I haven't done since...

The page had been ripped in half; it was a fragment only. But enough to leave Alice in no doubt whom Deb was referring to. Trembling, she slipped it into her pocket and resumed sweeping with grim energy. She must stay in control, for Timmy's sake. He was at the door now.

'You promised we could go today,' he said. 'To Mark's cave.'

She put down the broom. 'Alright. Go and get your jacket.'

An intermittent drizzle was falling as they set out in the direction of Sacromonte. It fitted her mood of despondency.

'This way, Mummy.' Timmy steered her towards a dusty track leading off the road to the left. A young couple, their lips, noses, ears and eyebrows pierced, were coming down, trailed by several loose dogs. Their bizarre appearance, the excess of metalwork, intimidated her and she instinctively moved to one side, letting them pass without speaking. The path, sloping gently upwards, ended in a series of rough steps cut into the hillside.

'Up here? They look very steep. Are you sure?'

Timmy grabbed her arm. 'Come on, it's easy.'

She followed him up, pausing once or twice to catch her breath. At the top, she was amazed to see in front of her a row of neat caves with proper front doors and even name plaques, almost like a normal street.

'Not these, Mark lives higher up.'

As they continued to climb, another line of dwellings became visible: about half a dozen caves with gardens in front and chimney pipes sticking up out of the hillside.

Timmy pointed to one of them. 'I think that's it, Mum.'

A dog started barking and two more emerged from one of the caves, bounding towards them and joining in what was now a chorus of yapping and growling. Alice took Timmy's arm and held him behind her, trying to appease the animals by muttering softly to them as they approached.

'Keep still,' she whispered to Timmy. 'They might be dangerous.'

A middle-aged man with unkempt beard, long straggly hair and some kind of kaftan appeared and called to the dogs. One of them was already jumping up at her; for all she knew, the animal could be rabid.

Frantic now, she shouted in English, 'I'm looking for Mark.'

The man stared at her then tilted his head at the cave Timmy had pointed out.

'Marco! *Una visita.*'

The dogs had retreated but one of them was still growling. She let go of Timmy and he ran towards the cave. The arched entrance was blocked by something solid, propped up against it from the inside. Timmy was squinting through a narrow gap to one side. 'I can't see anything,' he said as she joined him. 'It's too dark.' He put his mouth to the slit. 'Mark, can we come in?'

Silence. She banged her fist on the wooden barricade. She had no doubt he was in there. 'Mark? Are you alright?' She tried pushing but it refused to budge.

Alice was about to give up when the obstruction was suddenly pulled away and Mark peered out, blinking. 'What do you want?'

Instinctively, she put an arm around Timmy, shocked by the aggression in her nephew's voice.

'I wanted to show Mummy your cave,' Timmy said, cowering closer to her.

'Go away, leave me alone.' Mark's head disappeared inside and she heard a scraping sound as the barrier was wedged back into place.

Alice looked at Timmy and shrugged. 'Sorry darling, he's upset. We'll come back another day.'

The man in the kaftan was still watching as she let Timmy lead the way down to the road. They turned back towards the Albaicín, walking in silence now. The winding road was overhung with wild prickly pear trees while across the valley to their left rose terraced hills divided by deep gullies. A boy sped past on one of those little *motos*, fumes belching from its exhaust. He looked scarcely older than Timmy. On their right, cave after cave promised nightly flamenco shows. Alice remembered Deb dismissing them as tourist rip-offs, not 'the real thing' at all. A gypsy woman with bulging rolls of fat around her midriff stood, hands on hips, in the doorway of one cave and beckoned to Alice. 'You like to see gypsy cave?' *She* looked like the real thing.

Noticing a litterbin by the side of the road, Alice retrieved the scrap of diary from her pocket and dropped it in. Deborah's words were already imprinted on her memory: she did not need to read them again.

The minute Timmy was in bed, Alice returned to the diaries. Reading about Deb's early days in Granada fascinated her: there was so much her sister had never shared. Immersing herself in the diary was a way of recovering some of the missing years. They had been close before she left England but then the gap between their lives widened so much, it seemed they had nothing in common except their past.

Until Timmy came along. Then once again they could connect more deeply, their lives bound together by motherhood. She had never imagined herself bringing up a child on her own. *Single parent.* She remembered the prevailing attitude of disapproval, not just in the press but among her colleagues in Housing, some of whom thought girls deliberately had babies so they could get Council accommodation. She had never gone along with that, but neither – to her shame – had she been wholly free from prejudice.

27th March 1986

At last some progress with the house in London. Contracts were exchanged last week, which means it shouldn't be too long before my share of the money comes through. The big question is what to do with it. Now I'm certain I want to stay in Granada, the idea of buying a place makes sense. There are so many dilapidated houses that could be fabulous with some renovation and by London standards the prices are laughably low. I must keep my eyes and ears open because everything here happens by word of mouth.

3rd November 1986

It's 3am but I'm too excited to sleep. This afternoon Leonor took me to see an old carmen she'd noticed was for sale not far from Plaza Aliatar. Having only seen it from the outside, I should really reserve judgement but the location was perfect. The house itself is quite big and rundown; it's obvious no one is living there. I think you'd be able to see the Sierra Nevada as well as the Alhambra from the roof terrace. Peeping through a chink in the gate, I saw an interior patio overrun with greenery. First thing Monday morning I'll contact the agents.

4th November 1986

Love at first sight. This is it, the place I want. José Manuel, the agent was all for showing me several others but after two, I said no more. *Carmen de la Virgen* feels right (apart from the name). It's the place I've dreamt about ever since moving here.

The owner is Esperanza, a woman of ninety who lived there for fifty years until her husband died, when she moved in with her daughter. That was three years ago and it's been empty since, her children preferring the mod cons of an urbanisation in the suburbs.

7th November 1986

I've had another look round and remain as convinced as ever. As if fate were calling to me: "Deborah Hardy, your future lies here." I must have walked past six or seven times in the last three days. The bathroom and kitchen are very old-fashioned, all white tiles and antique plumbing and the rooms are filled with dark, heavy furniture: massive wardrobes and dressers but beds so short even my legs would stick out – made for pint-sized Andalusians. The whole house is dark, designed to keep out the enemy (the sun!) but José Manuel thinks bigger windows would be perfectly feasible. Once I let in some light, the place will be transformed. And the patio is enchanting, with fruit trees, vines, bougainvilleas growing up the wall and a flourishing wisteria that forms a canopy over part of the garden.

Mum and Alice will call me reckless and imagine every kind of disaster, but when it's all done up and beautiful, I'll invite them out here, serve them drinks on the terrace and they can sit gazing at the Alhambra with a backdrop of snow-capped mountains.

10th December 1986

I've put in an offer and am waiting on tenterhooks for a response. José Manuel has been instructing me on real versus official prices. It's absolutely taken for granted that the official price is only half the real price. That way you avoid paying a good deal of the tax. The notaries are all in on it and everyone I've talked to says it's standard practice, I'd be mad not to go along with it.

Deb had never breathed a word about this aspect of the purchase. It might be common practice in Spain but it sounded dodgy to Alice. What if it came out at some later date? Back then, she would have condemned it as corrupt. Now her concern was purely pragmatic. She had long ago given up the right to take a moral stance, having proved every bit as willing as Deb to lie and deceive.

21st January 1987

At my insistence, Robin took me along to La Platería again. This time it was a local singer, El Niño de las Almendras, accompanied by Rafalín, a young guitarist from the famous Habichuela (Bean!) family. I love the names chosen by these flamenco artists: the Child of the Almonds must be in his fifties. I see some of them around the Albaicín and feel a kind of exhilaration to be living amongst them. As if something of their passionate (admittedly macho) nature rubs off. When I come away from a performance, the outside world seems insipid and tame.

27th February 1987

Couldn't sleep at all last night, anticipating the big day. I was quaking when I collected the fat bundle of notes from the bank (counted out, stuffed into a brown envelope and handed to me without comment by the cashier in full view of others behind me in the queue). José Manuel was waiting outside and secreted the envelope in the inner pocket of his jacket. Then we walked together to the notary's. I saw every passer-by as a potential mugger – as if the money was shouting I'M HERE, COME AND GET ME!

All the formalities went smoothly; Esperanza's children invited me for an excellent celebratory lunch at Chikitos; the big bunch of keys was handed over. I still can't quite believe it. Carmen de la Virgen is mine. Now I'm raring to get on with the renovation so we can move in.

Alice gave up trying to hold back the tears. Deb's vitality, the spirit that came through in her diary was too poignant. What remained of that spirit now?

Mark felt bad about sending Timmy away. He was only a kid. If he'd come up on his own... It was Alice he couldn't hack at the moment. Those pitying looks – the kind of looks you'd give a starved kitten or a bird with an injured wing that you knew didn't stand a chance in hell of escaping the ravenous cat. He didn't want to see anyone, not even Tina. Other people got in the way of his remembering. They thought you had to say something. *Sorry about your mum.* Like she was already dead. It was just words, something to make him feel better. Except it didn't. The questions were even more fucking annoying. *Did she recognise you? Has she come round yet?* The worst was when they tried to pretend they were more genned up than the doctors: *Don't worry, she'll be fine.* That really really aggravated him. Timmy knew better; he knew to keep quiet.

The trouble with caves… It was no good, he couldn't hold out any longer or he'd wet himself. Mark shifted the barricade and checked no one was hanging around, then ran over to the trees. The rain had got heavier, which was good because it meant people stayed inside but bad because his *rastas* were soaked when he came back in and he was shivering. He rubbed a towel over his hair and neck and lit the *butano* stove. Mum said gas wasn't safe in a cave but he couldn't see how she figured that out. A cave had more ventilation than a house.

He thought about their house. Weird how it still felt like home – even though he'd lived in Sacromonte nearly two years. He was four when they moved in but he can remember going there before, when the builders were still working on it. This one time when he and Mum walked by, the roof had gone. He couldn't believe it – that you could just take a roof off like opening a can of sardines. It was raining that day and all the old furniture, the cooking stove and everything was getting wet. Juanito said as it was springtime, the birds would come and nest inside and we'd have baby birds hatching out. Next time they went, he looked all over, hoping to find a nest with eggs in but there was nothing. Mum said the noise would have scared them away. He liked the noise – not only the hammering and drilling but Juanito's singing and the way they shouted to each other.

Mum said he used to stand there watching them for hours and when she tried to drag him away he'd throw a tantrum. He can't remember that. But he can remember the mule they used to take away the rubble and he can remember later after they finished the job, seeing all three of them around the Albaicín or in Aixa. Mum said he would run up to Juanito as if he were his dad. He'd have liked to do a swap, trade Charlie in for Juanito.

The thought crashed into his mind like a bullet out of nowhere: what if Mum had come round? He could see his phone lying there on the ledge, useless bit of plastic junk. The mobile companies, they were all the fucking same. He didn't believe their excuses. If you could get a signal in houses, why not in a cave? They never told you that when they flogged you a phone. There should be a warning on the box: *Does not function in caves.* Suppose Paco had tried to call him? Suppose Mum had woken up and asked for him? What if she'd died? He'd be the last to find out. Mark pulled the door away enough to wriggle through and stood outside. He checked his messages, his missed calls. Nothing. He couldn't decide whether that was good or bad.

He'd like to hear her voice just one more time – even if it was only to bawl him out. *Mark, I despair of you! You're wasting your talents!* Or just saying his name... When he was little, she used to call him Markie or sometimes Markito. He can still hear her voice in his head, rabbiting on about Walladah with that manic look on her face or griping about small-minded *granadinos*. He can hear her all fired up, marching in the anti-war demos, shouting against Bush and Aznar. And her laugh – kind of husky, like there's grit in the back of her throat.

He'd never thought about Mum dying. There ought to be some sort of alert, a red danger light so you had time to get your head round it. She wasn't old, not old enough to die. But then most of them in the trains weren't old, they were just unlucky. It could have been him, it could have been anyone. And fucking Aznar with his evil eyebrows and stupid moustache, still walking around free like he wasn't to blame. What did he care?

21st March 1987

Spanish bureaucracy being what it is, says Vicente the architect, I must be patient. He has submitted the plans, now we have to wait. But how I hate waiting. I always want to harangue the functionaries with their endless forms and paperwork. I get mad waiting for them to come back from their breakfast. If I see them in the bar, tucking into their toast, reading the paper, I want to round them up and chase them back to their desks.

I've been over to the house every day, throwing out all that dreadful old furniture that makes it so gloomy. If I put it in the street by the rubbish bins, it soon disappears – probably to some cave in Sacromonte. Anything that remains is taken by the men who ride the bin lorry when it does its noisy rounds at midnight.

26th April 1987

It drags on and on: the forms, the inspections, the waiting for permissions. But yesterday Fernando the builder said we should just start. Yes yes yes, I said. So now it's full steam ahead.

Crimson flowers like small bells adorn our pomegranate tree. Each one will be transformed into a fruit by the time we move in. One of the neighbours hailed me and asked could I hear the nightingale? I listened to the trilling, so clear and melodic and took it as a good omen.

4th May 1987

I'm getting to know the three builders. Fernando is very sweet, a little shy with me. I see him measuring, doing calculations on scraps of paper, supervising the other two but he also works very hard himself. Rafa is incredibly strong and works steadily like a mule. He's an old *albaicinero* with an accent I struggle to understand. Juanito is quite different in every respect: quick in his movements and agile like a monkey. He's always joking and Mark adores him. It's a fallacy the Spanish are lazy. These guys work!

12th June 1987

Most mornings now, I pop into Aixa for a coffee so I can catch my builders at breakfast. We confer about different materials and anti-damp measures, wiring or plumbing options or the intricacies of roof-building (vast amounts of concrete are involved). God knows how many of the bar's paper serviettes Fernando has used to make sketches in an attempt to explain these things to me. I'm sure Alice would understand in seconds what it takes me half an hour to get into my thick skull.

19th November 1987

Yesterday, as I was sorting and packing, I found that appliqué bag Alice gave me one Christmas. She'd spent a vast amount of time and care making it. When I opened the parcel, beautifully wrapped as always, not sloppy and bodged like mine, I imagined her bending over the task, giving it all her attention, infinitely patient, refusing to leave it until every detail was perfect. It's not fair, Alice has all the talents: practical, creative, musical...

Alice found this appreciation astonishing. She remembered the making of that bag as if it were yesterday. Searching for suitable scraps of material, deciding on how to arrange colours and textures, keeping her stitches neat and unobtrusive, even wrapping the gift had given her enormous pleasure but she didn't think of it as a talent. All through her childhood she had followed in Deb's wake: not as bright, not as pretty, not as popular as her older sister. The only 'talent' she could claim for herself was playing the piano and in the sixties when she was growing up, that was considered square. To be with-it, you had to play the guitar.

She had started Timmy with piano lessons a year ago in the hope that he might have inherited some musical talent from one side or the other. It was a complete failure. He hated the lessons and refused to practise. After six months of battles, she had to admit defeat. 'He takes after me,' Deb had remarked with a laugh, 'Tone-deaf.' It was true.

3rd December 1987

We're in! Yesterday we left our little quarters at Ramón and Lola's and slept for the first time in Carmen de la Glicina, as I've renamed it (somehow the wisteria draping the outside walls survived all the coming and going, the chipping and rendering and painting). Fernando has moved on to another job but Rafa and Juanito are still here finishing off. Mark can't wait to get home from school so he can watch them at work. He gobbles down his lunch and no matter how tired, refuses to sleep until they leave at 4 o'clock.

There was someone at the gate. Alice had been immersed in the diary, immersed in the year 1987 – not her own but Deb's. For the whole year, her sister had written of little else but the house. Page after page of detail, most of which Alice skipped. All her sister's enthusiasms and frustrations were there, everything exaggerated, revealing a childlike impatience that was typically Deborah.

The buzzer went again. Alice stood, uncertain what to do. It was 9.30, late for visitors. She picked up the entry-phone. 'Yes?'

'It is I, Ignacio. I am friend of Paco and Deborah. Please, you open the gate?'

The name struck a chord but she couldn't remember meeting him. 'You prefer I come back tomorrow?'

'No, it's alright.'

He was tall and had a loping walk that caught her attention even in the few steps it took him to cross the patio. As he held out a hand to her, his other hand repeatedly pushed back a mop of distinctive grey curls that reminded her of that composer, Simon Rattle. He was nervous, she realised, and this endeared him to her.

'I call to see you are okay. Paco asks me... You must excuse my bad English.'

'It's very kind of you. Please come in.'

He was a kind-hearted man: she sensed it straightaway from the warmth in his voice, the compassion in his eyes. They sat at the table drinking tea. He worked with Paco at the university, he told her, and he considered them – Deborah as well as Paco – his closest friends. They had helped him through a difficult time... His fingers ran through his hair again. She wondered if he was aware of the gesture.

'I went with him to Madrid the day it happened. Driving here, there; to one hospital after another. Searching. *"No puede ser. ¿Qué voy a hacer?"* All the time Paco is repeating this. It can't be. What will I do?'

They sat in silence for a few minutes. Since the tragedy, every conversation about Deborah seemed to arrive at a point where words ran out.

Ignacio cleared his throat. 'Your son, he is already sleeping? Paco tells me you bring up the boy all alone. This is hard. Excuse me for asking but... the father he leave?'

Alice tensed. Why did people have to be so inquisitive? Wherever you went, it was the same. They thought they had the right to know everything. She nodded; experience had taught her it was the response most likely to stall further questions.

'Sorry, this is not my business.'

'Do you have children?' she asked, smiling to show she was not offended.

'No.' He did not return her smile. 'I cannot have children: this is my private sorrow.' There was a pause and although he tried to stifle it, his sigh did not escape her. 'Well, now I am separated – since last summer. My wife is expecting...'

'It's alright, you don't have to tell me.' Unintentionally, they seemed to have hit on each other's sensitive spots.

'But you are very sympathetic.' He rose. 'However I did not come here to talk about my troubles. Is there anything I can help you with? The gas bottles – you know how to change them?'

'Yes, Paco showed me. I'm fine, honestly.' She *was* fine, despite the faint echoes of a long-buried pain provoked by his words – the shock of seeing Michael's girlfriend patting her pregnant tummy with smug satisfaction as they were introduced in the Council car-park. That day had put a brutal end to her deluded hopes and still in shock, she had dived immediately into a new relationship – and a transfer to one of the outlying Council offices. But neither Andy nor a new job had been the answer.

She was aware that Ignacio had spoken again. 'Sorry, what did you say?'

'I ask if you are not afraid, alone with your son in the house? No one is bothering you, I hope?'

'Bothering me? Like who?' The question alarmed her. What did he mean?

'Nothing, only your sister was not so popular with all her neighbours and sometimes she felt...' Her unease must have shown because he quickly changed tack. 'No, no, there is nothing to worry about. It is perfectly safe here. But in any case, I give you my number.' He jotted it down on a scrap of paper and handed it to her. 'Call me any time. But I can see you are strong like your sister. It must be in the blood.'

No, I'm not strong, she wanted to shriek. *I'm weak and fearful.* But she said nothing as she saw him out, then double-locked the door. The sooner Paco returned the better.

Chapter Six

Bang bang bang like a fucking hammer, like one more thump and his head would explode. Mark tried opening his eyes: a bad mistake. Even the thin ribbon of sunlight sneaking in at the side of the door irked him. It must be late, maybe afternoon. As if the pounding head weren't enough, his stomach was churning and he had a foul taste in his mouth like vinegar dregs. He'd wanted to put her out of his mind; actually *chosen* to get smashed. But that was wrong and now he was being punished. He deserved to feel rough.

It was after calling Paco he'd started on the beer. The words were coming back to him now. 'There's very little hope,' Paco had said. 'We have to accept it.' In which case, what the fuck was he doing still hanging out in Madrid? It was obvious *he* hadn't accepted it. Was he waiting for the Virgin to perform one of her miracles? He'd been brainwashed by the priests at his school, he told Mark once. Now he was dead against religion, especially forcing it on kids – though he reckoned not all the priests were bad. Mark didn't believe in the Virgin but he liked the idea of miracles. He wondered if they could only happen to Catholics. If so, Mum would have no chance.

He shifted round on the bed and put down first one foot then the other; forced himself upright. He'd crashed out without getting undressed; his clothes stank. He poured water into a bowl and stripped off to the waist to wash. Splashing the cold water onto his face helped. He grabbed a T-shirt and his jacket and stumbled towards the door, almost tripping over a bottle. There were half a dozen of them rolling around on the floor of the cave. Outside he found the remains of another one, smashed to smithereens. Shit, he couldn't even remember doing that. The slivers of brown glass stared up at him, giving him the evil eye.

The day was bright, too fucking bright. And too cheerful: the way the birds were chirping and twittering, you'd think they had something to celebrate. The sound of drumming from across the valley put up some competition but the birds were definitely winning. He noticed a scrap of paper on the floor just inside. Someone must have shoved it through the gap. *José's cooked up some papas – come and join us. Besos, Tina.* Food didn't seem a bad idea; a plate of potatoes would go down well. He could see a bunch of them sitting round a table outside José's cave. There was a big pan in the middle but they looked like they'd finished their meal. Some of them were smoking: the wind must be blowing his way because he caught a whiff of it drifting across. It took him a few minutes to decide but in the end his hunger won out.

They all went quiet when they saw him coming. Good. Maybe they'd taken the hint. Either that or they didn't know what to say.

Tina handed him a plate and pointed to the pot. 'We left some for you.'

'Thanks.' It was nice to know they'd thought of him. The *papas* were cold but they filled him up. When he'd finished, Tina came up behind him and put her hands on his shoulders, started to massage them.

'Does that feel good?' she whispered, leaning in closer.

He just nodded because her hands were making him sad as hell.

After a few minutes he shook her off. You could have too much of a good thing – or that's what his granny used to say. Mum believed the exact opposite: that if something was good, you should go all out for it, no half measures. Except the rule didn't always apply. 'You'll be sick if you eat any more chocolate,' she used to tell him when they went to England at Christmas or Easter. Later, it was drink and drugs she thought he did too much of.

Pierre had just finished rolling another joint. Mark held out his hand for it and took a couple of deep drags before passing it on. Fabio, the little Italian guy was strumming a guitar. They were well chilled out, all of them. It wasn't so bad up here, afternoons like this. *Tranquilo.* That's what everyone said about Sacromonte and mostly they were right. He'd never choose to live in the city, no fucking way. This time of year everything was sprouting like crazy. Mum used to say you could see the plants growing: all it took was a few drops of rain and they'd be off, changing the colour of the hills from brown to green overnight. The scrubby almond tree still had a few blossoms hanging on along with a handful of blackened nuts from last year.

'I'd better be going,' he said when the sun moved round towards the city, sinking low and taking all the warmth out of the air. Too much of a good thing and it didn't feel so good any more, his gran was right. Listening to José's stories had been cool, but now they were laughing and joking. They'd forgotten. Fair enough: it wasn't their mum. A ripple of breeze caught Mark's neck all of a sudden, making him shiver. They didn't mean any disrespect, it was just they were on a different planet. They didn't understand you could only forget for so long. Then it all came back to you.

1st January 1988

The start of another year – I always feel a spark of excitement, that sense of infinite possibility, like holding in my hand a mystery parcel that may contain good or bad things but always intrigues. What surprises will 1988 bring, I wonder?

It had brought her Hassan and despite what happened later – or rather because of what happened later – Alice could not class him as a bad thing.

15th January 1988

I have a new role – as a landlady! Yesterday Pete and Linda from Manchester moved into my little upstairs apartment. They both teach English at one of the academies in town and have been living in a dark, damp flat with broken furniture and an aggressive alcoholic landlord, so they're ecstatic to be here for only 2,000 pesetas more in rent.

Now that's all settled, I must find myself some worthwhile occupation before my brain starts to rot.

Alice couldn't concentrate. She had found her bed disturbed, the covers lying in a heap instead of neatly pulled up as she had left them; as she always left them. The diary lay underneath, but one of the notebooks had been poking out for all to see. Was it Timmy or had someone else sneaked in and taken a look? Paco was in Madrid. To her knowledge, Mark was the only other person with a key. But how would she know? Her scatty sister could so easily have lost a set. When Timmy woke, she would question him. In the meantime, her nerves were on edge.

16th February 1988

At last a couple of prospects on the work front. Monika mentioned an academic she knows, a biologist. His articles have to be submitted in English and he wants a native speaker to translate. At our meeting, I pretended to have some experience in science translation – a bare-faced lie. I've also been asked to teach English to Alfonso the lawyer's children. It will be a start. In the meantime I'm observing, reading, absorbing, dreaming – and without the slightest feeling of guilt.

2nd April 1988

Spring here is beautiful, the countryside lush and verdant, hillsides bright yellow with flowering broom. On every patch of open ground a riot of wild flowers has sprung up, scarlet poppies standing out amongst all the other colours of the rainbow. My eye is drawn by the brilliant green of the fig trees as they burst into new life: those distinc-tive leaves with their tongues shooting out in all directions seem to grow visibly by the day, their colour deepening.

12th May 1988

For the first time since leaving Charlie, I've caught myself looking at men. Until now, I've felt good on my own, revelling in my freedom to do as I please. But it seems the yearning for a romance has been creeping up on me. I recognise it by the way I feel seeing Pete and Linda. Every day I observe them coming and going from their little love-nest (as I've started to think of it) and there's no denying the stirrings of envy I feel at their intimacy. I can't help hearing those little cries drifting from their window at siesta time. Yet I'm reluctant to complicate my simple, 'wholesome' life, to lay myself open once again to pain and to all those negative emotions that go – inevitably it seems

– with any relationship: jealousy, resentment, anger, disappointment…
So why not have a fling, Kay suggested. In her pessimistic view, most
Spanish men are either married or mummy's boys. I suspect she has
a point but Kay is cynical about everything. She thinks I am naïve in
my love affair with Granada, that more time here will open my eyes to
the downside. I am determined to prove her wrong.

Had Deborah fallen out of love with Granada in the end or did she manage to maintain her rosy view through all the trials and tribulations of the
last twenty years? Faced with half her sister's troubles, Alice would have
hotfooted it back to England without a second thought. Not Deb. Alice
couldn't recall her ever talking of leaving – not even in the worst of times.

As for Kay's theory about Spanish men… It was long forgotten
history now, but when Deb started seeing Paco, he was still married.
That particular snippet of information about her sister's new lover had
not leaked out for quite some time.

The message from Alice came through on Mark's phone as he was
walking back. *Lunch at 2, we'd love to see you.* She must have sent it
hours ago but he wouldn't have gone anyway. There was another bit
that said she was planning to visit Mum early next week, did he want to
come? He turned off the phone and squeezed through the gap into his
cave. He'd think about it later.

It was peaceful in here, in the dark. If he could just shut out Pierre's
laugh that came barging in on his thoughts every now and then, faint
but not faint enough to ignore. He wanted to carry on where he'd left
off with the remembering.

He tried to remember when the Walladah thing had started, how
old he had been. It was about the time Hassan moved in with them. He
remembered them talking about her, Mum ignoring him as if he didn't
exist, or as if she'd gone deaf. She'd forget to make lunch some days.
They'd end up eating about five o'clock, just when his friends were
going out to play. Once she even forgot to fetch him from school.

I must be about six. All the other kids have gone, there's only me
and Señor Antonio.

'Your mother isn't at home,' he says. 'I've tried to phone her. Any idea where she might be?'

I just shake my head. How would I know?

We sit there, me and Señor Antonio. He keeps looking at his watch and frowning. He asks me if I'm hungry and I say no, which is a lie.

About two hours later Mum comes running up, all out of breath. Her hair's sopping wet because she's come out without an umbrella and it's pissing down.

'Sorry, I didn't notice the time,' she says, and laughs like it's nothing, like it's only five minutes. 'You weren't worried, were you Markie?'

When Paco moved in, he brought a big clock and stuck it up on the wall. Not that it did any good. *You'd be late for your own funeral.* Fuck, who was it said that to her? Could have been Charlie... Mark reached for the jerry-can and drank some water. It tasted of plastic. He didn't want to be reminded of funerals, specially not Mum's. He remembered his granny's funeral, the only one he'd been to. It must have been about four years ago. The priest in the dog collar had talked a lot about Adele being rewarded with everlasting peace. She'd be with God, he said as the coffin went sliding along a track, swishing through a curtain to the furnaces. No way Mum would stand for anything like that. Jesus, the thought of it!

She wasn't dead yet. But you couldn't really say she was alive either. He thought about souls. If they existed, if she had one, it had probably done a runner by now – or a floater or whatever. He liked the Buddhist idea of reincarnation. Mum had explained it to him once and they'd imagined themselves coming back as animals. Mum fancied spending her next life as an eagle, soaring over the mountains on the wind currents, swooping down on the odd unsuspecting mouse or rabbit when she felt hungry. He'd said he wouldn't come back as a mouse or a rabbit then. He'd chosen a lion, which was too big to be eaten by anything else, though come to think of it, there was always the danger some rich bugger might shoot him for fun or capture him for a zoo. He certainly wouldn't fancy being stuck in a cage to be gawped at all day.

Were there eagles in the Sierra Nevada? There were loads of vultures, maybe buzzards... Over towards Cádiz and Tarifa there were definitely eagles. He'd seen them that time he went in *Semana Santa* with Mum and Monika. He remembered being practically blown over by the wind on Bolonia beach. The sand had been whipped up into giant dunes you could climb like mountains. Perhaps Mum was already flying high, eagle eyes glinting in search of live food – while her useless, fucked up body still lay in the hospital bed in Madrid like a broken doll. There was no point going back there. Alice could do what she wanted but he didn't have the stomach to set foot in that hospital again, not unless she woke up.

There had been no intruder of evil intent, just Timmy searching for a lost sock. All the same... Alice took it as a warning to be more careful. Timmy had a reading age of twelve, his teacher said. The diary was not for his eyes either.

> *3rd August 1988*
>
> A week in England, a week's relief from the heat. Alice was brilliant with Mark, taking him out, playing games, singing to him. She'd make a wonderful mother. I do so wish she would meet someone and have a child of her own.

Unknown to her sister, she had still been obsessed with Michael at that time, conscious of the fertile years slipping by but incapable of looking at anyone else. She and Deb had never talked about her longing for a child – the 'baby' arguments with Simon during their marriage had been too personal, too painful to reveal to anyone – yet Deb had recognised it. *A child of her own.* Alice put down the diary and glanced at Timmy in the other bed. She listened to his regular breathing, noted the pinkness in his cheeks visible even in the dim light from her bedside lamp, the lines patterning his outstretched palm where it rested on the pillow. So secure, so trusting. To preserve this innocence, this state of peaceful oblivion seemed to her the most important thing in the world. No one would convince her otherwise.

> *16th October 1988*
>
> Today in Bar Aixa I met a most interesting man, a Moroccan. I was talking to Manolo behind the bar about the campaign by local Muslims to get permission for their mosque and he joined in the conversation.

He's lived in Granada nearly as long as me but only recently moved to the Albaicín, which explains why I haven't seen him before (he's very striking – tall, dark and handsome). His name is Hassan and he's thirty-six. He lived in Paris before coming here and speaks fluent French and Spanish as well as Arabic. He's a journalist, I gathered, writing mostly for Moroccan papers. He also plays the oud, a stringed instrument that sounded from his explanation to be similar to a lute. He said he was trying to get a group together to play Arab/Andalusian music and asked if I knew any local musicians who might be interested. I promised to talk to Amparo's husband, Juan Antonio who plays the *tambor*.

10th December 1988

Hassan came round last night and we sat by the wood stove for hours, talking. I do love our conversations – he's interesting and a wonderful story-teller. His opinions and moods are not predictable, which I like. With English men – and most of the Spanish men I've met too – you know before they've even opened their mouths what their views will be on just about any topic. Frankly they're boring. Hassan has lived in different countries, he's had experiences, good and bad, that have forced him to think for himself, not merely regurgitate the opinions of others. And the breadth of his reading puts me to shame. He's not a practising Muslim but Islam has shaped him. Last night he was explaining how the Qur'an gives a whole set of instructions for living and that all Islamic civilisations are based on these. All the social structures, medicine, science, agriculture, the design of cities, everything was dictated by the Prophet. I was particularly fascinated with what he said about the Moorish civilisation here – how *al-Andalus* was by far the most advanced civilisation in Europe, most of which was still in the Dark Ages at the time. Yet the Muslim contribution isn't acknowledged at all by most historians and philosophers – not even Bertrand Russell.

After he'd gone, I felt wide awake although it was after two. I put more wood on the fire and stayed up another hour, just thinking.

15th December 1988

Hassan invited us to the *tetería* for tea this afternoon. I felt transported to North Africa, to some Berber camp in the desert. There was low, cushioned seating around small hexagonal tables with candles. The only other illumination came from those little lamps made from goatskin stretched over an iron frame and painted with traditional designs on a red, orange or yellow background. The tea was brought to the table in individual silver teapots to be drunk from delicate glasses. You could choose from a whole list of teas, some quite exotic – like *azahar* (orange blossom) or spicy combinations of cinnamon, cloves, ginger… Now if I need to chill out, I know where to go. Mark loved it too – the staff treated him like a star, spoiling him with little Moroccan cakes and juice squeezed from half a dozen different fruits.

Hassan is going to Morocco to see his family but promised he would be back before the New Year. Christmas will be lonely without him – though Mark may be pleased to have me to himself.

29th December 1988

Hassan is back and we've become lovers. He'd been so gentlemanly up till now, very respectful, keeping his distance. While I, impatient as always, was lusting after him, tempted to make the first move but held back by…what? His dignity? A kind of self-possession he has? Or simply his otherness, the fact he's from a different culture. Several times I almost grabbed him but I'm glad now that I waited. He wanted to be sure I was ready, he said afterwards. But perhaps he meant sure he was ready. With an instinctive feel for the right moment, he took me in his arms last night and kissed me – a long, slow, erotic kiss that reached every nerve end. Then he undressed me, making of that too a deliciously sensual experience. I had all my winter layers on so it took some time!

It's impossible to tell what kind of lover a man will be. Hassan has never talked of other women in his life and I haven't asked. But whatever his experience, he knew all the tricks – pleasuring me with his tongue, his fingers…exploring my body in detail, playing it like a musical instrument, in a symphony that lasted half the night. Is this Arab sensuality (you only have to look at the Alhambra to recognise their appreciation of beauty, of indulging all the senses) or is it just him?

Several times Alice put the diary aside; it was too personal. Deborah had not intended to share these intimate thoughts. What if she recovered? How

75

would she feel, knowing her sister had invaded such private territory? Yet even though what Alice regarded as her 'better side' demanded that she stop reading, she ignored the stern voice of conscience and continued. Deborah was not going to live: the silent phone confirmed it. Reading her words was all that remained, the only way of getting closer.

30th December 1988

I've been exploring him too. He has a brownish birthmark on his left buttock and these delicate little earlobes that come to a complete point at the bottom like upside-down pixie ears. When I nibble them it drives him crazy. I love every last centimetre of his body.

Upside-down pixie ears: how clever she was at capturing an image. Alice could picture Hassan – good-looking yes, with his dark, liquid eyes guarding their secrets, his honey-coloured skin, his long-limbed athletic body. Interesting too maybe, but his personality defects outweighed all the rest. In the euphoria of new love, Deb had seen only what she wanted to see. As always, her emotions were intense. And changeable: blind love turning to blind hate. Whereas Alice had disliked Hassan from the moment she met him. Long before he posed any threat.

Chapter Seven

It was difficult to keep track of the days but Mark thought it was Monday; or possibly Tuesday. Either way, it could be the day Alice was going to Madrid. She might be there now, sitting by Mum's side on that black chair that folded out into a bed. Suppose she told Mum he didn't want to come? Suppose Mum heard her and understood the words? Well too fucking bad. It wasn't his fault she'd got on that train. He'd always thought her precious research was a waste of time. All that effort, what was it for? He wondered if they'd still publish her book if she died. A right scam that would be – like someone working unpaid for years and then dropping dead just as the boss was handing over the dosh.

He'd moved the old door out of the way: it was getting claustrophobic being barricaded in like that. He didn't mind the dark but he needed some fresh air. The air in the cave stank of stale smoke and sweat. He'd never gone so long without company in his whole life. Prisoners were put in solitary as a punishment or to break them so they talked. Like torture. Too long on your own could send you *loco*.

He might go and see what Alice and Timmy were up to. Also he needed to lay in supplies: his tobacco, food and water were all running low. He checked the tin to see how much cash he had. There was a five euro note and a pile of change, mostly twenties, tens, fives and those useless little one and two *céntimo* coins. It was all he had left of the twenty euros Paco had pushed into his hand in the hospital *cafetería* the day he went to see Mum. If he'd kept the forty euros he nicked instead of giving them to Dani he'd be alright.

He looked at his guitar propped up against the wall. It felt like ten years since he'd gone out busking, though when he worked it out, two weeks was all it was. He hadn't done badly that day, working his way along Paseo de los Tristes and around Plaza Nueva, stopping to play at half a dozen restaurants. He reckoned the tourists were more generous when the sun was shining and they could sit outside.

The key to Mum's was in its usual place on the shelf. He stuck it in his pocket along with most of the money from the tin and slipped out into the brightness of the morning. It was still early, 10.33 according to his phone; no one was about yet. Once he got down to the Camino, he walked faster, heading up past Quique's bar onto Vereda de Enmedio. He passed a couple of women clattering their shopping trolleys along the cobbles and another swilling the patch outside her gate with soapy water. A black cat ran across the street in front of him. It better not bring him bad luck: he'd had enough of that already. In England black cats were supposed to be good luck or that's what his granny had told him.

When he got to the *carmen*, he unlocked the gate and stood for a while in the patio just studying the house, like he would if he was going to sketch a building (how long since he'd done that?). From the outside, it looked the same as always. Which felt wrong; felt like a lie. He let himself in and listened for signs of life but it stayed silent as a cemetery at siesta time. Alice must have gone to Madrid – alone or with Timmy. He wouldn't have minded looking after Timmy for the day but she hadn't asked.

In the kitchen, everything had been put away. The only time he'd seen it so clean and tidy was when Mum went away for a week and Paco had a blitz on it. The fridge was full of food: eggs and *jamón* York and two types of cheese; tomatoes, a cauliflower... There were some cans of coke and a bottle of *vino blanco*. Up on one of the shelves, in a tin, he found chocolate biscuits. Alice wouldn't mind him making some breakfast but first he needed a shower.

The bathroom spooked him. All Mum's gear was still on the shelves, her shampoo and shower gel by the side of the bath, that cream she put on her face for the wrinkles, the loofah mitt she used to scrub her skin. There was other stuff too that must belong to Alice: English toothpaste and shampoo and conditioner all neatly stood in a separate corner like it didn't want to be contaminated by alien Spanish brands. Stuck in a mug were two toothbrushes, one of them with little cartoon characters on the handle.

He stayed a long time in the shower. Then he tied a towel round his waist and went to his old room in the hope of finding some of his clothes still lurking there from before he moved out, but all he found was an old belt hanging over the rail in the wardrobe. Alice and Timmy were sleeping in his room; it was full of their things. He had no choice but to put on the same grubby T-shirt and jeans he'd been wearing before. He cooked up some scrambled eggs and ate them with two slices of the ham. It was the best food he'd eaten for days. Just so Alice couldn't complain, he washed up his plate and the pan and left everything tidy.

The radio was sitting there on the worktop. He switched it on and listened to the news on *Cadena SER*. There was going to be a state funeral for the victims of 11-M next week in the cathedral of La Almudena. Some of the injured had left hospital but another one had died last night, a man with three kids. The other thing he learnt was that the bombers had blown themselves up in a flat in Leganés when the police came after them. Good fucking riddance – assuming they'd got the right ones. You could never be sure.

There was nothing about Mum. He imagined them announcing her death: *una inglesa de 52 años con domicilio en Granada…* Maybe they'd mention him: *un hijo de 20 años*. They always gave the age, as if that was the most important thing about a person. If he heard on the radio that she'd died, if no one told him first…but that wouldn't happen. Paco would let him know, course he would. He'd fucking better.

In the bins by Spar you could find bloody good food thrown out for being a couple of days past the date. When he got up there, he saw the Irish guy, Paddy coming from the other direction. There were two bins so they took one each and rooted for treasure amongst the garbage. Mark was in luck: they must have just dumped a load of stuff in his bin. He found a whole *tortilla*, two four-packs of yogurt, some beef steak that smelt more or less okay and three cartons of fruit juice. Paddy got cream, a small *chorizo* and some cake that was already going mouldy. Mark gave him one of the packs of yogurt and a carton of juice to even things up.

With a couple of days' worth of food in his pack and all his dosh intact, he could easily afford a coffee. Aixa was quieter than usual: most of the breakfast crowd had gone and it was still early for *tapas*. He picked up *Ideal* and read some more news. There were stories about some of the victims on the 'train of death' – that's what they called it. One was a boy of seventeen from Ecuador who wanted to be a screenwriter. He was a fan of Arnold Schwarzenegger so his mother was going to take his ashes to Los Angeles where his idol lived. Another was a Bulgarian woman who was planning to get married. It said her first husband and brother had been killed in an accident. Talk about bad luck. Loads of the victims were immigrants, a good number of them Muslims. Some bodies still hadn't even been identified.

Mark looked up and Manolo caught his eye. He was standing there with the bottle of *Caballero*, about to pour a *chupito* for the old guy further along the counter.

'How's it going with your mother? Any sign of improvement?'

'Still the same.'

He nodded slowly with a sad look on his face. He was okay, Manolo. Mum liked him.

'*Paciencia*,' he said. '*Ojalá* we'll see your mother back here one of these days. A lot of people have been asking about her. We all wish her well.'

'Thanks.' Mark pushed the paper away and delved into his pocket for change but Manolo waved his hand to say no, he didn't need to pay.

At the tobacconist's he had to break into the five-euro note but even after buying bread, he still had a couple of euros left. Just as well because no way did he feel like busking.

'It's the uncertainty that makes it so difficult.' Alice had resorted to ringing Ginny every other day to relieve the isolation. 'No one has the faintest idea how long Deb will stay in this awful limbo... I don't feel I can leave when she might come round at any moment but on the other hand we could be stuck here for months and there's my job, Timmy's school....' Alice listened to herself moaning. It went against the grain – she prided herself on not making a fuss, on dealing single-handedly with any situation – but right now, Ginny's sympathetic voice on the other end of the phone filled a need it would be pointless to deny.

'Poor you. I can imagine how difficult it must be. And lonely too.'

'Yes, I do feel rather alone.' Alice jabbed at the rogue tear sliding down her cheek and flicked it away. She would not give in to self-pity.

'How's Timmy coping?'

'Timmy's been good as gold but he's bored; there's nothing for him to do here. He'd hoped to spend time with his cousin... And then I'm worried about Mark too. I told you, he's shut himself away in his cave incommunicado. Though actually I suspect he may have sneaked in here when I was out yesterday – the bathroom and kitchen were in a bit of a mess – but as usual, he hasn't replied to my messages. Anyway, I'm sure he needs help...'

'You can't support everyone, Alice. Concentrate on yourself and Timmy for the moment. Mark will probably come to you when he's ready – or maybe there's someone else he can turn to.'

'Thanks Ginny. I guess you're right, I can't force myself on him.'

*

How to occupy Timmy was a challenge she had to face every day. She could not rely forever on the kindness of Robin and Leonor or the dwindling novelty of their little sorties around the Albaicín or into town. If only she had some idea how long they were likely to be here... Limbo: the word seemed to describe her own state as well as Deb's. She considered its meaning and because she was thinking of her sister, she did what Deborah would have done and turned to the crammed bookshelves for an English dictionary. *The supposed abode of infants dying without baptism*, she read. That was hardly appropriate. But then came further interpretations: *an imaginary place for lost, forgotten or unwanted persons or things; an unknown intermediate place or condition between two extremes.* She was the lost, forgotten or unwanted person; while Deb was in that intermediate place between the extremes of life and death.

Alice snapped the dictionary shut and went outside. Wallowing in negative thoughts would help no one. Timmy was kicking a ball around in the patio where already half the plants had been bashed into their own precarious zone between life and death. Bright scarlet geranium petals, swept into small piles by the breeze, were gently decaying; fallen needles of rosemary littered the tiles around the bush and everywhere broken stems of limp foliage lay scattered like battle casualties. Now she noticed that one of the small earthenware pots had also fallen victim to the ball.

'Come on Timmy, let's go out.'

Timmy shrugged. 'Where to?' He let the ball roll off into a corner near the mimosa tree and turned to face her.

She gazed at him and wished as always that he didn't look so like his father. It was well over ten years since she'd last seen him. She did not expect to see him again ever, God willing.

'Anywhere you like. It's your choice.' As if Granada offered countless amusements for children.

'I don't mind.'

'Then let's just go. Who knows what surprises are lying in wait?'

Alice hadn't expected to be surprised so soon. As she closed the gate behind them, a thick-waisted, middle-aged woman in fluffy blue slippers emerged from a neighbouring house and called out to her. She looked vaguely familiar – had Deb introduced them once?

With an apologetic smile, Alice trotted out one of her stock Spanish phrases: 'No hablo español.'

'María.' The woman pointed to herself and beamed at them.

Somehow by a combination of sign language and guesswork, Alice grasped that María had a grandson around Timmy's age and was suggesting they might play together.

'Javier,' she repeated several times and held up eight fingers to show his age. Alice reciprocated with nine. If she had understood right, María fetched the boy from school each day and brought him to her house for lunch. His parents picked him up later in the afternoon. Indicating they should wait, María turned towards the open door of her house.

'Javi!' she called. 'Javi, ven aqui.'

Javier was about six inches shorter than Timmy and much slighter, with enormous brown eyes and a friendly, open smile. The two boys inspected each other.

'Do you want to play with Javier?' Alice asked.

'Okay.' Timmy's lack of hesitation made her realise how much he needed company of his own age. To a child, the language barrier was immaterial. She stood watching as he followed Javier into the house without a backward glance.

'I'll be at home,' she said to María. The free afternoon would give her an opportunity to tackle the next volume of Deborah's diary: the one she had been dreading but lacked the strength of mind to put aside. The one that finished abruptly with the ragged edges of those missing pages.

Before starting, she picked out a collection of Bach cantatas from the small collection of CDs she had brought and slid it into her Walkman. The familiar music soothed her as it always did.

3rd January 1989

A new year and I feel in my bones that it's going to be a happy one. On *Nochevieja*, I invited friends here to eat and drink and celebrate. There were so many nationalities: Kay and me from England, Kay's Canadian friend, Ruth who's here for Christmas, Monika from Germany, Hassan from Morocco, Sidi, a musician friend of his from Senegal, plus the Spanish contingent.

Hassan, Sidi and Juan Antonio provided the music. They played beautifully together, creating an atmosphere we all agreed was magical. After we'd gobbled our midnight grapes (I managed to do it for the first time this year – practice makes perfect), we all trooped out into the street and wandered round the Albaicín. Everyone was out and about, the bars packed, such a happy feel. Not the ugly drunkenness I remember from the London days.

Did Deborah have to be so negative about every aspect of life in Britain? Like anywhere else, it had its good and bad sides.

19th January 1989

Mark was enthralled by last week's snow. We watched it drifting down and settling in a fine layer of crystals over the patio. María clucked and said my plants would die; I should have covered them with sheets of plastic or brought them in. Within a couple of hours the snow was gone. Mark keeps asking when there'll be more and I have to tell him not to count on any – not in Granada. In the mountains there's plenty. Juan Antonio was telling me about the *neveros*, the men who used to trek high up into the Sierra Nevada in summer to fetch snow so that the city would be supplied with ice. They took mules and set out in the early hours, not getting back to Granada till dawn the next day with their panniers full of snow. Then refrigeration was invented. Now the only snowmen are the sort Mark likes to build.

5th February 1989

A rare flying visit from Charlie to see his son. I didn't tell Mark he was coming till the day before in case Charlie cancelled. I knew he'd get keyed up about it. Charlie had promised to bring him some particular toy he wanted. It turned out to be the wrong one, but anyway they went for a ride together in Charlie's hired car, which seemed to impress Mark – especially the electric windows – so he came home happy.

Every time I see Charlie I wonder what persuaded me to marry him and how we stayed together even the relatively short time we did. Perhaps his electric windows – or their equivalent (cool designer clothes, riverside apartment, swish dining) – impressed me too in the beginning. Mum and Dad were expecting me to shack up with some penniless long-haired rebel so I think they were relieved when I brought Charlie home with his smooth public school manners and easy confidence. He wasn't so arrogant then. He had energy and drive, he knew what he wanted. Unlike me, trying on different roles, different lifestyles, whatever took my fancy at the time. I thought of myself as free but now I see that I'd already lost my freedom by the time I met Charlie. I was already submerged in the business world (or I'd never have met him), already on the fringes of that yuppy London scene. From which thank God I've escaped. Charlie can sneer all he wants, I'm happy as I am.

She'd got one thing wrong. Dad had seen through Charlie almost immediately – long before Mum or herself. He had just kept quiet about it except for one solitary occasion when he'd let his true opinion slip out. Charlie had been boasting to the family about his latest money-making scheme while Deb was in the bedroom getting dolled up for some big dinner. Dad had listened in silence but she remembered his words after the two of them had gone out. As always, he had spoken quietly but from the heart: 'Deborah needs someone with more in his head than the ambition to get rich'. How right he had been.

Amparo works in the Faculty of *Filosofía y Letras* and she's swung it somehow that I can use the university library. I'm reading everything I can lay my hands on about *al-Andalus*. It was Hassan who started me off and now there's no stopping me. I had no idea how advanced the Arabs were in so many spheres. For example they had surgical instruments that are basically still the same as those in use today, they introduced paper and ink to Europe, they invented the binary system. Their agriculture was far ahead of anywhere else at that time. Scholars came to Spain from all over Europe to learn; they respected the Islamic culture.

The phone was ringing. Alice dropped the diary on her bed and hurried towards the *salón*, thinking it might be Paco.

'Hello?' The answering silence unnerved her.

'*Hola?*' she tried. No response. What was it they said? '*Dígame?*'

The caller was still there: she could hear his breathing, not heavy but detectable. She put down the phone, her own breathing fast, shallow, panicky. Was it him?

Don't be stupid, she told herself. *It's a wrong number*. She waited. If it didn't ring again, there was nothing to worry about.

I was half an hour late picking Mark up from school today. Poor thing, he thought I'd forgotten him – which to tell the truth I had. So swallowed up in my obsession was I that I completely lost track of time. What had absorbed me so thoroughly was reading about the social status of women. According to this writer, women in *al-Andalus* had access to higher education, they worked in medicine, in teaching, they were traders, they participated in political decision-making... If you think of Europe at that time (1,000 years ago) the contrast couldn't be greater. Yet now, Muslim women are covered and confined, they're controlled first by their male relatives and then their husbands and have none of the freedoms western women enjoy.

Hassan says we should go to Córdoba. I loved it the last time I was there (ten years ago?). I remember thinking I could spend days just taking in the *Mezquita*, absorbing its coolness, its spaces, its proportions; the perspectives created by those arches and columns with their unforgettable juxtaposition of brick-red and cream.

16th March 1989

The idea for a project is forming in my mind. I'd like to do some in-depth research into the position of women in Moorish Spain. So little is known, I may even succeed in publishing it. I'm itching to make a start. Material won't be easy to get hold of but I'm sure it exists somewhere. I may have to travel, I may even have to learn Arabic. But this is what I need, a project to really challenge me.

19th March 1989

What Hassan tells me about the blocking (or rather the reversal) of permission for the mosque here in the Albaicín enrages me. The Town Hall approved it five years ago but racist right-wing elements stirred up a campaign amongst local people, appealing to all their xenophobic instincts, with the result that the authorities reclassified the site as residential – which meant the *mezquita* couldn't be built. The Muslim community has no intention of giving up though. Hassan is involved in the fight – mainly in his role as a journalist, writing about it, raising awareness, highlighting the intolerance and bigotry that are the real reason for all these bureaucratic obstacles. He sees it as a matter of basic human rights. I said I'd join the campaign group and help in whatever way I could. Considering there were thirty-four mosques in Granada when the Catholic monarchs took the city, it seems wildly unjust. Practically all the churches used to be mosques, including the Cathedral, which was built on the foundations of the Great Mosque, and San Nicolás, right next to the proposed site.

30th March 1989

I've returned from Córdoba inspired! I saw the city quite differently in the light of my reading about the Caliphate, and also because I was with Hassan and he could supply so much background. This time, when I saw the statue of Maimónides, the 12th century Jewish philosopher and physician, it meant something. And I learnt that the synagogue in the *judería* wasn't 'discovered' till 1885, after being used for various other purposes including a hospital for rabies sufferers.

Córdoba was where the brave Walladah hosted her salons for poets, artists and musicians. I'm determined to find out all I can about her – a woman who openly took lovers! For an 11th century woman, this was daring indeed. Apparently she didn't give a fig about the conventions of the time.

Was it reading Deborah's enthusiastic accounts of Moorish Spain or an unconscious reluctance to face the pages to come that made Alice put away the diary and turn instead to her sister's research? Somewhere in this clutter of papers a draft of her soon to be published book must be buried.

Her eye fell on some stapled-together sheets lying on the desk. What had caught her attention was the portrait preceding the text. It was the same woman whose picture she had found crumpled up on the floor some days ago. Alice ran her eye down the text. Walladah was the daughter of a Caliph and lived in Córdoba. She was a poet and hosted soirées for intellectuals, both men and women, where she read her 'quite bold' poetry. She was outspoken, refused to wear the veil and defended her right to take lovers; she never married. On her sleeve, Walladah had stitched the words: *I am, by God, fit for high positions and am going my way with pride.* Alice was amazed that in the Middle Ages, Muslim society had tolerated such freedom for women.

As she read on, certain phrases leapt out at her: 'an irrepressible spirit; confident, economically independent and beholden to no one; free-spirited'. The more she read, the more this Walladah Bint Mustakfi sounded like an 11th century version of Deb. Even if she hadn't recognised the resemblance, it might explain her fascination with this obscure Arab poetess.

Alice switched on the computer. A folder with the name 'Women of Influence' looked promising. Opening it, she started to read the file on Walladah. Much of it seemed to focus on her rather 'licentious' sexual behaviour and in particular her love affair with a fellow poet called Ibn Zaydun, who in the end betrayed her with a black slave girl, one of her own protégées. Jealousy led her to exact a cruel revenge on him. She took as her next lover his political rival and arch enemy, which led to him being deprived of his property and jailed. He was released a broken man. Deaf to his pleas for forgiveness and to a further outpouring of impassioned love poetry, Walladah never spoke to him again.

The sound of the buzzer startled Alice so much she knocked a whole pile of papers to the floor. Her nerves must be more strung out than she thought. It would be Timmy of course. She pressed the switch on the entry-phone to release the gate and hurried out into the patio to meet him.

'Timmy?' she called as the gate swung open.

'*Perdona…*' The bearded man standing just outside must have noticed her shock. 'You speak Spanish?'

He looked Moroccan – nothing like Hassan but definitely a Muslim, despite being dressed more or less normally in a long overshirt and trousers with an open jacket. Why had he come? What if he was a friend of Hassan's sent to reconnoitre?

'No. Who are you?' Fear infused the words with a more hostile tone than she'd intended.

'My name is Mustafa.' He moved towards her and held out a hand. When she still hesitated, he added, 'I am friend of Deborah. I call to say how sorry we are – all of us at the *mezquita*.' His face dissolved into a sad smile. 'You are a sister perhaps?'

Alice did not take his hand but a wave of relief enabled her to return the smile.

'Thank you. You guessed right, I'm her sister. Alice.'

'So, Paco is not here?'

'He's been in Madrid at the hospital ever since…' Ashamed now of her suspicion, she invited Mustafa in. 'Sit down, I'll make some tea.'

'That is very kind. But first tell me, how is she? Do you have any news?'

'I went the day before yesterday. Nothing has changed. She's unconscious, in a deep coma. No one knows how long…or whether there's any real chance of her coming round.'

Mustafa bowed his head. 'I am very sorry to hear this.'

Over tea, he told her how Deborah had supported the local Muslim community, especially in their fight for the mosque. 'We are all very fond of her. She is good person.' He spoke quietly as if the words pained him. His sadness came across as wholly sincere. And yet... Alice couldn't ignore the fact that it was Muslim terrorists who had planted the bombs. The irony, the unfairness of it could not escape him, surely?

As if reading her thoughts, he withdrew from his jacket pocket a folded sheet of paper printed on both sides. 'Maybe you like to read the statement from our community? It is about our repudiation of this terrible act. Such crimes have no basis in Islam. Our religion does not support killing and destruction.'

'Thank you, I'll read it later.' His close scrutiny from across the table as they waited for their tea to cool made her add, in tacit apology for her initial distrust, 'I know most Muslims aren't fanatics.'

He nodded in acknowledgement and sat silently for a while, stroking his beard.

She remembered Deb's impassioned response a couple of years ago, after 9/11, when she'd carelessly let slip some derogatory remark about Muslims. 'But all the major religions have fundamentalist sects. What about the religious Jews in Israel, some of those fanatic born-again Christians in the States? Can't you see through the propaganda?' Deb had succeeded in making her feel guilty.

'The path of vengeance may appear sweet...' Alice assumed Mustafa was still talking about the bombings but he continued, 'Your sister rose above personal antipathy to do the right thing. This struggle with her conscience...was it only one year ago? She spoke to me about it afterwards. I understood how it tested her... But of course you will know far more of this than I do.'

Alice had no idea what he was talking about but before she could ask him to explain, the buzzer went again. 'My son,' she said as she opened the gate for Timmy. 'He's found a new friend to play with.'

'And Deborah's son? I am thinking often of Mark.' He was leaning forward, hands clasped on the table. 'Ah, I see from your face...'

Timmy bounced in, looking livelier than at any time since they'd arrived. Alice didn't need to ask how he'd got on with Javier. She introduced him to Mustafa.

'Mum, can I play with Javi again tomorrow?'

'Yes, if you want to.'

'Well, now I must go.' Mustafa stood and moved towards the door. 'But I would like to talk to Mark. Maybe our community can give him some support.'

'You can try… I haven't found him very receptive. You know he's living in a cave in Sacromonte?'

'Yes, I had heard this from Deborah.'

Alice gave him directions and promised to let Paco know of his visit.

'Javi's dad came to fetch him,' Timmy said after Mustafa had gone. 'He rides a motorbike and he lets Javi sit in front of him on it.'

'Really? That sounds very dangerous.'

'No it's not.' He leant back on his chair so that it almost tipped over. 'I said my dad was a pilot. I drew a picture of a plane so he'd understand. I said I'd been up in it loads of times.'

'Timmy, it's wrong to tell lies.'

He shrugged. 'Everyone does. Even you, I bet.'

Chapter Eight

Not everyone liked Mum: people either loved or hated her. That's what Paco said. He reckoned Mum made enemies because she wasn't afraid to say what she thought. If she believed in something, she'd fight for it; she was that kind of person, he said. Too right. She wouldn't take shit from anyone. Mark sometimes thought she was looking for trouble, the way she always took on other people's battles. Like the woman whose gypsy boyfriend beat her up and Mum let her hide in their house, and the illegals who got treated like scum just because they were from Africa. She spent fucking ages helping the Senegalese drummer, Sidi with his papers. The *fachas* on the right hated her: that PP guy who owned a whole chain of supermarkets told her to go back where she came from and not interfere in his country. What was it she'd said afterwards? 'He can take a running jump.' He'd pissed himself laughing at that; it was a new one on him.

Anyway, as Paco said, there were plenty of others who appreciated her. He doubted if he could count all the friends she had; there must be dozens. There were the other *guiris* in the Albaicín for a start: Monika, Kay, Robin... He'd known most of them all his life; they'd been here even before him and Mum. Then there were her and Paco's political friends in the IU, the crowd from the *mezquita*, people she'd got to know at the university, friends from the *barrio*...

But when he was little... Mark thought back to when he was at school. In primary, the other kids had given him a hard time. Because of her. It started when Hassan moved in with them. María José said his *mamá* was a *puta* who went with *moros*. He was seven years old; he didn't know what the fuck she was talking about but he didn't need to:

the spite in her voice was enough. Most likely she was just repeating what her parents said. When the rest of them saw how easy it was to wind him up, they joined in, trying to make him blub. They wouldn't leave him alone – even after he punched María José. All that did was get him into trouble with the teacher. Señor Felipe said it was cowardly to hit girls. Telling Mum would have made it ten times worse so he never did. She had no fucking idea what he had to put up with.

At first it was cool having Hassan around. They did more fun things, like going to the *tetería* for milkshakes and inviting people over to make music. Mum got him a guitar for his eighth birthday but it was Hassan who taught him to play. Mum was always in a good mood in those days. She laughed a lot and told him 'secrets' that went in one ear and out the other. Later, the laughs were what he missed the most.

Some evenings they'd sit around the fire in the dark, watching the orange flames dancing and leaping up the chimney, listening to them crackle and hiss while Hassan told stories about goblins, ghosts, hidden gold... He was a brilliant storyteller. Mark could still remember a few of them, mostly the scary ones. He'd pretended to be frightened but he wasn't really because Mum and Hassan were there, the three of them sitting close, him in his pyjamas... Times like that he didn't give a shit about the kids at school and what they said. It was a fucking shame those times didn't last.

Voices. He'd been so wrapped up in ancient history he hadn't noticed them. They sounded quite close, like they might be right outside his cave. Whispering, which meant they were talking about him. He strained to recognise the voices. One of them could be Pierre...

'Ahem. Mark, are you in there?'

'Who is it? What do you want?'

'*Soy* Mustafa. You remember me, don't you?'

Mustafa. Fucking hell, what was he doing here? How had he found his way? Mark shifted the door and peered out. Mustafa was standing there but not too close. *At a respectful distance*, that's how Mum would have put it. He was wearing a *djellaba* with sandals and socks. He looked like some kind of prophet, all sad-eyed and serious.

'I came to see if there's anything you need, anything I can do to help,' he said. 'And to let you know that all of us at the *mezquita*...

we are thinking of you, praying for your mother, that she gets better.'

Mark stepped out of the cave. Praying: he doubted that would do much good – about as much as throwing a wish on the bonfire the night of San Juan. Still, it wouldn't do any harm either.

'I'm alright, I don't need anything,' he said, 'But thanks.' He couldn't think what else to say.

'You know our community will always make you welcome. Those who come to us find love and compassion, an alternative to the material world...' He made it sound quite tempting. Like a new age commune but with Allah thrown in. 'We are very grateful to your mother, we have not forgotten how she helped us achieve our beautiful new mosque. She is a good person.'

'Yeah, thanks.' *Is.* He'd noticed how Mustafa said *is*, not *was*. *Es buena persona.* Little things like that, they were important.

'I'll leave you now.' Mustafa reached out and clasped Mark's hand in both of his, keeping hold of it so long Mark thought his arm would bloody well seize up.

After Mustafa had gone, Mark sat outside for a while, smoking and watching a line of ants streaming to their destination like they knew exactly where they were headed and why. He wondered if there was a boss ant who controlled them or if they were just obeying some powerful ant instinct.

3rd June 1989

Hassan eats here most days and often comes at night too. I've been wondering whether to suggest he gives up his flat and moves in. I don't think Mark would mind – he's used to having Hassan around. And there's plenty of room, we wouldn't be on top of each other.

I'm getting to know some of his *maghrebi* friends, mainly those fighting for the *mezquita*. Good, sincere people, most of them. Hassan got drawn in through covering their campaign for the Moroccan press. The real driving force behind it is actually a Spanish Muslim. I hadn't realised till I got involved that there's a whole community of Spanish converts to Islam spread throughout Andalucía. I was chatting to one of the women the other day (she calls herself Nur) and she told me that for her Islam provides an antidote to all the ills of western society, "a different, more peaceful and principled way of life through submission to the will of Allah," she said, quoting from one of their leaflets. It did make some kind of sense – at least I could see its attraction – but I don't think I'll be converting any time soon.

That was a relief; Alice had been starting to wonder. The thought of Deb secretly becoming a Muslim was laughable and yet... She was so unpredictable, you just never knew. Some obscure passion would take hold of her and all reason went flying out of the window. The more you tried to talk sense into her, the more determined she became.

20th June 1989

I've decided to shut up house and go to England for the summer. It's too hot to be outside and with no school from late June to mid-September, what will Markie do stuck in the house all day? Some families – those with a flat on the coast – swap the city for the beach but for us it makes more sense to spend the time in England. As well as seeing Mum and Alice, I'd like to catch up with my London friends, have a few nights out – if I can still stand the pace. I've slowed down so much since moving here. I'll probably turn into a typical Albaicín housewife by the time I'm fifty – strident voice, coiffured hair, thick waist, pulling a tartan shopping trolley behind me.

25th June 1989

Two months of separation from Hassan. Will I survive? Rashly, I told him he could move in here in the autumn. A kind of consolation for both of us, something to look forward to. I might just 'forget' to mention that bit of news to Mum. 'I've nothing against coloured people but...' If I hear those words again, I know I'll find it impossible not to react. Alice will have to swear secrecy.

Poor Mum, Deb was hard on her. She'd been no more prejudiced than most of her generation. And when it came to the real test, she had passed with flying colours. Deb hadn't given her nearly enough credit for that; for the huge adjustment Mum had been forced to make.

What joy to be home. Though I'm not sure Markie feels the same. He got used to England and all the attention from family. Mum and Alice between them spoilt him rotten. Almost as much as most Spanish grannies and aunts indulge their little ones, which is saying something. Now he'll have to make do with just me.

Two people asked, didn't I miss home, didn't I get homesick? Of course I thought they meant Granada but it turned out they were talking about England. Nobody seems to understand how Granada has wormed its way under my skin to become part of who I am. I'm not sure I understand it myself. All I know is that this is where I want to live, where I want to die.

I missed my house, my views, Hassan (*muchísimo!*). I missed the *alegría* and warmth of the Spanish, the earthiness of the Albaicín. I even found myself instinctively seeking out Spanish speakers in London – tourists, immigrants, anyone; trying to get into conversation with them. The London clubbing scene was where I felt most out of place – like a fish in a farmyard. Has it changed so much or have I changed? The best was spending time with Kate and Sally. It reminded me of my crazy youth, the high jinks we got up to – but also of the high-pressure, high-living London days. Perhaps I do need that link with the past, which I thought was entirely lost. If I break all the threads, I'm killing off a part of myself too. Strangely, family has become more important than when we all lived close.

It wasn't just distance that made those ties seem important. Birth and death brought them home even more strongly. If Deborah died... Alice's skin started to feel clammy. Her death would leave a gap that could never be filled. And on top of that, she must now bear the weight of their secret alone; face single-handed the consequences of their actions.

She shut the diary and put it away. Opening the door to the patio, she caught the sweet scent of the first wisteria blooms. It was late afternoon, the air already warm enough to go without a jacket. A walk would do her good and why not to Sacromonte? Her failure to get through to Mark still niggled.

As she took the now familiar road, she thought about those early years when she had 'spoilt him rotten'. She remembered the joy it had given her at a time when the prospects of having a child of her own looked uncertain. The wasted years languishing over Michael and then trying to make a go of it with Andy, who had 'been there, done that' and made it crystal clear she should look elsewhere if she wanted babies. But in any case, spoiling had always been the privilege of aunts and grandparents hadn't it? With Timmy she was less indulgent.

She saw Mark well before he became aware of her presence. He was sitting on a stool outside the cave, elbows resting on his knees, head bent as if the earth held some deep secret that would be revealed if he stared long enough at its rutted, stony surface. The sight of him made her want to cry. He cut such a solitary figure, sitting there still as a statue, lost in sorrow or so it looked. She tried to remember herself at twenty but there were no points of comparison. She'd been brought up in a stable family; she had a job, a fiancé, a comfortable rented flat shared with Judy and Pauline. She knew where she was going.

When Mark finally raised his eyes, she was only a few yards away. She waved and he gave her a curt nod, which she supposed was progress of a kind.

'I brought you some provisions,' she said, plonking down the plastic bag with tinned fish, chickpeas and a packet of rice from Deborah's store cupboard. She had no idea how Mark fed himself with no income – or none she was aware of.

'Thanks. I'll find you something to sit on,' he said and darted into the cave, emerging with a tatty but quite serviceable small armchair.

'Where's Timmy?' he asked.

'Timmy's playing with his new friend, Javier.'

'Oh right.' He fiddled with his pouch of tobacco, peering into it then stuffing it into his pocket.

'I went to the hospital,' Alice said. 'I'm afraid there's been no improvement. She's the same as when you saw her.'

Mark chewed his lip but said nothing.

'Paco is planning to come back for a few days. After the funeral.'

'Funeral?' Mark was sitting up straight all of a sudden. 'What are you talking about?'

'For the other victims,' Alice said, annoyed at her failure to make it clear. 'There's going to be a state funeral in the cathedral.'

He relaxed again. 'Oh yeah, I heard.'

'Paco told me the new Prime Minister had been to visit the injured. I think he spoke to Paco.'

'Zapatero? What did he say?'

'I don't know, you'll have to ask Paco when he comes back.'

They sat in silence for a few moments.

'I'd love to see inside your cave.' Alice was expecting a firm no but Mark immediately rose and beckoned to her.

'Can you get through the gap? It's a bit of a squeeze...'

'You managed to get the chair through,' she said with a smile. 'I'm not that large.'

'Wait a sec. I'll move the door, let some light in. Otherwise you won't see a thing.'

His cave was much less squalid than she had imagined. Pieces of coloured tile had been cemented into the floor and formed a kind of mosaic. In one corner was a primitive stove with aluminium tubing to take the smoke out through a hole above. Curtained archways in the thick lime-washed walls divided it into three separate rooms. In the 'bedroom', a rug had been spread beside the mattress, which was heaped with Mark's rumpled bedding. Casting her gaze around, Alice scrutinised the furniture: a small table and two of those straight-backed chairs with rush seats, an old trunk, a camping stove and a heater with bottled gas. There were a couple of washing bowls and a large plastic water container. Little alcoves had been cut into the rock walls, with ledges for what Timmy had described as 'treasures'. The walls were decorated with pictures and Alice noticed one of Mark's drawings amongst them.

'It's cosy,' she said, joining him at the table. 'I can see why Timmy was so impressed.'

'No one bothers you here.' He pulled a couple of cans from a six-pack of beer and offered her one.

'Not at the moment, thanks.' In her bag was the sheet of paper Mustafa had given her. 'I had a visitor from the mosque,' she said. 'A friend of your mother's.'

'Mustafa? Yeah, he came up here too.'

Alice waited for him to say more, to give an opinion perhaps, but the act of sprinkling tobacco and possibly marijuana onto a cigarette paper appeared to demand all his concentration.

'Mustafa gave me this,' she said, digging the sheet out of her bag and passing it to him. 'I wondered if you could translate it for me.'

Mark finished rolling his cigarette and took the page from her.

'It's about the 11-M bombers,' he said, running his eye down the sheet. 'It says they're not recognised by any Muslim community. What they did was totally against Islamic law that condemns and punishes such abominable acts... *Abominable*, is that a word in English?' He looked up at her. 'It says about 'the mysterious Al-Qaeda' that no one had heard of till the Twin Towers attacks, when the Americans decided they were to blame. There's a whole lot more...' He turned the page. 'Terrorism is against the interests of Muslims because it gives the West an excuse to detain Muslims without fair trial, to invade Muslim countries and grab their resources... Too fucking right.'

'Okay, thanks, I get the idea. Of course most Muslims are decent people. It's natural they want to disassociate themselves. How long have you known Mustafa?'

'You sure you don't want a beer?' he asked, ignoring her question.

'Well alright, maybe I will.'

'I should have a glass somewhere,' he said, getting up and poking around behind a grubby curtain in one of the alcoves.

'Oh please don't bother. I'm quite happy to drink from the can.' The standards of hygiene up here hardly inspired confidence. 'Shall we sit outside again?'

'If you want.'

'I've been thinking back,' she said when they were seated in what, at a stretch of the imagination, could be described as Mark's front garden, 'To when you were small and you used to come to Bristol in the school holidays. Sometimes you'd stay at Granny's, sometimes at mine. Do you remember?'

'Course I do.'

'We had some fun, didn't we?'

'I remember getting ice-creams every day. With chocolate flakes stuck in them.'

'They're called 99s.'

'Why?'

'Oh Mark, I've no idea!'

'And I remember one time we went on a steam train.' He looked pensive for a moment. 'I s'pose it was before Timmy was born... You had toys in your house though: there was a big red fire engine and a model village with little houses and trees and people.'

Alice laughed. 'I got those specially, so you'd have something to play with.' She looked up at the sky, now painted in swathes of bluish grey and pink; the hills bathed rose by the setting sun. Already the smell of wood fires was beginning to drift on the early evening air. Thin plumes of smoke curled up from some of the pipes sticking out of the hillside. 'I can see why you like it here,' she said. 'It's very peaceful.'

For a while neither of them spoke and yet in the silence she felt at last the barriers were beginning to dissolve.

'What else do you remember?' she asked. But her words were drowned out by a chorus of barking from what sounded like half a dozen dogs. So much for peace. Along with the dogs, various figures had appeared – from out of the caves, she supposed. But Mark's attention was fixed on an old tramp who was weaving his way unsteadily in their direction. He stood in front of them, an unpleasant leer on his face.

'Hey Mark, go'r a lady vishitor, eh?' The voice, so slurred as to be barely coherent, had an unmistakeably nasty edge to it. Now he was close, Alice realised he wasn't old at all – probably no more than forty. Alcohol and who knew what else had ravaged his face and what she could see of his body.

'Fuck off, Ed.'

'Paid up in the end, didn't yer?' His cackling laugh made Alice flinch. 'Took yer time though, tha's wha' I heard.'

She turned away in revulsion as he cleared his throat and spat.

'Go'r a beer for yer mate Ed, eh Mark?'

'Why don't you just fuck off, you pisspot?'

To Alice's great relief, he turned away and staggered down the hill, cackling to himself. She would have liked to ask Mark what he meant about paying up but this clearly wasn't the moment.

'I hope not all your neighbours are like that,' she said.

'No way. There's only him and Dani. The others are okay, they're cool.'

Alice noticed a bearded blonde boy pushing a wheelbarrow of stones towards one of the other caves and heard the sound of a guitar drifting on the air. The mood of menace had cleared now Ed was gone but Mark still seemed edgy, his eyes darting this way and that, one toe shifting the loose earth in pointless circles.

'I ought to be going,' she said. 'Timmy will be wondering where I am. Come with me if you like.' But she could tell from the turn of his mouth that he would not. 'Or come for lunch tomorrow if you prefer,' she added.

'I might do.'

'Good. And thanks for the beer.'

Mark had risen and she stepped forward to kiss him goodbye, half-expecting some resistance. There was none. On the contrary, he embraced her with warmth. Was it her imagination or did he cling to her with something akin to desperation? Like a child, a frightened, lonely child needing to be held?

After Alice had gone, Mark went back in his cave and pulled the door across. He lay down on the bed and closed his eyes. Two visitors in one day had done him in. Two visitors not counting Ed. Most likely Ed was the reason he felt so wobbly. Mark wished he'd drop dead, the cunt. That's what happened to Nico. The booze killed him. He got sicker and sicker till one day he just collapsed and died outside his cave.

Better not to think about Ed. He thought about Alice instead. He'd known her all his life: Mum's sister. Except for their looks, you wouldn't think they were sisters. Their personalities were way way different. For example, he couldn't imagine Alice forgetting to pick Timmy up from school or losing the keys every other day or exploding if someone made the wrong kind of joke. She was quieter than Mum – definitely not as mad – but she wasn't boring. It was true they'd had some fun when he was a kid. She used to play games with him, even football in the park, till he got too rough – or that's what she said. It was after that time the ball hit her in the chest. Getting hit in your boobs must be about as bad as getting hit in the bollocks.

Alice used to like taking him to the zoo as well. They'd stand watching the monkeys for hours. He thought it was dead clever the way they carried their babies about with no hands, the little ones just hanging on to their mothers' bellies, upside down as they ran around.

It wasn't just Ed who'd shaken him up. He'd already been feeling rattled. He wished Alice hadn't mentioned the funeral. He wanted to know...but then at the same time he didn't. Mum was just like before: that's what Alice had said. The vision of her lying there was still in his head; he couldn't get rid of it. He could still hear the sound of those monitors beeping away. It must be getting on for two weeks now. If they turned the machines off she'd die, and no amount of praying to Allah or the Virgin was going to make the slightest fucking difference. Knowing Mum, she'd hold out till after the funeral in the Cathedral. She wouldn't want to be there with the King and Queen and all the *politicos*. No way.

The thing about Alice was she made him feel like a kid again. Could be because she was his auntie or because they'd been talking about those times when he was little. When she left... It was bizarre but he'd almost cracked up. One minute he was itching for her to leave, the next it was like she was abandoning him and he wanted to bury his face in her neck and howl like a baby. Just as well she hadn't noticed.

11th September 1989

Hassan has moved in. He didn't need to remind me of my promise. The first two days after I arrived home, I wouldn't let him leave the house. We feasted on each other! Poor Mark, he must have felt horribly left out. Yesterday I suggested to Hassan that he fetch his stuff and give the landlady notice. No sooner said... Have I been too rash? But it feels right, it *is* right.

The next entry was the one Alice had read when she first discovered the diaries – that unrestrained outpouring of love evoked, it seemed, by Hassan's playing of the oud.

1st October 1989

Just re-read what I wrote last time – gushing or what? If anybody ever discovers my writings, I'll die! No, that's not true. A twinge, a blush, a self-mocking joke perhaps...but basically I don't care.

5th October 1989

Hassan told me that pomegranates, not apples were the original forbidden fruit from the Garden of Eden. When I saw them piled up on Trini's stall this morning I couldn't resist buying a kilo. No wonder Adam and Eve succumbed to temptation. Trini had cut one open to expose the rich red of the seeds, such a deep red they reminded me of rubies.

20th October 1989

Struggling to pick up the rhythm of my research again. Being away all summer, then the delicious distraction of Hassan... He steals up behind me in my sanctum, starts to tell me some fascinating story or anecdote of history and I'm not strong enough to shoo him away. I have to listen. Then it's time to fetch Mark from school and I've done nothing.

25th October 1989

'*Fuera moros*' scrawled in big black letters on the outside of my wall next to the gate. I felt so sick when I saw it. I've heard the muttered insults too, when walking in the street with Hassan and even once or twice when I've been alone. '*Puta*' spat out in a tone of utter disgust. I scrubbed at the wall like a madwoman, energised by my fury. I want to protect him from these insults. It's him I care about; they can say what they like about me. What is it here in Granada, that there's so much prejudice against Arabs? Is it their history? 'Moors out' – like a replay of the 16th century when they were expelled. The history books refer to them as invaders, talk about the *reconquista* but how can you call it a reconquest when they were settled here for nearly eight centuries and mostly co-existed peacefully and in cooperation with Christians and Jews and when they interbred widely? A good proportion of the population must be descended from *moros* (how I hate that word with its clearly pejorative undertone).

28th November 1989

Hassan has found me an Arabic teacher, an Iraqi woman called Fátima. She was a primary teacher in Baghdad and I don't think they've been here long. Hassan implied that she and her husband were political dissidents of some kind. Can't wait for our first class tomorrow.

I don't expect to reach a high level, but it should be some help in my research. Anyway, I just love the idea of being able to communicate in the language that was spoken here for 800 years.

It's war. Late last night, I sneaked round the Albaicín with a couple of others sticking up posters for the *mezquita* campaign. No doubt they'll be ripped down but we have to keep up the fight. I've already made one enemy amongst my neighbours. Two actually – the po-faced couple on the corner, who never ever return my greeting, just give me disapproving looks (I should have a husband). Narrow-minded bigots, secret admirers of Franco I wouldn't be surprised. He was out walking his dog last night and spotted me at work with my pot of paste and brush. The look he gave me! As if he wanted to consign me to the flames of Hell. Preferably *pronto*.

When I first arrived in Granada my eyes were open only to the charm. Now I am seeing the darker side. As Kay said I would.

So disillusion *had* set in and quite early on. Alice wondered if these were the neighbours Ignacio had been referring to. Thinking of him, remembering the gentleness and sincerity in his manner, his openness about his own sorrow, she felt a sudden impulse to ring him. He was someone she could talk to about Deb, someone with whom to share her grief. She found the piece of paper with his number and picked up the phone.

Chapter Nine

Mark woke up with a massive hard-on, the first for days. He'd been beginning to wonder if there wasn't something wrong with him. Tina had been on his mind when he went to sleep. He thought about her again now till his cock exploded in his hand, in about twenty seconds flat. He wished he hadn't told her he wanted to be alone; it was mostly the others who'd been pissing him off. It would be good to feel the warmth of her body next to him in the bed again, to smell her skin there even after she'd gone.

Last time Alice came over to Granada, she'd asked if he had a girlfriend and he'd said no. It was before he and Tina got it together. Not that she was really a 'girlfriend' now. You couldn't say they were *novios*; they just had a shag every so often. She was nice with him though, like she cared. And he looked out for her; he wasn't just into fucking her. Sometimes they'd lie in the cave and talk for hours. Her parents had split up too and her stepdad was a dirty bastard who couldn't keep his hands off her. She hated him. That was the main reason she'd left home in Glasgow and come to Granada – after working her way down through France and Spain.

He must have drifted back into a doze because the sound of hammering from somewhere not too far away found its way into his dreams and then out again, making him sit up with a start. As his brain got into gear, he remembered today was when Paco was supposed to be coming back. Two weeks he'd spent just keeping Mum company, though she wouldn't have known it. How could he sit there day after day and not go crazy? Was he remembering too? Flicking back through the years they'd been together? It was alright for Paco: he wouldn't have to feel bad about slagging Mum off because he never did. They hardly had any rows, not real ones. Which was a bloody big relief after Hassan.

Mum and Hassan were always fighting, specially the last couple of years. Mum never bothered to close the windows. She probably didn't twig that in the summer he could hear everything: the shouting and insults (every single fucking word); the sex... At first, when he was quite little, he thought Hassan was hurting her. Later he knew exactly what they were up to when he heard those little moans and grunts. Pablito had explained it all to him.

He'd better go up to the house again, see what Paco had to say. Yesterday, when he went for lunch, Álvaro and Maribel had asked him about the rent. If Deborah wasn't home by April, should they pay it to him? He said he'd let them know. Three hundred and fifty euros would be bloody useful but it didn't seem right to take it. Mum said they were the best tenants in the apartment since the Dutch couple; they always paid *pronto*, right at the beginning of the month.

On his way to the Albaicín, he remembered Paco wasn't coming till late. He thought about turning back but decided to head up to the *mezquita* instead. At San Nicolás, a huge party of Japanese wearing labels trailed across the square after their guide who held up this stupid little flag, like they were kids who might get lost. As usual, tourists were sat all along the wall, taking pictures of the Alhambra and each other, trying to ignore the old woman clacking her castanets in the hope of a sale.

Mark wandered into the *mezquita* gardens. The place was practically tourist-free, dead peaceful. It could be they were afraid of coming in, afraid of *musulmanes*. If so, they were missing out because the view was loads better from here and nobody hassled you to take their photo or flog you stuff. With the fountains spurting and a few oranges, lemons and olives on the trees, it was like paradise. He stared across at the snowy Sierra Nevada and thought it might be nice to get up there and see the virgin snow all around, the air so biting cold it cleaned you right through; cleaned your head of all the crap so you could start again like a baby. Pure.

'Alice?'

Startled, she looked through the window and saw Ignacio out in the patio, a large canvas bag slung over his shoulder.

'Oh... How did you get in?'

He held up a bunch of keys. 'Paco didn't tell you I had the keys?'

'No, he didn't.' Dammit, he should have done. Ignacio was honourable, not the type to go sneaking around in someone else's house. All the same, if he had keys, so might any number of others. 'Well... It's good of you to come so soon.' Her discomfort must be obvious. 'You don't have to go to work this morning?'

'Later. I have no classes till twelve. So, Alice, how are you?'

'I'm...' His eyes were on her, those kindly eyes that held hers and made platitudes pointless. Without warning, a tear rolled down her cheek. Embarrassed, she wiped it away with her hand. 'Sorry...'

'It is natural,' he said. 'Come, *un abrazo*.' He held out his arms. 'You know this word?'

'A hug?' In England it might have seemed inappropriate from a man she hardly knew, but this was Spain, where hugging and kissing were the equivalent of shaking hands. She let him hold her for a minute, resting her head against his chest. He was taller than she'd realised and bonier.

'Deborah often spoke about you,' he said. 'And about your son. Family was very important to her. In this, she was as the Spanish. You know, for us family is everything.'

Alice nodded. She had never thought of her sister as family-oriented. Of course once Timmy came along...

'It caused Deborah sadness that you lived so far apart,' Ignacio said, breaking into her thoughts. 'Look, I have brought photos to show you...if you like.'

They sat together at the table with the *brasero* – it was still cold at this hour – and looked at his photos. Most were of social occasions in restaurants or bars with a crowd of other people, including Paco and sometimes Mark. Ignacio passed them to her one by one. Seeing Deb's animated face, her smile as she raised a glass of wine or in one shot a speared prawn, made Alice weep. She allowed the tears to fall and accepted the comfort of Ignacio's hand on hers. He pointed out his wife, Conchita – a petite, elegant woman with ultra-short hair in contrast to his own unruly curls. A few of the photos had been taken on political marches: Deb holding up a placard or carrying one end of a banner strung across the road.

'Only a month ago,' Ignacio said of one. 'It's hard to believe. How ignorant we are of our fate, how helpless.' He swept the photos into a pile and pushed them aside.

'Why is life so cruel?' Alice spoke through her tears. 'I can't bear it, never to hear her voice or laugh again or see her as more than an inert body stuck with tubes.'

'Losing someone you love, it is the hardest thing.'

Alice turned to look at him and saw in his eyes that he was speaking for himself as well as her. 'I'm so glad you came,' she said. 'I hadn't realised quite how lonely I was.'

'Grieving is always lonely. Beyond the first days or weeks, it is expected you...contain yourself. And in your case, when the outcome is still uncertain and this uncertainty may continue during many months...' He released her hand and stood. 'I must go very soon but first you make some coffee?'

After he'd gone, she felt a little lighter, not quite so friendless. She went to her room and picked up the diary.

20th January 1990

When I talk to Hassan about Walladah, how free she was and how women in general had considerable influence and even a degree of independence in *al-Andalus*, he says how important it is that I should write about it, let all those censorious Europeans and Americans who denounce Islam know the truth: that there's nothing in the Qur'an that calls for the subjugation of women. Then a few hours later, he's telling me I shouldn't be arranging to go out and see my friends without consulting him. He's throwing jealous tantrums even if I'm only having a quiet drink with Amparo or Monika. I used to think he was different, that he'd overcome the machista mind-set. Not at all. Teresa says her ex-husband was the same: he hated her going out without him, especially at night. And he's Spanish. In fact they're just as bad; decades behind British men. I wonder what Walladah would think if she could come back and see Andalucía in the 20th century. She'd be horrified.

Nevertheless, for all his faults, I love him. I'm beginning to realise how deeply rooted we all are in the culture we grew up in. Where two cultures confront each other and attempt to fuse (or even co-exist) in a relationship, NOTHING can be taken for granted. Every action must be explained and understood; constant negotiation is necessary. It tires me out but I won't give up. Who wants a boring relationship with no energy, no life, no challenge? Not me.

25th January 1990

I am working at my Arabic, reciting the numbers, struggling to decipher the unfamiliar squiggles, dots and dashes of the script. I had no idea there was such a difference between the literary and spoken language. Tomorrow is only our fourth class but I am impatient, I want to be able to read, to speak, to understand now. But then I 'waste' half the class quizzing Fátima about her life in Iraq, what made her leave, how it is for women in Baghdad... Until she quietly reminds me of my purpose and we get down to work again.

12th March 1990

The number of Spanish words derived from Arabic is a continual revelation to me. It's not just those starting with 'al' like *alcazaba* and *alarma*, but numerous others too. Lots of foods introduced by the Moors kept their Arabic names: *espinacas*, *almendras*, *limones*, *azucar*...the list is endless. Then there are the expressions, like '*ojalá*' for 'if only'. Fátima explained how that came directly from the Arabic 'if God willed it'. And '¡*olé*!' derives from '*wa-Alla*' (for Allah). I'm disappointed when others don't share my enthusiasm. I was talking about these connections with Belén today and she just shrugged and went on to talk about the new dress she'd bought for her cousin's wedding.

2nd April 1990

Had a furious argument with Belén's boyfriend, Carlos in the Faculty cafeteria today, which I fear means my friendship with her is over because I was really very rude to him. We were having a moan – in a fairly mild way – about the Spanish attitude to time and Carlos says: Oh it's all due to the *moros*. We suffered their invasion for 800 years so it's not surprising their bad ways have persisted. I questioned his use of the words 'suffered' and 'invasion' and pointed out how many good things we'd inherited from them and how an invasion couldn't last 800 years. I resisted pointing out he was probably descended from '*moros*'. He compared the Arab invasion of Spain to the Romans invading Britain. I told him we didn't think of the Roman civilisation in those terms. Then he got extremely aggressive and I lost my cool completely and called him a racist. He banged his glass down on the counter and stormed off without a word.

Alice couldn't help smiling. Deborah was a match for anyone when it came to displays of temper. As a child, she had felt awed by her older sister's rages. Once Deb had even taken some empty milk bottles outside and deliberately smashed them.

19th April 1990

Having Alice here reminded me how I felt when I first arrived five years ago. I was seeing things through her eyes, things I take for granted now. Like Pepe, striding around the Albaicín every morning with his book of lottery tickets, shouting out his wares so you can hear him coming long before you see him, greeting everyone he knows – including me, even though I've never bought a ticket. Like the little grocery shops where you have to ask for what you want instead of the soulless supermarkets they have in Britain. Like the way people prefer to stand in the street and yell to the upper windows when they call on family or friends rather than use the doorbell.

I got the feeling Alice didn't like Hassan. I suppose all she sees is a good-looking but moody Moroccan. How can she appreciate his wide knowledge, his *cultura* (culturedness?), the interesting stories he tells, when they don't have a language in common? I did my best to interpret but after a while it gets tedious. She doesn't seem interested in learning Spanish, not even a few words; she'd rather rely on me. It doesn't take an enormous effort to say '*gracias*' and '*hola*' and '*como estás?*' Yet she's not lazy in other ways; I've always tended to be the lazy one. Hassan tried hard with the little English he has but her lack of appreciation didn't exactly encourage him.

Alice found it uncomfortable reading about herself, seeing on the page in Deb's familiar spiky handwriting the criticisms she had only sensed at the time. Knowing they were justified made it worse. She had asked herself many times why she disliked Hassan so much, had disliked him right from the start. She didn't consider herself prejudiced, despite what Deborah thought. At work, she chatted more to Rita, her black colleague than to anyone else; she considered her a friend. Then there was the Indian family with their three immaculate and well-behaved little girls, who lived a couple of doors away. She often stopped to talk to them. Once Sunita had brought round some delicious chicken curry and offered to teach her the recipe. So her antipathy to Hassan couldn't possibly be because of his race.

Now, of course, that initial aversion was overshadowed by fear, but why had she distrusted him so much in the early days? Picturing him in her mind, she realised that it was his eyes: you could tell from a person's eyes if there was a hidden side to them. Already the first time she met him, when Deb's adulation had been farcically over the top and he seemed equally love-struck, Alice had sensed something dangerous lurking beneath. At the time it was no more than a fleeting intuition that she couldn't have put into words. The conviction he would stop at nothing to get what he wanted. As proved later by his relentless pursuit of Deb after she threw him out. Even using Mark. First impressions counted: in her experience, they were nearly always right. It wouldn't surprise her if he *had* been involved in terrorism, whatever Deb might say.

*

'Mummy, wake up!'

Alice came to with a start, straight out of a dream in which she and Timmy were being chased through the streets by a gypsy with curly hair, a gold earring and a black waistcoat like the one that horrible alcoholic neighbour of Mark's was wearing. He was shouting *Olé! Olé!* and brandishing a knife. Mercifully it was Timmy shaking her and not the gypsy.

'It's been light for ages. Mummy, Paco's come back.'

'I know. I'll get up in a minute.'

Although it was a relief to escape from the dream, she had slept nowhere near long enough. Yet again Deb's diary had kept her reading late into the night. The clang of the gate sometime in the early hours had registered but Paco had insisted when he phoned that she should not wait up.

In the kitchen now, she found him standing by the window, a glass of coffee in his hand. When he turned to greet her, she found the change in his appearance shocking. He looked worn out, the lines of his face etched deeper, the hollows under his eyes darker and more cavernous. He had lost weight from both his face and body. The grey hairs flecking the dark seemed to have multiplied. Meeting him for the first time she would have put him in his sixties whereas before he had looked young for his fifty-one years.

'Alice, I am happy to see you.'

'Me too.' She meant it. His absence had made the house seem bigger and emptier, filled it with painful echoes. They held each other for a long moment – until the tears sliding down her cheeks forced her to reach for a tissue. Timmy was watching them. He looked anxious, uncertain. He was unused to seeing her crying.

'Mummy...'

'It's alright.' She pulled him close and gave him a cuddle.

Turning again to Paco, she said, 'Timmy has a new friend, María's grandson Javier.'

'Good,' he said. 'And you? Have you found a friend here? Do you speak sometimes with Álvaro and Maribel in the apartment?'

'I see them now and then.' To her shame, she'd been avoiding the tenants, embarrassed by her inadequate Spanish. They probably thought her cold and aloof. 'But your friend Ignacio came. It was thoughtful of you to ask him.'

'He is a good man,' Paco said. 'Now, there is a little coffee left in the pot and I can make more. I have already been to the shop for bread, if you like some toast.'

'Please don't worry about me. I'll see to myself.' She looked at Timmy. 'Have you had breakfast yet?'

'I had toast with jam. Can I play outside now?'

'Good idea. Just mind the plants with your ball.'

Alice poured the remains of the coffee into a cup and sat down. After a moment, Paco joined her at the table.

'It's very hard,' he said. 'Every day she is the same. Always I hope for some change, some sign of life, but...nothing.'

'What do the doctors say? Do they hold out any hope?'

Paco's shoulders drooped. 'They warn me not to expect...that even in the best case, she will not be...' He hesitated, struggling to articulate the painful truth. 'She will not be as before.' He lit a cigarette and put it to his lips.

She noticed his hand was trembling and wanted to still it, to offer some comfort, a vestige of hope even if they both knew it was false.

'I went with Teresa's daughter to the state funeral,' Paco said. 'For her there is no hope.' He drew on his cigarette and blew out the smoke, taking care to turn away. 'Many people were weeping; even Queen Sofía and others in the Royal Family were weeping. Outside, the rain... People were saying this was not rain but tears. Madrid was crying.'

'It must have been harrowing,' Alice said.

Paco did not respond but whether it was because the word was unfamiliar to him or he was too emotional to speak, she couldn't tell.

After a while she said, 'I went to see Mark.'

'And how did you find him?'

'He was more open with me, a little more willing to talk, but... Paco, I do wish he'd come and live here for a while. It can't be good for him to spend so much time alone. Also, his neighbours worry me. One of them came by while I was there, a drunk with a most threatening manner.'

'I'll talk to Mark again,' Paco said. 'But if he decides no, what can we do?' That expansive Spanish shrug, palms spread wide. 'His mother, she always...'

'Mummy, Mark's here!' Timmy came running in, his face alight with excitement. A moment later, Mark strolled into the kitchen. She was surprised by the warmth with which he and Paco embraced. It seemed entirely natural, reminding her that Paco was far more of a father to him than Charlie had ever been.

Seeing the two boys side by side, she looked, as always, for a resemblance. There was surprisingly little. Mark's features, although softer, were unmistakeably his father's: the same broad nose and slightly jutting chin, the close-set eyes of an indeterminate hazel that turned to pale green in some light. Only the narrow build came from Deb.

Timmy, with his darker hair and complexion, could have been taken for a local. Once or twice on previous visits to Granada, acquaintances of Deborah had assumed she was married to a Spaniard. No, she had replied, laughing it off, she would speak better Spanish if that were the case. In England, those distinctive physical traits he had inherited from his father were tactfully overlooked. Timmy had her nose, people would remark – the upturned Hardy conk that she and Deborah shared, that came from the paternal side of their family. And she would point out his stubby fingers, identical to hers. Only once to her knowledge, a horribly precocious girl in his class had upset him with some snide comment he didn't properly understand.

'Mark, we must talk,' Paco said. 'You will excuse us, Alice?' He beckoned to Mark and the two of them disappeared into Paco's study.

'Mark said I could sleep over in his cave tonight,' Timmy said. He stood facing her, head thrust forward, eyes staring fixedly into hers, challenging her.

'No.'

'Tomorrow then.' His stance made it clear he would not give up easily.

'Not tomorrow either. I'm sorry Timmy.'

'Why not?'

'Timmy…' She held out her arms to him but he pushed them away, his eyes flaring in anger.

'Why not?' he repeated.

'Because…I don't think it's safe up there. You're too young. Have you seen any other children in those caves?'

He didn't answer and she shook her head. 'There aren't any. It's not a fit place for…'

'You don't let me do anything!' He stamped his foot hard, so that the lace of his trainer, already half undone, came loose, snaking across the tiles.

His flashes of temper never failed to alarm her, though fortunately they were rare. She hated raised voices, arguments, aggression of any kind. Explosions like this were not something he had learnt at home. It upset her to think they might be in his blood.

'It's boring here. I want to go home.'

'I know, my love.' She was beginning to feel the same, to hanker after their normal peaceful existence, ruled by familiar routines rather than this constant uncertainty, the tension of waiting for news that could only be bad, worse or worst. What exactly were they doing here?

Three hundred and fifty euros in his pocket. Mark couldn't imagine it, he'd never had that much – not all in one go. More than likely he'd get robbed, carrying that amount of money around. It still didn't seem right for him to take the rent, but as Paco said, it wasn't any use to Mum and someone had to have it.

'I can't keep that kind of money in the cave. I'll have to leave it here, okay?'

Paco clapped a hand on his shoulder. '*Hombre*, for this we have banks. You don't have a bank account?'

'I don't know. I *did* have one. Mum used to put money in sometimes. It's been empty now for bloody ages; they might have closed it.'

'Then you go to the bank *pronto* and find out. Before 1st April.'

'Right.' He was waiting for Paco to say something about the funeral. He hadn't even mentioned it; hadn't mentioned Mum either. Like the money was more important. But the way he looked, all crumpled and grey, you could tell he had other things than the rent on his mind. Mark stared at Paco's books, neatly lined up on the shelves, the spines dead level as if they were never moved.

'Alice told me Zapatero came to the hospital,' he said.

Paco nodded and plonked himself down in his chair as if he'd collapse in a heap otherwise. 'He spoke to me briefly – and to the other victims and relatives. I felt he was sincere. At the Cathedral all the politicians were present, many from other countries too. Also the Royal Family, as you would expect...'

'I bet Aznar didn't go.'

'Aznar was there, naturally. There was an incident... The father of one of the victims made a scene just before the service started, pointing a finger at him, saying he held Aznar responsible for his daughter's death. It was a difficult moment. Emotions were very charged, as you can imagine.'

'Bastard. He should be fucking shot.'

'*Ay* Mark, I understand how you feel but what good would that do? The bombers are already dead. There has been enough violence done, don't you think?'

Mark turned away without answering.

After a while he said, 'So all that time you've been at the hospital, she hasn't spoken or twitched or fluttered her eyelids even? Nothing?'

'Now and then I see some small movement but the doctors say it means nothing. Your mother is the same as when you saw her.' Paco sighed. 'I am very sorry. You know I would prefer to bring you good news.'

'I wish she'd just fucking die!' The words burst out of him before he could stop them, as if it was someone else speaking. He couldn't believe what he'd said. The way Paco was looking at him – not angry or shocked, more kind of pitying – made it worse.

'I didn't mean that,' he said, but it came out with a loud hiccup. He kicked the door open and ran into the patio, head down so no one could see he was crying. He ran past Timmy, who was sitting there eating a banana, and right out of the gate. He hadn't meant it; of course he hadn't fucking meant it.

22nd May 1990

Six months since I started my Arabic classes and at last I feel I'm making some progress – if only in the spoken language. I can manage simple conversations with Fátima and with Hassan. My reading is coming on slowly but surely. If only writing were as easy. I just haven't the patience to perfect the strokes so that they're recognisable. In *al-Andalus*, the Umayyad chancery employed seventy women copyists and Qur'an calligraphers. I've seen copies of the Qur'an in museums that are true works of art – just like the old medieval manuscripts handwritten by monks in England. Does that kind of dedication still exist? To devote years of one's life's to such a task.

28th May 1990

Amparo and Juan Antonio took us to the mountains yesterday. We left the car at the ski station and walked up towards Veleta. Mark was my excuse for not making it to the top, though he could probably have done it. There were still patches of snow on the slopes and running streams of melted snow trickling down through the brilliant green moss underfoot. Tiny, delicate wild flowers were everywhere – you couldn't avoid trampling them. The altitude, the views, the remoteness made it almost a spiritual experience. I had a sense of being outside time, freed from all the petty detail of life. Hassan had decided not to join us, which I didn't mind at all initially, but then when I was up there, I wished he were with me, to share the experience.

Arriving home, my elation subsided like a pricked balloon. We found the house taken over by half a dozen of Hassan's friends. He had cooked a meal for them and there were dirty plates and dishes everywhere, empty bottles, glasses with dregs of beer, overflowing ashtrays... They were sitting round the table deep in some philosophical discussion, oblivious of the *dueña* and her hungry boy. They had eaten everything; the fridge was bare, though I'd stocked up with food the day before. Being Sunday, the shops were shut, leaving us no option but to eat in a bar.

To Hassan it wasn't an issue. He had brought his friends back, it was lunchtime, there was food in the house, of course he had to provide. He was sorry there was none left for Mark and me – his friends had been hungry and he thought we would have eaten at a restaurant. The fact I'd bought the food was irrelevant to him. Am I being taken for a ride? The way he sees it, what's mine is his (and, to be fair, vice versa).

I decided not to make a fuss. I'm trying hard to avoid conflict, which means curbing my criticisms, being meek. It doesn't come naturally – don't know how long I can keep it up – but if we're to mend the broken bridges...

31st May 1990

Monika says it's a cultural thing – she lived with a Syrian guy for a while. The hospitality rule is absolutely fundamental. I'm sure she's right. Hassan is admirably generous and takes generosity for granted in others. But in fact the Spanish are exactly the same. Could it be the Arab influence? When it comes to food and drink, there are no limits, and that's true even if they're poor. Whatever they have is for sharing. Meanness is despised here: I've heard people described with contempt as '*pesetero*' – the equivalent of penny-pinching.

116

H has been busy the last couple of weeks with a series of interviews. Seeing less of each other has helped. I'm appreciating him more, enjoying his company again. Yesterday he bought me half a dozen beautiful silver bangles. No reason – nothing to celebrate (birthday, anniversary, saint's day) – just the desire to please me. A spontaneous gift from the heart, or that's how it felt.

I came across a Moroccan saying: *The quarrel of lovers is the renewal of love.* I translated it into Spanish and wrote it on the wall (the one I'm planning to paint) for Hassan to see.

18th July 1990

Hot hot hot! Walking down Paseo de los Tristes today, the sun pressed down on my back like a hot iron. Mark is on the coast with Leonor and Robin for a week (much more fun than sweltering Granada, where the heat makes people bad-tempered). Hassan has just returned from another trip to Morocco. From his village near Rabat he brought back the usual feast of yummy cakes and sweets, rich with ground almonds, pine nuts, honey and dates. His mother told him she would look for a nice young girl; it was high time he got married. 'Always the same' he said, laughing. I can't imagine him with a village girl – he says his mother knows perfectly well he's not interested – so why does it still give me a jolt of insecurity?

6th August 1990

Mum, along with the heat, has finally persuaded me to spend a couple of weeks in England – for Mark's sake more than mine. He hasn't seen his father for nearly a year but Charlie has promised to take him out at least once. Alice will have him for a weekend and Mum wants as much time as we can spare. 'He's my only grandchild,' she said pointedly. I hope she doesn't make such tactless remarks to Alice, who would give anything to be able to oblige. At thirty-seven, she'll have to get a move on. She did mention a new man, Andy but whether he's the right one I don't know. A nice steady, homely type would suit her – someone who appreciates her caring nature and doesn't take advantage. Such a type would no doubt bore me to death.

Alice stopped reading and turned out her bedside light. She had never found that nice steady, homely type but in the end she hadn't needed to. *God works in mysterious ways*, their mother used to say. Whether or not God had a hand in it, the solution had come from a wholly unexpected direction.

Chapter Ten

Mark swung the empty plastic container as he took the path up to the fountain. He didn't blame Timmy for going ballistic. He was pissed off with Alice too. What harm would it do for Timmy to stay one night in the cave? Banning it meant she didn't trust either of them. He felt sorry for Timmy. Alice treated him like a five year-old; he needed more freedom. Mark didn't know any kids Timmy's age who weren't allowed to go out on their own. Did she think he'd get kidnapped or what?

Mum hadn't kept him chained up like that when *he* was young. They did lots of stuff together, but the rest of the time he could play in the street with his friends, go where he wanted, pretty well. It never did him any harm. Once when he was about six, he and Antoñito walked all the way to San Miguel Bajo because Jaime said someone was handing out free Chupa-Chups. It was a lie but when he got home and told Mum, he didn't get in any trouble. She just laughed and gave him twenty pesetas to buy one from the shop. Mum had a life and maybe that was the difference. He wasn't sure whether Alice had a life besides being Timmy's mother. Okay, she worked, but that didn't count.

Mum had a life. Mum had a life and Alice didn't. Had that thought really gone through his head? Without the irony of it striking him? What a fucking idiot. He splashed water from the fountain onto his face before starting to fill the jerry-can. Alice had a life and Mum didn't. Why couldn't it have been the other way round? As soon as he'd thought it, he felt guilty. What about Timmy?

He screwed the lid tight on the container and heaved it up onto his shoulder. Why was water so fucking heavy? He'd end up lopsided if he carried on doing this every day but it felt wrong on the other side. He legged it down the hill as quick as he could, only stopping a couple of times to give his shoulder a rest. If Alice had been the one blown up on the train, Mum would have looked after Timmy. She wouldn't have minded; in fact he reckoned she'd have liked it. They'd have been brothers then, he and Timmy.

Tina was waiting outside his cave when he got down there. She was sitting cross-legged, dead still with her eyes shut in what looked like a yoga pose. The sun on her hair reminded him of *castañas* – the ones they used to play with at his English school when he was ten. Conkers, they called them. He put down the jerry-can and crept up on her. He got so close he could have counted the freckles on her arms. He'd planned to surprise her but she opened her eyes a minute too soon.

'Hey,' she said, stretching her arms in the air. 'Where have you been?'

Mark pointed to the jerry-can. 'I'd run out of water.'

'No, I mean it's days since any of us have seen you.'

She was wearing a tight black top that showed the shape of her nipples and a little short skirt over leggings. She looked sexy as hell.

'Come here.' He reached for her hands, pulled her to standing and made a dive for her neck, nuzzling and kissing any skin he could get at then clamping his mouth on hers, pushing his tongue in; feeling her tits at the same time. He couldn't help it, all he could think of was getting her clothes off and shagging her.

'Hey, slow down Mark. I've been waiting half an hour. Don't I even get a cup of coffee first?'

'I'll make some coffee after.'

Tina wriggled free. 'Anyway, how's your mum?'

He broke off and pushed her away – harder than he'd intended. Wasn't he allowed to forget for one fucking minute? Why did she have to bring it up now of all times? His prick had capsized, like instantly; shrunk to a useless worm.

'She's not dead yet,' he said. His words hung in the air like a cloud heavy with spite; they made him ashamed. Tina was frowning at him like she was trying to solve a puzzle. He ought to say sorry, though he wasn't sure it would stop her going. But then a part of him wanted her to go.

He looked away, at the narrow paths of pale brown earth criss-crossing the hillside where feet had tramped away the grass leading to one cave or another. He never saw her move but miraculously, from one minute to the next, he felt her body pressed up against his, her hands stroking his back; and the fresh girly scent of her skin made him want to sniff and lick her as if he were a dog.

'Many people admire your sister.' Paco leaned across the table to fill Alice's glass from the bottle of Rioja. She wasn't sure whether his use of the present tense signalled an optimistic outlook or merely his difficulty with English. 'You have a saying, I think: *where angels fear to tread.* Is that correct?'

Alice nodded and he continued, 'This woman has no fear. She goes where angels fear to tread. If she believes in something, then nothing will stop her.'

'That's true. Even when we were children, she'd be the one to walk on a frozen lake or explore the haunted house in the woods. I was always the cautious one, pathetic in her eyes.' Alice helped herself to more salad.

Paco had laid down his fork. He looked deep in thought. 'You will perhaps know more about this than I do, Alice – I'm sure she spoke to you about it – but the moment I admired her most was when she made the decision to put aside her personal feelings at a time when revenge must have been a tempting option, in order to help another human being in need. This decision was brave, it cost her much. You know, of course, what I am referring to.'

'Well, actually no…'

The gate clanged and they both started. A moment later, Mark walked in carrying a football. He had more colour in his cheeks, as if he'd spent some time out in the fresh air instead of holed up in his cave.

'Where's Timmy?'

'Probably in the bedroom. He likes to escape our company once he's finished eating.'

'Okay if I take him up to the football field?' Mark's look was direct, challenging even.

Alice considered. 'Fine, go and ask him.' She began to clear the table, eager to continue her reading while Timmy was out. In the diary she would perhaps find clues to this act of bravery that had so impressed Paco.

25th October 1990

Last night Hassan presented me with a pomegranate, a luscious ripe *granada* already beginning to split and packed with plump seeds. We cut it open and the ruby juice ran out and made a big pool on the table. What a waste. I wanted to lap it up like a dog! Then we undressed each other (so as not to stain our clothes, he said) very slowly, one garment at a time, and sitting there naked, we fed each other the seeds. It felt like a sacred ritual. By the time we'd finished, we were both feverish with desire. We fell on each other and it was like a continuation of the rite, the ceremonial feast.

Today when I woke, I remembered a short story where a pomegranate is the symbol of a woman's new love for a man. It was by a Mexican writer, Elena Poniatowska. I managed to find the book, on the floor under a great heap of others. It was one Amparo had lent me and I should have given back long ago. I re-read the story, called *El Recado* (The Message) and loved it even more this time, remembering the sensuality of sharing that big juicy *granada*. She describes the cut pomegranate's shining red seeds as like a ripe mouth with a thousand sections.

6th November 1990

Sally wrote to me from London, moaning about her long working day, having to leave home in darkness and return in darkness. The gloom of an English November: the constant drizzle, the gusting winds, the fog. 'You're so lucky to have escaped,' she said. To think I could still be in that world! Slaving away for someone else's profit all day, then cramming into a tube train, rattling through tunnels under the city before scuttling home braced against the damp and cold, too tired to do anything except eat and sleep. Every day. Oh what joy to be free!

10th November 1990

Free? Today I don't feel free, I feel like a prisoner. Hassan made a huge fuss last night because I was out when he came home and

I hadn't told him where I was going. Teresa had called at 10 o'clock and invited me, along with a few others, to the little bar in Calle Elvira to celebrate her birthday. Mark was tired so I left him with Leonor. She said he could sleep there with Pablito and Antoñito and she'd take the three of them to school in the morning.

The moment I walked through the door, he grabbed me by the shoulders. 'Where have you been?' He reminded me of a bull with steaming nostrils, a bull provoked and angry, ready to charge. I refused to answer till he let go of me. 'Who were you with? Why didn't you let me know?' He gripped my wrist and pulled me towards him. 'Answer me, woman.' I broke away and glared at him. 'I don't have to account to you for my movements. You don't own me.'

He hadn't considered it necessary to let me know when he was coming back from Málaga. Of course that's different, he's a man. They must have absolute control. I told him he should go back to Morocco and marry a plump young village girl if what he wanted was subservience; if he wanted a meek, submissive woman who would prostrate herself at his feet and never leave the house without his permission. I slept in Mark's bed – the first time we've had a row and not made it up before bedtime. Now I'm waiting for him to apologise. Will he? I doubt it.

3rd April 1991

Narrowly avoided another outburst of H's groundless jealousy but only by lying (a harmless lie because I was completely innocent). One of his friends saw me having coffee with Richard, a friend of Kay's. He's here visiting and we happened to bump into each other in town. Kay was teaching all morning. I told Hassan he was her new boyfriend and that she'd just popped out of the bar for some *churros*. The ploy worked perfectly: instead of subjecting me to an interrogation, he brought out his oud and treated me to an hour of sweet music.

16th April 1991

Today it was back to school for Mark and I went into town happy to find the streets passable again, the normal city sounds replacing those sombre drumbeats of *Semana Santa*. No puddles of hot wax, not a whiff of incense in the air. I never saw it as offensive before meeting Hassan but now I think how provocative it must seem to those of other faiths. What must they feel when their path is blocked by all those interminable processions? As if the whole population wants to share in the anguish of Jesus on the cross. Hour after hour, night after night, they parade those statues of the Blessed Virgin, the Crucified Christ through the town.

Juan Antonio said it was much worse when he was a child. During the dictatorship all entertainment was banned for a week, radio and TV could only broadcast religious music, you weren't allowed out to play. His parents were on the left and non-believers but that made no difference, they had to conform. In those days any overt dissent could get you into serious trouble. The power of the Church was absolute. It may not be quite so bad now but still I shudder when I see the hooded penitents, the women in their black *mantillas*.

5th July 1991

At Mark's insistence (not that I needed much persuading), we've been going down to the beach on Sundays. Three weeks in a row now to Salobreña. The last time, Leonor and her boys came with us and we had a good talk while the kids played. Cultural differences in relationships turned out to be the main topic of the day. She started talking about Robin's English mind-set (everything has to be planned, pinned down, punctual, she complained), which led us on to my difficulties with Hassan (and his with me) and then the pitfalls of cross-cultural relationships in general. We decided they made life more interesting – but more difficult. She and Robin tend to laugh about their differences and misunderstandings. I can't say the same about Hassan and me: we're both too combustible. When we fight, it's deadly serious. Apologies aren't in our repertoire. But after the explosion, once the air has cleared, it's never long before I succumb to his charms or he to mine and all is forgotten. The attraction between us is too strong to waste time brooding.

13th November 1991

I'm beginning to get cold feet about Mum's Christmas visit. I want to see her; and Alice too, of course. What I'm struggling with is her likely reaction to Hassan. She knows I have a 'boyfriend' and that he lives here with me but she's assuming he's Spanish. 'Can't you send him away?' Alice suggested. The answer is no. Why should I? This is his home, he has every right to be here. I've been rehearsing in my head how to tell her: he's dark-skinned/ his family is Muslim/ he's from Morocco? I always end up asking myself why it's necessary to make an issue of it. What difference does it make whether he's Spanish or Moroccan, Christian or Muslim or atheist? I could give her a lecture on how the Andalusians are mostly descended from Arabs or Berbers or Jews. You only have to look at them to see that racially they're scarcely different. And for that matter, the English aren't so pure either.

Am I worrying needlessly? If I say nothing and let her find out when she gets here, will she faint from shock, refuse to shake hands with him, turn tail and book herself into a hotel? Or will she accept him as a fellow human being, the man her daughter has chosen to be with? I wish I knew.

7th December 1991

H is being such a sweetie, making a real effort to prepare for my family by learning English. Every evening he opens one of my Elementary level course books and pores over it, practising some of the words and phrases, asking me to test him. His knowledge of other languages helps – he's progressing a lot more rapidly than most of my students. Still, there's a limit to how far he can get in two weeks. Mark finds it hilarious when he gets a word wrong and delights in correcting him. Mum and Alice had better appreciate his efforts.

30th December 1991

Phew, ordeal over! They left this morning and I can breathe again. The visit was NOT a success. And it wasn't Hassan's fault. He was at his most charming, he tried hard with his little English; he behaved perfectly. Plus he spent hours in the kitchen, cooking yummy dishes like Moroccan chicken with lemons, which Mum found 'too garlicky', and *harira* soup ('too spicy – you know spicy foods don't agree with me'), though actually there was no heat in it at all.

Hassan isn't a difficult name but Mum insisted on referring to him as 'he'. Is he coming with us? Does he have family? When she did address him directly, she talked extra loud as if that would help. The only positive thing she said about him was that he was nice-looking.

On Christmas Eve, after a truly festive and delicious meal, Mum and Alice said they'd like to go to midnight mass. 'He won't be coming to mass, I presume,' Mum said with a titter, as if she were being amusing. When I told her I wouldn't be going either, her response was 'Oh dear, I hope he isn't trying to convert you to his religion.'

They returned from the service at San Salvador shocked by the behaviour of the congregation. Alice reported how they were chatting away, coming and going whenever they felt like it. One woman was even talking on a mobile phone and another breast-feeding her baby. Mum 'could have sworn' she'd seen a man drinking from a hipflask...

Cultural differences: what a mountain of misunderstandings they can create.

I think Mark was the only one of us to enjoy Christmas. For Mum, for Alice, for Hassan and for me it was testing, to say the least. An experiment not to be repeated.

Alice closed the diary, unable to go on. Obviously Deb hadn't expected her harsh comments to be read, but the fact remained, she had been unforgiving in her judgement. Although it was four years now since Mum's death, Alice still missed her. No one could replace a mother. The criticisms hurt.

Partly to distract herself from these painful thoughts, she wandered into Deb's study and sat down at the desk, picking up a folder at random. On the second page, a couple of paragraphs had been marked with asterisks: *The taifa king, Abdullah Ibn Buluggin wrote about the role of women in his memoirs, The Tibyan. He notes that in the leading Berber families, women of the household participated in a shura council that made collective political and military decisions, which the ruler would enact.*

The Berber commander Yusuf Ibn Tashufin relied heavily on his wife, Zaynab, for strategic advice. He trusted her to oversee and protect his realm from political rivals.

She visualised Deb sitting here in this same chair, highlighter pen poised over the page; imagined her excitement at what she was reading. Perhaps she had called out to Paco, eager to share the details of her research with him. Or did these pages, photocopied rather than printed, date from earlier, from the years with Hassan?

In one of the desk drawers, she found a book of Arabic grammar, a photocopied article in Arabic with English words scribbled in the margin and a notebook with Deb's own attempts to write the script. She gazed at the strange, indecipherable marks and felt awed. Could her sister really have learnt to make sense of them?

A shadow fell across the room and Alice looked up to see someone standing at the door, which she'd left slightly ajar: a rather dumpy woman with fair hair pushed back under a bandanna.

'Hi,' she said. 'I'm Kay, a friend of your sister's. I wondered how you were coping. If there's anything I can do…'

'Oh hello, I remember her mentioning you.' Not quite true; what she remembered were Deb's comments in the diary about Kay's cynicism. Had Paco let her into the house or did she have a key too? 'It's kind of you to call.'

Kay plonked herself down on a corner of the desk, pushing aside the clutter of papers, some of which dropped to the floor. 'Poor Deborah, I was devastated when I heard. My first thought was to get on a bus to Madrid but then I asked myself if there was any point when… I gather it's not looking good.'

Alice shook her head. What was there to say when someone lay unconscious, unchanging, day after day with little prospect of improvement?

'She was such a positive, vital person. And clever – I admired her hugely – even if she could be naïve at times. You know, rushing into things, often getting the wrong end of the stick, carried away with some ideal…'

'That's true, but there's nothing wrong with being enthusiastic, is there?' Kay's critical tone made Alice rush to defend her sister.

'No, but she saw…sees everything and everybody as either black or white. That's what I mean about her being naïve. For example…did you ever meet her ex, Hassan? Yes of course, you must have done. Well, I warned her but…'

'What do you mean? Warned her of what?' Alice frowned, trying to disguise the anxiety that always gripped her at the mention of Hassan's name.

Kay kicked off her shoes and slid her bum round to face Alice directly. 'Hassan knew how to spin a tale. And Deb was so besotted she believed every word. She found him exotic, that's what made her fall for him. And he impressed her by seeming to know a lot. It took her ages to see through him.'

'Through him to what?'

'Oh you know, underneath that enlightened facade he was just a typical man, he had to be in control. And he knew exactly how to manipulate Deb. Easy peasy.'

'I heard he was in prison.'

'Yes, he's still awaiting trial. It's anyone's guess whether he'll get off or not. Though knowing him, he'll talk his way out of it.'

'But do you think he's guilty?'

'Actually I don't. No more guilty than Taisir Alouny, the guy who interviewed Bin Laden for al-Jazeera. But when justice and politics conflict... Well, we'll see what happens. Anyway, as far as Deb's concerned, Hassan is history. Since Paco came on the scene... To be honest, I'm envious. Men like him are one in a million here in Spain: men who treat women as equals. And he loves her to distraction.' She turned and stared out of the window. 'I remember when Deb first saw this place. It was autumn and that tree over there was laden with ripe pomegranates. I think it was the garden she fell in love with more than the house.'

'You've known her a long time, I guess.'

'Nearly twenty years. If she doesn't...you know. I'm going to miss her like hell.' She jotted down a number and handed the sheet of paper to Alice. 'Here, call me if you feel like some company.'

Chapter Eleven

12th June 1992

Can people ever throw off their culture, what they've absorbed from infancy? I will not be controlled by a man. It may be normal in Morocco, it may be normal in Andalucía but I'm not going to be told what to do or be ordered around – even if it's only to bring him a glass of water. I won't be subjugated just because I'm a woman. Hassan thinks he's different – modern and enlightened; that he's left his *machista* attitudes behind. No way. Perhaps he's not as bad as most. He doesn't beat or bully me; he even listens to my views, but deep down (actually not so very deep), he thinks of me as inferior. He'd never admit it but he thinks I belong to him. He watches me when other men are around, accuses me of flirting and flaunting myself. It's not true. I'm just behaving in the way normal to my culture. I refuse to change, to lower my head, cover my body, give up my independence. 'That blouse shows your breasts,' he said today. 'I don't want you to wear it.' I replied with a quote from Walladah, which he didn't like one bit. Too bad, that's his problem.

Once, on a visit, Alice had overheard the two of them going at each other like cat and dog. She had heard Deborah scream: 'Get your hands off me!' Frightened, she had rushed in to rescue her sister. But instead of being grateful for her intervention, Deb had given her a cold look and told her to keep out of what didn't concern her. After that, she never entirely believed Deb's assurances that Hassan was not physically violent.

Mark is in tears and I'm in a quandary. I have the right to withdraw him from *Religión* at school. It's not compulsory to put him through the preparation for First Communion. But but but... All the other children in his class are doing it as a matter of course. 'This is a Catholic country' his teacher Marta reminded me (as if I'd forget). He doesn't want to be singled out, left alone in a room to do extra sums or pointless copying of texts. Up to now, I've let him go to the Religión classes despite my reservations about their indoctrinating nature. But *Primer Comunión* is something else. Initiation into a religious community shouldn't be part of the school syllabus, I told Marta. She shrugged and said, 'In our country this is how we do it.' Implicit was: 'If you don't like it, go back to your own country.'

Mark stomped out of the house today and I can't blame him. H and I were at each other's throats again. My crime this time? I hadn't told him my new hairdresser was a man. Alberto is as gay as they come but I wasn't going to placate Hassan by telling him that. I just laughed – until the insults and insinuations became too much and then I completely lost it.

Yet there are lulls in the tension when I still feel a little of the old attraction, when we can talk without rancour and discuss philosophy, religion, ideas... But mostly the house is like a pressure cooker about to explode. Little things about him that I once loved now infuriate. For instance, that high-pitched Arab giggle that used to charm me I now find effeminate and irritating. He finds fault with me for everything, but what really inflames me is when he criticises the way I'm raising Mark. 'You don't move from that table till you can answer every question on the page without mistakes,' he screamed at Mark on Sunday. Poor boy had been studying half the weekend for yet another school test. Then he attacked me: 'You're too soft with the boy, he must be disciplined.' I have to remind Hassan that he is my son.

Timmy wanted to go home to England and Mark could see why. It must be dead boring hanging around in the *carmen* all the time with

130

Alice. Even school would be better, Timmy said. He had a teacher called Mr Jenks. They didn't use first names there; it was always Mr or Mrs whatever. Mark remembered when he went to the English school having a teacher called Mrs Porter. He must have been about the same age as Timmy. He didn't know why Mum had suddenly decided they should go to England. She was in a bad mood most of the time there, crying a lot. And then she went away for ages but not back to Spain – at least she said not. Granny had looked after him mostly.

Thinking about it now, the reason was obvious. It must have been because of Hassan. He'd changed – or maybe it was Mum who'd changed. Or both of them. At any rate, they'd ended up hating each other. Remembering that part of his life before they went to England, it was like a bloody thick fog had come down and he was groping about, trying to figure out what was going on all around. No one bothered to explain anything to him; they just forgot he was there. It was like being trapped in a war zone where you were invisible. The 'secrets' Mum told him were different, not happy ones like before: ugly secrets that he couldn't forget, even if he didn't understand them properly. So at first he'd been relieved to get away from here, away from all the slamming doors and angry voices. The English school wasn't too bad. The other kids thought he was cool because he could teach them Spanish swearwords.

'Mark, you're still here?' He hadn't heard Paco come up the steps to the terrace.

'Listen. The English publishers have been in touch. I thought you should know.'

Mark nodded, his eyes focusing first on the clay-tiled rooftops of the Albaicín, then shifting to the far-off snowy peaks, topped by the hook of Veleta. It was a view he pretty much knew by heart: he could have drawn it from memory without a single mistake.

'They hope Deborah will be restored to good health by the launch date on 22nd June. But in the opposite case...' Paco folded his arms and hugged them to his chest, taking a deep breath and then slowly letting it out. 'They wanted to know, should they delay publication till she is well or go ahead as planned?'

'June! *Joder*...that's three months away.'

'I told the Editor her condition was very grave, that we should not count on anything. I said I would keep them informed.' He pulled a pack of ciggies out of his pocket and offered it to Mark. The two of them stood side by side, smoking not talking. There was nothing else to say.

Paco went down once it got dark but Mark stayed, watching the stars come out and remembering how Mum had taught him their names a whole fucking lifetime ago.

'What did you think of Hassan?' Alice had been itching to ask him but tonight was the first time she judged Mark to be suitably receptive. Something had definitely perked him up.

'At first I thought he was cool but when he and Mum began yelling at each other all the time I went right off him. I couldn't stand it when he called her names, though she was just as bad. One time she called him a something something pig – she said it in English but he understood *pig* and he went totally berserk 'cos pigs are, like unclean to Muslims. He was usually okay with me though. Once, when Mum wasn't around, he said he'd like to have a son of his own one day. I remember he looked kind of sad and said it'd be better not to tell Mum. I'd forgotten that till now.'

Alice darted a quick glance at Mark, hoping he hadn't noticed her sudden intake of breath, the tensing of her muscles, but it seemed not, because he carried on without a pause.

'Still, I can tell you I was well happy the day she kicked him out. Then he tried using me to get back with her, bringing me presents, acting all soft, like I was too thick to see through it... If I saw him coming, I'd run the other way.'

'He didn't hit her or anything?'

'No, it was just words, but they scared me; I think they might even have scared Mum. Well, maybe not... It took a lot to scare Mum. She was the one who'd throw things: plates and one time a baked potato. She always missed. The potato made me laugh – the way it went splat on the wall – but most times I'd just clear right off when they started. The last year or so I used to stay out practically all the time.'

Poor Mark, it must have been a poisonous atmosphere for a child. Alice remembered thinking so at the time. Reading her sister's diary and now hearing Mark's memories of it confirmed her view.

4th December 1992

Looking forward to England and a break from all the tension; a break from Hassan. Spending a few days apart will give us both a chance to cool down. Mark is excited too about seeing his granny and his aunt.

Had a little panic in case Hassan finds this diary while I'm away. His English may be minimal but he'd understand enough. I'd also hate Mark to read it. So I'll have to search for a good, safe hiding place where no one would dream of looking. Either that or burn it and stop writing, but I've become rather addicted to putting my feelings down on paper.

Not such a very good hiding place, Alice thought. She had found it easily enough.

8th January 1993

The break did some good and we managed to be civil to each other all the way through Christmas and New Year. I was determined to keep things calm for Markie's sake. Hassan gave me a beautiful silver necklace. A peace offering? I accepted it as such and have been wearing it these last two days, partly to please him.

13th February 1993

Focusing on my research is keeping me sane. But only just. For an hour, sometimes more, I can shut out the mess of my life with Hassan and feel composed, close to 'normal'. Then I lose concentration for one short second and it all comes flooding back, drowning me in a sea of despair.

7th May 1993

Tomorrow is Mark's *Primer Comunión* and I have to dress him up in a ridiculous sailor suit (luckily Leonor still had the one her Antonio wore last year). I'm dreading it: all these children gathered in church, the girls dressed up like brides, the boys in sailor suits; all promising to be good Catholics. Then the party in a restaurant, the treats and presents. Proud relatives taking photos, making a big fuss. There won't be much of that for Mark, I'm afraid.

12th June 1993

I know I have to end this relationship, it's destroying me. Every time we have a row, it reduces me to a horrible pathetic pulp, but then afterwards, my heart hardens at the edges like freezing ice-cream as I detach myself just a tiny fraction more. He goes out, often for hours – I've no idea where, probably he hangs out with his friends in a café – and when he returns, he acts as if everything is fine and hunky-dory between us. He smiles at me and those edges begin to melt all over again. That smile (of eyes and lips and delicate tilt of head) that he knows I can't resist. The smile alone does for me, but once I feel his touch, that's it, I'm lost. And he knows his power. Sometimes I hate him with such passion it's not so far from love. All the energy I once put into loving now goes into hating him. But it's not that straightforward because a part of me still loves him too, so it's like a battle raging in my heart, love against hate. If I believed in a god, I'd pray for the strength to finish it.

7th July 1993

I caught myself yesterday actually wanting him to hit me. It shocked me afterwards that I'd considered deliberately provoking him to violence – just to give me the impetus, the strength I need to throw him out. He never has hit me, I don't think he would, but sometimes I can see the shaking of his body, the tension in his clenched fists and the way his mouth contorts and I know it's an effort for him to restrain himself. Strangely, the contained violence feels worse. There's a pulsating energy that I sometimes see like a glowing red aura surrounding him. His anger used to alarm me, now I wonder if a violent act wouldn't at least bring some kind of catharsis. It's almost like a death wish (but is it my death or his that I'm courting?).

12th August 1993

Ants have invaded the house – millions of them. They are tiny, harmless Hassan says, but I find them disturbing beyond all reason. My attempts to defeat this new enemy seem doomed to failure. Nothing works: not boiling water, not the hoover, not blocking their holes (they always discover new ways in)… Mark finds them fascinating and watches their endless streaming for hours while I see them as symbols of my helplessness, the inability to take control of my life.

19th September 1993

I can't believe it, he's gone! Out of this house and out of my life. The relief is overwhelming. I'm sure Mark feels it too. The house is our own again, we can relax. We've been playing games together as we did years ago; he's had friends to stay (I don't have to worry about them overhearing our rows); he can mess around or be a little cheeky and get away with it because I see it as perfectly normal for a ten year-old.

Today Monika came to paint on our terrace as she used to before Hassan.

23rd September 1993

So, it was too early for rejoicing. Today, when I opened the gate to go out, Hassan was lying in wait. I'd demanded his keys (he threw them at my feet when he left) but I was naïve to assume he would disappear so easily. Seeing him standing there nearly gave me a heart attack. And the fact he was relaxed and smiling made it worse somehow. As if he didn't take the split seriously and expected me to relent and fall into his arms. I tried to ignore him and walk past but of course he wouldn't let me. We can have a coffee together, he said. '¿*Porqué no?*' Because I don't want to, I told him. He was still obstructing my way so I pushed him quite hard and told him to go to hell. '¡*Puta!*' he hissed but he let me go. He'll get over it, he'll soon tire of hanging around me. I just have to be strong; to show any sign of weakness now would be fatal.

28th September 1993

Five days late and I'm trying not to panic… I must occupy my mind with other things; fill all my waking hours with busyness so there's no space for fear to creep in. Five days is nothing, I tell myself. The body's natural response to stress.

That man is still plaguing me – and even worse – using Mark. Yesterday he came home with a bunch of roses. Hassan had intercepted him on his way back from school and thrust them into his hand '*para tu mamá.*' Roses for me and (he confessed later) *chicles* for him. Okay, chewing gum isn't a big bribe but I was incensed. 'Don't speak to him, don't take anything from him,' I told Mark. I threw the roses straight in the bin – with some regret because they smelt divine.

Five or six times in the last week I've had silent phone calls. I know it's him and he knows I know. If he carries on like this, he will drive me insane.

4th October 1993

Eleven days and now I can no longer pretend. If I don't start today, I'll get a kit from the *farmacia* and do the test. But I don't need proof, the signs are all too clear. I curse my stupidity, my useless bloody memory. The pack of pills sits here mocking me. How could I have forgotten two nights in a row?

Hassan would rejoice if I told him. A son! Or even a daughter, though naturally a son would be preferable. The pomegranate is a symbol of fertility, he told me once, and I heard the veiled meaning behind his words. I daren't tell him, he would never allow me to… I can't even write the words though I know it's the only solution. With a child by Hassan, I would live in constant fear. A baby can't be kept secret for long. He would claim his child, insist on moving back in or else spirit the baby away to his family in Morocco. A symbol of fertility but also of blood. Better to end the wretched business now – in England where it's legal and safe.

Chapter Twelve

Mark had expected it all to change once they were back home. But Mum was just as moody in Granada as she had been in England. She still cried a lot. Now and then she'd have a mad burst of energy and drag him off on some long, pointless walk – even if it was teeming with rain – or they'd take a bus down to the beach and let the grey, churning winter sea come rushing up to their feet so they had to jump back. She'd laugh then but soon enough he'd catch her crying again. He was worried she might be ill; Monika said she looked ill. Mum said there was nothing wrong, she just felt a bit sad, but when he asked why, she wouldn't say. It lasted ages and ages. He spent a lot of time at Antonio and Pablito's house. Leonor stuffed him with food. *Es tu casa*, she kept saying. But it wasn't his house. Robin said he must look after his mum; she was going through a bad patch.

He wondered what had happened to the set of drawing pencils Alice gave him that year he was in England. He'd sharpened some of them so often they were no more than stubs but still he'd like to see what was left of them. They'd come in their own wooden box that he used to carry around with him everywhere. Mrs Porter told Mum he was outstanding at art. She put all his paintings up on the wall and said it was a great shame they didn't do art at his Spanish school. He thought so too.

One time he'd done a drawing of Plaza Larga: every building along one side of the square. He'd spent hours putting in all the detail. Buildings were what he was best at. He liked to draw in practically every brick, all the squiggly bits on the balconies and railings. He'd been really proud of this particular drawing. When he showed it to Mum, she just glanced at it without noticing a thing. 'Very nice, Mark,' she said; that was all. Then she started going on about fucking Arabic writing. On and on and on, till he walked out of the room. He'd felt like tearing the picture up but instead he gave it to Monika because she looked at it properly and said he had 'real talent'. He'd always remembered those words. Real talent.

Paco said Monika had been to see Mum in the hospital, which was more than you could say for most of her friends. Not that he blamed them: unless she woke up, it was a waste of money going all that way. But Mum and Monika had been friends for years and years – for as long as he could remember. Monika had come looking for him at the house; she'd also sent him a couple of messages. One of these days he'd call round at her place. If he was in the mood.

He certainly wasn't in the mood to talk to his dad, who was hassling him with texts every other fucking day. Didn't he have anything better to do? *Son, are you alright? Please ring me. Mark, aren't you getting my msgs? Ring your father asap.* Charlie was about the last person he felt like talking to.

His guitar was leaning up against the wall near the *chimenea*. He hadn't picked it up for weeks. He reached for the instrument now and the familiar shape of it against his chest felt kind of comforting. He tried a few chords, just by way of experiment. Then it was like his fingers decided for him – his fingers and the strings together – and that was it: they were away.

Alice found her breathing and heartbeat had speeded up. Volume three of the diary ended abruptly with the remaining pages ripped out, leaving an irregular line at the centre where it was stapled. Odd fragments of words could still be seen on the two or three peaks that jutted from this line in a wad, close to the stapled centre. Alice took a sip of water from the glass by her bed, wishing it was something stronger, and put the diary away.

She'd had no idea, not the faintest glimmer. When Deb arrived on her doorstep at only a day's notice, Mark in tow, it did not strike her as abnormal or out of character. Deb was a great believer in what she called spontaneity. And her twitchiness, the desperate, haunted look in her eyes, was a natural reaction to the stressful split from Hassan. True, there was something fishy about her mysterious 'appointments' but Alice's suspicions centred on a secret lover rather than a baby.

So there had been nothing calculated in the unburdening of her heart to Deb that second evening. The bottle of wine they'd shared, followed by 'nightcaps' of whisky, no doubt helped. She had given way to tears as she confided to Deb how reaching the milestone of forty that year signified for her the end of hope. She would never be a mother. Deb had sat there smoking one cigarette after another but snuffing them out with a disgusted look before she was halfway down; saying nothing, her eyes blank, distant; the tension visible not only in her face but in every muscle of her body. *I'm wasting my breath*, Alice remembered thinking. *Deb is not even listening.* At some point well after midnight, Deb announced she was going to bed: she had another 'appointment' the next day and would have to get up early to take Mark to Mum's. Alice remembered how bitterly let down she had felt at her sister's lack of empathy.

She had scarcely slept that night and she would not sleep tonight. The memories were too vivid – as if she had been transported back ten years and was reliving the drama of that day, the day that changed her life. The day Deborah phoned her at work at eleven in the morning, hysterical. Begging her to feign sickness and come home because she had a proposition to make. Refusing to listen to reason. No, it couldn't wait till five o'clock. 'Pull a sickie for heaven's sake!' She had never pulled a sickie. The first little lie that had led to so many more.

She's having a breakdown, Alice thought, and finally agreed to come home. The scene was still imprinted on her memory: Deb throwing herself on the bed, crying, desperate, absolutely beside herself. 'I was at the clinic, I went to get an abortion.' Alice would never ever forget those words. 'But I had a better idea.' Deb's face was white even through the Spanish tan; her eyes stared like those of a madwoman. 'If you'll help me.'

Alice glanced across at Timmy, sleeping oblivious through the storm of her emotions. *A better idea.* By teatime they had it all worked out. The immaculate conception, Deb had called it with grim sarcasm, attempting a smile, choking back the tears. Together they were carrying the embryo of a secret; a lie. But were all lies bad? Surely this was a lie that would benefit all concerned. A sob escaped her. She managed to stifle the next as she listened for a change in Timmy's breathing, but he had not woken. What was conceived that October day was a lie but also the miracle of a child who would call her Mummy. She had never for one second regretted it. Had Deborah?

Mark kept his hand in his pocket all the way down to town, gripping the fat wad of notes he'd collected from Álvaro and Maribel. It made him jumpy carrying so much dosh; it made everyone he passed look like a thief. The sooner it was in the bank the better. Except for the fifty he'd decided to keep back so he could take Tina out. He'd take her somewhere special, not one of those fancy hotels Dad went to but a restaurant like Chikito's that everyone knew was good. Then they might go on to a club or the disco at El Camborio. He hadn't told her yet, he wanted it to be a surprise. And he'd have to swear her to secrecy because no way did he want evil tossers like Ed and Dani to suss out he was rich.

He thought about Alice at the hospital. She'd gone yesterday, just for a couple of days. Timmy had two whole days of freedom. Fucking amazing that she'd agreed to leave him here. Then it was going to be Paco's turn again, carrying on with his guardian angel act in Madrid. They'd tried to talk *him* into going and he'd almost said yes, but then the vision of her with those tubes stuck up her nose and needles stuck in her arm and machines bleeping and sounding their alarms made him change his mind.

Mark joined the queue in the bank. Most of them were tourists buying tickets for the Alhambra. They wore a uniform of cream or white trousers that always looked brand new; you could tell them a mile off. The guy behind the counter gave him a funny look when he handed over the cash – like he thought it was stolen. Wanker. He had a nose as long as Pinocchio's with an enormous wart on the side of it.

There were posters everywhere for *Semana Santa*. Mum usually found a way to escape it – like going to England. Not like locking her head away in a fucking coma. Easter in England had suited him when he was a kid because what it meant there was stuffing yourself with chocolate eggs. He'd never worked out what that had to do with Jesus dying on the cross. The only thing he could think of at the time was that when Jesus went up to heaven, it was like a chocolate factory with God as Willy Wonka. Alice used to read him that book, Charlie and the Chocolate Factory. It was his favourite for years. Maybe she'd read it to Timmy too.

A thin rain was starting to fall as he came out of the bank. The Africans were already in position on the street flogging their umbrellas. They were the same ones who came round the bars with pirated CDs. According to Paco, they were controlled by the mafia and earned fuck all for themselves.

She'd better be in, Tina. It was a couple of days, maybe more, since he'd seen her. He pictured her eyes lighting up when he told her. She might do that thing, putting her hands on his shoulders from as far away as her arms would reach, looking into his eyes and then suddenly kissing him hard on the mouth. She'd want to tart herself up... Thinking about Tina, he'd forgotten to stop off for a bottle of wine. It was too late now, he was already at Peso de la Harina. Once the road flattened out, he put on a spurt. He'd show her the fifty-euro note in his pocket. That's for us, he'd say, we can blow it all tonight, no sweat; there's more in the bank.

Mum wouldn't mind, he was sure she wouldn't. Once he'd overheard her talking about him to Paco. 'A girlfriend would settle him down,' she'd said.

'*Depende*.'

'*Sí, depende pero...*'

And then they'd shut the door and he hadn't heard any more.

*

He knew straightaway something was wrong. There were four of them sitting around in Tina's cave, drinking. She called for him to come and join them but the way she said it sounded phoney like she didn't mean it. Could be because he was the only one sober...

'We're celebrating,' José said. 'Tina's got herself a job.'

So why was she looking guilty? Mark couldn't work it out. You'd expect her to be smiling.

141

'She's off to *las Canarias*.' Fabio nudged her. 'We'll miss you.'

Mark gaped at Tina. 'What for?' It was fucking unbelievable.

'I'm hacked off with Granada,' she said. 'My friend Amy's been working at this hotel in Lanzarote for a year. She says there's a job for me and I can share her flat. It's warm all year round and the social life is brilliant.' She wouldn't meet his eyes. 'I feel like a change,' she said.

So what about us, he wanted to ask, but what was the fucking point? She'd made up her mind.

'Come with me if you want,' she said.

'Fuck that.'

As he pushed his way through the curtain, she shouted, 'Don't be like that, Mark.' But she didn't come after him.

Outside, the rain had got heavier; it was coming down in sheets from up the valley. He walked slowly back to his cave, not caring how soaked he got. The fifty-euro note in his pocket was sodden too and he didn't care about that either.

Paco had been surprised by her decision to take the bus. 'Why you don't fly, Alice?' But she was glad she'd chosen the slower, cheaper alternative. It gave her more time to think, to pluck from her memory the missing months in her sister's diary – five hours to focus on those crazy hours and days of talk and more talk; the hatching of the plan. The lie. Would her own recollection of events differ much from Deb's? Their feelings had been different of course, but the facts remained.

She could remember every detail of those conversations. Deb's frantic pleading: 'If he finds out, he'll steal the child away; he'll take it to Morocco, to his family.' There'd been hundreds of similar cases, she claimed. The law was no use: all over Europe mothers had been left grief-stricken and helpless. They'd talked once, she and Hassan, about a Spanish woman they knew whose son had been kidnapped by her Syrian ex-husband. 'He's the father: he has a right,' Hassan had said. 'In his position I would do the same.'

'I'd rather terminate the pregnancy now than lose my child to Hassan or his relatives. I couldn't bear it. I'd kill myself. Don't you see, Alice? In England the child will be safe, Hassan will never know about him – even if he's the spitting image of his father.' She was convinced long before any scans that the baby would be a boy.

A boy in the image of Hassan. But even as Deb put her thoughts into words – 'You realise he may be dark-skinned?' – any fleeting misgivings melted away. It made no difference to her. Good enough that this was her sister's child. Half the genes would be from their family.

It was to be a secret between the two of them. 'Absolutely no one must know. Do you agree?' Alice remembered how Deb had gripped her shoulder, the muscles of her forearm clenched; her eyes burning with intensity. 'If anyone asks, you had a brief fling, a holiday romance that was over in a week.'

Endless rows of olive trees stretched away in all directions as the bus wound its way through the hills towards Madrid. Alice gazed unseeing at the TV screen, at scenes of a car chase, angry confrontations, a woman in high heels running. The elderly man sitting next to her reeked of tobacco. She fiddled with the vent above her but failed to increase the flow of fresh air.

They had worked out the detail between them. Deb would go to a trusted friend in Leeds for the last two months of her pregnancy, saying the child was to be adopted. In a month or two Alice would hand in her notice at work. 'Stuff a cushion up your jumper; whatever it takes!' Mark would stay with Mum and attend a local school till the summer. Mum... The thought struck them both at the same moment: without Mum's help, their plan could not work. She would have to be told.

'You mean I'm going to have a half-caste grandchild?' Alice was glad she had volunteered to break the news. Deb would have muffed it completely, losing her cool the moment she saw that pantomime look of horror on Mum's face. Alice had talked calmly, laid out the choices in a rational manner and, to their mother's credit, she had accepted the idea within a day or two, supposing – albeit with weary resignation written all over her face – that their plan was for the best.

The bus was pulling into a service station. As the passengers queued to get off, Alice noticed two men of Moroccan appearance who must have been sitting just behind her. One had the same high cheekbones and tight curly hair as Hassan. Panic seized her, constricting her chest and forcing her to grab at the nearest seatback for support. What if

Hassan was out of prison, loose in Granada? The Albaicín was so small. But Kay had said he was still awaiting trial. She would know, surely? And in any case, Timmy was safe in Paco's care.

Alice forced herself to breathe deeply and count to ten as she'd taught herself to do whenever these irrational anxieties took hold. It was Deb who had always been prone to 'freaking out' as Charlie used to call it disparagingly, but Alice could no longer claim to be exempt. She was too aware that the fragile tower of lies on which her life with Timmy was built could topple from one day to the next.

She had never imagined herself breaking the law. Deb was the errant one, the rebel. But amazingly, she had committed what amounted to fraud without a second thought, registering Timmy as her own. The ease of it had been mind-boggling. 'Just change your name back to Hardy like I did when I divorced. Do it now!' And Deb had been right, it was a doddle. Later there had been a few awkward questions from health service staff and others but the more she lied, the easier it became. She had learned the art of deceit. Anyone could lie and cheat if enough was at stake and once you started out on that path, there was no end to it.

Their driver was leaving the bar. She pushed aside her neglected cup of coffee and followed the other passengers already piling back onto the bus. What was Timmy doing now? It was unsettling to have so little control, to place all her trust in another person. She sank back into her seat as the bus moved off, determined not to give way to worry. He would be fine.

Five days after her birthday, May 20th 1994, six in the morning, Deborah's voice on the line jubilant. Laughing as she broke the news. 'Your birthday present – late as usual. He's a darling, seven pounds exactly, perfect down to the last fingernail.' And Alice had suddenly been afraid, fearing her sister would change her mind and decide to keep the baby. If she was so scared of Hassan, what was to stop her moving to England with Mark, bringing the child up herself?

The drive north had seemed endless. *What if...? What if...?* Desperate to reassure herself, she had stopped at a motorway service station somewhere near Doncaster and listed the reasons, writing them down on the back of an old till receipt: Deb's love of Granada, the research she was so passionate about, her friends, her beautiful *carmen* in the Albaicín... Of course Deb wouldn't give up the life she had made for herself in Spain. Logic told her so, yet the fear persisted. When had her sister ever been predictable?

She remembered turning the paper over, running her eye down the list of items from Mothercare; it stretched half the length of her arm. They were all ready and waiting in her spare bedroom – the cot, the buggy, the bath; the pile of tiny babygros and vests; the packets of nappies.

Now here she was on another motorway, heading for another hospital. This time there would be nothing to celebrate. A stone lay in her chest, where once a quivering bird of hope and joy had dared to flutter its wings. There would be no happy end to this journey. But that day in 1994 when she first set eyes on Timmy, the clinical hospital ward had been transformed into a fairy-tale grotto, a place of wonder and magic. Was he real, this delicate creature sleeping in the cot by her sister's bed? 'But he's so tiny!' Deb had laughed. 'Big enough to hurt. It was bloody painful, I can tell you.' She knew he was real when she picked him up and felt the warmth of his little body through the blanket as she kissed and kissed the velvety-soft skin of his cheeks, his smooth forehead; stroked his fine, dampish hair, breathed in his sweet infant scent.

They had argued over his name. Deb wanted to call him James after their father, always known as Jim. But Alice had insisted *she* must be the one to choose. In the end they had agreed on a compromise: Timothy James. *My son Timmy,* she had whispered to herself over and over as she lay in bed that night in a small hotel near the hospital. *Deb's nephew, Mark's cousin.* Practising her story.

Glancing at the road signs, Alice realised they were already on the outskirts of Madrid; the last two hours had passed in a daze. She was shocked to spot to her left a vast area of waste ground crammed with makeshift shacks. The scene reminded her of TV images she had seen of third world cities. Lines of colourful washing were strung out between the miserable dwellings of corrugated iron, cardboard and plastic sheeting. '*Inmigrantes,*' she heard the woman in front of her mutter to her neighbour.

It was time to return to the present, to prepare her mind for the hospital visit ahead. Yet her mind refused to budge. It was stuck ten years in the past – as if she had to relive every last detail of those months. The final question that neither she nor Deb wanted to face: whether – and if so, when – to tell Timmy the truth. For the time being, he would know Alice as his mother, obviously. But what about the future?

Surprisingly, it was Deb who had insisted he must be told. It was his right, she said. 'Even if he hates me for abandoning him.' Alice had assented grudgingly, ashamed to voice her selfish reservations. So it was agreed: they would tell him, but only when he was mature enough to understand. In his teens perhaps. Suitably vague, comfortably distant, the moment of truth lay too far in the future to threaten her peace of mind – or had done until now. But he was almost ten; his teens were no longer so far off. And more important, his mother was dying. Driven by her hunger to be the centre of his world, she had deprived him of both mother and father. In adolescence and adulthood, would he forgive her for not revealing his true origins until it was too late? For lying and deceiving him? Would he reject her as an impostor? The thought was unbearable. She closed her eyes and tried to calm her troubled thoughts.

And then it hit her: if Deborah died, she would be free to decide for herself whether or not to tell Timmy. No one would be any the wiser. She breathed a huge sigh that made the man next to her turn and stare. After all, what did the biology matter? She would be sparing both Timmy and herself a massive burden of unhappiness. The truth is overrated, a friend had once said, and she had been shocked – but that was in her younger days. Now a favourite expression of her mother's came to mind: *why rock the boat?*

Chapter Thirteen

As usual, Sacromonte was packed out on the Wednesday night of Semana Santa, everyone waiting for the *gitanos* procession. It was only eleven, which meant there was about three hours to wait, but no one cared because the bars were all open. Later they'd be lighting fires on any patch of ground they could find, even in the street. Mum always said it was dangerous. Too right. If the wind got up, that'd be it. A fire engine would have no fucking chance of making it through the crowds.

People were shoving past each other, trying to stake a place. Drinking, playing with their cameras, shouting and laughing. You couldn't escape – not even in a cave. Mark had enough beer to knock him out cold but after the first two cans he didn't feel like drinking any more and the wind must have been blowing the wrong way because the wailing trumpets, the drums with their two long, three short booms that echoed in your brain for days afterwards, the shouts of ¡*Viva*! ¡*Guapa*! to the statue of the Virgin like she was a real chick, the clapping and cheering, all got through somehow.

Next morning there were still a few drunks wandering about on the road. Mark picked his way through the bottles and broken glass, the food cartons, plastic bags, patches of sick... He felt sorry for the garbage workers who'd soon be along to clean up the mess. His head ached as bad as if he had a hangover. Could be because he'd hardly slept, even after the procession passed.

He hadn't intended to go to the *mezquita* but finding himself there felt right, like he'd been guided by some kind of invisible magnet. That was how birds knew where to migrate: he'd seen a TV programme about it once. The gate was open so he went and sat on a wall in the gardens, just chilling out. The place was deserted. All he could hear was the birds chirruping away and a soft rustling of leaves in the breeze.

He must have been sat there for ages – could even have dropped off to sleep – when a hand on his shoulder made him jump.

'¡*Joder*! What the..?'

'Sorry, I should have spoken first. You're Mark, aren't you? Deborah's son?'

It was that guy, Bashir. Mark remembered him coming to the house once with Mustafa and some others. They said he spoke Arabic and knew all of the Qur'an by heart, though he was Spanish and grew up in the Albaicín. Mustafa had introduced him as an *imam*, whatever that was, and Mum had been dead impressed because he was only nineteen.

'Yeah, we met once,' Mark said, 'When you came to our house.'

'That's right, it must have been just after Mustafa was released. You know, he'd been detained by the police – him and a few others. ¡*Que tontería*! But these things are no joke.' Bashir clapped Mark on the back. 'You're welcome here,' he said. The *mezquita* is open to everyone, whatever their beliefs. Your mother is in our thoughts and prayers along with all the other victims. If there's anything we can do to help…'

'Thanks. Mustafa's already been up to see me.'

'I know. We were concerned about you.'

'I'm alright.'

'If you'd like to learn more about Islam – the truth, not the lies and propaganda put about by the media – we've got loads of books and pamphlets…' Bashir pointed to some racks near the mosque entrance. 'Or if you just want to chat to one of us…'

'Thanks, I'll keep that in mind.'

After Bashir had gone, Mark sat there a while longer. It was a cool place to hang out. Relaxing. Mum was always going on about *harmony*. The Muslims liked to create harmony, she said. Like in the Generalife gardens. They'd done it here too. Maybe that was why it felt so peaceful.

It was unbelievable they'd taken Mustafa for a terrorist. Bloody idiots. Mum had gone mad when she heard. It was like any Muslim was fair game, she said. They'd had to let him go after a few days though. It was the journalists they kept locked up. That al-Jazeera guy, Taisir

Alouny, for example. Mark was pretty sure he was still in jail, waiting for his case to come up in court. And hadn't someone mentioned Hassan? Not Mum – she refused to speak his name after all the aggro she'd had from him – but he'd definitely heard something about Hassan being detained... Paco would know.

Mark wondered what Timmy was doing today. Alice had said they were leaving in a week or two so Timmy could go back to school after the Easter holidays. Well there wasn't much point in them hanging around here for ever. He'd miss his little cousin though. It was like having a kid brother, someone who looked up to you.

'But what about Auntie Deborah?' Timmy asked when Alice told him they would go home before the start of the summer term.

There is no hope for your mother. That would have been the honest answer. Alice took a deep breath before replying. 'You have to go back to school,' she said. 'They don't expect Auntie Deborah to get better for a long time. Possibly not ever.'

'Oh.' Timmy looked at the floor. 'What will Mark do?'

'Mark is grown up. He'll be very sad but he knows how to look after himself.'

Alice had left the hospital shaken and in tears. After seeing her sister again, unchanged, as if made of plaster not flesh and blood and bone, all hope had ebbed away. A return to consciousness was not impossible, the solemn young doctor said: her heart was still beating, but with the damage to her brain... He had left the sentence unfinished.

Now the two boys were out together. Alice had no idea where; she had decided to place more trust in her nephew. In less than a fortnight she and Timmy would be back in England. It seemed mean to deprive them of each other's company for the short time remaining. Half-brothers or cousins, was there so much difference? What would they gain by knowing their true relationship? Nothing, she concluded. Her conscience could cast off that burden.

She picked up the next part of the diary, but without the burning curiosity she had felt before. With less guilt too, now she was convinced her sister would not recover. It appeared to start several months after

Deborah's return to Granada, in January 1995. The first page described a New Year's party with friends, but the writing had not a glimmer of life or energy in it. Alice was surprised Deb had even bothered to put pen to paper with such a flat account. In the pages that followed, it was impossible to make out more than the odd word or a date. Nothing to give any hint of what had passed. Yet her sadness seeped out in the blanks as much as in the few words that remained. The whole of that year was a mess. Even Deb's handwriting had deteriorated. The next legible entry, on a page of its own, was dated 27th January.

> This morning I found an old Arabic proverb translated into Spanish:
> *'Lo pasado ha huido, lo que esperas está ausente, pero el presente es tuyo.'*
> 'The past has fled, what you await is absent, but the present is yours.' If I can keep that in my mind, maybe I'll feel better.

Deborah's old spirit was more apparent on the following page, written only a few days later.

> *4th February 1995*
> Hassan has gone back to Morocco, Fátima told me today. What joy! I can walk in the street without fearing he'll suddenly leap out in front of me or sneak up behind me. I hope he marries that plump young virgin his mother was always threatening and never comes back.

So Hassan had continued to persecute Deb after her return to Granada. She'd never said anything. More black felt-tip and the ragged edges of some missing pages, then a jump to late March.

> *24th March 1995*
> I'm trying to sink myself in work. It's the only way to defeat this depression. I've got three translations to do, one of them urgent and I'm longing to get back to my research on Zaynab, wife of Berber commander Yusuf Ibn Tashufin. According to my source, he trusted her to 'oversee and defend his kingdom from political rivals'. If he wanted advice on strategy, she was the one he turned to. History must

be littered with strong women like her who remain nameless; whose influence has never been acknowledged because their men take all the credit.

10th April 1995
Ten years. A whole decade in Granada. I only realised when a friend of Kay's asked me how long I'd been here. I worked it out: ten years and two days – we arrived in Granada on 8th April 1985. Kay said I should throw a party, but even the idea of it makes me feel tired. So the partying will have to wait till we've got another decade to celebrate. 2005! Mark will be twenty-one by then and I'd rather not think about how decrepit I'll be.

8th April – wasn't that today's date? Reluctant to dwell on this sad coincidence, Alice turned to the next page.

2nd May 1993
Talking to one of the doctoral students in the library today, I let myself get rather heated. He claimed the *convivencia* was a complete myth, there'd been no collaboration between the communities, and referred me to a couple of articles in academic journals. Later I read them but I wasn't convinced. My own research suggests not just tolerance but cooperation between the three religions of *al-Andalus*; even some inter-marriage.

Alice could just hear her sister. 'Rather heated' would be an understatement. Deb thrived on argument – the intellectual kind especially. Alice had never understood it; she would do anything to avoid a confrontation. If someone upset her, rather than engaging in a battle of words, she would go to the piano and take out her feelings that way. Twenty minutes of Beethoven or Mendelssohn or her favourite Chopin Nocturne was usually enough. She would get up from the piano stool purged of the hurt or resentment or anger – as if those difficult emotions had flowed out through her hands, leaving her free of them. She missed her piano.

As she browsed through the messy, fragmented pages of the diary, the passing months of Deborah's life, the writing regained some of its former vitality and, perversely, Alice found it more painful to read. The vision of her lifeless body intruded, superimposing itself on the images conjured by the diary. She put it down and wandered into Deb's study. This was where her sister had taken refuge from difficult emotions.

She switched on the computer and from a folder named 'Women in the Qur'an' opened a document at random. Her eye was drawn to a passage where the word 'prophets' was highlighted in turquoise: *Andalusi scholar Ali Ibn Hazm (died 1064) advocated a literal reading of the Qur'an. In his opinion, women could have been prophets of God in the past. He also asserted that women could play a role in leadership.* She was struck again by the contrast between this relatively enlightened view of women's roles and the restrictions imposed on women in Muslim countries nowadays. Had there really been women prophets? She couldn't recall hearing of any. Not in any religion.

If only she could have discussed this with Deb. How remiss of her to have wasted the opportunity. She had let her sister gush forth, only half-listening; noting her enthusiasm but allowing much of the substance to float by unheeded because, after all, what did it have to do with real life? Now, she felt less sure of that. The popular view of Muslims as oppressors of women, violent fanatics, terrorists, just didn't fit with what she was reading. Knowing what to believe was difficult, almost impossible. Politicians rarely told the truth, you couldn't necessarily trust the newspapers or TV...

The phone interrupted her reading. It was Paco calling from Madrid. He had set off only hours after her return as if he couldn't bear to be separated from Deborah a moment longer. His devotion moved her to tears.

'I call you to say maybe you should change your mind about returning to England,' he said, speaking faster than usual, a little breathless.

The urgency in his voice made Alice's heart lurch. Had Deborah taken a turn for the worse? 'What's happened? Is she...?'

'No no, she is the same. Only, the doctor he says that any time... it is perfectly possible that at any time she might...how do you say ...wake up?'

'But Paco...' Waking up wasn't the point. Her brain had been irreparably damaged. That was what *she* had understood from the doctor's sparse words. How could Paco retain such an optimistic outlook?

'He says the progress of coma patients cannot be predicted and so I think…'

'If she wakes up, I'll get a flight back immediately,' Alice said. 'But I can't take any longer off work and Timmy has missed more than enough school.'

Paco sighed and hung up, disappointed perhaps at her lack of faith. But she couldn't go on hoping indefinitely, lying to herself as Paco seemed to be. What was the point? In the end you had to face the truth.

Timmy was kicking his legs against the wall they were sat on up near San Miguel Alto. Mark had brought him here because it was a cool spot to sit and have a smoke while you watched the sun go down over Granada. At first the place had been practically deserted but now there were people strung out like pegs all along the wall. The sky above the city was lit up orange and the blue-grey clouds had edges like they'd been outlined in gold paint. Mark blew out a mouthful of smoke. He was sticking to tobacco so Alice couldn't accuse him of being a bad influence on Timmy but the sweet smell of cannabis hung in the air from other people's joints.

'Was your mum strict?' Timmy asked, right out of the blue.

'Strict? You mean when I was your age?' He thought for a moment. 'No, not really. Not like your mum.' After they came back from England, she'd let him do what he wanted most of the time. He used to go out a lot because he couldn't stand seeing her sitting there blank as hell, not talking, not doing anything, just kind of staring at nothing. She didn't notice what he did; he guessed she didn't care. Though now and again she'd suddenly grab hold of him and hug him till he was nearly smothered to death. She'd whisper his name over and over. *Markie, Markie, what have I done?* How was he supposed to know? Not that she seemed to expect an answer; it was more like she was talking to herself. She'd better not have murdered someone, he remembered thinking. What if the police came knocking at their door? He didn't want his mum in jail.

'I'm allowed to go to the shop on my own,' Timmy said. When I'm ten, my mum says she'll let me ride my bike on the road – not the big road though. I can play out with my friends if I tell her where I'm going.'

'Sounds fair enough.' Mark noticed José and Fabio heading up the path and turned away, hoping they wouldn't spot him. He didn't much feel like talking to them. Tina had come over yesterday to say goodbye. She'd be on the plane now, flying to fucking Lanzarote.

'Mummy won't let me have a TV in my room,' Timmy went on. 'Everyone else has. And a computer.'

'No?' Mark shrugged. 'Well you've seen my cave. No electric, not even a bloody mobile signal, let alone a telly.'

'That's different. A cave is fun.'

Timmy was pissing him off today. What did he have to whinge about? 'So your mum's strict – most likely 'cos she cares about you.' Mark took a last drag on his ciggie and tossed the *colilla* away. 'At least she's alive.'

Timmy went very quiet for a couple of minutes. He was still swinging his legs and Mark noticed one of his trainer laces had come undone. He pointed to it and Timmy stuck his bony knee up and fastened it. Then he said, 'Is your mum going to die?'

The sun had slid down out of sight and the hills were losing their reddish tinge. Soon all the colours would melt away into a grey murk. 'Come on,' Mark said, getting to his feet. 'Let's go.'

Alice flicked forward through the pages of the diary in search of happier times, the first mention of Paco. When and where had they met? How had she dealt with the fact that he was married? Had he told her straightaway or concealed it to begin with? She recalled her own experience with Michael, his cowardly deceptions and evasions; but Paco was a different person entirely. He would not have lied, she felt sure. He would have told her, perhaps, that it was impossible: he had a wife and family. How would Deb have coped with this further dose of pain, the bitter-sweet emotion of a love that was mutual but forbidden?

Skimming rapidly, Alice came across the first reference to Paco in May of '95. It seemed they had crossed paths at some political meeting.

17th May 1995

In the faculty library yesterday, I was chatting to Carmen, the professor of Semitic Studies and she invited me to go along to a meeting of the *Izquierda Unida*. She's an active member of the party and says that what with the PSOE having broken so many of its election promises and moved way to the right, plus all the recent scandals, the IU has been gaining support. I've no intention of getting involved in party politics (of whatever persuasion) but I agreed to go along.

It was much as I'd expected. Lots of interesting lefty types there, everyone talking at once, the usual dominating male egos you get in any organisation but also some strong women with energy and ideas, Carmen among them. She introduced me to various people, whose names I've already forgotten. I also bumped into a guy called Paco Molina, who I've seen around the Faculty. He's a lecturer in Contemporary History, not one of those dominant types but passionate in his beliefs when he does speak. We were discussing the corruption, Felipe González, Garzón, all the hot topics. Sadly I couldn't go to the bar with them afterwards as I had to collect Mark from his friend's house. Everyone here seems to have mothers, sisters, cousins or other family on hand for babysitting. With neither husband nor family, I feel at a definite disadvantage.

The next mention of Paco was some six months later, sandwiched between problems with the tenants in her apartment, the persistent attentions of a friend's husband, triumphs and setbacks with her research and the odd passing reference to Mark.

5th November 1995

Went to another meeting of the IU. A really stimulating evening, lots of committed people with ideas and energy. Bumped into Paco again, also César and Marisol. We went to the bar afterwards and talked politics for hours. I'm learning more about the Second Republic: some of the personalities involved and what all those initials stand for. Paco is incredibly knowledgeable, rather shy but once he gets talking...

And then three months later:

A productive day's work in the university library (some exciting new material about a female physician) and an interesting chat with Paco, that history professor I met at the IU. But by now she had succumbed to her married pursuer, Curro.

Alice remembered the words of Walladah, highlighted in one of the articles she'd found. *I will take what lovers I choose.* So, it seemed, had Deb. Curro's wife Rosa found out and, not surprisingly, it ended badly. Had her sister's life ever been free of drama? Maybe towards the end, but then…Madrid, the train, the bomb. Trust Deborah.

Alice turned the page and was instantly transported back to June 1996, the time of her first visit to Granada with Timmy, the moment she had been half-dreading for months. It had been Deb's idea not to see her baby before his second birthday. 'I'm not sure I could stand it,' she had said and Alice, fearful always that Deb might change her mind, had been relieved; happy to wait.

12th June 1996

Tomorrow they will be here, Alice and Timmy. I am excited, terrified, edgy as a teenager anticipating her first date. Smoking far too much.

The rest was blocked out. Alice peered at the thick black ink covering three pages. Impossible to make out a single word. She remembered watching Deb's face, noticing the fleeting sad smile as she held Timmy, played with him, bathed him. And her own wariness – well hidden, she hoped. *He's mine. No going back.* But neither then nor later had Deb expressed any regrets at her decision. Her feelings were another matter. Alice noticed now that some of the black felt tip was smudged. How many tears had her sister shed over these pages? How much pain and loss did the blacked-out lines conceal?

They had stayed nearly two weeks. After the heightened emotion of the first days, both she and Deb had relaxed and she remembered feeling that they had never been closer. Watching Mark and Timmy playing together one afternoon in the patio, pushing toy cars across the tiles, they had looked at each other and exchanged conspiratorial smiles. Another image came into her mind of Deb holding Timmy up to the mirror after his bath, kissing his damp curls. 'Look, it's Timmy and Auntie Debbie!' And of his delighted giggle as he pointed to the mirror. 'Timmy! Bebbie!'

Reading on, Alice realised that for whatever reason – the reunion with Timmy or her growing friendship with Paco – some kind of turning point had come over the summer of that year. A subtle shift of tone, a more positive outlook – as if Deborah's life had finally got back on track.

1st September 1996

First day of the month and already the new tenant, Miguel has been down to pay. Not just the rent but two sample packets of coffee for me. He's a sales rep for Bonka and travels a lot. When he's here, he's quiet, clean; the model tenant. He told me he had recently separated from his wife but they seem to be friends still: she sometimes brings his daughter round, a sweet little girl of about four with ribbons in her hair and the kind of summer dresses we used to wear on Sundays in the 1950s. She runs up the steps calling '*Papá*!' and Miguel picks her up, twirls her round and covers her with kisses while she squeals with delight.

11th October 1996

My project is suffering serious delays and I blame it squarely on Paco Molina. Every time I go to the library to work, we seem to run into each other, and end up talking for hours. The truth is I'm fascinated by him. He's perceptive, a thinker, very confident in his opinions but not at all arrogant. He'll listen to my views with total attention and then make some highly pertinent comment that takes my thoughts in a new direction. Today we stood talking at the top of the staircase for almost an hour – about freedom and censorship, class and privilege – oblivious to the noisy gaggles of students walking past. By the time we parted, my brain was incapable of focusing on Walladah.

18th October 1996

Is fate throwing us together? I enter the lift and there he is. Twice in the last week it's happened. He asked if I was going to the next IU meeting and I said yes even though I knew nothing about it. Carmen looked surprised when I called her for the date and time. Does Paco know I'm going only because he is? I hope not!

21st October 1996

Went to the meeting and he wasn't there. Had to hide my disappointment and feign interest through the whole of what turned out to be a very boring meeting. I left early, took the bus up and comforted myself with a glass of wine and *tapa* in El Torcuato on the way home.

23rd October 1996

Not fate, not coincidence, I've realised I'm actually seeking him out deliberately now. *CUIDADO!* DANGER! I hear the warnings in my head and choose to ignore them. This morning we had breakfast in the cafeteria (his suggestion but craftily engineered by me). He was telling me about his morning meditation routine, twenty minutes to start the day. He says it has kept him sane for the last six years. I didn't ask what would otherwise be driving him insane, but I'm curious. He comes across as very composed, very sorted; self-sufficient. I know nothing about his life.

From the moment Deb introduced her to Paco, Alice had been struck by the difference in their temperaments. Chalk and cheese, as Mum put it. He was not an easy man to know. He kept his emotions hidden – unlike Deb, unlike Hassan.

26th October 1996

He is married, as I'd half-guessed but didn't want to believe. ¡*No me digas*! The words leapt out of my mouth when he told me. From his silence, the look in his eyes, I'm sure he thought I was being sarcastic: 'You don't say'. When what I meant was literally 'Please don't tell me that!' My response was over the top, pure reaction after the Curro and Rosa thing. Nothing can be taken in isolation. Experience is cumulative, coloured by what has happened before: the last relationship, the last hurt, the last failure.

Nothing has happened yet with Paco; nothing has been said. Maybe I'm even imagining the warmth in his look, the extra *cariño* in his touch, his parting kiss; the improbable flukiness of our 'chance' meetings. But I'm not imagining my own feelings for him. I daren't say anything. Even less so now I know for sure that he's married.

158

I should keep away. After what happened with Curro... But this feels so different. That was craziness, a purely physical obsession with no depth. And this???

I think about Walladah, how she did exactly as she liked. 'I will give my cheek to my lover and my kisses to anyone I choose.' Would she have suffered these qualms? The truth is I am powerless. Incapable of staying away from him.

'Mummy, I'm back.' Alice leapt to her feet as the bedroom door burst open. She had been so absorbed in the diary, in Deborah's life, that she had no idea of the time. Now she realised she'd been reading in the half-gloom; that the day was all but gone.

'Did you have fun?' she asked Timmy, at the same time slipping the diary under the bedclothes. 'It's late, nearly dark.'

'You didn't say a time.' Timmy's voice was defiant.

'It's alright.' She reached out to him. 'But where's Mark?'

'He went home. He got a message from his dad and it put him in a bad mood.'

'But he brought you here first, I hope?'

Timmy kicked off one trainer and then the other. 'Yes, course he did.'

His eyes skidded away as he spoke and for the first time ever, Alice doubted his word. She said nothing but a sudden chill rising from the pit of her stomach worked its way through her veins and made her shiver.

Chapter Fourteen

It was fucking unbelievable his dad coming over. Just like that without any warning; without even asking. *Arriving tomorrow 11.30*, the message said. Mark guessed he'd be staying at that posh hotel in town like he did the last time. The rooms had fridges stacked with booze: little miniature bottles of vodka, rum, whisky, gin... You could just help yourself and pay later.

He hadn't felt like telling Timmy about his dad's visit. Timmy would have just asked him a load of questions he didn't want to answer. That was the trouble with kids: they were always interrogating you. So he'd taken Timmy down the hill to Calle San Luis and let him find his own way home. He was old enough for fuck's sake.

Mark thought about the first time he'd seen Timmy. Alice brought him over when he was about two. It must have been summer because he was always asking for ice-cream when they went out. Half of it would get smeared over his face. He could talk a bit, though sometimes it was only Alice who understood what he was saying. The weird thing was, Mum hadn't even told him Alice had a baby – not till Timmy was about one year old. Then she'd shown him a photo of this curly-headed kid holding a toy telephone to his ear like he was talking to someone. 'This is your cousin,' she'd said. Like he'd only just been born or like it hadn't occurred to her for a whole year that he might want to know he had a cousin. Bizarre.

Mum had hired a car and they'd gone to Málaga airport to meet Alice and Timmy. It was a shiny red one, brand new, and Mum had overtaken every car and truck on the motorway so they wouldn't be late. In spite of that, Alice and Timmy were already sat there waiting and when she saw them, Mum burst out crying and then Alice did too. You'd think it would be the kids crying but it was the fucking grownups. He and Timmy were fine.

After that they used to come over every year though they never stayed long. Mostly it was in England he saw Timmy – either at Alice's place or at their granny's, before she got ill and died. She was quite old and she must have been going a bit wrong in the head because she'd get confused about simple things. Once she thought Timmy was Mark's brother and Alice got all het up about it, which just made things worse. Another time she said it was a shame Alice hadn't married and had children. Right in front of Timmy! Luckily he was too busy playing with his Lego to take any notice, but both Mum and Alice went bananas. He'd felt sorry for Granny; she couldn't help getting mixed up. Lots of old people did. Tina said her gran didn't even know who she was sometimes. She'd think Tina was her daughter or her sister. It was a disease with a proper name and everything but you didn't die of it. His granny had died of cancer.

Mark checked his phone. It was 11.40. Charlie would be here by now, picking up a car at the airport or else getting a taxi into town. Any time now there might be a call or text from him. Shit, he'd have to go. You couldn't tell your own dad to fuck off, not when he'd come all this way. But Charlie had better keep his mouth shut about London. Why the fuck would he want to go there? Even Mum thought it was a bad idea. Not that she could back him up now… Basically, he was on his own. He picked up his guitar and played a few chords. For some weird reason he thought about that priest at school, the one who taught *Religión*. Jesus is always with you, he used to say. But most likely that only applied if you were a good Catholic, which cut him right out.

'So tell me Alice, what's the news about Deborah? Will she live?'

Charlie stood facing her across the *salón* in that typical stance of his, legs apart, hands in his pockets, hips swaying slightly. The willowy blonde hung on his arm, eyes roaming round the room. He had introduced her but already Alice had forgotten the woman's name. 'Sit down, won't you?' she said.

He ignored the invitation. 'I'd like to know the situation before I see

Mark,' he said. 'Don't want to put my foot in it.' That rueful smile that might, she thought, charm some women.

'Deborah is still in a coma. We don't know what the outcome will be but it's not looking very hopeful.'

'Hmm, that is bad news. Well now, if she doesn't pull through, Mark stands to inherit the house and, presumably, other assets of his mother's. He'll need some sound financial advice.'

This is my sister you're talking about, Alice wanted to scream. He'd better not talk so coldly to Mark. But he surely couldn't be that insensitive, could he? She counted to ten in an attempt to calm herself. 'I think you're being rather premature, Charlie.'

'Prepared, I'd call it.' He cleared his throat, gave a little cough. 'If the worst came to the worst, you know. Anyway, how *is* the boy?'

'Up and down, as you'd expect. It's hard, very hard...' She turned as Timmy poked his head around the door. 'Come in, Timmy,' she said. 'Meet Charlie and...'

'Suzy,' the woman said, holding out a hand to him.

Timmy took it but his eyes were on Charlie. 'Are you Mark's dad?'

'Indeed I am.' Charlie looked questioningly at Alice.

'This is my son,' she said. 'Timmy.'

'Do you know, I'd completely forgotten you had a son. Now I think of it, Mark did mention a cousin, but my memory...' He was staring at Timmy. 'You're a dark horse, Alice.' He shook his head, seeming to find something faintly amusing in the idea of her having a child. 'Well, he's certainly caught the Spanish sun. Either that or...'

How dare he? Furious, Alice glared at him and the smirk disappeared from his face. 'I expect you'll be wanting to settle into your hotel,' she said. 'And I'm rather busy today. So if you'll excuse me...'

'Actually, we've tickets to visit the Alhambra this afternoon. I promised Suzy.' He turned to face her. 'Didn't I, darling?'

'It's my first time in Granada,' she said, flashing Alice a smile as she snuggled up to Charlie's leather jacket.

As if this were just a sightseeing trip, Alice thought. Or perhaps he viewed it as killing two birds with one stone: show concern for Mark and give the girlfriend a treat, a weekend away. 'So you won't be seeing Mark today?'

'We thought tomorrow. I've sent him a message but you know what the lad's like. He takes his time replying.' Charlie pulled out his phone. 'No word yet. But don't worry, I won't leave without seeing him. That's the main purpose after all.'

As they said their goodbyes, Alice realised that Timmy's eyes had hardly left Charlie the whole time.

'What's *my* dad like?' he asked as soon as the gate had shut behind them. 'It's not fair. Why can't he come back? Just once so I know what he looks like.'

*

Alice threw herself on the bed. The conversation with Charlie had brought on a dull headache and left her devoid of energy. His visit was unlikely to help Mark either; probably the contrary. And it was only luck – an urgent banging on the gate from Timmy's friend Javi, inviting him round to play – that had saved her from more awkward questions.

She reached out and retrieved the diary from its hiding place, eager to read more of Deb and Paco's story. At some point before leaving Granada, she must make a decision about what to do with the diaries.

30th October 1996

So, now I know it all. He is married, his wife suffers from depression, she gobbles pills that do nothing to help, she won't sleep with him. It's been like this for three years... He doesn't know what to do, how to help her. And the children – two girls and a boy – are affected; naturally he worries about them. Their mother keeps them close, controls them through emotional blackmail. Paco feels trapped: if he leaves, he may lose the children. All this spilled out last night in a little bar in the Realejo over a couple of glasses of Rioja.

When we left the bar, it was already too late. Without any words, any decisions, we kissed – in a way that left nothing in doubt – and headed back here in wild haste as if the anticipated banquet would be snatched away before we could taste a morsel.

And in fact it was snatched away. Paco was mortified. '*No sé qué pasa.*' When my efforts proved useless, I tried to reassure him that caresses were enough, the rest could wait. It might be guilt, I suggested, or the fear of waking Mark.

163

So now he has gone and I can't sleep for thinking about him, wanting him, willing tomorrow to come soon so I can see him again. I should feel guilty but all I feel is a tender aching love that includes desire but is much more than that.

1st November 1996

Another failure last night and the confession that he has resorted on occasion to prostitutes. Should I not mind? '*Es normal*' he said, '*En mi situación.*'

Is it normal in Spain? I've no reason to doubt the fact. Someone must visit all the *clubes de alterne*, those neon-lit brothels you see outside every town, and call up the girls who advertise in the small ads of the newspapers: big-busted Susi, hot Juanita, Sylvi who's into S-M. If Paco has used their services, I don't want to know. Today is All Saints and we can't meet. I'm glad. Mark and I have been invited to a restaurant in Pinos Genil with Amparo and Juan Antonio, his sister and her English husband. For one day I would like to forget Paco.

7th November 1996

Suddenly the difficulties are resolved and we agreed the pleasure was all the more intense for being denied us till now. Relief, release or some other unknown reflex made us laugh aloud, laugh till we cried: first Paco then me. And even now, sitting alone here in my den writing, a giggle escapes me. *Paco, te quiero.*

Alice squirmed. What she had in front of her was private, embarrassingly so. Deb might be beyond knowing or caring but these were Paco's secrets too. How would she be able to look him in the eye when he returned from Madrid in a few days' time? She went to the kitchen and made herself an infusion of camomile. She shouldn't be reading the diary, she knew it was wrong, and yet... The truth was she found it compulsive. She would skip the intimate parts, she decided. And then destroy all six notebooks. It was her duty to her sister.

16th November 1996

It isn't enough, the portion I'm allowed. I want all of him, all of the time. Alice used to tell me I was greedy. She was right. I am greedy: I want Paco to myself, not shared with a depressive, manipulative wife who makes him unhappy and guilty. And by association makes me feel unhappy and guilty. Paco is so highly principled. He hates – but really really hates – lying. I know he will tell her. Very soon, I think. Poor Nieves, it isn't her fault. I am the 'other woman', the thief, the interloper.

4th December 1996

Another big let-down. It's becoming a pattern: Paco appears at my door, we embrace, kiss, remove what clothes the temperature will allow and make ourselves comfortable. Then just as we reach the point where the cold no longer matters because our bodies are generating more than enough heat, his phone rings. 'I'm sorry,' he says. 'I have to leave.' He cannot be argued with: family comes first. 'My son...' he begins, or 'My daughter...' and I don't want to hear the rest. If only he were free.

9th December 1996

Miguel, my perfect tenant, has given me notice. He's going back to his wife – a reconciliation in time for Christmas, he told me, smiling. I'm pleased for him and not at all surprised. At the same time I'm terrified that Paco will succumb to the same sentiment and desert me. He has promised to confess to Nieves – who already suspects – and announce he is leaving, but always his courage fails him. She once took an overdose and the threat of her doing so again hangs heavy, along with the fear of losing his children. I cannot now imagine a life apart from him and I know he feels the same. So I must have faith, I must trust him, I must be patient. That is what he tells me. I am trying.

28th December 1996

Christmas is over, thank God. Christmas with only '*tapas*' of my Paco: stolen moments, precious BUT NOT ENOUGH. I want a meal, not crumbs. Now there is New Year and then *Reyes* to endure without him. After that, so he has promised, when all the family parties are done with, the children back at school, he will talk to Nieves. The dishonesty, he says, is killing him.

165

He came to me wordless and shaking, a small overnight bag slung over his shoulder. He looked so shrunken in his black overcoat, as if swallowed by it, hunched up against the freezing air – or was it the numb cold of loss, the icy wastes of exile from his children's lives? When I lifted the coat from his shoulders, I saw his shirt was torn at the hem. His face is like a bruised fruit – her doing, I have to assume.

Later, in bed, as I held him and tried to breathe warmth and love into his unyielding body, he began to talk. Not of the violent scene with his wife but of how Ana, his daughter woke and shouted for them to stop: '¡*Basta, ya basta!*' Enough. She was distraught, fists pressed to her ears. It was worse even than he had imagined. Nieves will make them hate me, he said, blinking back tears. Impossible to comfort him.

Can what we have make up for the loss of his children or will he later hate me for what he has sacrificed?

2nd February 1997

Whole nights together instead of that dreaded abandonment in the early hours, the desolation of waking without him. At last he is here, he is mine, and if it weren't that he still suffers so pitiably on account of his children, I would be perfectly happy.

19th February 1997

Today Mark said he liked Paco and I was ecstatic, disproportionately so. His response to an 'interloper' moving in had been cool despite my attempts to give him more attention. Now he is beginning to come round, thanks also to Paco's efforts. I like to think that because I feel at peace, this is somehow transmitted to Mark and he benefits too.

3rd April 1997

Our first big row and it was all my fault. I thought Paco was so calm and laid-back that it would be impossible to argue with him, but no. It takes a lot to provoke him but I did, I pushed him too far and discovered that he can get angry, like anyone else. I chose a bad moment, forgetting that his other worries still consume him, however

166

hard he tries to hide them from me – the financial arrangements with Nieves, the girls' rejection of him. Lots on his plate and then on top of that, just when I should have been most supportive, I had a go at him for something so idiotic and petty I can't even bring myself to write it here. He was deeply upset, as if I'd undermined him in some fundamental way. I apologised – over and over as I never could with Hassan – but that kind of wound can't be kissed away like the minor bumps and bruises of a child's tumble.

6th April 1997

It's still not quite right with Paco. I feel he's disappointed in me, no longer sees me in such a positive light. There's a coolness in our relations and we haven't made love for three days, which is unusual. My attempts to seduce him have been kindly but firmly rejected. Another day, he says. It feels like a punishment. I can't bear the thought of losing him or even losing his respect. I MUST restrain my temper; learn from him about staying in control.

18th May 1997

We are getting accustomed to each other's routines and foibles, finding ways to live in harmony. Living together takes effort, Paco says. I know not to disturb him in his morning meditation (though usually I'm still fast asleep); he knows I don't take kindly to him tidying up my papers. (I have solemnly promised not to clutter up the *salón* with my stuff.) Learning each other's limits is the key.

And recognising the moments when all can be solved with a kiss.

29th May 1997

Paco has shown me that a man can be interesting without being difficult, calm without being bland. It hit me like a revelation how misguided and blind I've been all these years.

Yes, and unnecessarily patronising about *my* choice of men, Alice thought with some satisfaction. Deb had always implied that her own lovers were infinitely more interesting. Thinking of that manic-depressive poet she'd got involved with in her early twenties, of Charlie and Hassan, Alice felt vindicated. Ted, Simon, Andy... Deb may have found them boring but they'd all been basically decent men. It wasn't their fault the relationships hadn't lasted. The truth was that in her experience, sooner or later, a man always seemed to disappoint. A child was a better bet. Timmy had given her a purpose in life that no man had ever been able to provide.

So Deborah's prediction had been wrong. 'You're much more likely to end up with a stable, sensible partner, a substitute father for Timmy.' It was Deb who had settled with Paco – as stable and solid as one could wish – and Timmy had been denied a substitute father. Did it matter? She had always thought not, but now she felt less sure. Was it selfish of her to deprive him just because *she* had no need of a man? Troubled by these thoughts, she plunged back into the diary.

10th September 1997

Four months without writing; I had no idea it was so long. The reason can only be contentment. Now Paco is free and Nieves has stopped harassing him so much, we're both feeling more settled and secure. If something is troubling me, I share it with Paco, simple as that. It was never so easy with Charlie and certainly not with Hassan. Thinking back, it's the first time I've had a lover I trust completely. Yet I'm always conscious of the one great secret that separates us. I hate it; I hate the thought of anything coming between Paco and me.

Yesterday I was on the point of telling him. It was only that wise poet Kahlil Gibran who saved me from blurting out the truth. I'd been reading my little volume of his works at siesta time and the book just happened to fall open at these apt words:

"If you reveal your secrets to the wind you should not blame the wind for revealing them to the trees."

I trust Paco a hundred per cent, and yet... He could so easily give away to friends (or worse still to Mark) some small hint, a mere sliver of truth that is nevertheless enough to set the ball of doubt rolling. And I would live in fear that he might – quite unintentionally – let slip to Alice that he knows. We swore faithfully to each other never to break the confidence. It mattered to her as much as to me. So I will remain silent as I promised; as Kahlil Gibran bids me.

Alice put down the diary, aware all of a sudden how her muscles had tensed as she was reading. Had it come so close? She shut her eyes and let the relief wash over her. Their secret was safe, Paco didn't know. And now he never would.

Was his dad showing off or what, bringing that good-looking blonde with him? Like he wanted to prove he could still pull? Mark had to admit she was quite a stunner. And she seemed to be into Charlie, though it might just be for his money. At his age, it couldn't be for his looks.

They were staying at that fucking enormous red brick hotel up at the top of the Realejo, the Alhambra Palace but Charlie must have thought he was too scruffy to show up there because he'd suggested meeting in town, in the Plaza Bib-Rambla. He sneaked a look at them across the table now, heads together over the menu, knocking the English translations, as if they could do better. Mark had already decided what he wanted. He was going for a great big *buey* steak. It was the most expensive item on the menu and like Charlie always said, you had to take your opportunities.

He looked around the square. It was nice sitting outside this time of evening, now the clocks had changed. The light was kind of golden. It was about now the birds always went crazy. The row they made, you'd think you were in the jungle. It was *paseo* time, families strolling about. A dozen or so kids were running around the fountain, squealing and shouting. At the next café a little kid about five was sitting with his granny, spooning ice-cream into his gob. Only the tourists ate dinner this early.

Mark told the waiter what they wanted because neither Charlie nor the girlfriend, Suzy spoke any Spanish. They were trying to decide on the wine. He could tell the *camarero* was getting pissed off at how long it took. As if one red was that different from another. The minute they'd ordered, Suzy cleared off to the toilet for about twenty minutes. He thought Charlie would start on about London then but he didn't say a word. He said he'd seen Alice and Timmy, which wasn't exactly news because Timmy had already told him. Timmy seemed to think

Charlie was cool, which just showed he had no fucking experience. Well you couldn't expect a kid of nine to know any better.

The *camarero* came with the wine and Charlie swigged a mouthful like he was considering spitting it out, but he nodded in the end and let the guy pour three glasses. It tasted alright to him.

'Um, you won't forget your father,' Charlie started, shifting about in his chair. 'If you need advice in the future – I mean about your financial affairs. You'll remember I'm there to help, won't you?'

What the fuck was he on about? 'My financial affairs? Well I haven't been doing a lot of busking just lately. Or did you mean the rent for Mum's apartment?' Usually Dad went on about jobs and careers. *Financial affairs*: that was a new one. Get real, he felt like saying.

Charlie still hadn't said a word about Mum. It must be Suzy distracting him with those nice tits of hers. She was heading back now, clutching her little gold handbag. She gave him a sort of sad half-smile as she sat down.

'I'm so sorry about your mother,' she said. 'Terrible, what happened. Absolutely shocking. But we mustn't give up hope.' She looked about to burst into tears.

We! As if it mattered to her. Still, at least she'd said something, unlike his dad. She was trying to be kind. 'Thanks,' he said.

It was a relief when the food came and they didn't have to talk any more, except about how the fucking wine complemented the meat and why there weren't any vegetables and would he please help eat some of Suzy's chips.

Alice examined her face in the bathroom mirror. It was paler than when she'd arrived in Spain and her eyes were cupped by plum-coloured shadows like half-moons. As for her hair, it was a total mess, much longer than she liked it with the fringe straggling into her eyes, a constant annoyance. She reached for Deborah's scissors and snipped in what she hoped was a straight line across her forehead, letting the ends fall into the basin.

Sunlight streamed in through the open door but all this spring weather was passing her by: she had scarcely been out for days. No wonder she looked pallid. *I'm becoming a recluse*, she thought. Deb's friends, Leonor and Robin had taken Timmy out for the day to their little *cortijo* in the country. She'd been invited too but had declined, choosing instead to shut herself indoors with the diary. She should have gone.

She walked out into the patio and breathed in the heady scent of the wisteria, now in full bloom. To her surprise, it was warmer outside than in. Why spend her last days here cooped up in the house? There were parts of the Albaicín she had never explored: cobbled squares and narrow alleyways, flights of steps that might end in unexpected views of the Alhambra or the hills. It was Saturday mid-morning; she had nothing urgent to do.

The market in Plaza Larga was loud with activity. At the fruit stall, women pushed forward, clamouring for Trini's attention, their tartan shopping trolleys standing at the ready. Through the open door of Bar Aixa came the clatter of crockery, the roar of the coffee machine and a buzz of conversation. The rattle of trolleys being wheeled over the cobbles, along with the shouts of the lottery seller and the revving of an occasional car or motorbike fighting its way through, competed from outside. All this colour and bustle cheered her. Here in the streets was life and Alice wanted to be part of it – if only as an observer. She'd had enough isolation.

A tap on the shoulder made her jump. She turned and saw it was Deb's friend, the tall woman with a German accent who had come to the house a week or two ago to offer her sympathies and ask after Mark.

'I'm Monika, do you remember me?'

'Of course.' They exchanged kisses.

'I wasn't sure if you'd still be here.'

'Not for much longer. We're going home in about a week – unless my sister's condition changes.'

'You're very brave to stay so long, all alone in her house,' Monika said. 'You know I went to see Deborah in the hospital? I expect Mark told you.'

'No, actually he didn't. He's not very communicative, to be honest. He worries me. I'm at a loss how to help him...'

'Have you time for a coffee?' Monika steered her into Bar Aixa, grabbed a couple of stools and pushed one towards Alice. '*Café con leche*? Toast?'

'Just coffee thanks.'

The little barrel-bodied barman put two half-full glasses of coffee on the counter and topped them up with frothy milk from a jug.

'I miss Deborah too,' Monika said. 'She was my best friend; we had no secrets from each other.'

'Oh really?' Did Monika notice the tremor in her hand as she put down her glass, slopping coffee onto the saucer?

'Mind you,' Monika continued, 'I'm not sure someone as open as Deborah would be capable of keeping a secret – or not without good reason.' She turned to Alice, for confirmation perhaps, and added quickly, 'I don't mean I didn't trust her, just that she isn't the type to have secrets.'

Doubtless Monika meant it as a compliment, whereas Alice, fully aware of her sister's openness, had seen it only as a liability. Alice was not just more discreet by nature; she was also experienced at keeping secrets. Those years of hiding her feelings about Michael had served her in good stead.

'It's okay, I understand what you're saying.' The man next to her spread his newspaper over the counter, poring over the sports pages. Behind them, several people were pressing forward, shouting orders for toast.

'But getting back to Mark,' Monika said, leaning closer to make herself heard above the din, 'Deborah was very concerned about him. Maybe I shouldn't tell you this but she suspected him of stealing money from her. And the obvious conclusion was that he wanted it for drugs, though I've never seen any evidence that he's into more than marijuana, which hardly counts. The conflict between them was wearing her down; he could be quite aggressive with her.'

'Oh? She never said anything to me. I thought they had a good relationship.'

'Until a couple of years ago, yes. But recently not so good at all.' Monika broke off to greet a couple standing further along the bar. 'Neighbours of mine,' she said as Alice tried to absorb this new insight into her sister's life.

Then, lowering her voice so Alice had to strain to hear, Monika continued on a new tack. 'Poor Deborah, she seemed to face one problem after another. And yet she always bounced back. I'm thinking of her dilemma over Hassan. She found it incredibly hard, as I'm sure she told you. I didn't put my oar in, I just listened. It was Paco who convinced her in the end to forget her antagonism and speak up for him. But anyway, when he was acquitted she felt strongly that she'd done the right thing.'

Alice froze. 'Acquitted? So he's out of prison then?'

'Oh yes, didn't you know?' Monika finished her coffee and put two euros on the counter. 'I've got to run,' she said. 'But it's been good to talk to you.'

'Wait a minute...' She had to find out more. 'Hassan... Is he back in Granada then?'

'I don't think so. I certainly haven't seen him around. No, I've a feeling he went to live in Madrid, or could have been Barcelona.' She picked up her bag. 'I'll try and keep an eye on Mark when you've gone. It's the least I can do for Deborah.'

Chapter Fifteen

Timmy. As Alice turned the pages of the diary, his name leapt out at her. Late December of 1997, the year Deborah, Mark and Paco spent Christmas at Mum's. Although it had been her idea for Deb to come over to England, stupidly, she hadn't thought through the implications. Of course Paco wouldn't be left behind. She remembered spending the whole of their visit as well as the preceding weeks in an agony of nerves in case Mum gave the game away by some indiscreet comment or slip of the tongue. It irritated her that Deb seemed so oblivious to the danger. Reading her sister's account, she wondered why this page hadn't been blacked out or torn out like most of the other incriminating references to Timmy. An oversight probably.

It took me a while to realise why Alice was so nervous all the time. The risk of Mum putting her foot in it about Timmy just hadn't occurred to me till it actually happened. I wanted her to meet Paco, I wanted her to like him. That was all I thought about – that and the fact that I didn't want to be separated from him at Christmas. Thank God Alice was out of the room when Mum dropped her clanger; she'd have thrown a fit. I almost did. 'He's good with his little brother, isn't he? A shame they don't see more of each other.' The boys were too busy playing, I don't think they even noticed, but Paco looked at me as if to say… I think, though I've never been a hundred percent certain, that he put it down to confusion, the beginnings of dementia. That's what I'm banking on. I managed to keep my voice steady as I reminded her they were cousins and steered everyone's attention to the plate of delicious mince pies still warm from the oven. I decided not to say anything to Alice, though it's possible she overheard from the kitchen. But on second thoughts, she would surely have said something to me afterwards...

Wrong. Alice had overheard. But she knew it would have spoilt Christmas for all of them if she'd let her anger show. Hiding her feelings had taken a colossal effort but after all, what could she say? *You shouldn't have brought Paco.* No, that would have been most unfair.

Alice wandered out into the living room. She thought about Monika's words: 'You're brave to stay alone in the house for so long.' No one had called her brave before. She had always thought of herself as rather cowardly. Yet it dawned on her now that the last ten years of her life had taught her to be brave. Circumstances had demanded of her the kind of guts and daring she would previously have associated only with Deb.

Today, however, she felt far from brave. The news that Hassan was out of prison half paralysed her with dread. She wished there were not seven whole days to wait for their flight home. At the same time, leaving Spain felt like giving up on Deborah. She admired Paco's determination to stay with her sister to the end. It was irrational – but then reason hardly came into it for either of them. They were both driven by emotion, reacting with pure instinct to their worst fears.

As she glanced round the room, a framed photo on one of the shelves caught her eye: three children, a boy of about thirteen and two younger girls. She'd barely noticed it before amongst all the Hardy pictures. Now she looked more closely at Paco's children and saw how the boy in particular strongly resembled his father. They would be much older now, almost grown up. She reproached herself for having forgotten this private sorrow of his. It crossed her mind that most people carried some secret font of sadness which only those closest to them knew anything about.

Returning to the diary, Alice found the next entry, dated a few days later, decorated with doodles of hearts and stars. Paco had bought her a computer for *Reyes*, the Three Kings holiday when presents were exchanged. 'It will take me months to learn its magic tricks,' she wrote. 'I am in awe.'

By March she had got the hang of the computer and her research was advancing 'at full tilt'. She was happy with Paco. Mark was settled and doing well at school. Often a month or more would pass without her writing anything – an indication, Alice assumed, that all was hunky-dory. There was no mention of Hassan. When she did write, it was mostly to enthuse about her research, describe a social event with friends or recount some detail of Spanish life or language that particularly fascinated her.

1st June 1998

I've been thinking about the Spanish way of describing people as either good or bad: '*una buena persona*' or '*una mala persona*', whole families as '*buena*' or '*mala gente*'. I hear it said so often, it usually just washes over me. No doubt Paco's ex and his children think I'm '*mala*'. In fact ever since childhood I've been cast as the bad one: the wild child, the wayward teenager, the trouble-maker, while Alice was seen as sensible and responsible – younger but more 'mature'. I called her the goody-goody girl. Now I see what nonsense it is to label people like that. We're all – including Alice – capable of both kindness and cruelty, altruism and selfishness. I wasn't really bad, not then. A little crazy at times, thoughtless maybe... The bad things I've done in my life are on a different scale altogether, measured in pain, the pain I've caused to others. But I don't believe there's anyone who hasn't hurt those close to them – or been hurt.

A fair comment. Alice had never considered herself morally superior to Deb. The goody-goody label, thrown at her like an insult, was not just uncalled-for but infuriating. As for 'sensible', her idiocy over Michael showed just how wide of the mark her family's view of her had been.

Six months on, Christmas time again and Paco's relationship with his children seemed to be a source of grief and guilt to both of them.

15th December 1998

As last year, Paco is sad. He would like to see his children at Christmas but only Juan has consented to meet him (on an indeterminate day between New Year and *Reyes*, possibly just to receive his present, or so Paco suspects). The extended family has ostracised him – he is excluded from the family parties, the Christmas dinner. Only his sister Marina sticks up for him. We went to visit her and her husband in Guadix last month and they made a big fuss of Mark, embarrassing him with their compliments on his good looks. They are more open-minded than the rest, Paco says; they understand.

I so want to make him whole again, to heal the hurt he still suffers over his children. I'm hoping that with time they'll understand and forgive him. He is happier than he was but there is damage – damage on account of me.

Could I learn from Alice? I used to think she deliberately went for damaged men: Simon with his back injury, Andy recovering from a breakdown after his wife left... It was like a mission to care for them, to put everything into the task of making them better, even though the damage hadn't been inflicted by her. And she did make them better. She was brilliant at it.

Alice paused in her reading. It had never occurred to her that she chose men who were damaged. Thinking about it now (even Michael had been scarred – by a tragic loss in childhood), she saw that Deb was right. But she had nothing to teach her sister. *Brilliant at it.* Yes, so brilliant that they stopped needing her. And then it all fell apart. Well now she no longer needed *them.*

Mark hadn't expected a visit from Monika. She used to say she had bad knees but she'd managed to get up here yesterday. When he showed her his cave, she was dead impressed. She said it was a painter's paradise and no wonder so many artists chose to live on the hill. 'So many' was an exaggeration, but there were one or two Mark could think of. She'd asked if she could come up again today because she had an idea for a painting and wanted to get going. 'Fine by me,' he'd said. He liked Monika. Anyway he didn't own the hill; there was no way he could stop her.

When the dogs started up, he stuck his head outside to see who it was. They always went mad if someone was coming. It was her. She was climbing up the path carrying a wooden easel under one arm and a big stripy bag on her shoulder. He went to help her because she looked like she was struggling.

'I've brought you these,' she said and took a sketchpad and some brand new drawing pencils out of her bag. 'It's about time you started again. I can't believe you haven't got a single new work to show me after all this time.'

It was true: he'd given up drawing bloody ages ago, well before he came to live here. There was no particular reason he could think of. He'd just stopped doing it. Maybe Monika was right and he should have another go. He thought about the time he was sketching down on Paseo de los Tristes and this tourist – an old guy with grey hair – came up, looked at his drawing and asked if it was for sale. The man offered him thirty euros. Fucking crazy, he'd have given it him for nothing!

Financial affairs. His dad's words came into his head all of a sudden and he laughed. 'Hey Monika, do you think I could make a living out of it?'

'You could try, though most artists are poor like me.'

'Mum wanted me to study, but stuff that! If I can get thirty euros for one drawing…'

Monika had that look, like she was thinking. 'Have you ever considered going to art school?' she said.

'Go back to school? You must be joking. I want to be free. And now I've got the rent from Mum's apartment every month, I'm loaded.'

'Well fine, but I've spent good money on these pencils so you'd better make use of them or I'll be seriously pissed off with you.'

'Okay, fair enough. I will use them.' He meant it too. He was well pleased.

'I brought you some fruit, just so you don't starve.' She pushed the curtain out of the way and walked into his cave. 'I'll put them on here, alright?' Her bag was full of apricots, *nísperos* and oranges, plus a load of broad beans. She tipped them out onto the table. 'These beans are from a friend's plot in the *Vega*,' she said. 'He gave them to me, but what am I going to do with five kilos of beans?'

'Thanks.' Mark picked up an apricot and bit into it. They were Mum's favourite, apricots. He wished he could take some to her in the hospital; wished she'd get better enough to eat fruit again. She used to eat a ton of it, every day.

Monika was taking photos of the cave with flash. 'Right,' she said,

178

'Now make me a cup of tea and then I'm going to set up my easel somewhere over there and get to work.' She meant higher up the hill.

He took his new pencils and sketchpad – mainly to please Monika – and carried the easel for her. She wanted to paint the hillside with all the caves and in the background the old wall marking off the Albaicín. He let her get on with it and wandered on upwards. He couldn't stop thinking about Mum. It was the apricots had started him off. He kept getting these visions of her stuffing herself with fruit: slurping on a mango or spooning out the flesh of a *chirimoya* like custard apples were her idea of heaven. She loved figs too. In the summer she'd buy them all the time off Trini – the little green ones and the massive great purple *brebas*, so ripe they'd be squashed to pulp by the time she got them home and you had to eat the whole kilo in one go. Then in the autumn they used to go up to Güejar Sierra to collect chestnuts and walnuts – bags and bags of them; she wouldn't stop. They'd both be staggering under the weight and Mum would be moaning about her back for days after. Same with oranges when they went to the Lecrín valley. Eating fruit was the best way to stay healthy, she used to say. Fat lot of good it had done her.

She was always telling him what was good or bad for him, like drink water or juice not coke, eat up your veggies, don't smoke, don't drink, don't take drugs. She and Paco smoked like fucking chimneys. And they drank, though not a lot. He'd seen her smoking joints loads of times, especially with Hassan but other friends too. Including Monika, he remembered now. So course he wasn't going to take any fucking notice.

If she hadn't gone on at him so much, he'd have been nicer to her. If she hadn't rubbished his friends all the time... They were bad for him too, according to her. That was why he'd moved out. He wanted to live his own life. It wasn't as if he was still a kid; he was eighteen. Up here in Sacromonte he could do whatever he wanted. He was free of all that crap: studying, taking exams, or else working for fuck all so some rich bastard would get even richer.

Timmy thought Alice was too strict. Maybe she was. Maybe Timmy would have to break out same as him when he was older. Mum always used to say what a good child Timmy was, how polite and well-behaved.

But he wasn't always good. Mark had seen him being stroppy, stamping his feet and screaming. It made him feel shit when she said those things, like she preferred Timmy to him.

He stopped walking and looked over towards the Albaicín. From where he was standing, he could see the houses all jumbled up together, with the odd patch of green and then the dark cypresses sticking up like rockets between the rooftops. The tower of San Nicolás stood out way higher than anything else. He could draw that scene – not now, he wasn't in the mood today – but he might come back another time and have a go at it. He sat on a patch of dry earth and skinned up. When he'd finished his smoke, he'd go down again, see what Monika was up to.

It was late. Timmy lay fast asleep on his side, head resting on the pillow, exposing one darling ear with its sweet pointed lobe. Alice stood over him for a moment, observing his closed eyelids, the hairline more familiar than her own. A couple more pages of diary then she'd turn out the light and, with any luck, drift off into oblivion.

4th May 1999

Sometimes I feel so elated I could dance for joy. After all the problems, all the fights, my life is serene at last. I'm happy. As if I've ridden a violent storm at sea, tossed by foaming waves, attacked by barracudas, sharks, medusas…and now the storm has passed, leaving a calm but sparkling ocean, an ocean clear to the depths. I stand on the terrace in the still of evening, watching the swifts swoop and dive and I feel my heart overflowing with peace and gratitude. It takes me back to when I first came here, the liberation I felt after leaving my old life and discovering how simple and sweet life could be here in the Albaicín.

May 1999, the month they had diagnosed Mum's cancer. Of which Deb was blissfully unaware because she and Mum had decided not to tell her. 'Not yet,' Mum had pleaded. 'Wait till she next comes over.' And Alice had agreed. Another secret. By the time Deb visited again, in August, Mum's illness was obvious.

Arrived home last night after six weeks in England, six weeks of fake brightness and optimism. Mum has cancer. Her illness was obvious to me the minute I saw her. I was furious with Alice for not telling me. They'd known for three whole months. She looked so haggard, her face drawn, her clothes hanging on her, the pain written in her eyes that made her smile feel like a lie. It wasn't a lie, I realised afterwards. She was truly happy to see us, but at the time I was too shocked to understand that.

Six months to a year, the doctor told Alice. There's nothing more they can do; the cancer has already spread too far. I felt guilty leaving her, coming back home. Alice is taking time off work and she's so capable, such a wonderful carer, it makes me feel useless. But at least I'm confident Mum is in good hands. I don't know how Alice manages to hide her real feelings and put on that cheerful smile. She just gets on with it, throws herself into whatever needs doing, whether it's cleaning windows, preparing Mum's pitiful bland meals or keeping her spirits up by sitting with her for hours while Timmy's at school. And Mum is amazingly controlled, dignified, accepting. If it was me, if I knew I'd be dead in a few months, no way could I stay so calm. I'd be fighting against it, scared witless, railing against fate.

Alice couldn't bear to read any more. Nearly four years had passed since Mum's death and the pain of losing her had diminished, but now she was about to lose her sister as well. And no amount of railing against fate would help.

*

She woke with a start from a dream, a nightmare. She could feel her heart thumping in her chest. Terror, and then the relief of dawning reality: the feel of the cotton sheets, the slightly saggy mattress; the glass of water on the bedside table; the faint sound of Timmy's breathing in the bed close to hers. He was asleep; safe. Still the dream remained with her, vivid and ominous. They were in some foreign bus station, she and a much younger Timmy. It was vast, chaotic, packed with people rushing about or sitting amongst piles of luggage. Then, all of a sudden, Timmy was gone. She was frantic, stumbling over suitcases and people

181

as she searched and begged for help. The faces were blank, indifferent: no one had seen a small boy. Then an older woman in a black *burqa* came up to her. 'He'll be alright, he's being cared for,' she said. Alice seized her by the shoulders. 'Give me back my son!' she screamed. Lying in her narrow bed, Alice could still see the woman's cold smile.

She sat up and drank some water, willing the morning with its reassuring routines to come soon. No ribbon of daylight peeked from under the door but that meant nothing: the sky never lightened before eight. Timmy stirred in his sleep – a soft sigh and a rustling of the bedclothes – but from his breathing she could tell he had not woken. Alice lay on her back, focusing on concrete plans for the day: cleaning the house, shopping for Paco's return, giving Timmy a few sums to do or listening to him read.

She must have drifted off to sleep eventually because she was aware now of sunlight streaming in through open shutters and Timmy's bed empty, the duvet thrown back. He was sitting at the kitchen table, still in his pyjamas with a bowl of breakfast cereal and a glass of milk.

'What day is it?' he asked. 'Is it Easter yet?'

'It's Monday. Why?'

'I haven't had any Easter eggs.'

'I don't think they have them in Spain,' Alice said, bending to plant a kiss on his head. He needed a haircut too. 'You'll have to wait till we get home.'

The dream came back to her as she stood soaping herself in the shower and she was gripped again by that sense of panic, of desperation at finding Timmy gone. She let the hot water run over her body, warming her right through, driving out the fear. Was it too early to ring Ginny? She needed to hear her friend's calm, down-to-earth English voice even if she couldn't tell her the whole story.

It was ridiculous to get so wound up over a dream, she told herself, but it didn't help. So she shut herself in Paco's study where Timmy wouldn't see her tears. Ginny took a long time to answer but just as the recorded message was starting, her sleepy hello cut in.

'Oh Ginny, I'm so glad you're there. I hope I didn't wake you.'

'It doesn't matter. You sound upset. Your sister, is she…?'

'There's not much hope for Deb but she's still alive, still in a coma. The thing is, it could go on for weeks or months; we've no way of knowing. So I'm coming back on Sunday. Timmy has already missed too much school and I need to get back to work.'

'It must be hellish for you, just waiting.'

A sob rose in Alice's throat. She tried to stifle it but her usual self-control had deserted her. 'Yes, I'm finding it very difficult here, very lonely. I can't wait to be home.' She blew her nose. 'Sorry about this. I think I've been holding everything in for too long.'

'I don't know how you've coped. Having to stay in one piece for Timmy as well, and keep him occupied...'

'He'll be glad to get home too. What we both need is a strong dose of normality. Just the boring routines of work, school, going to the supermarket on a Saturday morning, taking Timmy to football practice. You don't know how I long for them. And my piano; I miss my piano.'

'I can imagine. Well, ring me the minute you're back. I've missed you.'

It was only a month. Unbelievable, it felt like fucking years. Mark was reading the paper in Bar Aixa. According to El País, there were forty-six *víctimas* of 11-M still in hospital but fourteen of the injured had already died. Mum could be the next – or the last. He didn't know which would be worse.

If Mum died, who else was there? His dad had gone back to London; Alice and Timmy were leaving next weekend. That was it: that was all his family. He was practically an orphan. A memory from way back popped into his brain: Mum going ballistic, ranting on at Hassan because she'd read somewhere that in some Arab countries an orphan was a kid whose dad had died. 'So the mother doesn't count? But that's outrageous! I've never heard anything so idiotic!' Like it was Hassan's fault. She'd gone on about it for hours – even after he stomped off in a mood.

Mark thought about Paco, who'd been pretty much like a dad to him. Paco had three kids of his own. He'd never talked about them, not at first. It was Mum who told him – but only ages after Paco moved in. He'd been fucking amazed. Three kids! She said that was why he was sad sometimes. His ex wouldn't let him see them. There was a boy called Juan, a couple of years older than Mark, and two girls. No one had asked the kids if they wanted to see their dad. He knew that because Juan had told him. He said he'd managed to sneak out and see Paco a few times but his sisters were too young. It was different now; their mum couldn't stop them any more. Juan said the girls were mad with her: she'd told them a load of lies about Paco.

The three of them came up to the house sometimes, not always together. Mark got on fine with them though Juan said they used to hate him – for having *stolen* their dad (that's how they thought of it, which wasn't exactly fair). Cristina, the older girl was nearly his age. She had masses of dark curly hair that came halfway down her back, and great legs. She wore these very short skirts with high boots, dead sexy. Too bad she had a boyfriend. If they ever split up, he'd be in there like a shot.

He finished his coffee, folded the newspaper and passed it back to Manolo behind the bar. No one asked him any more about Mum. You couldn't blame them: the answer was always the same so what was the point? Instead, they gave him these long sad looks, so he knew they hadn't forgotten.

Alice stood on a chair and reached up with the brush to disperse the fine threads of gossamer that stretched from one ceiling beam to the next, clinging to corners and crevices, sticking to her hand whenever she touched them. She'd already cleaned the kitchen and both bathrooms while Timmy tackled the three pages of sums she'd set him. Deb had never understood the satisfaction it gave her to transform a grubby object or room to sparkling cleanliness. Getting stuck into practical tasks invariably soothed her, stilled her mind – with the added benefit of achieving something useful. Her dream had faded and she saw it now for what it was: just a dream, a reflection of her irrational fears rather than a premonition.

The floor was next. As she mopped, her mind slipped back to the conversation with Monika – in particular what she had said about Hassan. At the time, she had paid attention to only that one word 'acquitted', which meant he was out of prison, loose. But Monika had said more. She had spoken about a dilemma facing Deborah, about her speaking up for Hassan, presumably in court. Alice remembered no more; her alarm had blanked out all the rest. Could it be true that Deb had actually defended Hassan? Got him out of jail even? She couldn't imagine what would have induced her sister to help him. Deb hated her ex-lover. She dredged her memory for Monika's exact words. Hadn't she implied that Paco persuaded her? Alice twirled the mop, pressing down on it, squeezing every last drop of dirty water out through the holes and back into the bucket. Deb should have told her. But she would find out, one way or another. She had a right to know. When Paco arrived later today, she would ask him directly.

*

The minute she caught sight of him walking across the patio, tote bag slung over his shoulder, she knew there was no possibility of interrogating him. Not today and maybe not ever. His gait was like that of an old man – weary, sapped of all energy. He moved slowly, head down, shoulders bowed. She ran out to greet him and they embraced. He had lost weight. She could see it in his face, the flesh of his jowls hanging loosely, and as they held each other she was shocked by how insubstantial his body felt compared to before.

'So, I am back,' he said. 'And you are still here, holding the fort – isn't that what you say?'

'That's right,' she said, feeling once again that she was betraying him, betraying Deb by having booked their flights home. 'You look exhausted. Come inside and sit down. Would you like tea? An infusion of camomile? If you're hungry, I've made a stew with pork and beans…'

'A glass of camomile would be perfect,' he said. 'Later I might eat some of your stew. But tell me, how are you and Timmy? And have you seen Mark? I'm afraid I have neglected him.'

'We're all alright, coping as best we can. Mark has been here a few times, though he doesn't say much. I think he prefers Timmy's company. And Charlie came over for a couple of days, for what that's worth. It would help if he'd make some effort to understand his son instead of criticising. Poor Mark, he gets a raw deal.'

'I must go and see the boy as soon as possible – maybe this evening.'

'But Paco, first you should rest. And eat something.'

'*Bueno*, perhaps you are right.' He flopped down on the sofa and gave a long sigh. '*Ay* Alice, your sister has not improved although sometimes I think so – when her eyes open or she moves. The doctor tells me she is in a "persistent vegetative state." That is the term they use. You see, this can go on for many months and still there is the possibility of recovery. Only after a year… When twelve months have passed they consider it a "permanent vegetative state." And then…' He fell silent, unable or unwilling to continue.

As Alice waited for the water to boil, it came to her that she still had time to visit Deb once more, a last chance, perhaps, to say goodbye. Not just goodbye. There were other important words to be said: sorry and I forgive you; thank you and I love you. She needed to voice these sentiments. Next time might be too late. If she caught the plane from Granada, she could easily get there and back in one day. Paco was here to take care of Timmy… By the time she had poured the tea, her mind was made up. She would go on Friday.

'Paco, your *manzanilla*.' She held out the glass to him.

'Put it down on the table.' He patted the space next to him on the sofa. 'Come, sit with me for a minute.' His arm was resting along the back of the sofa and as she sat down, he moved it to encircle her shoulder. 'Sometimes I think touch is the most important of our senses,' he said. 'The loving touch of another human being. Without it…'

She turned towards him and compassion made her respond in a way she would never have dreamed of had she stopped to consider. She was responding to his need but also, she realised with surprise, to her own. Afterwards she could not remember how it happened that all of a sudden their bodies were locked together in a feverish embrace, their lips and tongues frantic.

'Timmy!' Alice pushed Paco away and shot to her feet. 'He might come in at any moment. This is crazy, we must stop!'

'Ay, I had forgotten.' He was breathing heavily, staring up at her with a fixed gaze. She looked away as he reached inside his trousers to rearrange himself. 'You are right. But I am thinking… Of course you can tell me no, *por supuesto*… Alice, I would like to sleep with you tonight. Just one night. It will change nothing, only give us both a little comfort, a little human warmth. Think about it. Only if you are sure.' He picked up his glass of camomile. 'You tell me later.'

Chapter Sixteen

Mark came to out of a long straggly dream that had Mum in it. She was going frantic trying to find something in her study, which was a tip as always. Piles of paper and books kept slapping and thudding onto the floor. His job was to pick them up and shove them back on the shelf. He was thinking how hopeless she was, that she ought to get organised. When he told her, she said not to be so boring.

He opened his eyes. There was enough light coming through the crack to see the shapes of things. He reached for his mobile and checked the time: 10.04. Mum was already fading away like dreams always did – the good ones more than the bad, which was fucking annoying. Closing his eyes again, he tried to conjure up her face but it was just an out-of-focus blur, shifting all the time so he couldn't catch hold of it. Same with her voice – he couldn't hear it any more, it came out totally wrong. He grabbed his trousers and stuck the phone in his pocket before heading out for a piss. Mum had bought him these trousers just a few weeks ago. They had about ten pockets. She'd been nice to him that day; he must have done something right for once.

His phone sprang into life with a message beep. It was from Paco. *See you Casa Pasteles at 11 for breakfast.* He must be back from Madrid, maybe with news about Mum. Good news, bad news, any fucking news would make a change.

Paco was sitting at a table in the corner smoking when Mark got there. His face was grey and pasty, like he hadn't seen the sun for weeks. He stood up when he saw Mark. The look in his eyes was kind of shifty so Mark knew it wasn't going to be good news.

'I'll go and order,' he said. '*¿Café y tostada?*'

Mark nodded and sat down. Waiting at the bar, Paco kept hitching up his trousers but they'd just slip down again like they were a size too big. The place was quieter than usual. There wasn't much space at the counter but only two of the tables were taken. A couple of oldish women with flabby arms and thin orange hair sprouting out of their heads were sitting at the next one talking loudly about their husbands. One of them said hers went crazy if he found a bone in his fish, he said it was her job to take them all out; the other said she had to cut up her husband's meat like you would for a child. Then they started on about a neighbour with a black eye. She claimed she'd walked into a door but they blamed it on her ex-boyfriend. He wished they'd shut the fuck up.

Paco stubbed out his ciggy in the ashtray and took a couple more out of the pack, passing one to Mark. 'I'd like to bring you good news,' he said as he held out the lighter, 'But unfortunately... Well, her condition hasn't changed.'

Mark wondered what he thought about, sitting there by her bed hour after hour? How could he stand it?

'Thirty-four days.'

'Yeah?' Why even bother to count? The two women were getting ready to go, scraping their chairs across the floor and gathering up their plastic bags of shopping.

'As you know,' Paco went on, 'Alice and Timmy are leaving at the weekend. So, if you'd like to move back in for a while...'

'No way. I'm okay where I am.'

'Think about it Mark. I know you're fine in the cave but a house is more comfortable.' He took a deep drag and turned away to blow out the smoke. 'The truth is I could do with some company. And your mother would be pleased if she knew.'

If she knew? He had to be kidding. 'Well she isn't going to know, is she?'

'Who can tell? I talk to her. Maybe she hears something of what I say. In any case it makes me feel better.'

The waiter came with their coffee and toast. Paco wasn't eating. All he had in front of him was black coffee and a *chupito* of some liquor. 'The day before she left for Madrid, we had an argument,' he said in a kind of choked up voice.

Paco too? Talk about shit timing. Considering Paco and Mum hardly ever had rows. He knew how to handle her. When she blew her top with him, he had this way of calming her down. Sometimes he just smiled and pulled her towards him – gently like he wanted to kiss her even though she was bawling him out. He'd even seen Paco laugh at her when she was angry – and get away with it. Fucking amazing to watch. Before you knew it, she'd be laughing too, laughing at herself. So it was unbelievable that just that day...

'What was it about?'

'She wanted us to spend *Semana Santa* outside Granada, go to the Alpujarra or some other quiet place away from the crowds and processions. But I'd promised my nieces in Almería they could come to stay. They get on well with Cristina and Bea. I should have discussed it with Deborah first. I was in the wrong... But you know, my girls were so looking forward to seeing their cousins, they had all kinds of plans...'

'Yeah well...' Mark didn't know what to say. It was all fucking irrelevant in the end. Like him fighting with Mum over the forty euros. How could you know? You couldn't think every time you were pissed off with someone or got into an argument, what if they get blown up the next day?

'We were still angry with each other when we went to bed. And then the next morning when she left for Madrid, it was such a rush, I didn't have a chance to apologise. I tried to call her that evening, the evening before the...but her phone was switched off.' Paco looked like he was about to burst into tears. 'So now, when it's too late, I tell her I'm sorry and hope she hears me.'

Mark picked up his toast and took a big bite out of it in case Paco was expecting him to answer. The oil was dribbling down his fingers and no bloody *servilletas* on the table. He got up and fetched some from the counter. Just when he'd managed to almost forget his fight with Mum, Paco had to go and remind him. Though bizarrely, it helped in a way, knowing Paco was in the same boat.

'Maybe she *can* hear,' he said – not because he believed it but because he felt sorry for Paco, sitting there looking miserable as a duck in a drought. The irony of it suddenly hit him, the irony of Paco and him both feeling shit for what they'd said all those weeks ago, giving themselves hell over it when in reality Mum's brain was so shot to pieces she wasn't going to remember any of it even if she could hear.

Paco knocked back his *chupito* and said, 'We must keep it in mind that Deborah is a fighter. She won't give up easily.'

He did have a point. If anyone could cheat death it would be Mum. She'd told him once she was like a cat with nine lives, she'd had so many lucky escapes. Like when she was seventeen and her boyfriend smashed into a tree on his motor-bike with her on the back and she just walked away while he broke every bone in his body. Another time she was swimming in the sea and the current pulled her under. Lots of people had drowned off that beach and she saw her life flashing by. Next thing she knew, she was lying on the sand with a crowd of people standing around her. Someone had pulled her out just in time. The only thing was, she might have already used up her nine lives. Even cats didn't get ten chances.

Paco stood up and pulled a handful of change out of his pocket. 'I have to go,' he said. 'My sister in Guadix has invited me for lunch. You'll think about my suggestion, won't you?'

'What suggestion?' Then he remembered. 'You mean about moving into the *carmen*? Yeah okay, I'll think about it.'

He thought about it for all of five seconds after Paco had gone. No way was he going to risk losing his cave. If he left, that Dutch guy with the trumpet would be in there like a shot. Him or someone else.

When Alice woke in the early hours, Paco had his back to her, though her last conscious memory was of his warm body clasping her from behind, his hand lightly resting on her breast. From his breathing she could tell he was deeply asleep. The unfamiliar intimacy of waking with a man after more than ten years alone felt surprisingly natural.

They had undressed in the dark and climbed into bed from opposite sides like a long-married couple. No grand seduction, no passion, none of the urgency of their earlier encounter. In the intervening time, they had both, she assumed, been reflecting: weighing up the meaning of their actions. Nothing would change, Paco had promised. And she understood. It meant no more than the fulfilment of a mutual need for consolation in the bleak landscape of loss that each of them inhabited. It would not be repeated.

He was gentle with her, taking his time, making sure she was ready for him. They were both aware of what they were doing; the boundaries. For her and also, she thought, for Paco, the comfort of being held and caressed was more important than the act itself. After he came, his hot flesh lying heavy on hers, his face buried in her hair, she felt the wetness of tears on her neck.

He lifted his head. 'There is nothing wrong with making each other feel good,' he said. 'Deborah would have understood.'

She continued to stroke the smooth skin of his back, and a moment later he asked, 'You don't regret it?'

'No,' she said. 'I expected to feel guilty but actually I don't.'

Sleep had come easily, with no dreams that she could recall; certainly no nightmares.

Now she slipped out of bed and tiptoed back to her room in case Timmy should wake early and come looking for her. She lay in the dark, the covers pulled loosely over her. She thought with disbelief: *I slept with my sister's partner while she lay dying.* It sounded terrible – others would judge it as the most appalling betrayal. Yet to her it did not feel like that. Her sister's partner but she felt no shame. Who would understand that what bound them was their grief, their love for Deborah? Superficial judgements, she realised, were so often wrong, yet she had been as guilty as anyone else of judging people without knowing the full facts.

*

Once again Alice was alone in the house. Paco had gone to his sister's for the day; the boys were at *Abracadabra*, a magic show they'd seen advertised in town. The last volume of the diary lay open in front of her: four years of Deb's life still to be read.

25th April 2000

Mark is fascinated by the 'hippies' who live in the Sacromonte caves. I wish he would study more instead of spending all his time up there or shutting himself in his bedroom playing the guitar. His teachers say he is intelligent but wastes his talents. He says school is boring, he is sick of learning by rote, it's all irrelevant. Soon he will have his final exams of the ESO and I fear he will fail. He did well in the first stage two years ago but at fourteen he was happy to study... Last night he told me he doesn't want to do his *bachillerato*, he's had enough of education. So what will you do, I asked him. He has no idea. In desperation, I threatened to talk to his father – a bad mistake because I know Charlie will be furious and blame me. As if I could force Mark to study.

22nd July 2000

Charlie is coming over to talk to his son. He wants to know why Mark failed in three subjects and persuade him either to retake them or – ultimate threat – go and study in London. I suspect Mark will tell him to fuck off and Charlie will do just that, threatening not to give him another penny – as if he was ever generous.

28th July 2000

It happened exactly as I predicted. Including the lecture I had to endure about having allowed Mark to 'run wild'. Paco says perhaps he needs time out and if left to himself, will resume his studies later. Maybe, but in the meantime Mark takes it for granted that I will provide for all his needs, including beer and tobacco, while he loafs in bed till lunchtime and then hangs out in the street with his equally idle friends.

24th November 2000

Two months since Mum died and I still think about her every day. At the moment I can only see her as she was in her last year, faded and feeble. How would I like to remember her? Sitting on the bed with Alice curled up on one side of her, me on the other, for our nightly bedtime story. On seaside holidays, in her flowery one-piece swimming costume, laughing as, hand-in-hand, we jumped the waves. Holding her new-born first grandchild with a look of absolute awe on her face. I should have appreciated her more. I wasn't the sweetest of daughters. Ever.

And if Monika was right, Mark hadn't always been the sweetest of sons to Deborah. Alice wondered how much that was weighing on his mind now. She wondered too, not for the first time, whether Timmy would become less sweet once he reached adolescence. Even the most perfect parents were not always appreciated by their children. Would she be able to handle the changes in store? A long-ago conversation with Andy came to mind. Teenage boys need a father figure, he had said, thinking of his own sons, who lived with their mother. At the time she had agreed.

The number of '*immigrantes*' is multiplying. Half the shops are being taken over by Moroccans. This is what people are muttering – or in some cases complaining loudly about. They sell teapots and glasses along with small packets of tea, spicy or fragrant; camel-skin lamps, pointed leather slippers dyed bright yellow, red or purple, baggy tops and trousers; and the tourists flock to them. Meanwhile, the other immigrants – those from England, France, Germany and Japan – have also multiplied these last few years but no one complains about them. Unlike the *maghrebis* who are here from economic necessity, the '*guiris*' have come for sunshine and simpler ways, just as I did aeons ago. No one hassles or abuses them. Nor does anyone claim – as one of Paco's university colleagues did about the '*moros*' – that they are being paid by the Saudis to reproduce, with the aim of eventually outnumbering the 'authentic' *granadinos*. Who is it that invents these lies and lets them loose so they can spread like malignant cells through the population?

Alice and Timmy are here and it makes me so happy to see the two boys playing together. Ten years between them but my fears that Mark would scorn a younger child (as I scorned Alice at times) proved groundless. I suspect Mark enjoys being looked up to. And Timmy is really quite adorable. He is grown up for his age, a little on the serious side like most only children (including Mark at that age), but given the right encouragement, his normal six year-old sense of fun spills out and several times I've heard shrieks of laughter from the patio where he and Mark are playing.

With me he is affectionate – once he loses his initial shyness, which can take a couple of hours or a couple of days. Alice observed that I couldn't take my eyes off him. She's right. I study him as if learning him by heart. I love looking at him, despite certain resemblances... Physically he and Mark are thoroughly different. Both take more after their fathers in appearance – though not, thank God, in character.

Suddenly a breakthrough with the *mezquita*. The Emir of Sharjah came to visit Granada and has promised his support. Meaning – we presume – the money to finish building it. The work has been paralysed for so long, we are all very excited. Now when I walk past the site, I'll see activity, development, new additions to the half-built shell. Already I look at it and imagine the prayer hall full of people, the minaret standing proud, the garden planted with fruit trees and fountains. The vision is so pleasing I'm tempted to become a Muslim myself. Not seriously of course. I don't need imams or priests to tell me how to live, and if God exists, it won't be in any form devised by men.

Alice was reminded of that man from the mosque (Mohammed? Mustafa?) who had come to see her during her first week here. Thinking about that encounter, a forgotten fragment of their conversation came back to her. Something about resisting the temptation of revenge... about Deb overcoming her antipathy and doing 'the right thing'. He must surely have been referring to Hassan, to her defence of him. At the time, his words had meant nothing to her. Now they tied in with what Monika had said. And also...she had a vague memory of Paco saying something similar, admiring her 'bravery'. Neither of them had mentioned Hassan by name so she simply hadn't made the connection. What struck her now was that all three of them – Monika, Paco, the man from the mosque – seemed to admire Deb for having helped Hassan.

Alice sat there with the diary open on her knee, thinking. Trying to put herself in her sister's position; imagining Deb's struggle with her conscience; wondering if *she* would have done the same thing. And concluding that probably she wouldn't.

Monika had been sending him messages: *Have you started drawing yet? I hope I didn't waste my money on those pencils.* Stuff like that. So he didn't have a lot of choice. The idea had come to him last night, to draw the *abadía* from above. Mark stood looking down at it now from the top of a grassy slope dotted with olive trees. You could see all the angles of the intersecting roofs, the bell tower of the church and then the abbey part on the right with its totally caved-in roof. He tried to picture it with flames licking up into the night sky. He'd have liked to see that but it was years ago, before they'd come to Granada. Half the roof tiles had just melted away and other bits were blackened and burnt. Through the window bars he could see piles of rubble from walls that must have collapsed in the fire. Everything had just been left. He wasn't going to paint that side; it was a mess.

Now he'd made the effort to climb up here, he couldn't wait to get going but it had to be the right spot. He mooched about till he found a good place and sat down on the grass for a smoke while he took in the view. Over to the left, he could see the peaks of the Sierra Nevada: Mulhacén, Alcazaba, Veleta, still thick in snow. Across the valley straight in front of him, the hills were in shadow, black as death. It was weird because his side was in bright sunshine. No one would choose to live over there, which could explain why there were hardly any caves that side. He opened up his sketchpad and picked out a pencil to start with.

His first attempt was crap. He screwed up the paper and began again on a new sheet, hoping he hadn't lost the knack. He wanted to get it right so Monika would be impressed. He thought about her idea that he should go to art school. It wouldn't be like secondary, having to learn a load of facts and do exams every week. Maybe you could just paint and draw all day and they'd teach you techniques and stuff. But he doubted if they'd have him. You probably needed to do the *selectividad* exam to get in, like for university. If it meant he had to study at college for two years first, no way.

He stopped for a break and a smoke and looked at the rough outline he'd done. It was working out better this time. He felt chilled alone here with no one to bother him and the only sounds the wind in the trees, the birds calling to each other and now some church bells in the distance, faint so they didn't get on his nerves but were kind of soothing. In nature, you could forget the ugly things for a while.

Also, drawing made him feel good; it always had. He'd tried to explain it to Mum once but she didn't get it. She said Alice was the arty-crafty one. Alice liked making things. She knitted sweaters for herself and Timmy and she always sent home-made Christmas and birthday cards. Once she'd made him a scarf, purple and green and black. She said it would keep him warm in the freezing Granada winter. He'd worn it loads but then he lent it to a girl he liked and that was the last he saw of it – or her. She was from somewhere up north and she'd expected Granada to be warm.

It was late when the boys returned but Alice had been absorbed in Deborah's writings and scarcely noticed the time.

'The show was brill, Mummy. He did this trick with a rabbit and…' Timmy went off into a long, detailed description of each act as Alice prepared their supper. She realised how long it was since she'd seen him animated, the corners of his mouth turned up in a smile instead of drooping. She put the plate of aubergine fritters, a bowl of salad and some bread on the table and the three of them sat down together to eat. A normal family sharing their evening meal – or so it would look to an outsider. For a short while Alice could almost believe it herself. Until her eyes fell on the empty chair and the illusion was abruptly shattered.

Once Mark had left, Alice could tell from the way Timmy lolled on the sofa that the afternoon's excitement had taken its toll. For once the word 'bedtime' seemed to come as a relief to him. Within seconds of her goodnight kiss, he was sound asleep and Alice was back with the diary.

12th September 2001

I didn't know a thing about it till Paco phoned from the conference. I was deeply immersed in the 11th century and couldn't make any sense of what he was saying. A plane, two planes…? Blazing towers in New York? Turn on the TV, he kept repeating. So I did. And found myself mesmerised by the endlessly replayed images of planes flying into skyscrapers, smoke, rubble, panic, figures falling, figures running… It was surreal, like watching a disaster movie. I had to remind myself these were real people, not actors. Paco came home and we watched together, shocked into silence, as the full horror emerged.

Later we talked. 'The Americans thought they could screw the rest of the world and get away with it,' Paco said. 'This is the result of their arrogance.' He's right but, as always, it's the innocent who suffer. The world is instantly a much more dangerous place – because the story doesn't end here. There will be revenge on a terrible scale. I am filled with dread for the future. The cycle will go on and on – possibly for generations. I fear for Mark and Timmy. Mark seems more excited than afraid. He doesn't understand the implications. Even in Granada the effects will be felt, I told him but he just looked at me with an expression of disbelief.

Alice had been at work – though once the news filtered through, work was abandoned as they all crowded around a small radio Steve kept in his desk drawer to listen to the cricket scores. Imagining those poor souls consumed by fire or jumping to their deaths, she had felt physically sick. Her colleague Martin had a brother in New York and was desperately trying to make contact. At the time they'd been talking of up to ten thousand dead. In the end it hadn't been quite so bad, but then there was Afghanistan and Iraq – the wars that led to countless more deaths. The wars and then another round of revenge. Deb had predicted a more dangerous world and feared for the boys but, ironically, she had been the one to fall victim. On that day in 2001, the terror on the News had seemed remote; nothing to do with real life. Timmy, who was only seven at the time, thought it was an action film that held her glued to the set all evening.

This time there was no escaping reality. The terror had penetrated her, become part of her. A feeling of menace seemed to linger in the air, vague but ominous. What had happened to Deborah, her fear of running into Hassan, the uncertain future – it was impossible to separate the different elements.

Turning back to her sister's diary, there were several pages about the aftermath of 9/11. She and Paco had taken part in demonstrations against the invasion of Afghanistan and also some protest at the local office of a national paper, which had implied there were al-Qaeda cells in Granada. According to Deb, it was a cynical attempt to plant suspicion in the community. She sounded furious.

It's sick – as if there isn't enough prejudice already. How could a responsible paper like El País stoop so low?

Alice wasn't entirely surprised to find Deborah half-believing some of the conspiracy theories starting to circulate: the Jews who hadn't turned up to work that day, the idea that Bush and his cronies were behind it all, a general distrust of the facts.

There's no doubt we are being manipulated, she wrote. But how can we know what to believe? Where does the cynicism end? Is everything a lie?

21st October 2001

With the protests growing (the revulsion at so many civilian deaths, the failure to capture Bin Laden, the sheer pointlessness of it all), a new reason for the Afghanistan war has been manufactured. One that cannot fail to hook western women and liberals in particular: the fanatic Taliban, those evil chauvinists who prevent girls going to school and women working or even leaving the house without male protection; who force them to cover their faces and bodies; who deny them all rights. Now people are confused: is the war a revenge attack for September 11th? A way of protecting the citizens of the US? An attempt to 'get' Bin Laden and bring him to trial? Or is the purpose of the war to oust the Taliban and secure human rights for Afghani women and girls?

It's a clever ploy. How can anyone not wish to bring down such a brutal regime? (Never mind that Saudi Arabia is equally oppressive – they are our friends, they buy our arms and sell us their oil.) Who in the West has read the Qur'an? Islam is now seen as a religion that decrees the oppression of women and therefore a religion to be fought against by all decent, self-respecting folk. There is NOTHING in the Qur'an to say that women should not be educated or allowed to work. Like Christianity, Islam has been subverted by men, interpreted to suit their own agenda.

22nd October 2001

Why didn't I see it before, the links with my own research? Paco says it's so topical, I should write a book on women in *al-Andalus*, aimed at the popular rather than the academic market. It's a brilliant idea, something to counteract the deliberate misinformation being spread about Islam as a religion. That's if I can find a publisher open-minded and brave enough to go against the current… Walladah could have her day; she could become famous again – proof that in a Muslim society a woman can stand up for herself. She would be the focus but I'd include all the others too, all those with power and influence. I'm already thinking of titles. 'Liberated Women in the Spain of the Moors' or 'Fit for High Positions: Walladah and other strong women in Muslim Spain'.

Alice remembered Deb prattling on with typical enthusiasm about this 'brilliant new idea'. It wasn't a good time – she'd been reading Timmy his bedtime story when the phone rang – but Deb was oblivious to her repeated attempts to cut short the conversation. Well, to her sister's credit, the brilliant idea was now a real book, soon to come out in print. Somewhere in Deb's study, the final proofs must exist. Even if no printed copy came to light, it shouldn't be difficult to find the document on the computer. She wondered what title Deb had settled for in the end.

Paco had not yet returned and the house was in darkness. Alice closed the shutters and switched on some lights before entering the study. There were several towers of paper and folders on the desk. Most she had scarcely looked at. She chose one at random and started rifling through it but found nothing of interest. The second pile toppled the moment she touched it, littering the desk and floor with an unruly mess of scribbled or printed sheets, the odd photo, drawing, chocolate wrapper and even a flattened cigarette packet.

At her feet were a couple of photos, partly covered by a green folder. She picked them up and found herself face to face with Hassan. In one, he was sitting at an outdoor café table, smiling as he held up a glass of beer (though funnily enough, he had always claimed he didn't drink). The other photo was taken from fairly close up and included Deb. He had his arm around her and they looked happy, perhaps newly in love. Hassan was dressed identically in the two pictures, which suggested they'd been taken the same day.

Alice laid them on the desk and gazed at Timmy's father with a kind of queasy fascination. He was good-looking, she couldn't deny it: high cheekbones, those hypnotic brown eyes, a sensuous mouth with full lips. His teeth were visible when he smiled and she remembered having secretly admired their gleaming whiteness and regularity. He would be much older now of course. These pictures probably dated back fifteen years. He must be around fifty like herself; possibly going grey. All the same, she had no doubt she would recognise him instantly.

'Who's that, Mummy?'

Alice instinctively slapped the photos face down before turning to Timmy. She had no idea how long he'd been standing there behind her; long enough, obviously.

'What are you doing here? You should be asleep,' she said, unable to keep her voice from rising.

She saw Timmy's eyes fill. 'I had a bad dream. An alien with a massive head was trying to get me and my legs wouldn't move to run away. He shouted and then I woke up.' In his slightly too small jungle pyjamas, his bare feet pale on the reddish tiles, Timmy looked forlorn. 'Don't be cross with me.'

'I'm sorry darling.' She scooped him up onto her lap and hugged him close. 'It's alright, I just didn't hear you come in and it gave me a fright.'

'Did you think it was a burglar?'

'Yes, I thought it might be.'

'I want to see the photos,' he said, wriggling out of her grasp and reaching forward to where they lay on the desk. He turned them over and stared at them.

Helplessly, Alice sat waiting while he studied the pictures of his father. Her forehead and armpits were clammy; she thought she might be sick.

'That's Auntie Deborah,' he said. 'But I don't know who the man is.'

Alice wiped the sweat from her forehead with a tissue. How did a child's mind work? Could he guess? Did Timmy spend long enough in front of a mirror to spot the likeness?

'It's an old boyfriend of your auntie's – from a long time ago, before she met Uncle Paco.'

Timmy ran his finger over Hassan's face in the photo. 'He looks nice.'

She realised she'd been holding her breath. 'He was alright,' she said, 'But Uncle Paco is much nicer.'

Chapter Seventeen

Ed was outside somewhere. Mark could hear him, shouting and cursing in the dark, smashed out of his head as usual. Then a yelp and a thud – sounded like he'd hit the ground hard. Good, he could fucking stay there all night. If he'd broken a leg or an arm or his head, serve him right. Mark turned over in bed and tried to go back to sleep but Ed was moaning and groaning like he was bloody dying. Selfish bastard, waking everyone up.

He thought of that time he and Mum had passed this old guy lying in the street, out cold with an empty bottle rolling around just by him. You could smell the booze on his breath from way off. It was the middle of winter and he didn't even have a coat, just a thin jumper. Mum said he'd freeze to death by morning. When they got home, she fetched a blanket out of the cupboard and they walked all the way back to the Realejo and covered him up. She'd probably saved the man's life.

'Why don't you shut the fuck up?' Soon as he'd shouted, he knew it was a mistake. He wouldn't have, only remembering what Mum did to help that old drunk was making him feel guilty. Suppose Ed died. On the other hand, why should he care? He hated Ed. Mum would hate Ed too if she knew the kind of things he'd said about her. His life wasn't worth saving.

After about half an hour, it went quiet. Stupid bastard must have passed out. Good. Now they might all be able to get some sleep. He couldn't sleep though. Too many thoughts were crowding into his head; it was like a fucking invasion. Thoughts and also people: a procession of them stalking him. He didn't know where they'd come from. Some of them were from way back, some he'd rather forget – like that priest with a bald head and big belly who said he should pray for his mum because she was on the road to hell, living in sin with a *musulmán*. Tina barged in with an annoying grin on her face and then another of his exes, Anabel, showed up, together with that *cabrón* from Galicia she shacked up with after.

He started thinking again about Paco's idea that he should move back into the *carmen*. It was a crap idea. He'd be surrounded by all Mum's stuff – her red sandals and ancient straw hat, that big tub of aloe vera skin cream on the bathroom shelf, the yellow rubber gloves she always wore to wash up... It would be creepy having her gear staring him in the face the whole time; like living with her ghost. That could explain why Paco preferred to stick around at the hospital. And also why Alice was going a bit nuts, which was fucking obvious despite her trying to hide it. Her lips must be sore as hell, the way she kept biting them, and her eyes reminded him of a frightened rabbit's.

He was bloody lucky to have the cave. Some people in the Albaicín reckoned you went barmy if you spent more than a couple of years up here but it was a lie. He was living proof and so were Pierre and Fabio and José. Fabio had been hanging out in Sacromonte for seven years at least and there was nothing wrong with him. You got used to it.

He'd never understood why Mum tried to talk him out of leaving home. You'd have thought she'd be over the fucking moon seeing as just about everything he did was wrong in her eyes. They were always at war. It was like she'd find any excuse to get at him or knock his friends. It pissed him off; she should have shown more respect. But what really blew it was that time he invited some of his mates round for a bit of a *fiesta* while she and Paco were away. She totally lost her rag the minute she walked in the door, claiming they'd trashed the place even though he'd spent hours clearing up and the only things broken were a couple of glasses and an old chair. Then she started on about how they'd helped themselves to her food and booze and fags – as if she was too skint to buy more. That did it for him. He had to bloody get out.

Sharing the cave with Mani had been okay at first. They'd got on fine till he brought back that *chica* with the huge tits and irritating laugh and he had to listen to them shagging every night. He was well happy when the two of them moved out. Once he had the place to himself, he could get it straight. Even Mum admitted it wasn't bad, which was about the best he could hope for from her. She even bought him a new mattress to sleep on instead of the lumpy stained one Hugo had left. He was lying on it now but the fucking thing wouldn't let him sleep. He turned over and thought how nice it would be if he could reach out and find not empty space but a warm body, a girl he could nuzzle up to and fondle. Fat chance of that.

'Paco, come and eat. I've grilled some fish.' He was staring at the computer screen as he had been all morning, shoulders hunched, face tense with concentration. Alice counted nine butts in the ceramic ashtray on his desk; the room stank. She hovered at the door, trying not to show her disgust. 'You'll waste away at this rate.'

'I don't understand what you say but yes, one moment and then I come.'

Over lunch he told her of half a dozen 'miracle cases' he'd found on the internet where patients in a persistent vegetative state had suddenly risen from their beds after being almost written off for dead. Alice listened in silence. What could she say? The more his face brightened with deluded hope the sadder she felt. A quick death would have been easier, kinder to them all. In a couple of days she would see her sister – possibly for the last time. She was dreading it, unsure where she would find the strength. The constant tension of the last few weeks had drained her hollow. Like Timmy, all she wanted now was to be home in England. Four more days.

'Do you think Trixie will still remember us?' Timmy had finished eating and was playing about with the fish skeleton on his plate.

'Of course she will. Cats don't forget.' A month – it was nothing in normal circumstances but if to her this month had felt like a year, to Timmy it must have seemed an eternity.

'The cats here climb on the bins and eat rubbish,' he said.

Paco smiled at him. 'There are many cats living wild in the Albaicín. They must forage for food where they can.'

'Our cat's a tabby,' Timmy told him.

Alice left Timmy to explain the meaning of 'tabby' while she cleared the table.

By the time she'd finished in the kitchen, the house was quiet. Timmy sat absorbed in his Game Boy in the *salón*; Paco had retired to his room for a siesta. She retrieved the diary and her sunglasses and climbed the steps to the terrace.

27th October 2001

I've been expecting it for some time now: Mark has finally chosen what he calls freedom, which translated, means a cave in Sacromonte. He is eighteen, old enough to decide for himself, but I still worry. Things happen up there in the caves: fights, accidents, an unintended overdose... Paco says I must trust him, he's an adult now, and I am reminded (by the briefest of shadows passing across his face) that Paco has children too and is excluded from their lives.

Odd things have gone missing from the kitchen: a jug, the sieve, knives and forks, a chopping board. We have fewer towels, I've noticed, and the pile of sheets in the cupboard seems to have lost height. This morning Paco reported that the dustpan and brush had disappeared. These signs of Mark's home-making, although inconvenient, amuse rather than irritate me.

24th November 2001

For practically the first time in my life, I am working in a disciplined way with a proper routine. Every morning from around 9.30, I'm at my desk, researching or writing. Most days I keep at it till 2 o'clock when I tear myself away to prepare the lunch. Sometimes I go back to it in the evening, occasionally till late at night if I'm particularly inspired. Last night Paco literally carried me off to bed at 2am. He insisted I needed my sleep, but that was just an excuse, I discovered because he then kept me awake another hour, making sure I was relaxed, as he put it. My cries of protest soon gave way to more appreciative noises. By the time we finished, the bed was in complete disarray and we were both not only relaxed but worn out. Then Paco decided he was hungry and I made the ultimate sacrifice of abandoning our warm nest for the freezing kitchen to make toast for him. What greater proof of love could there be?

My friends, *guiris* and Spanish alike, are amazed when I talk about my project. Yesterday I was telling Leonor about how girls in *al-Andalus* would go to the *madrasa* and receive the same education as boys, often in mixed classes, and that far from being confined to the house, they became poets and singers, translators and copyists, teachers and administrators. Women had their own property and could get divorced. Leonor wanted examples so I told her about the doctor from the Avenzoar family, renowned for her work on the scarring of wounds; about Yamila, who fought alongside her brother in cavalry battles with rebel groups from Mérida and was praised for her bravery; and about Fátima, famous for her eloquent odes, who worked in the library of Al Hakem II and renounced marriage, preferring to devote herself to books and keep her independence. I explained how we're deliberately encouraged to equate Islam with the kind of repression imposed by the Taliban, which is at best a distortion of the truth.

Leonor went very quiet for a while. Then she said that in their history lessons at school, the 800 years of Muslim rule were just skipped over, in the same way as the second Republic, the Civil War and certain aspects of the dictatorship. She was only now beginning to realise what a biased and incomplete view of history she and all her generation had. But it's not just her generation, as I pointed out. Our children – Mark, Pablo, Antonio – were fed a similarly partisan version of events. 'All the more need for a Spanish edition of your book,' Leonor said. Paco thinks so too. He thinks I should start sounding out publishers now while it's a hot topic. The truth is I'm so immersed in the lives of my bold heroines, I'm loath to tear myself away to more mundane tasks like writing to editors. How I'll miss them when I finish.

Alice walked over towards the railings. The sun was still high, forming stark patterns of light and shadow in the cobbled streets below. All Deb's enthusiasm, all those years of work and then just when she was about to reap the rewards... It was so unfair. Unfair and cruel.

'Cristina wants to see me.' As usual I was absorbed in my work and didn't take in Paco's words at first. Only when I looked up and saw his dazed expression did the meaning sink in. So many years he's been waiting for this, for some sign of softening from his daughters. As I hugged him, he gave a little sob and my eyes filled too. The message had come via her brother Juan, who told Paco she would call him at the weekend. Now he is nervous, wondering about her motives, afraid he'll disappoint her. I am almost as edgy as he is, jumping whenever I hear his mobile ring.

29th March 2002

For the third time, Paco has gone out to meet his daughter, this time with hopes much diminished. The first time she cancelled half an hour before. The second time she didn't show up. But he has been gone two hours now, which must be a good sign. It won't be easy for either of them but she'll surely see that her *papá* is not a bad man. And if Cristina forgives him, maybe the younger one will also come round. A reconciliation would make him so happy. Dear Paco, I am keeping my fingers crossed for you.

Deborah was right: the reconciliation took time and effort, as the next few diary entries showed. But by September of that year, both Cristina and Bea had accepted their father and Paco was seeing all his three children regularly. It took a little longer for them to accept Deb. That was only natural, Alice thought, remembering her own experience with Andy's children, who had tolerated her but with a chilling disdain that made her curl up in pain every time they visited. The affection she had hoped for never came.

20th July 2002

¡*No a la Guerra*!' I spent an hour today painting the words on an old sheet, which Paco then strung up from the terrace railings. The anti-war banners are multiplying – adding to those still left from the Afghanistan invasion. There is no justification for waging war on Iraq. Not one of the 'reasons' stands up. So what is the real motive? Is it about 'regime change' or their as yet undiscovered weapons of mass destruction? Or is it greed for their oil?

No matter what the rest of the world and their own citizens think, Bush and Blair will do as they please with Iraq – and now it seems likely Aznar will join them in this war that begins to look inevitable. I thank God the *mili* has been abolished. When I think that Mark could have been sent to fight there... Both Paco and I are depressed and angry, as are many of our friends. We go to rallies and demonstrations, we shout loudly... What more can we do? Freedom and civil liberties are being whittled away on the pretext of security. Muslims – some most certainly innocent – are kept caged like animals at Guantánamo with no prospect of a trial. Every day we are fed lies and more lies... On this subject Mark is with us all the way. Complete harmony reigns while the talk is of politics. So, ironically, the prospect of war has brought a kind of truce.

Mark stuck his head out of the cave soon as he woke up, wondering what the fuck he'd do if he found Ed's stinking body lying there. But there was no sign of him so he couldn't have died – unless he'd crawled off somewhere else to do it like animals did.

It was late – he could tell by the sun – but he still felt shit. He'd slept nowhere near long enough. You were supposed to get eight hours and he couldn't have slept more than five or six. Cooking smells wafted in his direction from one of the other caves, making him hungry and he could hear the faint sound of drumming in the distance.

'Hola.' The voice came from his left – a girl's voice, quite close. He turned his head and there was this gorgeous *chica* with short spiky hair the colour of cherries sitting on the ground with a cardboard box in front of her and some kind of tool in her hand like she was making something. '*Soy* Racquel,' she said.

He thought he must still be dreaming. It was unreal, as if that ugly frog Ed had morphed into a beautiful princess only without the kiss. He rubbed his eyes, half expecting her to vanish but she was still there smiling at him.

'Mark,' he said, hoping she wouldn't come too close, seeing as he hadn't had a chance to wash. But she'd unfolded her legs and was walking towards him like in a slow-motion film. 'I haven't seen you before.' It was the only thing he could think of to say. He wondered if people who had visions of the Virgin felt like this, lost for words.

'I've only been here a couple of weeks,' she said. 'I was living on the coast in Almería but I fancied a change.' She looked around her. 'It's cool here; I love it.'

Her neck and wrists and ankles were strung with beads on leather thongs – masses of them. 'I make jewellery to sell,' she said when she noticed him looking. 'Do you think the tourists here will go for it?'

'Yeah, definitely. They'll love it.'

'Just what I want to hear.' She shot him a big smile. 'Is that your cave? Can I see it?'

'Sure.' He turned and lifted the old door further to one side. 'Where are you living?'

'I've just moved in up there,' she said, pointing in the direction of the Albaicín but higher up the hill.

Then he saw where she meant. No fucking way! He stood staring at her, totally stunned. He couldn't believe it, she was pointing straight at Dani's cave. As if that cunt of a cokehead deserved a girlfriend like her. Come to think of it, he'd never seen Dani with any girl. He was devastated. 'Are you with Dani then?' His voice came out flat as a pancake, like all the air had gone out of it.

Her face had scrunched up into a frown. 'What's up? Who…?' Then suddenly she was smiling again. 'Oh I know, you mean that dealer who used to live there. Yeah, someone told me about him. But he's gone. They said he left Granada in a hurry; some guys had threatened to kill him. Could be he was working on their patch.'

'I didn't know.' Dani gone was the best news he'd had in a long time. He felt like hugging her just for that.

'The cave was a disgusting mess; it took me well over a week to get it sorted – some friends from Almería came to help – but it's great now. We painted it and everything.'

'Cool.' If he was lucky, she might offer to show it to him. 'Are you coming in then? I could make some coffee.'

'Excellent. Just what I need.'

He stood to one side so she could go in first but just at that moment her bloody phone went off.

'*Díme* Miguel,' she said and moved away like she didn't want him to hear.

When she came back, everything had changed. 'I've got to run,' she said. 'My friend's waiting for me in the Albaicín.'

'Oh right.' So she had a boyfriend. He might have guessed. 'Well, see you around then.'

'Sure.' She leaned towards him. '*Un beso.*' Her lips hardly brushed his cheeks as she took off like the wind, heading down to the road.

He stood there watching her till she was out of sight. It was only then he noticed she'd left her box. Which meant, unless it was empty or just trash, she'd have to come back. He picked it up and carried it into the cave. Inside were a load of coloured beads, some metal clasps, wire and lengths of leather cord. He reckoned she'd need those pretty soon. Cool – even if she did have a boyfriend who could whistle her like a dog.

It was all history now, Alice thought as she flicked impatiently through page after page of politics in her sister's diary. Iraq had happened, was happening, despite all the anti-war feeling: the meetings and marches, the massive opposition from around the world, the lack of a UN resolution. Deb, along with Paco, was heavily into the protests: her indignation seemed to be reflected even in the sloppiness of her handwriting in this part of the diary, as if she could barely contain her rage. For months during the run-up to the war, Walladah and the rest of them got only the occasional mention. But buried somewhere in here, Alice was convinced, must be a reference to Hassan's arrest. When was it Deb had told her? The information had been casually dropped into some rant about the demonising of Muslims during one of their long phone conversations, but was it in the spring of 2002, later that year or even early 2003? All she could recollect was her relief at the news, along with the feeling that he must have done something to deserve it.

25th January 2003

I can hardly believe it, they've taken Mustafa in for questioning. Not just him but several others too from the Muslim community in Granada. They spent last night in police cells, Nur told me. She was distraught. Nobody seems to know what provoked this, what they're accused of, whether or not they've been charged with anything...

I asked her what we could do to help but she says we must just wait and see what happens. I was all for marching down to the police station and demanding their release but Paco persuaded me it would be counterproductive and might result in me being arrested too. I don't care about myself but I agreed, reluctantly, to wait until we know more.

27th January 2003

They have been released without charge. This afternoon Nur called me with the good news. Apparently they'd been picked up on some ugly rumour without the slightest shred of evidence and questioned about 'links with terrorism'. It makes me seethe. How could they even think of suspecting Mustafa? He is such a good, gentle person, absolutely opposed to any form of violence. Thank God (or should I say *insha'Allah*), he was able to convince them.

Still nothing about Hassan, unless he was one of those arrested with Mustafa... Alice read on, skimming, until at last, in early March, his name appeared on the page.

2nd March 2003

More disturbing news, this time about Hassan. It was Fátima who told me. She said he'd been detained in Madrid and charged with having links with al-Qaeda. They are keeping him in custody, though an appeal for bail has been lodged by his lawyer.

I am shocked. For all his sins, Hassan is no terrorist. He isn't even a practising Muslim let alone a fundamentalist. Fátima thinks these 'links' are merely journalistic contacts found by the police in his address book. It seems to me a likely explanation. Much as I loathe the man, I have no doubt these accusations are a lie.

Alice closed the diary. Deborah seemed very sure of Hassan's innocence. How did she know he hadn't changed since they separated? Wasn't that how these extremist groups worked: recruiting perfectly ordinary people with their clever propaganda? She tried to think rationally, to put aside the strong emotions his name provoked. The law had found him not guilty, after all. Hassan was entitled to his freedom.

He was Timmy's father. The unwelcome recall of this fact brought with it a familiar bitter taste. She knew it was illogical to resent it, unfair to wish him ill, but how could she remain dispassionate when he – and only he – had the power to wreck her quiet life with Timmy? If Deborah died, he would be legally entitled, as Timmy's only surviving parent, to take his son away. There had been no lawful adoption, only a lie. A lie that a simple DNA test would lay bare. She had no rights whatsoever. On top of that, Timmy would hate her forever for keeping him in ignorance.

And yet... There was more than one way to look at it. Who had the right to judge her? *I saved your life.* That was her trump card – the indisputable truth she clung to and would exploit if necessary to convince Timmy or Hassan or the authorities... She had committed a small deception but in doing so had saved him from the far worse fate of abortion.

In the *salón* she found Paco watching TV but no sign of Timmy. The urge to see her son, to hug him to her and be reassured that nothing had changed was overwhelming.

'Timmy went to play with his friend Javi,' Paco said, 'At the house of María opposite. Is okay?'

It took a conscious effort to quell her unease. 'Yes, of course.'

If Paco had been a little unhinged by the tragedy that had hit them, he wasn't the only one. To panic when they had only two days left here was ridiculous. Two more days and Timmy would be safe in England, far beyond Hassan's reach.

Chapter Eighteen

Mark stopped to catch his breath. He'd been legging it up the hill like a dog on speed and his lungs wouldn't take it. He put down his two bags of shopping. He must be getting old – unless it was the smoking. Well there was no way he was going to give that up. What was the point when you could just as easily get blown to bits on a train or knifed by some *loco*. You had to die sometime. He was hoping he hadn't missed Racquel. If she didn't show up today, he'd take the box to her, seeing as he knew exactly where she lived.

The best thing now was he could go where he liked without having to figure out how to dodge Dani. Going the long way round to avoid him and Ed had become a habit. You never knew what state they'd be in, specially Dani when he'd done a few lines of coke. That was when you really had to watch your step. Fucking manic he was then, and even worse when he'd come down and was obsessed with scoring his next fix.

Mark had only done cocaine a couple of times. It made you feel great, like you could do anything. But afterwards when it wore off, you felt shit. It wasn't worth it. Tina had gone mad at him, asked if he wanted to end up like Dani. Fucking Dani. 'You can pay me later,' he'd said. 'Go on, give yourself a high.' Talking nice to him, like he wanted to do him a favour! He only got nasty when it came to paying back the money. 'No hurry,' he'd said. 'Pay when you can.' Fucking liar. Five days later it was 'Give it me now!' Whispered in a voice that scared the shit out of him. Serve the bastard right if he got knifed by some other cunt of a dealer.

Mark reached his cave and lifted the door aside. Home. Everything was as he'd left it. You never knew. He kicked off his boots and sat down on the mattress. That was the worst thing he'd ever done: getting in debt to Dani. He should never have accepted the coke. Then he wouldn't have owed him money, he wouldn't have had to hassle Mum for it or nick it when she refused. He wouldn't have had that row with her.

Alice could hear the rain even before she opened the shutters. It was lashing down, bouncing off the tiles in the patio; soaking the cushions she'd left out last night; dripping from the gutters where they didn't quite join up. Timmy was still asleep, on his back with one arm flung wide. Having lain awake much of the night, depressed and anxious about her hospital visit, she envied him his state of oblivion.

Paco was in the kitchen, waiting for the coffee to bubble up in the pot.

'Are you going to work today?' she asked him.

'Yes, it is necessary,' he said. 'Maybe already they don't remember who I am.'

'It'll be the same for me next week.' Alice had hardly given a thought to work. She tried to picture the Council building, her desk with the photo of Timmy pinned on the wall above it, the faces and voices of her colleagues, the catching up she'd have to do; and found it impossible. After years working there, the office should be as familiar as her own house, but from here it felt unreal, like the set of a film. A thought struck her. 'But Paco, you will be at home tomorrow to look after Timmy, won't you? I'm going to the hospital, remember?'

'Yes, Alice. I'll be here, don't worry. Mark also.'

'I'd prefer...' She hesitated, knowing she must sound paranoid. 'I'd prefer it if you stayed in the house. Um...I don't want Timmy catching a chill just before he goes back to school.'

'*Bueno*, if the rain continues like this, it's certain we don't go out.'

'I wondered...' Again Alice hesitated. 'Would you like me to go through some of Deborah's personal things? I mean her clothes and such-like.' It was one of the questions she'd been chewing over during the long sleepless hours of last night. Now she watched his face for signs of outrage or distress, fearing he might find her offer tactless. She only wanted to be helpful but if he still held out hope for Deb...?

'Would you like coffee? There is enough in the pot for both of us.'

His expression remained bland, as if he hadn't heard her question.

'No thanks. I'll have tea this morning.' She busied herself filling a pan with water, wishing she hadn't spoken. Paco was already pouring coffee into a glass, its powerful aroma pervading the kitchen.

'I am not stupid, Alice.' Paco eventually broke the silence that had stretched into several long minutes. 'I know the chances of a recovery are small. But she is not yet dead so...I cling to my small fragment of hope. You understand?'

'I understand. I'm sorry if I upset you.'

'No, no, it is okay.' He drained his glass and took it over to the sink. 'Well, tomorrow you will see her for yourself. Now I must hurry.' At the door, he added, 'I will miss your company – yours and your son's also. You have done well with Timmy. Bringing up a child – this is no easy task without a husband to help you.'

'Thank you Paco.' She wondered how he would feel if he knew Timmy's true parentage; if he knew that his beloved Deborah had lied to him all these years. With luck, she would never know the answer to that question. Paco and the rest of the world would continue to assume Timmy was hers, fruit of a brief fling best forgotten.

*

Timmy was still asleep though it was long past his usual waking up time. Alice suspected he'd been reading under the covers till late into the night. Yesterday, by a stroke of luck, she had found a stash of Mark's old story-books in a box at the back of the wardrobe. He was an avid reader – taking after Deb perhaps – and had pounced on them with glee. The books meant she was freed from the burden of finding ways to occupy him. For her there remained a year of Deborah's life to be read. Skimming rapidly, she ignored her sister's predictable outpourings of anger and dismay over the invasion of Iraq to concentrate on the diary's more personal themes.

10th April 2003

An English researcher working with one of Paco's colleagues has passed on the name of her agent. As well as academic works, this woman writes for the popular market, mostly on the First World War: the role women played and how they were affected. Paco happened to mention my work in progress and she immediately scribbled down the agent's details. 'Write to her today,' Paco urged me. Everyone says contacts are more important than anything else so I will take his advice and write, now I am close to the end. The Yamila chapter needs to be finished, the introduction revised and I'm there.

30th April 2003

After reading my outline and a couple of sample chapters, the agent, Rita Jennings, has asked to see the completed manuscript. I am over the moon – an expression I had to explain to both Paco and Mark. Now I must work flat out to finish. In two weeks, if I can shut out the world, this insane war and my worries about Mark, and focus on Walladah and co, I should be able to do it.

11th May 2003

I have worked like fury and this morning walked down to the Post Office to send off, at great cost, my precious manuscript, which Ms Jennings insisted must be hard copy. Now all I can do is await her verdict.

20th May 2003

No word yet and I'm mad with impatience. Several times I've picked up the phone and put it down again. Paco says I must not pester her, these things take time. I wander around the house, looking for distractions, smoking more than usual, checking the *buzón* for post half a dozen times each morning.

28th May 2003

Today again, I noticed there was money missing from my purse after Mark had been here. I'm not absolutely sure, I could be mistaken, but it's the second or third time… I'm not going to accuse him; not until I'm certain. I don't want to believe it. I've always been generous with him and it makes me wonder what he wants the money for. Drugs, for example? Otherwise, why not just ask me, as he always has? It hurts to think I can't trust him.

He's become moodier since he went to live in the cave, so I never know what to expect. He can still be affectionate and loving, yet there are times when his hostility smacks me in the face. It's as if he wants to punish me, but for what I've no idea. When I see the crowd he hangs around with these days, I shudder. Some of them are okay – arty types and musicians who scratch a living selling their handicrafts on the street or busking like Mark – but others are into dealing or are addicts beyond all hope of redemption. I see them off their heads in the street and it fills me with fear.

20th June 2003

Paco has taken his children to the beach for a couple of days over the Corpus holiday. He invited me too but I thought it better they had time alone together. The girls adore their *papá* and Juan comes to eat here often, sometimes staying till late into the evening. All is forgiven, it seems. Paco is happy and my conscience lighter.

24th June 2003

At last a letter from the agent and she's willing to take me on! I was all prepared for rejection but no, she liked it and already has a couple of potential publishers in mind. So next week I'll go to London, discuss the manuscript with her and hopefully sign a contract. When I phoned her to fix a time and date, she asked about future projects and I improvised wildly, pouring out enough ideas to keep me writing for years to come. Unbelievably, these seemed to impress her. Paco is almost as excited as I am and says he'll have a bottle of champagne waiting for my return.

3rd July 2003

The champagne has been drunk – every last drop. I have an agent and she thinks my chances of publication are good. She has suggested some minor revisions – mainly in how it's organised – but nothing too radical. By the end of the month I should have the new version ready. Then it will be up to her. I'm walking around in a dream. Yesterday I passed Kay in the street and was so absorbed in fantasies of seeing my book on the shelves of Foyles and Waterstones, I didn't even notice her until she grabbed my arm.

Alice had visited Granada towards the end of that month, when Timmy broke up from school. She remembered Deb frantically finishing off the manuscript, barely taking notice of either Timmy or her until their fourth or fifth day when she finally sent it off and began to relax. They went to the coast for a few days then, exchanging Granada's heat for the cooler sea breezes in Almería – just Deborah, herself and Timmy. Mark had declined, much to Timmy's disappointment.

For nearly a week they spent every day on the beach, taking a break for lunch at one of the small beach restaurants: fish fresh from the sea, with salad and bread. The place was called Agua Amarga, which Deb translated as Bitter Water. Sweet would have been more apt. From the beach, it looked a glassy greenish blue. She had never seen such translucent water. Deb said there were often jellyfish (*medusas*, she called them) but all they saw that week were harmless tiddlers darting about in the shallows. Timmy cried on the last day. Couldn't they live there, he asked. So hard to believe it was less than eight months ago. Perhaps she should feel grateful for those idyllic days they had shared; perhaps one day she would. But right now the memory brought only pain. Why did happiness always come with a built-in expiry date?

11th July 2003

Yesterday my work on the manuscript was interrupted for several hours, but happily so. I wouldn't have missed the inauguration of the *Mezquita* for anything, despite almost passing out from the heat. (When my personal invitation arrived in the post, I did spare a brief thought for Hassan, languishing in prison. He should have been invited too – though he is the last person on earth I'd want to run into. Was he even aware of the opening, I wonder?)

I don't know what the 'enemy' (those bigots who were to blame for the twenty-year delay) made of it all. I saw one or two neighbours peeking out of their windows at the crowds gathering in the square of San Nicolás: men in *djellabas* and red *fez* hats, women in headscarves – some wearing *chadors*, others in European dress; officials from the town in suits and ties (they must have been suffocating) and a ridiculous number of police. For once the tourists were outnumbered. We were all clutching our bottles of water and fanning ourselves furiously. I think the odour of human sweat overwhelmed the more subtle scents of the *mezquita* garden's aromatic plants.

The Emir of Sharjah, whose financial backing had been crucial, was there along with representatives from Turkey, Syria, Lebanon,

Saudi Arabia, the Palestinian Authority, Indonesia... However, the mayor of Granada did not attend (his absence was noted in today's papers). How rude of the man to snub such an important event in his town. As one speaker said, the *mezquita* will be a resource for the whole population of the Albaicín, a meeting point for all cultures. Tolerance was the key word in most of the speeches.

I met many old friends I'd been involved with in the campaign. Salma and a whole contingent of helpers were fighting their way through the crowds with trays of lemonade and Moroccan pastries. I talked briefly to her and to Rashid and Mustafa and Nur; also to one of the Spanish journalists, an acquaintance of Hassan's, who asked if I had any news of him.

Everyone was quietly jubilant; it felt like a true celebration. I left when the *muezzin* started his call to prayer from the minaret, by which time I was dripping so much I thought I'd dissolve into a pool of tepid water like a snowman exposed to blazing sun.

There were no more entries till mid-August. Deb had written nothing about their beach holiday – as if it weren't important to her. As if the mosque, the political situation, her writing career mattered far more than Timmy and herself. It hurt that Deb had regarded their time together as too insignificant to write about. The next entries revolved around Mark and bore out what Monika had hinted at.

14th August 2003

When Mark turned up this afternoon, I noticed three of his friends – two youths and a girl, all with multiple piercings – standing outside the gate waiting for him, along with their mangy dogs (which seem to be a must-have accessory for the cave people). He was only here a few minutes and hardly spoke a word, just helped himself to juice from the fridge, fetched some clothes from his room and left. I found I was watching him in a way I'd never done before and afterwards I felt horrified. I thought about those months when the builders, Fernando, Rafa and Juanito were working here on the *carmen* every day and it never once occurred to me to watch them in case they stole from me. Yet today I was watching my own son, suspecting him of being a thief.

218

No word yet from Rita at the agency. It's holiday time, she pointed out when we last spoke, but still I am impatient. Most of my friends are away in cooler climes. I am restless and dwelling too much on my fears about Mark. If only he'd talk to me.

9th September 2003

Rita has been in touch but the news is disappointing: two publishers have rejected my manuscript, for entirely different reasons. One editor said it was 'against the current' (which I take to mean she has a different political agenda); the other that it fell between the academic and the popular so would be difficult to market. The manuscript is now with a third publisher and Rita says I should not feel discouraged. Easy for her to say: she hasn't spent years of her life working on it. Paco is unsympathetic, pointing out that I enjoyed the work. Both tell me I should start something new. I have a couple of ideas brewing. Perhaps one day soon…

'So what have you been up to since I last saw you?' Monika clapped Mark on the shoulder as he stood outside Spar. 'I was thinking of paying you another visit. Those pencils…you do remember I gave you some pencils?'

'Course I bloody do.' Monika could be aggravating at times. 'I've done a couple of drawings already. If you don't believe me you can come up and see them.'

'I believe you but I'd still like to see them. If you're interested, I can show you my finished painting too – you know, the one I started that day near your cave.'

'Yeah, cool. I'd like to see it.'

'Come round now if you've no other plans. Seeing as we're so near my place.' Her eyes shifted all of a sudden, looking past him down the road. 'There goes one of your neighbours,' she said. 'Looks like he's been in the wars.'

Mark turned and there was fucking Ed, leaning on a pair of crutches with one foot in plaster and his arm in a sling. He must have crawled to the hospital.

219

'He's a sad case, isn't he? Monika said, staring at Ed. 'If he carries on like that, he won't last long.'

'Fucking bastard, I hate him.'

Monika gave him a look like she thought 'hate' was too strong. 'Come on,' she said. 'Let's go back to my place before it starts raining again.'

Monika shared a bloody great big *carmen* with three other women. They each had their own rooms and there was a studio in the basement where Monika worked. He'd only been down to the studio once before. It was like a den of colour, with a workbench covered in messy tubes of oil paint and daubs of different colours she'd been trying out. Her paintings took up nearly all the wall space. Most were landscapes or street scenes he recognised from the Albaicín but there were also some portraits. One was of an old gypsy woman he'd seen around quite a bit; another was of Monika's ex-boyfriend. There were a couple of her too that she must have done from photos or in the mirror.

'Have a look round while I make some coffee,' she said now. 'Over there on the easel – that's the Sacromonte one I've been working on. You'll recognise the view.' He moved closer to look at her painting and that's when he saw it, on the far wall: his mum staring down at him. It was like a fist in the belly; it stopped him dead in his tracks. He never knew Monika had done it. You could tell it was Mum even though her face was all different colours: blue and mauve and yellow and red. You could tell by the eyes and the mouth. She had that look – a little bit fierce but not in an angry way, more like fired up; *animada*. Like just what she wasn't now. He supposed that was why it fucking hurt.

'What do you think? Oh...' Monika was back, carrying a tray with steaming coffee. She must have noticed what he was looking at. She put the tray down and came over to him. 'Yes,' she said, putting a hand on his arm. 'I painted that last year, from a photo I took at one of the anti-Iraq war marches. I'm sorry if it...'

'No, I'm alright.' He shook her off and turned away so she couldn't see it was a lie. 'Good painting.'

'Do you think so? I wanted to catch something of her character, her essence, rather than just a physical likeness. But your mother said it was awful and threatened to throw black paint all over it. I wasn't sure if she was joking or serious.'

'Yeah well, you wouldn't want to take any chances...'

Monika poured the coffee and handed him a cup. She pointed to a couple of old chairs covered in splatters of paint. 'Shall we sit down? There's *bizcocho* too.' He took a piece of cake and bit into it. He was fucking starving.

'That sad old drunk we saw this morning...what's his name?' Right out of the blue she starts on about Ed. 'He hasn't been bothering you, has he? I mean, drink can make people aggressive. My older sister was an alcoholic so I know.'

'You talking about Ed?'

Monika nodded. 'Him and others. I've seen a few of them around the *barrio* – addicts of one kind and another.'

'They used to try and get money off me, Ed and Dani. They thought I was rich.' He hadn't meant to tell Monika; it just kind of slipped out.

'Rich?' She laughed. 'What made them think that?'

'It's bloody obvious isn't it?' The words came out hard, he couldn't help it. 'Because of Mum having the *carmen* – like here's this foreigner buying up property, a woman on her own... She's got to be rich. That's how they think. And if she's rich, it's like I am too. Like I can get hold of her dosh any time I want.'

'Right.' Monika went very quiet. Then she said, 'My sister used to steal from me and from our parents: money, jewellery, anything she could sell. It all went on drink.' She pushed back her hair and squeezed a clump of it on one side like she was wringing out washing. 'Her liver was completely destroyed; she died at forty-nine.'

'I didn't know.'

'It'll be five years next month.' She picked up the plate with *bizcocho* and offered it to him. 'Have another piece.' His mouth was full of cake so he almost choked when she said, 'So, you tell me these guys were hassling you for money. Did you give it to them?'

Monika was looking straight at him. He thought if he told her a lie, she'd know. 'Sometimes,' he said. 'You would too if someone had a fucking blade in their hand.'

'They didn't cut you, did they?' Like she was shocked.

'No, but if I hadn't come up with the money...'

'And to come up with the money you had to borrow from your mother…?'

The way she said 'borrow' it was obvious she meant steal. Mum must have told her. 'She could afford it,' he said. 'It was never much; ten euros was nothing to her.'

'You sound angry,' Monika reached out and took hold of his hand. He let her because he didn't want to seem rude and anyway it was kind of comforting. 'Deborah would have understood. If you'd talked to her, explained you were being threatened…'

'Yeah, maybe. Well it's too fucking late now.' He let go of her hand and stood. 'I've got to get back.'

'Okay, I'll come up and see your drawings in a day or two. You offered, remember?'

'I remember.'

He was halfway home when he realised he'd left his shopping at Monika's. He couldn't be arsed to go back for it now; he had other plans. Racquel's box was still sitting on his floor and every time he caught sight of it, his mind conjured up her face. She had a turned-up mouth, like one of those smiling sun symbols. Her eyes were dead round, he remembered, and sort of shiny. There was something about her voice too that had stuck in his mind: it was deep for a girl's but warm, and when she laughed you could tell it was for real, not put on like some people's. He hoped her boyfriend wouldn't be around when he went up there. He hoped she'd be on her own; that she'd invite him in to see how she'd transformed Dani's filthy squat and made it nice.

It was late when Alice picked up the diary again. Her reading had been interrupted by domestic tasks and by playing with Timmy; by preparations for tomorrow's flight to Madrid as well as their journey home to England early on Sunday. Then Paco had asked for help with an article he was writing in English.

22nd September 2003

Rita has just phoned to tell me the third publisher is 'extremely interested' and asked that I go to London to discuss the manuscript. It would still have to get past the 'hard-nosed' marketing department so

222

I shouldn't consider it a done deal but... I could tell from Rita's voice she was optimistic. I am so excited I can barely sit still. I can't wait to tell Paco but apparently he's in a meeting and then has two hours of classes. I've left a message for him to phone back... I could go this week, tomorrow even, if I can get a flight and if the editor has time. Who said patience was a virtue?

Things had moved at an impressive pace after that. Deb had been to London, made some changes to the manuscript demanded by the publisher (not without a certain amount of haggling, it seemed) and within two or three weeks signed a contract. They promised to speed up the publication process as much as possible, given that the subject was so topical, aiming for June or July 2004.

No wonder Deb was in such a state of euphoria when she came to Bristol last October, fresh from signing the deal. Alice remembered how she couldn't seem to stop smiling. Or talking. The way she'd skipped along the woodland path the next day in the Forest of Dean. Like a teenager, Alice had thought, watching her.

3rd November 2003

When I saw his handwriting on the envelope, I very nearly tore it up without opening it. I could think of only one reason Hassan might write to me. I was shaking so much I had to sit down. How could he have found out? No living person knew except Alice.

This was it. Alice felt shaky herself, imagining the fear that must have gripped her sister before she opened the letter.

In my panic, I'd even forgotten he was in prison. I put the letter on the table and lit a cigarette. I smoked two before I summoned the nerve to open it. If it wasn't about Timmy, could it be a declaration of love? Or hate? A plea to resume our relationship? No, impossible after all this time... In the end, curiosity got the better of me.

'*Querida* Deborah...'

He was on remand in a prison outside Madrid, he wrote, on trumped up charges of having links with al-Qaeda. He recognised he hadn't always behaved well towards me and hoped I would accept his apologies. His feelings for me had made him a little crazy. Now he wanted to ask me a favour – as someone who knew him well and who had once loved him, someone whose word might count for something. 'You must know these charges are ridiculous. The addresses they found were contacts, mostly in my country, passed on to me as potentially useful for some features I was working on. A couple of these men I had interviewed; others I had merely written to. You know I am no fanatic, nor even a practising Muslim; that though I have my faults – like all of us – I am not a bad person. Do you really think I would support the murder of innocent people?'

I put the letter down before turning to the next page and smoked another cigarette. I could guess, more or less, what was coming, what the favour might be. The case against him is absurd. Hassan is no terrorist or terrorism sympathiser. He's a journalist doing his job. I believe in his innocence a hundred per cent. But that doesn't mean I want to get involved.

I read on. What he's asking is for me to vouch for his character, to attend the trial and testify in his favour. 'If you agree, I will write to the judge, giving him your name and address. Then it's up to him whether or not to allow it.'

Now I wish I hadn't opened the letter. I don't think I can face seeing him again, being reminded of all our battles; or the inescapable fact that he is Timmy's father. I am afraid. I would rather he stayed in prison – even though I am ashamed of such feelings. Should I talk to Alice? But I know what she would say. Better not to worry her. I must keep this to myself, try and forget it. He can surely find someone else to speak for him.

So what, Alice wondered, had changed her mind? If only Deb *had* talked to her. Then maybe she'd have been able to convince her sister not to give in to him. It was unfair of the man to appeal to Deb's conscience in that way.

6th November 2003

Against my better judgement, I talked to Paco. He could see I was agitated about something and begged me to confide in him. I resisted at first but he was so sweet and solicitous, I relented.

'You once loved this man,' he said after reading the letter. 'You believe he is innocent. I think you are being unreasonable in refusing to help him.'

But Paco doesn't know about Timmy. He doesn't understand why I'm so reluctant to get involved. He thinks it's just spite. The way he put it, I felt unable to argue. He implied it was my duty to support Hassan.

'Deborah, you know the charge is a nonsense. We should be fighting this hysteria about al-Qaeda, the excuse 9/11 has provided to brand Muslims as terrorists. Even Mustafa and Rashid were detained. Whatever you feel personally about Hassan, he is not a bad man – or so I understand.' We were lying in bed and he held me close, stroked my hair in that tender way of his, kissing my neck and ears. 'Perhaps he behaved badly, but aren't we all capable of behaving badly when we find we are losing the person we love? Jealousy is a fundamental human emotion; it makes us irrational, maybe a little unbalanced. He was not violent, you say. Hassan's only crime was to behave like a jealous lover. Isn't that so?'

This was last night and I am still torn. My head says I must do what is morally right; what Paco urged me to do. But my heart cries out in protest. When love turns to hate, its power is slow to fade. So much time has passed and yet still I am not free of him. I had hoped writing might clarify my mind but no. Last night I scarcely slept; tonight will be no different, I fear.

Alice already knew which path Deb had chosen. *Against my better judgement.* She re-read those words and felt a bitterness rise in her throat. Paco had had no right to interfere; Deb should never have listened to him. The diary made it absolutely clear that what had swayed her in the end was Paco's inflated moral sensibility. No wonder he had admired her decision.

Chapter Nineteen

Mark knew it was daft but walking up to Dani's cave took some nerve. He had to remind himself it wasn't Dani's cave any more, it was Racquel's. It spooked him all the same – not only in case Dani came back but because bad vibes often lingered; even after a death they hung around, haunting the place. Animals and some humans could sense it: a massive drop in temperature like walking into a freezer; or a prickling feeling that made their hair stand on end. Still, Racquel hadn't said anything about the cave feeling creepy or cold. She would have noticed, which meant Dani's evil aura must have cleared off with him.

There was no one about when he got there. A thick brown curtain had been pulled across the entrance. He stood outside with the box in his arms and called her name though he already knew there'd be no answer. The rain was still tipping down, turning the cardboard to mush. Water dripped off his hair; it trickled down his neck and crept inside his shirt. His trousers were sticking to his legs. He thought about lifting the curtain and sneaking a look inside. He could leave the box for her, save it getting any wetter. She'd know it was him.

The edge of the curtain felt damp. Peering inside, all he could make out at first were the outlines of objects. When his eyes adjusted, he could see at the far end a double mattress on the floor, which was bad news. It most likely meant her boyfriend, Miguel shared the cave. The paint on the walls – white with sky-blue in the alcoves – was fresh; you could still smell it. She had a load of rugs on the floor, covering the concrete. They made it kind of cosy. There was a table with a mug on it and a bowl full of beads like the ones she wore round her neck. A black hat, the sort with a wide brim, hung on a nail on the wall – it could be hers or it could be a man's, he couldn't tell. Near it was a mirror with a wet sheep staring out of it: a wet sheep that was him, with his *rastas* sodden and stuck to his head. Closing his eyes, he imagined Racquel's face in the mirror instead of his, the black hat sitting on her head, tilted to one side, and a big smile on her face.

A sudden draught whipped in from under the curtain, making him jump. It better not be Miguel showing up: he wouldn't be too happy at finding an intruder in his cave. Mark put the box down and stepped outside sharpish. No one in sight; must have been a gust of wind blowing the curtain. Still, he'd better push off. Racquel would see the box on the floor soon as she got home. Too bad he didn't have a pen or he could have left his phone number.

Mum always carried half a dozen pens on her in case she had an 'idea' while she was out and about. *My head's like a sieve*: that was one of her expressions. She meant her memory was lousy, which was true. Usually the 'ideas' were to do with her writing, not useful stuff. They didn't stop her running out of milk or forgetting to fetch him from basketball or locking herself out of the house. She wrote like she talked, fast, and her handwriting was crap – all spiky where it should be rounded. If he'd written like her, his teachers would have given him a rollicking.

He followed the path across the hill, not rushing because he couldn't get any wetter than he already was.

'Hey Marco, someone was looking for you.'

He'd been walking head down and hadn't seen Pierre coming towards him. 'For me? Who was it?'

Pierre grinned. 'A girl. Shortish, very pretty. Said she'd left something…'

Shit, it had to be her. 'Did she give you a name?'

Pierre frowned and swiped a hand across his beard, sending a shower of raindrops down the front of his jacket. 'Let's see…maybe Maribel? No, something similar…'

'Racquel?'

'That was it. Racquel. Said she'd pass by another day.'

'Right, thanks.' Talk about bad timing. Leaving the box at her place had been a mistake. He should have held onto it and waited for her to come looking.

He'd already moved off when Pierre shouted after him: 'Hey, there's a load of tiles been dumped up the Camino if you know anyone who needs them…'

Mark didn't bother turning round, just waved his hand to show he'd heard. All he wanted now was to get out of the fucking rain and into some dry clothes.

Just inside his cave he found a scrap of paper someone had pushed through the gap. It was wet and covered in his muddy footprint where he'd accidentally stepped on it. *Hola Mark, do you have my beads? Call me. Racquel.* Underneath, she'd written her number. Cool. He stepped back outside. The rain was easing off now and to the west the sky looked brighter – a silvery grey instead of the heavy charcoal that still hung over the hills in the other direction. He punched the keys on his phone and waited for her to answer.

Alice had set her alarm for six. The taxi was booked. She needed a good night's sleep to help her cope with tomorrow's hospital visit but the more she chased sleep, the more elusive it became. Her mind refused to rest, spinning from one worry to another in an endless circle. She was becoming a nervous wreck.

Reading the diary just before bed was partly to blame. She pondered the last words she had read. *Revenge is not sweet*: Deborah's conclusion after twenty-four hours agonising about how to respond to Hassan. Ludicrously, she had been swayed in the end not by Paco but by Walladah. As if the sufferings of a promiscuous 11th century poet could teach her anything!

Alice had already put the diary in her bag to read on the plane but now she switched on the bedside light and reached for it again.

7th November 2003

At eleven last night I sealed the envelope and took it to the post-box in Plaza Fátima. For three hours I'd sat alone in my sanctum tormented by indecision. Instinct told me to ignore the letter and do nothing. What could be simpler? But then Paco's words came back to me and I thought how disappointed he would be if I took the easy way, the selfish way. Still I wavered and dragged my heels, or rather my hands; resolutely not picking up my pen.

Walladah's proud eyes stared at me from the board above my desk. She lived to old age but her later years were far from happy. After Ibn Zaydun betrayed her, she never spoke to him again despite all his pleas for forgiveness and all the passionate poetry he wrote from his prison cell. Taking his enemy and rival as her new lover (and getting her betrayer jailed) may have brought some initial satisfaction but I'm convinced she never loved Ibn Abdús in the same way. Although there's no evidence for it, I'm convinced she still secretly pined for Ibn Zaydun and regretted what she'd done. Pride had driven her to revenge but at what cost to herself? I wish I could have found a portrait of her in old age – I imagine her eyes would have reflected some sadness, even bitterness. Thinking about Walladah, it occurred to me for the first time that her stubborn spirit may have worked against her in the end.

I picked up my pen. The cost to me would not be so great, surely. Hassan was out of my life and testifying for him wouldn't change that. I had no need to punish him. Revenge is not sweet.

Alice just couldn't see the parallels. It wasn't about revenge; it was about protecting Timmy and herself. And while Walladah may have still loved this Zaydun character, Deb certainly didn't harbour any secret longings for Hassan; she was blissfully happy with Paco. Okay, maybe she didn't need to punish him but she didn't owe him any favours either.

The next few entries were about her book. She appeared to have put the thing with Hassan to the back of her mind once she'd sent off the letter. Alice flicked through the pages: another trip to London, discussions with the publisher about cover picture and illustrations, payment of a small advance, the setting of a publication date for 22nd June of this year...

She got out of bed and put the diary back in her bag. The night was silent yet in the silence she felt a tension, as if the house or something within its walls were waiting, like a cat poised to pounce on its prey. She was overwrought, she told herself. The stress of these last few weeks had pushed her to the limits, affecting both body and mind. Her breathing was too shallow, her heart beating too fast; her imagination was playing tricks on her. She must sleep and in the morning everything would look different.

He was leaning on the bar in La Fragua when his phone went. 'Hey Mark, I've only just got your message; there's no signal in the cave.'

He'd given up trying to make contact with Racquel and left a voice-mail instead.

'Nor in mine. *¿Qué tal?*'

'I'm good. I wanted to thank you for bringing my stuff.'

'No problem. I thought you might need it.'

'I did. That's why I came by your place. I'd been tramping about on the hill getting soaked, trying to remember exactly where I'd left the box but then I thought maybe you'd picked it up. I was mighty pleased to find it waiting for me.'

He missed what she said next because what with the TV blaring, the clatter of glasses being washed and too many people bellowing, he couldn't hear a bloody word.

She repeated it for him. 'What I said was I've just cooked up some lentils. Why don't you come over? There's way more than I can eat.'

'Yeah, that sounds good but… You sure your boyfriend won't mind?'

'What boyfriend?'

'Miguel, was it?'

She laughed. 'He's not my boyfriend, just a friend. What made you think…? Oh well, never mind. Are you coming then? My credit's about to run out.'

'I'll be over in ten minutes.'

He finished his beer, paid and legged it back to Sacromonte. The rain had stopped and puffs of wind were dissolving the cloud so that by the time he reached her cave, white was losing out to blue and snatches of brilliant sunlight were making all the colours glow like they could blind you if you looked too hard.

She was sitting outside, threading beads on a leather thong.

'I'll get another chair,' she said and disappeared inside. The curtain was pulled back and he could smell hot food wafting out.

'I hope you're hungry,' she said, putting a chair down for him. She looked cool, in a little top that showed her navel with a silver stud in it, and baggy trousers like the ones in the Moroccan shops. She had sandals on and her toenails were painted turquoise.

'Starving,' he said.

She brought out two steaming bowls of lentils with potato and carrot and garlic and spices. It was better than Mum's, which wasn't hard, but better than Leonor's too, and that *was* saying something. 'Where are you from?' she asked. 'You look like a *guiri* but you don't sound it.'

'England,' he said. 'But I've lived in Granada practically all my life; I was just a baby when we came.'

'That explains it. Is your family still here then?'

His answer came out all on its own and much too quick, before he'd even had a chance to think. 'It was only me and my mum who came over and my mum's dead.'

When he heard what he'd said, the spoon dropped right out of his hand. He was stunned: he couldn't believe he'd told her that. The words kind of hung there pointing the finger at him, making him feel like he'd killed her by voicing them. Mum wasn't dead. He remembered Alice was going to see her today; she might be in the hospital this very moment. He wished he could take back what he'd said. It was a lie.

Racquel had stopped eating and was watching him, not saying anything, just looking kind of sad.

He picked up his spoon and shovelled some more lentils into his gob. It was an effort to swallow them: they swelled and stuck in his throat.

'When did she die?'

'Not long ago.' He couldn't look at her.

'My mum's dead too.'

'*Your* mum...?' He had to look at her then.

'She died when I was eleven, of cancer.'

'Oh.' That made him feel even worse, like he'd been lying to get her sympathy when she was the one whose mum was dead. He felt like a fraud. If she ever found out... He just wanted to get up and leave. Or else rub out the last ten minutes and start the conversation again. He fished around for something to say but the lie had scrambled his brain and made him go dumb. 'So your dad...?'

'My dad looked after us at first and my aunt helped too, but then after a couple of years he got married again.' She went quiet for a minute and fiddled with her earring but you could tell her mind was far away and not in a good place. 'His new wife had three girls of her own and they came first. Me and my brother…she didn't treat us the same. She didn't like us and her daughters didn't like us either. So I got out when I was seventeen and came south – to Almería first. It was about as far as you could get from Asturias. I miss my brother though. And my dad.'

'You're all on your own then.'

She nodded. 'Like you, I guess. But I've got good friends. Hey, d'you want some more lentils?'

'I'm stuffed, thanks. But I'd like to see your cave.'

'Sure. There's still work to do on it. For one thing, the floor's just concrete. I've put some rugs down but I'd like to tile it before the winter.'

Soon as she mentioned tiles, a bell rang in his head and he remembered what Pierre had said.

'If you want tiles, I know where to find some – if no one else gets there first. A load of them have been dumped down on the Camino.'

'Oh cool!'

She'd need help, he reckoned: first bringing them up here, then mixing the concrete and laying them. He was about to offer her a hand when his phone went. It was Paco.

'Mark, I have to go into the Faculty for an hour or two – just an administrative matter but it's urgent – and as you know, Alice is in Madrid. Could you come and look after Timmy while I'm gone?'

'Yeah, I s'pose so.' It wasn't the best of timing but he couldn't really refuse. 'Right now, you mean?'

'As soon as you can, Mark. Thanks. I won't be away long.'

'I've got to go,' he said to Racquel. 'But I'll come back later and we'll bring the tiles up. If you want,' he added in case she was one of those independent chicks who preferred to do stuff without a man's help.

'*Estupendo*,' she said and moved closer to give him a kiss. Her cheeks felt warm and either her skin or her hair – he couldn't tell which – smelt of coconut.

The laid-back feel of Granada's small airport only pointed up Alice's own far from laid-back state, making her intensely aware of her stretched nerves, her throbbing head. She had not slept and her face in the mirror showed it. If Deborah were able to see her, she would be shocked by the dark pouches under her eyes, the creases and folds in her skin. A haggard, old woman's face. Once her skin had been smooth and unmarked like Timmy's. She remembered the silkiness of his sleep-warm cheek as she kissed it before leaving; he had stirred but not woken.

She washed her hands and held them under the dryer. Her flight wouldn't be called for another hour. In the bag slung over her shoulder, the diary seemed to pulsate, demanding to be read. She returned to the precinct and ordered a coffee at the bar. Choosing a table in the least occupied part of the café area, she sat down and started reading.

27th November 2003

Paco put the letter in my hand when he came home for lunch. I hadn't checked the post, having been hard at work on a translation I'd promised for tomorrow. I knew immediately it was from Hassan. Paco kissed the top of my head and left the room while I read it. As last time, it had the prison stamp: of course it would have been censored. And who knows? Maybe my name has been added to some list of terrorist sympathisers. The letter was brief. He presumed I had already heard from the judge that his request for me to testify has been granted. He was grateful and hoped I would not find it too much of an ordeal. His wife also wished to pass on her thanks. So he is married! Was it the plump virgin his mother promised, I wonder?

I have yet to hear from the judge. Knowing how slowly the wheels of bureaucracy turn and the erratic nature of the Spanish postal system, I am not surprised. '*Está bien,*' says Paco but to me it's not good news, even if it should be.

30th November 2003

Today the official letter – in pompous legal language – finally arrived. The trial, to be held in Madrid, was scheduled to start on 8th January but I would not be required till the following week. I must write to confirm my attendance.

I have done so but my fingers on the keyboard dragged in protest.

Doing the 'right' thing brings no prize, nor pleasure.

Alice continued reading but she scarcely took in the words. Her mind lagged behind, gripped by the news that Hassan was married. She wasn't sure why it should make a difference, yet it seemed significant. A moment's thought gave her the answer: if he was married, he might also have children. For some reason, the possibility had never occurred to her before. Whether this would make him more or less of a threat was unclear but if Timmy was not his only child, she would dearly like to know.

4th December 2003

It does not help that while I am preoccupied with the trial and feeling at my most vulnerable, Mark has taken to verbally attacking me with the most ridiculous accusations: I am too rich, selfish, exploitative, snobbish… Where does he get these ideas? At the same time he pesters me to 'lend' him money and helps himself to my 'riches' in the form of food, drink and (I suspect) small amounts of cash.

I try to cheer myself up by looking ahead to June and the pleasure of seeing my book in print. It helps, but actually I miss my women now they have left me and sit instead with the publisher. For such a long time Walladah, Yamila, Fátima and the rest were my constant companions. Now they are gone and beyond my control. I had grown as fond of them as if they were here in the 21st century with me.

Reading about Deborah's difficulties with Mark reminded her of what Monika had said that day they met in Plaza Larga. There was more too: he had spent Christmas drinking with his disreputable friends and not even bothered to come down for the festive meal she had prepared. Poor Deb. As if the impending trial and the prospect of coming face to face with Hassan in the courtroom weren't enough to ruin her Christmas.

Yet casting her mind back now… She distinctly remembered her sister recounting the 'lovely time' they were having: the family meal on Christmas Eve, the pleasant stroll in bright sunshine followed by a relaxed lunch on Christmas Day. Had it been a complete fiction? She felt hurt that Deb had not trusted her sufficiently to share her problems. She had revealed none of her anxieties; had lied through her teeth, in fact. So much for their close relationship.

'Iberia Vuelo... Madrid...' Her flight was being called. She followed the other passengers – mostly dapper Spanish businessmen – through Security and joined the queue. Madrid: a word that sounded too much like dread. She couldn't wait for this day to be over. The contrast between Deborah sentient and spirited in the diary and Deborah lying inert as a dummy in the hospital bed was too stark to bear. She felt hollow, as if all the strength she prided herself on had gradually seeped away in these last few weeks, just when she needed it most. She feared she might faint and imagined the concerned faces of staff and fellow passengers as they crowded round her. How had Deborah felt when she made this same journey to Madrid for Hassan's trial? She too must have felt dread and misgiving. Yet she had found the strength to go through with it, to do what he asked of her.

Alice let out a deep sigh that made the woman in front of her turn round and stare. Embarrassed, she looked away and was relieved when, a few moments later, the queue started to move. She would have to get a grip before she arrived at the hospital – even if her sister remained oblivious to her presence. She had realised in the course of the long sleepless night that it hardly mattered whether or not her words were received. What she had to say was as much for her own benefit as Deb's and the words could be spoken aloud or silently.

She needed to ask Deb's forgiveness for reading her diary and try to explain what it had meant to see things through her eyes, with all the intimate details, the petty secrets and small deceptions laid bare. Even though at times she had been angered or hurt by what she read, seeing Deb exposed and vulnerable had aroused a compassion that far outweighed any negative emotions. For the first time, she felt she understood her sister fully. And with that came the recognition that she had never loved her so much. The irony of this made her want to weep.

As soon as the plane was airborne, Alice retrieved the diary from her bag and resumed reading.

It's over and I feel a great weight has been lifted from me. Tuesday 13th, considered unlucky in Spain, was the day for my testimony, the day I'd been dreading. Without Paco's support, I'm not sure I could have gone through with it. He insisted on accompanying me to Madrid and held my hand for the whole flight. Knowing he was there in the public gallery of the court gave me courage as I prepared to read my statement.

But then…I stood there with my sheet of paper. I knew its contents by heart, I didn't need to read. My eyes were glued to Hassan. I wanted to look away but felt powerless: he drew me like a magnet. I had expected to see him gaunt and aged. Although Spanish prisons are supposed to be relatively civilised, I'd presumed the soft regime would not apply to suspected terrorists. (When I commented on this to Paco later, he was indignant: we're no longer under the dictatorship, he said.) In fact Hassan looked healthy, well-fed and still handsome; too handsome. The extra ten years had given him a certain dignity that made him even more attractive. Facing him in that small courtroom, I was taken back to earlier days when I loved him with a passion beyond all restraint. I remembered our ritual with the pomegranate seeds (repeated more than once); the poetry and romance he could conjure up using words that held me entranced for hours on end. And I was totally unprepared for my reaction. I heard my voice waver. Then I looked over at Paco, the man I would always love; at his wise, kind eyes – and the spell of Hassan was broken. I knew it for a brief madness that already had disappeared without trace.

I didn't hear the testimonies of Hassan's colleagues and fellow journalists. The trial continued but I was escorted out to where Paco stood waiting. We headed straight for the metropolis and had a long and rather alcoholic lunch in Casa Ciriaco before returning to Granada.

News of the verdict came through this afternoon – earlier than I was expecting. Hassan has been acquitted: he is free. Paco was elated. Justice has triumphed, he said. And although at first I felt ambivalent, now I've had time to think about it, I see that he's right. Obeying my conscience does, I find, give me some comfort. It will make no practical difference: he's not in Granada; he's safely married. What have I to fear?

Alice waited in vain for some reference to herself, to Timmy. Surely it must have occurred to Deb that she would want to know, that she had a right to know about Hassan's release. But there was nothing: apparently it hadn't even crossed her mind. The next entry was about her book.'

20th January 2004

Good news! My wonderful agent, Rita has been talking to a Spanish publisher, who is 'very interested' in the possibility of a translation. She will keep me informed.

The very familiarity of the trek from bus station to hospital was depressing. Alice felt she could have done it in her sleep. The descent into the Metro, the clean, well-lit carriage, the female voice announcing the stations, the busy road leading to the hospital: all these produced a sensation of déjà vu that made her weary. Entering the foyer, she was hit by that antiseptic hospital smell so intimately associated with illness, and immediately a vision of Deb as she'd appeared the last time lodged itself in her mind. As she waited for the lift, she tried to prepare herself; to call up the necessary strength.

The first thing she noticed on reaching Deb's bedside was that her hair had grown; it showed most in the bald patch where her head had been shaved. Alice drew close and spoke her name, unable for the moment to find more words to say. As she stood there, Deb turned her head and coughed. The sound was so unexpected (and unexpectedly moving), it made Alice gasp and look round for a nurse. But then she recalled Paco telling her that Deborah moved, blinked, smiled and gave other signs of life (once she had even sneezed), which led him to hope... Although the doctors, he said, tried to persuade him that these reactions were automatic and meant nothing.

A doctor was coming towards her now. She introduced herself and he shook her hand. His grave face gave her little hope.

'We think there is too much damage to the brain,' he said. 'This cannot be repaired. If she lives, it will be without higher brain function. She will remain in what we call a vegetative state. I tell her husband...'

'Partner,' Alice corrected and instantly wished she hadn't – what did it matter?

The doctor ignored her. 'I tell him,' he repeated, 'But he doesn't hear me.'

This revelation was hardly a surprise to Alice. 'So what you're saying is that there's no hope, none at all...?'

'Of a meaningful life...I am sorry to say the honest answer is no.' He spoke quietly, as if he found it an effort conveying this news.

She swallowed. 'In that case wouldn't it be kinder to...?'

'The time may come when you, the family...must decide.' The doctor rubbed an eye and Alice, glancing at his face, saw the dark shadows of fatigue. He was probably at the end of a long shift. How dispiriting his job must be.

'Thank you for your honesty,' she said.

'I am sorry,' he said with a sigh. 'So many families, so many shattered lives.' He bent over Deborah and adjusted a tube dripping something into her veins. 'At least she feels no pain or discomfort,' he added. 'As always, it is those left behind who suffer.'

When he had gone, she sat down beside the bed. She wanted to take Deborah's hand but didn't dare, fearing she might dislodge one of the drips or drains or monitors attached to her sister's wasted body. As she drew the chair nearer, Deb opened her eyes and Alice saw how easy it would be to believe she was awake and aware of her presence; to dismiss what the doctor said.

'It's me, Alice.' She spoke softly, leaning close to Deborah's ear. 'You're not alone. We're all rooting for you, willing you to pull through.' She began to talk of the happy times they had spent, of occasions she remembered from childhood; of funny incidents and of those moments when she'd felt particularly close to her sister. Dropping her voice even more, she reminded Deb of Timmy's birth and their shared elation; of the gratitude she still felt. 'I'll always love and protect him,' she said, wiping away the tears she could no longer hold back.

She reassured Deb about Mark too. However difficult his behaviour, she should never doubt that he loved her. 'I'll make sure he's alright. I promise.' Deb shifted slightly in the bed but her eyes remained blank.

Two nurses were hovering. Alice wondered how long they had been standing there. She understood from their gestures that they were waiting to wash Deborah.

'It's okay.' She mimed raising a cup to her lips. 'I'll go to the cafeteria while you're busy with her.' They smiled in acknowledgement and moved their trolley alongside the bed.

It was lunchtime but although she'd scarcely eaten all day, she did not feel hungry. She ordered a mint tea and a small pastry. Her mind had been entirely focused on Deborah since arriving at the hospital but now her thoughts turned to Timmy. She reached for her phone and was relieved when Paco answered almost immediately.

'Don't worry, everything is fine,' he said. 'You like to speak to Timmy?'

'Please.'

'Okay, but first tell me, how do you find Deborah? Does the doctor report any progress?'

'Well, not really...'

'*Ay*, I should not expect... So, now I pass you to Timmy.'

It calmed her to hear him chattering in his high child's voice about the book he'd been reading. Paco had promised to make chips for lunch, he told her. And later, Mark might come.

'Well that's lovely. Be a good boy for Paco and I'll see you later, my darling.'

Reassured, she bought a baguette and managed to eat half of it before returning to Deb's bedside where the nurses were just finishing. Her eyes were closed now; she looked peaceful, at rest. Alice sat there for a long time, sometimes speaking, often silent. Different emotions swept over her in waves: rage with the bombers; grief for herself and Timmy; pity for Deb, but also – though she knew it was unfair and illogical – resentment with her for deserting them.

She tried not to be distracted by the monitors beeping away and occasionally emitting what sounded like an alarm. Staff came and went, checking on Deb. One nurse spoke to Alice in English: kind words that made her cry.

When it was time to leave for the airport, she kissed Deborah's sleeping face, took one last look and slipped away, fighting to control her emotion. Tears half-blinded her as she retraced her steps to the Metro station. Was it disloyal of her to go back to England? Sometimes reason and common sense were no help, she thought, understanding better now why Paco refused to accept the truth.

While she waited for her flight, Alice called the house again. The ringing continued until the answer machine kicked in. Alarmed, she tried again but no one picked up the call. Where could they be? It was silly to panic but... She tried Paco's mobile.

'*Hola* Alice, I'm just on my way home from the Faculty. An urgent matter but soon resolved.'

'So what about Timmy? Where is he?' She heard the rising note of her voice.

'Don't worry, Mark is looking after Timmy. I passed on your wish that they don't go out. All is well, please do not be anxious. In five minutes I will be home. If you like, I phone you back.'

'Please do.' He must have noticed the anger in her voice, the abruptness with which she ended the call, but she didn't care. He had promised; she thought she could rely on him.

Even when he phoned back a few minutes later to tell her he was home and Timmy fine, she could not shake off the suspicion that something was wrong. All through the flight, her mind was not on Deb but on Timmy. Fear gripped her and although it was hot in the plane, she felt shivery, as if she had a fever. Hurry up, she silently urged the pilot, the bus-driver, the taxi man who drove her up to the Albaicín. She would have liked to shriek at them. Whatever Paco said, her intuition was telling her a different story.

Chapter Twenty

'Let's play football,' Timmy said the minute Paco had gone out the door.

'Alice says we've got to stay in.'

Timmy made a face. 'We could play in the patio,' he said.

'Okay, go and get your ball then.'

'It's already out there. Come on.'

Timmy kicked it hard against the wall, showing off like kids always did. At the same time he was chattering away about being in his school's under-11 football team and how he'd scored two goals in their last match. Mark was only half-listening. He was still thinking about Racquel, hoping Paco wouldn't be too long, so he could go back and help her get the tiles.

When the buzzer went, he couldn't be arsed to go inside to pick up the entry-phone, he went over to the gate and opened it.

Then he saw who it was. For a moment they just eyed each other up, he and Hassan. He felt stunned. What the fuck was Hassan doing here? Mum would go mad, that was his first thought. It was years since he'd seen the guy but he hadn't changed at all, apart from being a bit greyer.

'Mark?' Hassan held out his hand like they were strangers.

Mark ignored it. 'What do you want?' If he was looking for Mum, he was going to be fucking disappointed.

Timmy had come up behind him and had his eyes glued to Hassan. 'I've seen a picture of you,' he said. 'You're...'

'Mark, I heard about your mother,' Hassan said, interrupting Timmy. 'I wanted to say how sorry I am and to ask for news... Forgive me, I wondered...is there any hope of an improvement in her condition?'

Mark moved out of the way to let Hassan into the patio. He couldn't see what difference it would make. From the look on his face, it was obvious he cared about Mum: when he said he was sorry, it wasn't just words.

'There's no good news,' Mark said. 'It doesn't look like she'll come round.'

Hassan kind of sucked in his breath and blew it out hard. 'What can I say? Your mother is such a special person; a wonderful person. It is a tragedy. You know, I was on the point of writing to her when I heard. I wanted to tell her how much I appreciated her help. To think it was only a few weeks ago...'

Mark hadn't a clue what he was on about. They'd had nothing to do with each other for years, Mum and Hassan. The last he'd heard, Hassan was in prison and the idea of Mum secretly visiting him was just too off the wall to be believed. No way she'd have wanted to help him.

Hassan glanced at Timmy, who'd gone back to kicking the ball around. 'Last time I saw you, you were about his age,' he said.

'Yeah, I s'pose so.'

'Who is he?' He was gaping at Timmy now with the same face he used to put on years ago when he was telling ghostly tales by the fireside and something scary was about to happen. But he didn't look scared as much as shocked. Like it wasn't Timmy he was seeing but some kind of spook. The way his eyes bulged, you could tell he was really rattled. It was bizarre.

'He's my cousin.'

Hassan was still gaping. 'Your brother, did you say?'

'*Joder*, have you gone deaf or what? I said *primo hermano*. He's my Auntie Alice's son.' Mark switched to English so Timmy could understand. 'Tell him, Timmy. You're my cousin, aren't you?'

Timmy nodded. He'd suddenly gone shy.

'*Mi primo*, okay?' Mark was fed up with repeating the word but he wasn't sure if Hassan had got it even now.

'How old is he?'

'He's nine.'

'And when is his birthday?'

'What is this, a fucking interrogation? Why are you so interested in him?' Mark didn't like the way he was staring at Timmy. What was the matter with the guy? If they'd tortured him in prison that might account for it, for him being a bit cracked in the head.

'Tell him your birthday, Timmy. Maybe he'll give you a present.'

'The 20th of May.'

'20th of May,' Hassan repeated. '*Veinte de mayo*. So, nearly ten... And he's Alice's son?'

'I've already said he is.' Jesus, did he have to repeat every fucking thing?

'Well, where is your aunt then? I remember Alice well. I'd like to see her and offer my sympathy.'

'She went to the hospital in Madrid. She'll be back later.' He said it mainly to get rid of Hassan but straight after, he realised he shouldn't have done. Alice might not be too keen on seeing him, even if he wanted to see her. 'Paco, Mum's *pareja*, will be back any minute,' he added, hoping that would put him off. For all Hassan knew, Paco might be the jealous type.

'*Bueno*, I'll leave you now but please call me if your mother...? Or better, perhaps, if you give me your number and I'll call *you*. I would prefer to know – even if the news is bad.'

Put like that, it seemed mean to refuse. Hassan got out his mobile and keyed in Mark's number. He'd better not bombard him with calls every fucking day.

'Goodbye,' Hassan said in English to Timmy. 'Perhaps we meet again.'

Fat chance of that, Mark thought. 'Timmy's going back to England the day after tomorrow.'

'Oh yes? Well, I too am only in Granada for a couple more days. *Adios* Mark. And courage. We must stay optimistic till the last.'

Alice could hear their voices – Mark's and Paco's – as she fumbled in her bag for the key: they must be in the patio. She did not hear Timmy's voice but as she pushed open the heavy iron gate, she was relieved to see him sitting on the low wall under the pomegranate tree. How foolish to have let panic get the better of her. What had she expected?

Paco came forward to embrace her. 'So how did you find Deborah?'

Unable to conjure up words, Alice just shook her head. I'm too tired, she thought; too tired and too sad. There's no comfort to be had.

She went over to Timmy and hugged him. 'I hope you've been a good boy.'

'He has,' Paco said.

Mark was moving towards the gate. 'I'm off. *Hasta mañana*.'

'Mummy, that man came: the one in the photo.'

'Which photo, darling?' There was more than one photo, more than one man. It didn't have to be him. *Stay calm, don't give yourself away.*

But then Mark turned. 'Yeah, he wanted to know your birthday, didn't he, Timmy.'

'Who?' Did the terror show on her face, in her voice?

'Hassan. He was hoping to see you.'

'But what did he want?' It came out like a wail. No wonder all three of them were staring at her.

'Just to say he was sorry about Mum. Look, I've got to be away.' Mark opened the gate and was gone, letting it bang shut behind him.

'Alice, is something the matter?' She was aware of Paco by her side, peering into her face with concern as if she were ill. 'You are overtired and distressed after your visit. That is natural.' He put an arm round her. 'Come, it is my turn to make you a cup of tea, English tea with milk.'

She let him lead her into the kitchen, sit her in a chair, bring her weak, milky tea and biscuits.

'Were you here?' she asked him, 'When Hassan came?'

'No,' he said. 'I did not see him. Mark was taking care of Timmy at the time.'

'Timmy...'

'Mummy, ow! You're hurting my hand!'

'Sorry darling, I didn't realise...' She loosened her grip. 'Now, I want you to tell me exactly what the man said.'

'He was talking in Spanish mostly.'

'But he spoke some English to you? Mark said he asked about your birthday...'

'He asked how old I was and if I was Mark's cousin... I think that was all.' Timmy pulled away from her. 'You don't like him, do you?'

'I...really, I don't have an opinion. It's years since I've seen him.'

'Mummy, I want to go and read my book now.'

She let him go and sipped at her tea.

'Alice, he is not a bad man,' Paco said. 'There is nothing to fear.'

'I was thinking,' she said, choosing her words with care, 'That it might be nice to spend our last night in Málaga. We could take a bus in the morning, go up to the castle – Timmy would love that – and stay in a hotel for the night.'

Paco shrugged. 'As you wish. But this can be decided tomorrow. Now I think you must relax while I prepare some supper.'

Everyone around him seemed to be cracking up. Mark couldn't wait to get back to Sacromonte. At least you knew where you were with people up there. He should have brought Timmy with him too. He felt sorry for his cousin: poor kid would most likely grow up warped unless Alice got her head together.

He texted Racquel to say he was on his way and went to look for the tiles. He found them straightaway: a big stack of them just past the old house with the palm trees. Half of them were broken but that didn't matter: it was best to build a mosaic. The Romans had the right idea. In a cave, where nothing was straight or level, it made a lot of sense. What he needed now was to get hold of Fabio's wheelbarrow...

When he reached Racquel's cave, she had two big guys with her, Miguel and Nacho. He'd never seen either of them before.

'I thought we'd need help with the carrying,' she said.

'Oh cool.' He told her about the wheelbarrow and asked them to wait while he went for it.

Fabio wasn't around but the wheelbarrow was there, half-full of rubble and a cat munching on what could have been a mouse or could have been the leftovers of Fabio's lunch. Mark tipped out the rubble; the cat had already scarpered. He knew Fabio wouldn't mind him taking the barrow – long as he bought him a beer after. That was the good thing about life up here. People were always cool about lending stuff.

It was bloody hard work pushing a barrow full of tiles up the hill, specially with all the ruts and bumps in the path, but having Miguel and Nacho to help meant it was only two trips each. They all mucked in with the loading and unloading, Racquel included. By the time they'd finished, the sweat was pouring off him; he'd need a few beers to replace all that liquid. A shower would be good too, but you couldn't have everything. He might get one at the *carmen* tomorrow when he went to say goodbye to Timmy and Alice.

The sun had gone down while they'd been working; the hills to the east were already that inky blue, the trees just dark silhouettes against the skyline.

Racquel looked well pleased with the evening's work. 'Come on,' she said, 'Let's hit the Albaicín and I'll buy you guys a beer. You deserve one.'

When they left La Fragua a few beers later, Miguel and Nacho decided to go down to one of the bars in Calle Elvira. He said he didn't fancy it and Racquel said she didn't either, which suited him just fine. He wanted to be alone with her so he could come clean about the lie he'd told; the lie about Mum. It was sitting in his head like a bloody great stone, but he couldn't think how to start.

'You're very quiet,' Racquel said. '*¿Qué pasa?*' He had his hands in his pockets and she put an arm through his. The strings of beads moved up her wrist; he could feel them digging into his arm.

'Nothing,' he said. But then he thought: that's another lie and a fucking obvious one. So he just came right out with it. 'My mum's not dead.'

Racquel stopped walking so he had to stop too, though he'd have liked to carry right on.

'I know,' she said. 'Someone told me what happened.' She didn't sound angry. He was too surprised to answer and after a while Racquel added, 'I guess it feels like she's dead.'

That was about right, he thought. 'She's...you can't really call it alive, the state she's in. When I saw her in the hospital...' He pulled away from Racquel and walked on a few paces. He couldn't put it into words, it was too hard.

He didn't even hear her come up behind him. She moved like a cat, silent in the night. But he felt her arms go round him from behind; turn him to face her. He felt her lips soft on his. She didn't open her mouth; it wasn't that kind of kiss. But he wasn't in the mood for that kind of kiss. 'It's okay,' she whispered and the way she said it made him feel like she understood. Like he could tell her anything and she'd understand.

It was just a matter of willpower, Alice told herself. She could do it, carry on for the few hours that remained – nearer twelve than twenty-four – as if everything were normal. This time tomorrow they would be gone. Their bus tickets were reserved, the hotel in Málaga booked. She was doing well, routines coming to her aid as always: sitting down to supper; clearing the dishes away; Timmy's bedtime rituals. She had talked calmly with Paco before making her excuses to retreat. She must pack their things, she had told him, so that all would be ready in the morning. Now she intended to read the few remaining pages of her sister's diary. She would not allow thoughts of Hassan to distract her. Hassan had seen his son and left. He had not spirited Timmy away. There was nothing more to fear.

11th February 2004

Mark consented to come down to the centre with me today and I rewarded him by buying two new pairs of trousers to replace the ripped and shabby (only?) pair he owns. We had a coffee in Café Central and I realised how little time we spend together these days. It felt like a treat, I'd almost forgotten what good company he can be. Have I been too hard on him?

13th February 2004

The Spanish publisher is 'on the verge of signing' according to Rita. Already the manuscript has been sent to one of their regular translators for an opinion. I can't believe how quickly it's all happening. Everyone tells me such momentum is rare in the publishing world, that it means they must expect to make serious money from my book, but that I can't believe.

5th March 2004

Another wretched argument with Mark yesterday. This time he wanted forty euros but when I asked him what for, he lost his temper and swore at me, said I wouldn't miss 400 euros, let alone forty, I was just tight-fisted and selfish. In his circle, you shared everything. If you only had four euros in the world, you'd still buy your buddy a beer rather than let him go thirsty.

When Paco came home, he was really sweet and supportive (he'd noticed immediately how upset I was). He said it was wholly reasonable of me to refuse Mark if he wouldn't tell me what the money was for. He thinks Mark could be under the influence of some of the harder types up there – druggies or alcoholics – and that they might be putting pressure on him. My worst fear is that he wants the money to buy cocaine. I haven't any real grounds for suspicion, just that there's a lot of it about in Granada and I feel he's vulnerable at the moment. We were on the edge of that scene in London – some of the parties Charlie and I went to – and I know the impact it can have on those who are susceptible.

I wish he'd do something with his life – anything, I honestly don't care what. He says he can make enough money from busking and that his freedom is what matters but if that's the case, why does he need to keep borrowing from me?

7th March 2004

The deal with Golondrina is signed and I am to meet the translator in Madrid on March 11th. Teresa (despite my being so remiss about keeping in touch) says I can stay with her in Alcalá the night before. She commutes to work in the centre so we can take the train together in the morning. It must be three years or more since Teresa moved to Madrid and we haven't met since. No doubt we will be up till the early hours drinking wine and swapping news and gossip.

I feel so lucky. Only my worries about Mark stand in the way of complete contentment. 'One of these days he'll settle down,' Paco assures me. I must believe him and allow myself to be happy. Life is too short.

End of diary. And how poignant those last words. But tonight Alice had no time for musing on life's sad ironies. If she opened the gate to emotion even a crack, she would crumple like a paper tissue. Her task now was to destroy the diaries: a task that had become imperative since Deb, typically, had given the game away in a few careless words in the entry of 3rd November: *the inescapable fact that he is Timmy's father*, she had written of Hassan. All her conscientious tearing out of pages and blacking out of incriminating lines had been for nothing. Well, in the end it didn't matter: before the night was over, a pile of charred embers would be all that remained of the diaries.

As she sat on the bed with the six notebooks lined up in her hands, she became aware of voices: Paco's and...another male voice but too faint to identify. *Please no!* She tried to stand but her legs had turned to jelly. Her heart was thumping in her chest as if a large bird were trapped inside her, beating its wings against her ribcage. It was him; the certainty came from within, too strong to question. Her instinct was to grab Timmy and run – out of the house, out of Granada, out of Spain. If he'd been a baby still, too young to require explanations, perhaps she would have done. But he was not, and in any case it was already too late. Someone was knocking softly at the bedroom door.

'Alice, sorry to disturb. It is Hassan, he wishes to speak with you – just a few words, he says. You are not in bed yet, I hope?'

She wanted to barricade the door, to crawl under the bed and hide; to make both Timmy and herself invisible. But instead she opened the door and followed Paco into the *salón* to face Hassan.

He came forward with outstretched hand. 'I am sorry,' he said. 'Your sister...'

She took the hand – politeness was too deeply ingrained in her to refuse it. '*Gracias.*'

'We sit down?' he said.

Not trusting her legs to support her for long, she sank with relief into one of the armchairs.

'Now. The boy...'

'He's asleep.' Her voice came out unnaturally high. It belonged to someone else.

'The boy,' he repeated. 'Timmy you call him?'

Alice said nothing. She felt light-headed, insubstantial. Her guts were rumbling in protest. She thought she might have to run for the bathroom any moment.

'I think...' The intensity of his stare terrified Alice. 'I think that he is my son.'

249

Now Paco was also staring at her. She saw herself lift a hand to her mouth.

'I think…that Deborah is his mother.'

'*Hombre, ¿qué dices?*' But the initial look of disbelief on Paco's face had changed to one of shocked recognition.

'I see him. This afternoon I see him. I see his dark skin. I see his…' Hassan pulled at his pointed earlobe. 'I see his hair…*rizado.*' He pointed to the tight curls on his head that were now, she noticed, beginning to grey.

'Alice is this true?' Paco sounded angry, but with whom she wasn't sure.

She took a deep breath and nodded.

Nobody spoke. Silence filled the room, crushing her with its weight.

Then the two men were talking in rapid Spanish that left her lost and helpless.

'Alice,' Paco said. 'Hassan asks that I interpret. His English is… limited.' Paco wasn't angry, she decided. Just shocked. His face had gone pale; he kept rubbing his eyes. 'You need something? A glass of water?' He sat down next to her and reached out a hand.

She shook her head as Hassan began to speak, addressing Paco, who then conveyed the words to her in English.

'He wishes to tell you that although his first reaction was anger at the deception, you need not be afraid of him. He will not seek to…to remove his son. He has a family now – a wife and two children: one boy, one girl. His home is in Valencia.'

Hassan paused and Paco took the opportunity to light a cigarette.

'After being in prison, he has little money. He cannot offer support for Timmy. He has been thinking, he says. And what he would like, what he asks is that you tell Timmy. He wants recognition that he is the father. He wants contact…*de vez en cuando*…from time to time.' He looked questioningly at Hassan, who muttered something. 'Yes, for example, three or four times a year?

'He says this is a big shock to him. He had no idea…'

In Paco's eyes she read: *a big shock to me too.* She read the question forming in his mind: *Why didn't Deborah tell me?*

Hassan addressed her directly now. 'I love Deborah,' he said. 'Always

I continue loving her. Many years. I never stop...thinking of her.' He spread his hands. '*Ay*, my English...' He turned to Paco and resumed in Spanish.

'He says...' Paco's eyes dropped. Alice could see how much this was costing him. 'He says she always provoked strong feelings in him, that at the end, when he knew he was losing her, he became desperate. He behaved badly... After she threw him out, desperation drove him to behave in a way that now makes him ashamed. He...lost his mind a little, he says. Love, jealousy, these are emotions that can destroy...

Watching Hassan's face as Paco translated his words, she was amazed to find herself moved. The man she had loathed for ten years – no, more like fifteen – was not the monster she had constructed in her mind. She could see the lines of suffering, the pain of hard experience in his eyes. She did not doubt his sincerity.

'He says his wife is a good woman and he considers himself fortunate but...' Paco took a deep drag on his cigarette. 'Deborah was the great love of his life.'

Hassan sank his face into his hands as if overcome with emotion. This was so utterly different from the scene she had imagined. She realised how fear had distorted her thinking, had prevented her seeing Hassan as a human being. He raised his head and turned to Paco again.

'Always he wanted a child with Deborah, but she would not consider it.' Paco's voice was hoarse. 'He is still... He cannot take it in fully, that he has a son: a son from Deborah.

'He says this will be a shock to his wife, his two children. It will not be easy for him to tell them, but he must do it. They will all need time to adjust to the knowledge.'

Alice felt dizzy: her head was swimming with thoughts that formed and dispersed and re-formed in different shapes. Her resolve not to concede to Hassan was weakening. She had been determined to refuse his demand for contact with Timmy but now... She was beginning to see that might be unreasonable. Unreasonable, and yet...*I can't face it*, she thought. *I can't face telling Timmy*. The vision of Hassan and Timmy (*her* Timmy) walking off hand-in-hand – laughing, chatting, eager – was too painful to bear. She had never had to share him with anyone, she realised. Now he would discover he had not only a father but a half-brother, a half-sister. He would find that Mark was more than a cousin. He would know she had lied to him.

A few metres away, Timmy slept, oblivious of the scene unfolding here. She imagined sitting down by his bed in the morning and telling him: the man in the photo, the man you met yesterday is your father. His name is Hassan; he is from Morocco. But that was the easy part. Infinitely harder…too grim even to contemplate: I'm not really your mother. Your mother is Deborah. *No!* A voice inside her screamed in protest. *I can't! I won't!* It was too cruel: a mother about to die; a father who didn't even speak his language. Surely ignorance was preferable. The truth would devastate him. And make him hate her.

'Alice, you are okay?' Paco was regarding her with pity.

They were waiting, the two men, looking to her for answers. Pain was written on both their faces. She heard the voice of Mrs Adams, her old primary school teacher, the sarcastic one. *Lost your tongue?* But she knew that if she spoke, she would lose her grip completely. What suffering they had caused, she and Deb between them. And now Deb was not here to share the responsibility. *She* was the one having to deal with it alone.

'Alice,' Hassan said. 'Think of Timmy. He has a right to know his father.'

Paco was nodding in agreement. He said, 'You must have known that one day… Always the truth comes out in the end, no?' It was an accusation – framed gently but still an accusation.

'We always intended to tell Timmy,' she said, 'When he was older.'

'Is difficult, I understand. For all of us is difficult.' Hassan's gaze was direct, his voice firm. He was not going to let her off.

'But he's still so young…' A last plea, but she knew it was hopeless.

Hassan turned and spoke to Paco.

'He says the boy is not too young to know his father. He will come back tomorrow…'

'No, I need more time. Listen, I will tell him, I promise.' She spoke slowly, each word an effort. 'I will allow the contact you ask, but I must break the news to him gently in my own time. We'll come back to Granada… Soon, I promise. You can meet him here; that is, if Paco agrees.'

'Of course.' As Paco translated her words into Spanish, she kept her eyes on Hassan's face, observing the series of conflicting emotions that crossed it: relief (had he expected more resistance from her?), disappointment at having to wait and, finally, a reluctant acceptance.

Another long silence hung between them but the tension had lowered. She felt sapped – as if her will, her energy, even her capacity to speak had deserted her.

Hassan rose to his feet. 'Okay,' he said. 'I go now.' From his jacket pocket he produced a card and handed it to her. 'Here, this is my email address. You write to me when...after you speak to Timmy, okay? You tell me date of your visit. We meet here.' The trace of a smile played on his lips as he added, 'I try to improve my English.'

'Okay, agreed.' She held out her hand to Hassan and the gesture seemed perfectly natural. She felt no repugnance. His grip was firm, confident. It struck her for the first time just how much trust she was asking of him. Because what was to stop her simply disappearing with Timmy? They could move house, even change their names... But no, that would be too spineless: a coward's way out. She would stick to her word. 'Actually,' she said, 'Timmy has picked up an impressive amount of Spanish from his friend Javi. He puts me to shame.'

After Hassan had gone, Paco fetched the whisky bottle and poured two large shots. They sat in silence for what seemed a long time. The whisky, searing her throat with each swallow, tasted like nectar; it tasted like the medicine that might save her life.

'I thought she had no secrets from me,' Paco said eventually. 'Can we ever know another person truly? We think we do, but then...' He picked up the bottle and refilled their glasses.

'She wanted to tell you,' Alice said, recalling from the diary how tempted Deb had been to confide in Paco, 'But we'd sworn to each other not to tell anyone.'

Paco sighed and took another sip of whisky. '*Bueno*. So you will keep your promise to Hassan.'

She heard it as a statement, or possibly even a command. Later she wondered if Paco had meant it as a question.

Epilogue

7th March 2005

OBITUARY

Deborah Hardy 1951—2004

Deborah Hardy, who was fatally injured in the Madrid train bombings of March 11th and died on November 14th, was the only Briton among the nearly 200 victims. Author of the acclaimed 'Bold and Free: Walladah and other liberated women of Muslim Spain', published in June of this year, she was in Madrid for a meeting with the translator working on a Spanish version of her book. She had spent the night at the home in Alcalá de Henares of her friend, Teresa López, who was also a victim.

Hardy, a linguist and translator, had lived in the Moorish Albaicín quarter of Granada since 1985 and was fully involved in the life of her adopted city, sometimes in controversial ways. Although not a Muslim, she had campaigned vigorously for the mosque in the Albaicín, which after years of obstructions and delays, finally opened in 2003. She was fascinated by the Moorish civilisation in Spain and had spent many years researching the so-called 'convivencia' of Muslims, Christians and Jews. The influential roles played by some women in al-Andalus particularly interested her. Much of her book is focused on Walladah Bint Mustakfi, an 11th century Muslim poet who hosted literary salons in Córdoba and made no secret of her love affairs.

Hardy is survived by a son, Mark from her marriage to Charles Fenton, dissolved in 1984, a sister, Alice, and her Spanish partner, Francisco (Paco) Molina.

Mark had kept the newspaper cuttings Alice sent him about Mum: the obituary and a couple of reviews of her book. She'd been in the Spanish papers too. There was a whole page on her in *Ideal* and a column in *El País*. He'd put them all in a plastic folder along with the letter (sellotaped together where he'd ripped it) telling him Timmy was his brother.

It was almost the anniversary of 11-M: they were talking about it on the news. He couldn't believe only one year had gone by; he felt about ten years older. Just those two weeks in November when he'd been trying to decide, when Paco and Alice said *he* should be the one to have the final word on whether to turn off the life support, those two weeks had seemed like a fucking lifetime.

At first he'd said no, it wasn't fair dumping all the responsibility on him. But when he thought about it some more, he was glad. It made him feel respected, like his opinion was important. They'd discussed it a lot, the three of them. They'd agreed Mum wouldn't see the point of being alive if she couldn't think or talk or do anything for herself. Alice said it would be kinder to let her die and she'd live on in people's memories the way she was before, not as a helpless victim. You couldn't argue with that. Paco said how happy she'd be that her book was out and people were reading it, which meant her ideas would live on. That's what he said, but you could tell by his face that he hadn't quite given up on the idea of a miracle. If it had been left to Paco to decide, Mum would most likely still be lying there in the hospital bed waiting for him to face up to reality.

As far as Mark knew, no one had asked Timmy for an opinion – even though she was *his* mum as well. Alice said he was too young and that anyway he couldn't get his head round the idea of his auntie being his real mum. Mark had asked Alice why Timmy wasn't mentioned as her son in the obituary. 'It doesn't have to be *public* knowledge,' was what she said in answer to that. 'We can choose who we tell.' She said Timmy preferred to think of *her* as his mum. That figured, seeing as he'd spent ten whole years believing she was. And with his real mum being dead, it probably seemed a better deal.

At first, when Alice wrote to tell him Timmy was his brother, he'd been fucking mad. He'd torn the letter in half and kicked a table over, which was a bad idea because he'd stubbed his toe so badly it got infected and he could hardly walk for a week. To think the pair of them – Mum and Alice – had been lying all these years. Lying to him, lying to Timmy, lying to Paco… Hassan didn't even know Timmy existed and he was the father.

Once the truth came out, a lot of things made more sense – like them going to England for half a year and Mum crying all the time. She should have kept Timmy. Everyone would have been happier – except maybe Alice, but she could always have had a kid with someone else. He didn't see why Timmy couldn't have lived with them. It made him feel kind of cheated. All those years he had a brother and didn't know it. He'd have loved a brother. It seemed like a cop-out giving him away. Alice said Mum was afraid Hassan would kidnap him and take him off to Morocco or else blackmail her into letting him move back in. That didn't wash, not in his opinion.

It was weird the way things worked out. He'd lost his mum but he'd got a brother in exchange. It wasn't the same, course it wasn't. Sometimes the pain of missing her was so sharp it was like a knife twisting in his guts. He'd always miss her. From his bed he could see Monika's portrait of her in the alcove. He'd thought she was joking when she said he could have it for nothing. It was her best painting. Racquel said it needed more light and would look better in the apartment. She had a point, but he was still weighing up whether or not to go for the move. He liked his cave and he liked the outdoor life up here. He'd told Racquel they'd shift after the summer. She was happy to go with that.

By then he'd be making enough from flogging his artwork so they'd be able to get by without the rent from the apartment. Three different shops were selling his drawings, though they took a bloody big cut, which seemed unfair when he'd done all the work. He did better from selling on the street and at the *mirador* like Racquel; she knew all the best places.

Charlie thought he ought to get rent from Paco seeing as the *carmen* belonged to him now. He'd told Charlie to fuck off. No way was he going to charge Paco rent – even though Paco *wanted* to pay. They'd had a big row about it, but in the end Paco had backed down. Mum would have gone berserk at the idea of him ripping Paco off.

Mark hadn't told Charlie about Timmy being his brother. It was none of his fucking business. Last time he'd seen his dad was at the funeral. It was unbelievable how many people had turned up for Mum's funeral – people she'd known way back in the past, people from all over. He didn't even know half of them. Hassan was there. He was sat next to Timmy and you could see what Charlie was thinking: that Alice had been messing with her sister's *pareja*. Seeing Hassan and Timmy together, you'd expect everyone to notice the likeness but no one said a word.

There was a lot of talk about Mum's book. Most of the Spanish crowd were waiting for the translation to come out in May but the English ones had all read it. He felt bad because he still hadn't got round to it; he'd just looked at the pictures and read the reviews. At the funeral, he pretended he had read it. Everyone seemed to think the book was brilliant, which made him feel proud of Mum. He hoped she was hovering up there somewhere, maybe as an eagle, and could hear them. He hoped she'd heard Monika when she said it should be compulsory reading for all the politicians who tried to stir up hatred against Muslims and justified it by claiming Islam robbed women of their rights.

He liked to think of Mum reborn as an eagle. Not that he really believed in all that but sometimes he'd look up at the sky just in case. Back in November, not long after the funeral, he'd watched a lone buzzard soaring on the air currents above Güejar Sierra and it made him feel good, almost happy. As he sat there following its flight, he got to thinking how in one year he'd been ambushed over and over: hit by a long run of surprises and not all of them bad. After the first, the terrible one of losing Mum in 11-M, the rest had been mostly good. Like Timmy turning out to be his brother; like Racquel appearing outside his cave that day; like Dani's disappearing act and then after him, Ed. The latest surprise was finding he could get good money for his sketches. It was fucking amazing: he'd never have guessed at a single one of those things. Which meant, just about anything could happen.

Timmy was juggling with two balled-up pairs of socks while Alice stood over the open suitcase deciding what to pack. Their trips to Granada were becoming something of a routine. This would be their fourth since the tragedy. Hassan had suggested they fly to Valencia instead but she was resisting for the time being. It was so much easier to stay at the *carmen* with Paco and also meant they could see Mark.

'My dad said he'd bring Omar and Amina with him next time we go to Granada. Omar likes football too. He's only six but...'

'You don't mean *this* time?' She still found it difficult hearing Timmy talk about his other family. He hadn't yet met his younger brother and sister but he'd seen photos and seemed to know an awful lot about them.

'No, I mean when we go at half-term in May.'

'That will be nice.'

How adaptable children were. How matter-of-fact in coping with change. Alice remembered waking sick with dread on the morning she had chosen to tell Timmy. He would be furious, he would reject her as a liar and imposter; it would be the end of everything she cared about. But her fears had been groundless. He had taken it all in his stride – as if he saw only the positives. He was thrilled to have a dad at last, to have Mark as a brother. 'Can't you still be my mum?' he had asked and when Alice said yes, of course she could and pulled him to her, a flood of relief had drowned her in sweetness. Laughing and crying at the same time, she had kissed and squeezed Timmy, until he screwed up his face in boyish contempt. 'Mumm*ee*,' he complained. 'You're making me wet.'

After the anguish of their first visit and then the funeral, it could only get easier. They had returned to Spain as promised, a couple of days after Timmy's tenth birthday. She recalled her increasing misery as the plane made its relentless progress towards Granada, Timmy assailing her with one question after another. His eagerness and impatience to see Hassan felt like a punishment. She had forced herself to respond, made every effort to sound cheerful. Hassan was waiting for them at the airport. She would have preferred to be met by Paco. In the taxi they were all subdued, even Timmy reduced to silence by an understandable shyness.

'So now I take the boy for lunch. We need some time together.'

Abandoned at the *carmen*, she had searched her mind for a way to distract herself during the fraught hours of Timmy's absence. Paco was still at work. He had left the key, but sitting alone indoors was the worst possible option; much better to take a walk. Disappointingly, Mark had not replied to her letter about Timmy. She had only Paco's word that his initial anger had melted away; that he had forgiven them. But he would have to be faced at some point, so she'd plucked up courage and walked to Sacromonte.

Finding him with a girl had come as a complete surprise, though it shouldn't have done. Racquel was exactly the kind of girlfriend he needed. Her support had given him a new confidence and belief in himself – though some of the credit must go to Monika too, for encouraging him to take up drawing again. Alice had no idea where this talent had come from. As far as she knew, no one in the family was artistic. If only his mother could see him now, she would be proud of him. The thought made her sad.

Mark had matured so much in the space of a year. Alice considered the last words Deb had written in her diary: *Only my worries about Mark stand in the way of complete contentment.* What damage words could cause. If Mark had read them, he would have been mortified. She had no regrets about destroying the diaries.

Later on that evening of their first visit, when Timmy was asleep in bed, she and Hassan had talked. He'd been working on his English, he said, and seemed pleased when she told him about her Spanish class. It made communication easier being able to switch from one language to the other. They had even laughed at some of their own and each other's mistakes. As they talked, she observed his long, slender fingers (quite unlike Timmy's) dancing an accompaniment to his words. She recalled that he played an instrument; a stringed instrument. Deb had mentioned it in the diary though she couldn't remember its name.

He was remarkably open about his feelings. 'I tell my wife,' he said. 'This is not easy. But she is *comprensiva*. She understands. She would like to meet Timmy, to welcome him into our family.'

His wife, it turned out, wasn't Moroccan (Alice had imagined a veiled Muslim lady) but Spanish, a nursery teacher much younger than him. Of course her nationality didn't make any difference. What mattered was that Timmy should feel at ease with her. As Hassan talked, she found herself beginning to understand what Deb had seen in him, to appreciate his sensitivity and frankness. They were qualities she had never noticed before. She had closed her mind to him right from the start, she realised, exaggerating his faults, refusing to see any good in him. Kay had accused Deb of seeing everyone in terms of black or white. Perhaps she was guilty of the same.

In the months since that first visit, she had thought a lot about Hassan. It was true she hadn't given him much of a chance. She didn't expect ever to like Timmy's father but Paco was right, he wasn't a bad man. And when he assured her he wanted to do his best for Timmy, she had no doubt his words were sincere. He had even hinted that if he received compensation for his wrongful imprisonment, some part of it might go to Timmy.

A vision of Hassan's grief-stricken face at the funeral swam into her mind now. She had been shocked to see how affected he was. Paco too, naturally. Both men had loved Deborah, loved her to distraction. She couldn't help feeling a twinge of envy at the devotion her sister was able to inspire. No one, she was quite sure, had ever felt that way about *her*.

Alice looked at the clock. It was almost time to go out and she still needed to shower and change. In spite of their early flight tomorrow, she had no intention of missing her Spanish class.

'Ginny will be here any minute,' she called to Timmy. 'Is there anything else you want to take? Before I shut the case.'

'Can I give Dad my old Man United shirt for Omar? It's doesn't fit me any more.'

'Yes, of course. I think it's in the bottom drawer in your room.' Dad. Spoken with pride but also – still – a trace of self-consciousness.

Alice opened her wardrobe and took out the new trousers she had bought at the weekend. They were a good fit that flattered her figure. Black, so something bright to go with them: the turquoise blouse from Zara and a silk scarf in multiple shades of blue and green on black. Examining herself in the mirror, she wondered why she had stuck for so long with the same old hairstyle: straight, evenly cut to chin-length, a straight fringe. Most of her life. It was too severe; Deb had always said so and she was right. The shorter, layered look took ten years off her age. She applied her make-up with extra care and dabbed just a soupçon of perfume on her wrists. The doorbell rang as she was gathering up her books.

'Very nice,' Ginny said, looking her up and down. 'You'll have all the men clamouring to sit next to you.'

'Oh come on!' But Alice couldn't hide the glow of pleasure she felt. *All the men* were irrelevant. It was Neil she hoped would notice her appearance and sit next to her so that they could be partners in the speaking exercises. It was the last thing she'd expected when she joined the Spanish class – to meet someone like him. He was tall with bushy eyebrows and greying crew-cut hair and he never seemed embarrassed by his mistakes, as she was. He would merely laugh, tap his head as if to say: *what an idiot*, and continue undaunted. 'I want to understand the jokes when I go down to my local bar in Mojácar,' he said. He had a holiday home inland from the resort but only twenty minutes' walk from the beach, and was hoping to spend more time there after taking early retirement in July. 'You'll have to nip down from Granada sometime.' He sounded serious. Like her, he had been on his own for a long time.

After the last two classes, a group of them had gone for a drink at the pub down the road. She hoped it was now an established ritual and that Neil would again accept her offer of a lift home. He usually cycled to the college but last week he had arrived on foot because of the rain. Glancing out of the window, she was pleased to see it was still pelting down as it had been all day and for most of the last fortnight. She regretted having turned down his invitation to come in for a coffee. Was it her imagination or had his goodnight kiss hinted at something more? This time she wasn't going to let obligation to the babysitter deter her. She had warned Ginny she might be late – just in case he repeated his proposition.

It was such a long time since she'd regarded men with any interest: the kind of interest she was beginning to feel now. It was much simpler to take care of her own needs. Alone in bed at night, her fingers served perfectly well to provide the modest pleasure her body demanded. The night with Paco had been an anomaly, a one-off that she'd almost forgotten about. Neither of them had referred to it since. In the emotional meltdown that followed, what happened between them that night simply didn't signify. If she felt closer to him as a result, it was for reasons that had nothing to do with sex.

But over the last few months she had noticed a change: small stirrings of desire which took her unawares. In Granada she had caught herself eyeing up smartly dressed young men with smooth olive skin and black hair as glossy as patent leather. She had suddenly become self-conscious with Paco's friend, Ignacio, whom she'd chatted to a dozen times without ever noticing how attractive he was.

She put it down to the liberating effect of no longer living a lie. For ten years she had felt like a criminal on the run, unable to wholly relax her guard with others. Always lurking at the back of her mind was the fear their secret would be blown. She had got used to it, not realising how it weighed her down. Had it warped her personality? Possibly. Dishonesty did not come naturally to her. Deb, she thought, had coped better.

In the car, she pressed play to start the Spanish CD at track 14: the conversation in a restaurant between Marta and José. She practically knew it by heart. *A ver... Para empezar, la sopa de picadillo. Y luego, merluza a la plancha.* Her pronunciation was improving, she thought as she repeated aloud each line of the dialogue. Later, with luck, she would role-play the scene with Neil.

Pulling up in the college car-park, Alice was seized by that familiar tug of sorrow. Would she ever stop missing her sister? She ached with the desire to show off her Spanish to Deb. How pleasantly surprised she would be. But even stronger was the longing to confide in Deb about Neil. And to tell her: *He's not damaged, he doesn't need looking after*! She had worked through all that; Timmy had satisfied her need to nurture. She was ready now for an equal relationship, one of openness and trust.

The last year had been the worst of her life, yet she had come through it. More challenges – some predictable, others unknown – lay ahead. She felt rather like a bird newly released from captivity and exposed to all the dangers posed by freedom but eager to fly regardless. An image came into her mind of the swifts that chased each other in play, wheeling and diving in endless movement above the terrace of the *carmen*. One day, if her friendship with Neil developed, she would like to take him there, to stand beside him on the terrace with a glass of wine, watching the swifts. The locals call them aeroplanes, she would tell him: *aviones*.

Acknowledgements

My sincere thanks to the Fundación Valparaíso for awarding me a month's residency at Mojácar to work on my novel; to Jill Foulston for critiquing my first draft; and to my friends: Lily MacGillivray, Graeme Symons, Gavin Smith and Lucius Redman for their helpful comments and encouragement as the novel progressed. I am particularly grateful to Lily for her detailed criticisms on successive drafts. Thanks also to Paul Roberts for passing on his knowledge of Granada in the 1980s and Jirka Jahoda for showing me his cave.

Lightning Source UK Ltd.
Milton Keynes UK
UKOW02f0414140415

249589UK00002B/74/P

9 781781 323694